Joseph Texte

Jean-Jacques Rousseau and the cosmopolitan spirit in literature

A study of the literary relations between France and England

Joseph Texte

Jean-Jacques Rousseau and the cosmopolitan spirit in literature
A study of the literary relations between France and England

ISBN/EAN: 9783337204792

Printed in Europe, USA, Canada, Australia, Japan

Cover: Foto ©Andreas Hilbeck / pixelio.de

More available books at **www.hansebooks.com**

JEAN-JACQUES ROUSSEAU

AND THE

COSMOPOLITAN SPIRIT IN LITERATURE

Jean-Jacques Rousseau

AND THE

COSMOPOLITAN SPIRIT IN LITERATURE

A STUDY OF THE LITERARY RELATIONS BETWEEN
FRANCE AND ENGLAND DURING THE
EIGHTEENTH CENTURY

BY

JOSEPH TEXTE
PROFESSOR OF COMPARATIVE LITERATURE AT THE UNIVERSITY OF LYON

TRANSLATED BY

J. W. MATTHEWS

LONDON
DUCKWORTH & CO.
NEW YORK: THE MACMILLAN COMPANY
1899

To

M. FERDINAND BRUNETIÈRE

DE L'ACADÉMIE FRANÇAISE

In token of gratitude

Preface

In submitting this translation of my book, *Jean-Jacques Rousseau et le cosmopolitisme littéraire*, to the English public, mention should be made of the fact that a considerable number of errors have been corrected in view of the present edition. Several books and articles published during the past three years have been laid under contribution, as will be seen by reference to the notes. In short, I have done my best to bring this translation up to the level of the latest publications upon this immense subject.

Nevertheless, having said so much, I am fully aware that the book must needs still present more than one lacuna. Studies in the comparative history of modern literatures involve, by reason of their complexity, peculiar difficulties, which have hitherto prevented them from attaining the development they deserve and are destined to receive in the future. Those, at any rate, who have prosecuted researches of this nature, will know how especially difficult it is to be complete in the matter of bibliography. I have repeatedly been made aware of this fact while writing this essay in comparative literature, and am still more sensible of it now that the book is about to appear in a new form.

I must acknowledge that I have incurred obligations

towards more than one of the critics who have spoken of this book. I would at any rate tender my thanks to Mr W. M. Fullerton for his constant sympathy, and to my translator, Mr J. W. Matthews, for the conscientious care which has enabled him to correct certain errors in points of detail, particularly in the matter of quotations.

JOSEPH TEXTE.

LYON, *January* 1899.

Introduction

"THERE exist two entirely distinct literatures," wrote Madame de Staël in the closing year of the eighteenth century, "that which springs from the South and that which springs from the North": on the one hand, the group of romance literatures, derived from the Latin tradition, with the literature of France as its chief representative; on the other, the group of "Northern," that is to say Germanic and Slavonic, literatures, free—or so, at least, thought Mme. de Staël—from this absorbing Latin influence, "the most remarkable" among them, in her opinion, being the literature of England.

To-day, however, we no longer divide the literatures of Europe, with the same assurance as did Mme. de Staël, into two groups separated by a hard and fast line. We have learnt that among "Southern," no less than among "Northern" literatures, there are essential distinctions to be drawn. In a word, we have multiplied the data of the problem, and obtained glimpses of more complex solutions. Have we shaken ourselves free from the central idea of Mme. de Staël's theory? Have we given up contrasting Latin with non-Latin tradition, Southern literature with Northern, "humanism"—as we say now-a-days—with "exoticism," or "cosmopolitanism"?

Clearly, we have not. Quite recently a brilliant discussion was started upon this question,—to-day more real than ever before—as to the influence of the "Northern literatures" and of "cosmopolitanism" upon the literature of France, and all who took part in it, whether opponents of "exoticism" or its partisans, were agreed in distinguishing the "Latin tradition" from what M. Jules Lemaître has wittily named "septentriomania."[1]

[1] Articles, by M. Jules Lemaître on "L'influence des littératures du Nord" (*Revue des Deux Mondes*, December 1894), by M. Melchior de Vogüé on the "Renaissance latine" (*ib.* January 1895), by M. André Hallays on "L'influence

M. E. Faguet, a few months earlier, seeking a definition for the
"classical" spirit, declared that the direction which French
literature is henceforth to take is at the present moment disputed
by two conflicting influences, namely, humanism on the one hand
and exoticism on the other.[1]

Is France to remain faithful to that veneration for antiquity to
which the national intellect has adhered for three or four centuries? Or will she allow herself to be carried away by the
movement which, for a hundred years and more, has been urging
her in the same direction as literatures which are younger and
more independent of classical tradition? Will she come back to
Greece, to Rome, to the French classics? Or will she turn to
England, to Germany, to Russia, to Norway,—in short, to the
North? Since the question can be asked, it is clear that the
distinction formerly drawn by Mme. de Staël still holds good in
substance: whether founded upon reason or not, her theory has
been, for nearly a hundred years, one of the leading ideas of
nineteenth century criticism.

But how did that theory come to be formulated? What are
the facts upon which it was based? How, and where did it
arise, and under the influence of what circumstances? Such is
the problem which I have attempted to solve.

It seemed to me that the origins and successive forms of the
influence of the classical spirit upon the French genius had been
studied repeatedly and at great length, but that the origins of
the cosmopolitan spirit, which had assailed and threatened to
supplant that influence, had been less frequently—and very
inaccurately—dealt with.

What then was it that cosmopolitanism, or "exoticism,"
represented at the outset? Few of the historians of French
literature have asked themselves the question. By some of the
greatest, Nisard for instance, it has been evaded; others have
touched lightly upon it, as a side issue, when treating of the

des littératures étrangères" (*Revue de Paris*, February 1895). See also M. F.
Brunetière's essay: *Le cosmopolitisme et la littérature nationales*, reprinted in *Études
critique sur l'histoire de la littérature française*, 6th series.

[1] Study on Alexandrinism (*Revue des Deux Mondes*, May 1894).

origins of romanticism or of Mme. de Staël. The majority, after devoting a few hurried pages to the anglomania or the "germanomania" of the romantic school, assert that this fashion had no very great vogue, and hasten, as Nisard expressed it, to "restore the true guides of the French spirit," namely, the ancient writers, to their rightful place.

Unfortunately, however, the present is an age in which the French mind, rebelling—rightly or wrongly—against the counsels of criticism, refuses adherence to its old masters, and when—as Emile Hennequin observes—French literature "is less than ever adequate to express the prevailing sentiments of French society." Not only so, but French society "has found its own feelings more faithfully expressed, and has taken greater pleasure, in the productions of certain foreign writers of genius, than in those of the poets and novelists to whom it has itself given birth." Whence it follows that between minds there exist "voluntary bonds, at once more free and more enduring than the long-established community of blood, of native soil, of speech, of history and of custom, by which nations appear to be formed and divided."[1] The question of race is therefore at the basis of the question of cosmopolitanism; it is the existence of the national genius of France that exoticism leads us to consider, at anyrate in so far as this genius is conceived as the lawful and privileged heir of the genius of antiquity.

In the present work I have endeavoured to determine the origins of this movement, and it has seemed to me necessary to go back not merely, as is usually done, to the romantic school, but to the eighteenth century and to Rousseau.

True, it was the romanticists who, if I may say so, let loose the cosmopolitan spirit in France; but the master of all the romantic school, as well of Mme. de Staël,—the man whose aspirations they did but formulate, whose influence they did but extend and strengthen—was Rousseau. He it was who, on behalf of the Germanic races of Europe, struck a blow at the time-honoured

---

[1] E. Hennequin, *Ecrivains francisés*, p. iii. *Cf.* H. M. Posnett, *Comparative Literature* (London, 1886), book iv., ch. 1 (*What is World-literature?*).

supremacy of the Latin races. It was he who, in the words of
Mme. de Staël, united in himself the genius of the North with
the genius of the South. It was from the day when he wrote,
and it was because he had written, that the literatures of the
North unfolded themselves to the French mind, and took possession of it. Jean-Jacques, said Mme. de Staël once more, although
he wrote in French, belongs to "the Teutonic school"; he
impregnated the national genius with "foreign vigour." Employing the same idea, and giving it greater precision, M. de Vogüé
has recently said: "There is one very cogent argument, and one
only, which can be brought against those who would see in
French romanticism a product of foreign influences, and that is
that the germ of all our romanticism exists in Rousseau. But
this precious fellow, who is lawful father to Bernardin and
Chateaubriand, and grandfather to George Sand and the rest of
them, actually has the presumption to be a Swiss. *Has he not a
very strongly marked foreign appearance, one which in many respects is
already of a northern cast*, even on his first irruption in the midst
of French tradition? It is painful to have to confess it, but in
order to defend ourselves from the reproach of having been
poisoned with German and English virus, we are constrained to
recognize that Swiss blood has, for a century past, been flowing
through our inmost veins."

The whole object of this book is to exhibit Rousseau as the
man who has done the most to create in the French nation both
the taste and the need for the literatures of the North.

In the first place I have endeavoured to show that Rousseau
profited greatly by the influence which had been exercised in
France, ever since the commencement of the eighteenth century,
by "the most remarkable of the Germanic nations"—the only
one, in fact, of which that century acquired a thorough knowledge
—namely, England. During the interval between his arrival in
Paris in 1744 and the publication of *La Nouvelle Héloïse* in 1761,
English influence strengthened its hold upon the French alike in
science, in philosophy, in the drama and in fiction. A contemporary, struck with the current of ideas which connected the
two countries during those decisive years, remarked that if at

that time France had brought a telescope to bear upon the things of the mind the instrument would have been constantly directed towards England; and Buckle once declared that this union of the French with the English intellect was "by far the most important fact in the history of the eighteenth century."[1] I have studied the origins of this movement; I have tried to show how the revocation of the Edict of Nantes, by driving the national genius abroad, if I may say so, paved the way for the advent of the Northern literatures, and I have reminded the reader of the way in which the work of Protestant criticism was carried on by Muralt, Voltaire and Prévost, all of whom Rousseau had read and closely studied. Disseminated by these men of talent or of genius, English influence had, at the moment when Jean-Jacques began to write, become a power. It was the secret hope of all who, more or less vaguely, were dreaming of a revival of French literature. To Diderot, the friend of Rousseau, and to the whole of Diderot's school, England seemed the home of liberty of thought : "The Englishman," wrote one of them, borrowing both metaphor and thought from Rousseau, "never bows his head to the yoke which the majority of men bear without a murmur, but prefers freedom, however stormy, to tranquil dependence."[2]

This stormy freedom of the English genius was destined to captivate Jean-Jacques. By his foreign descent, his religious convictions, and his literary aspirations, he was sooner or later to feel himself drawn towards this eighteenth century Salentum. We shall see the extent to which it actually fascinated him, and how his admiration for England, while it did not in his own mind take the form of a protest against the classical tradition of France, was rendered such by force of circumstances.

But the anglomania of his contemporaries was not enough for Rousseau. His most celebrated work is in part an imitation of a famous English novel. Every writer of his day remarked that, as an English critic has expressed it, the soul of Clarissa

---

[1] *History of Civilization*, vol. ii. p. 214.
[2] *Journal encyclopédique*, April 1758.

had "transmigrated into the heroine of *La Nouvelle Héloïse*." [1] I have endeavoured to specify Jean-Jacques' debt to Richardson, and to show why the latter, too little known at the present day, is the precursor of the former in the history of European literature. The whole of the *bourgeois* literature of modern times, and this is saying a great deal, has sprung from this English novel, and, as has been excellently observed, " it is undeniable that *Clarissa Harlowe* stands to *La Nouvelle Héloïse* in this same relation as *La Nouvelle Héloïse* stands to *Werther*, *René* and *Jacopo Ortis*." [2] For the first time a great English writer had served as model for one of the great writers of France. Can we wonder that Rousseau's contemporaries remarked the fact as a sign of the times ?

Thus Rousseau felt an instinctive admiration for the English, and imitated them. He was the brilliant personification of all that was most original and most independent in the English genius. Thomson sang the praises of nature thirty years earlier, and with no less feeling, than he ; twenty years before the publication of *La Nouvelle Héloïse* Young had given expression to that "enchanting sorrow" which so charmed Saint-Preux ; while old Ossian revealed the sweet springs of melancholy simultaneously with Rousseau. The works of these writers made their appearance in France when his literary career was at its height. In truth, he owes them nothing. But their influence became blended with his ; in them French readers, betweeen 1760 and 1789, found the same aspirations, the same unrest, the same lyricism as they had found in Rousseau,— everything, in short, which they thirsted for but had failed to discover in the classical literature of France. How could they help being struck with the kinship between the genius of Rousseau and that of the northern writers? How could they help regarding this as an instance, to use the expression of a contemporary, of " cross-fertilization " in the intellectual sphere ? Was it not inevitable that Mme. de Staël should have said that

[1] Leslie Stephen, *Hours in a Library*, 1st ed., p. 68.

[2] Marc Monnier, *Jean-Jacques Rousseau et les étrangers*, in *Rousseau jugé par les Genevois d'aujourd'hui* (Geneva, 1879).

he had infused the French intellect with "foreign vigour," since it was from his school that it learned to enjoy foreign works in preference to those of purely French origin? If the idea was an illusion, we can at any rate both account for it and excuse it.

It was through this school—that of Rousseau and the English —that our fathers learned to appreciate what Mme. de Staël calls "the genius of the North." They became, or began to be, "cosmopolitans"; that is to say, they grew weary of the pro-tracted supremacy of the literatures of antiquity. The ancients, wrote the author of *De la Littérature* not long afterwards, "leave little regret" behind them, and five-and-twenty years later the romantic school, through the medium of Stendhal, added the opinion that "*spite of all the pedants, Germany and England will win the day against France.*"[1]

It is true that cosmopolitanism did not take shape as a theory until after the Revolution, with Mme. de Staël. I hope I have succeeded in showing that as an aspiration, already well-defined, it dates from the previous century, and that, in contrasting the Teutonic with the Latin genius, the new criticism simply carried the revolution effected by Rousseau to its inevitable consequence. The influence of the northern literatures has increased or diminished during the past century in proportion to that of Jean-Jacques; the reason being that the former is but the latter in another form.

It should further be observed that the French were not awakened all at once to an interest in northern literature. Just in the same way eighteenth century France failed to under-stand Shakespeare, and the critics treated this as a proof of its inability to appreciate the literatures of other nations. Not only, however, is it difficult to recognize Shakespeare in the crude versions of that day,[2] but between the eighteenth century and Shakespeare there is something more than the mere differ-ence of race, there is the gulf that separates two epochs. Not

---

[1] Stendhal, *Racine et Shakespeare* (1823), p. 246.

[2] Observe that down to 1776, the year in which the first volume of Letourneur's version appeared, the only manner in which French readers could become ac-quainted with Shakespeare was through the grotesque parody of La Place. See J. J. Jusserand, *Shakespeare en France sous l'ancien régime* (Paris, 1898).

all at once did the French mind, which could no longer appreciate either Ronsard or Rabelais, succeed in understanding the English Renaissance.

Nevertheless, even in the eighteenth century, it both understood and appreciated the novels of Richardson and Sterne, and the poetry of Young, Thomson, and Ossian, all of them thoroughly English writers and anything but "classical." They form the escort of Rousseau, who is greater than them all. Some are his models, others his predecessors or contemporaries. All are bound to him by a family likeness: Mme. de Staël constantly speaks of "Rousseau and the English", and she is right. The cosmopolitan spirit was born, during the eighteenth century, of the fruitful union between the English genius and that of Jean-Jacques.

Such is the thesis of the present work.

The reader will be good enough to observe that I do not identify the cosmopolitan spirit with the influence of any one in particular of the literatures of Europe. The chief place is allotted to England, because she was the first, and, for a century, practically the only, country to exercise an influence upon France. Of German literature nothing was known during the eighteenth century beyond a few names, and Gessner was the only writer with whom Rousseau was acquainted. Those who read *Werther* or the *Robbers*, which owed their inspiration to him, could discern in them one more proof of the kinship between his genius and that of the Germans. Only a few of the more inquiring minds paid any attention to the writings of "the Danes and Swedes" mentioned by Mme. de Staël. England was thus the first country to exercise an influence upon France; an influence which gave the cosmopolitan movement the tendency it has maintained throughout the present century—namely, to raise a protest, in the name of foreign and modern literature, against the influence of the classical spirit.

But is there such a thing as a "classical spirit," a "French spirit," or an "English spirit"? And what right have we to distinguish a "Germanic" from a "Latin" genius? Are not these expressions simply empty formulas, which have no real import, and but faintly disguise the vagueness of the ideas for which they stand ?—I confess that more than once, in the course of these pages, I have asked myself this disturbing question.

"There are naturally," said Taine in a famous passage, "varieties of men, just as there are varieties of bulls and horses; there are the brave and intelligent, and there are the timid and feeble-minded; those who are capable of lofty conceptions and productions, and those who cannot go beyond rudimentary ideas and inventions; some who are especially fitted for certain kinds of work, and more richly endowed than others with certain instincts, just as certain races of dogs are better qualified, some for running, some for fighting, some for the chase, and some for the protection of houses and flocks."[1] Taine was the successor of Mme. de Staël, and since his day the history of literature has been above all an ethnological problem.

But since Taine wrote these lines we have learnt to distrust the more positive conclusions which some writers have attempted to draw from moral ethnography, assuredly the most difficult and the most complex of all the sciences.   Nay, in many intelligent minds, this distrust has turned into absolute scepticism.   Only recently the author of a splendid work upon *Robert Burns* asserted that the idea of race is " fluctuating, ill-established, and open to dispute."   Admissible, perhaps, in the physical sphere, that idea is unreliable in the moral sphere, and for two reasons : firstly, because there is nothing to show that a few differences in physical characteristics, faint and superficial as these, moreover, are, such as the outline of the nose, and the colour of the eyes or hair, carry with them differences, and important differences, in the intellectual system; and, in the second place, because the psychology of races seems still more problematic.   You cannot obtain a conception of the soul of a portion of humanity by merely supplementing certain ethnological labels with a few vague adjectives."[2]

These are specious objections, and I confess they do not strike me as conclusive.

---

[1] Introduction to *English Literature*.
[2] Angellier, *Robert Burns*, vol. i. p. vii.

In the first place, we are not here concerned with "the colour of the eyes" or "the shape of the nose." It is allowable to speak of the "French spirit" or of "the Italian genius" because, in Italy as well as in France, a long succession of writers of talent or of genius have had a certain more or less definite idea of this national "genius" and this national "spirit." Whether that idea was true or false is of little consequence; even an illusion may produce good results. Enough that from the whole assemblage of French or Italian works it is possible to select certain common features which differentiate them from the productions of Spanish or English writers. The excellent observation made by Nisard in respect to his own history, that it was possible "only because there exists a clear conception of the French intellect," might without hesitation be applied to French literature. In other words, this conception—or, if you will, this illusion—is the collective work of all those who for centuries past have wielded the pen in France, and the reason why the French spirit exists is simply that hundreds and thousands of writers have willed that it should exist. Could Robert Burns be called "the great poet of Scotland," if he had not set before himself a certain ideal of the "Scotch genius"? It has been maintained that, in his poems, he shewed himself independent of the necessities of race and blood. But while this may be, we must at least admit that with all the strength of his soul he believed in the originality of his country—that he gloried in being, through an act of his own free will, a "child of Scotland."

Doubtless, the idea of race, like so many other ideas essential to science of any kind—like that of heredity, or that of moral liberty—is neither absolutely clear nor perfectly definite in range. Does it therefore follow that there is no reality which corresponds to it? Not only would such a hypothesis contradict every scientific notion of things, but it would also infallibly land us in the strangest paradoxes, and when Taine expressed the idea that race is "the primary source of historical events" he did but enunciate a law from which it will long be impossible for the history of literature to escape. By eliminating this essential notion of race, we surrender, at the very outset, all possibility of accounting for anything beyond the individual. But what is the individual without his environment? What is Dante without Italy, Burns without Scotland, Ibsen without Norway? The inadequacy, the futility, of any attempt to study the genius of these men without paying due regard to the idea of race, is palpable. On the other hand, will any one deny that the literature of Greece, taken as a whole, represents an entirely distinct type of the human intelligence? Will anyone maintain that the whole mass of the works which have been written in Latin might equally well be attributed either to the Arabians or to the Chinese? Could the Alhambra be the work of the architect of the Parthenon, or the Discobolus of a Hindoo sculptor? Those who scoff at the absurdity of such questions thereby admit that the history of literature and art is before all things an ethnographical problem. Nisard, in his account of the literary productions of France, states that his aim was to write "the history of the French mind." He was right. A history of French literature which did not set that aim before it would be no more than a shapeless congeries of materials.

It is thus in vain to point out the obscurity of the conception of race, to protest that genius removes all barriers, or to expose the dangers and difficulties of the "psychology of peoples"; there is no escaping the fact that this idea of race is now, and long will be, the guiding principle of all fruitful historical research. "Humanity," said Vigny, "is delivering an interminable discourse, and every distinguished man is one of the ideas it expresses." When, therefore, the historian studies a man, he is studying humanity; but in order to go back to the origins of humanity, he must of necessity study the ethnological group to which the man belongs. For each nation, in its turn, utters a portion of the "interminable discourse" delivered by humanity.

But in reality it is only the discourse of humanity that can be called "interminable." The discourse which each nation delivers lasts, on the contrary, only a few centuries at most. It is this fact that enables the historian of Greece or Italy to speak with confidence of a Greek genius or a Latin spirit. These nations have said their say, and we can determine the nature of their genius. Their civilizations are dead and gone; they are organisms whose evolution has run its course. How much easier it is to study them than to examine a living civilization, the development of which will continue for centuries! By what right, logically speaking, can we give a definition of the French or of the German spirit, so long as there is a Germany or a France still in existence? What science authorizes us to classify, to judge and to define that which still lives and moves, and every day advances towards an end of which we cannot as yet obtain a glimpse? In a few centuries the vital force of our race may have exhausted itself; we, in our turn, may have ended our discourse; and then, and then only, will it be altogether permissible to say what we were. Meanwhile we are confined to conjectures and to probabilities.

Such is one reason for caution. Here is another.

The races of men are no more invariable and no more proof against the intrusion of alien blood than are the species of animals: interbreeding takes place between them, as between those species, and thereby they become transformed. " For the past eight or ten centuries there has been, in a sense, a traffic or interchange of ideas from one end of Europe to the other," so that Germany has been nourishing itself upon French thought, England upon German thought, Spain upon Italian thought, and each of these nations successively upon the thought of all the rest. The study of a living being is to a large extent the study of its relations to its neighbours. Similarly not a literature can be found of which the history does not carry us beyond the frontiers of its native country. Look where we will among modern literatures, it is always the same story of alternate lendings and borrowings; as Voltaire said : " Almost all literary work is imitation. . . . It is with books as with the fire on our hearth-stones : we obtain kindling from our neighbours, light our own fire with it, pass it on to others, and it becomes the property of all." There is, as it were, a fluid form of matter which flows successively into different moulds, runs from mind to mind, and always, as it passes on to the next, carries with it a fresh principle of life and movement.

The difficulty of these racial problems having been ascertained, it is none the less incumbent upon the historian of literatures, and of modern literatures in particular, to treat each one of them, " not as an entirely distinct and self-contained history, but as a branch of European literature in general."[1] This is what I have endeavoured, to the best of my ability, to do, in these pages, for Rousseau.

In their moral no less than in their political life, nations have their periods of concentration and expansion. I have attempted to show that for a century and a half the cosmopolitan spirit in literature has manifested itself in the reaching out of the French mind, according to the example set by Rousseau, towards the literatures of northern Europe.

The present volume owes much to the teaching and advice of M. Ferdinand Brunetière. He has said somewhere that it " would be well to subordinate the history of individual literatures to the general history of the literature of Europe." It is his opinion that " by adopting this standpoint in our study of the history of French literature, we shall find it no less original, and least of all less classical," but we shall assuredly "reconstruct it in part." Such, also, was my own opinion, and still is. Now that I have experienced the difficulties of the undertaking, and have had my own incapacity fully brought home to me, I cannot but feel the deepest gratitude to the generous teacher, but for whose encouragement these pages would never have been written, and whose instruction has been one of the chief favours I have received at the hands of fortune. Would that this book were less unworthy of the interest he has taken in it.

I wish also to acknowledge the useful advice I have received from M. J.-J. Jusserand, from my old master, M. A. Beljame, professor at the Sorbonne, and from the professors of Oxford University generally, who have made me their grateful debtor.

[1] F. Brunetière, *Revue des Deux Mondes*, 10th May 1891.

It gives me much pleasure to add to these names those of M. E. Ritter, M. H. Carré, and above all that of the late M. Guillaume Guizot, who was generous enough to place at my disposal his manuscript notes upon the literary relations between England and France during the eighteenth century.

LYON, *April* 1895.

Table of Contents

Book I

THE INFLUENCE OF ENGLAND UPON FRANCE BEFORE THE TIME OF ROUSSEAU

Chapter I

THE REVOCATION OF THE EDICT OF NANTES AND THE FIRST MIGRATION OF THE FRENCH SPIRIT

Chapter II

WRITERS RESPONSIBLE FOR THE DIFFUSION OF ENGLISH INFLUENCE: MURALT, PRÉVOST, VOLTAIRE

Chapter III

THE CAUSES WHICH, BEFORE THE TIME OF ROUSSEAU, PAVED THE WAY FOR THE SUCCESS OF THE COSMOPOLITAN SPIRIT IN FRANCE

Book II

JEAN-JACQUES ROUSSEAU AND ENGLISH LITERATURE

Chapter I

ROUSSEAU AND ENGLAND

Chapter II

Chapter III

Chapter IV

Chapter V

JEAN-JACQUES ROUSSEAU AND ENGLISH FICTION

Book III

ROUSSEAU AND THE INFLUENCE OF ENGLAND DURING THE LATTER HALF OF THE EIGHTEENTH CENTURY

Chapter I

ROUSSEAU AND THE DIFFUSION OF THE LITERATURES OF NORTHERN EUROPE

Chapter II

ENGLISH INFLUENCE AND THE SENTIMENTAL NOVEL

CONTENTS

Chapter III

ENGLISH INFLUENCE AND THE LYRICISM OF ROUSSEAU

Chapter IV

THE REVOLUTION AND THE SECOND MIGRATION OF THE FRENCH SPIRIT. JEAN-JACQUES ROUSSEAU AND MME. DE STAËL

Conclusion

Book I

THE INFLUENCE OF ENGLAND UPON FRANCE BEFORE THE TIME OF ROUSSEAU

Chapter I

THE REVOCATION OF THE EDICT OF NANTES AND THE FIRST MIGRATION OF THE FRENCH SPIRIT

I. Ignorance of the seventeenth century with regard to England—Prejudices and prepossessions—Ignorance of the language—Instances of English books which were known in France during the seventeenth century—Why these instances prove nothing—Paramount influence of humanism.

II. The French colony in London—Propaganda of the refugees on behalf of English philosophy and English political institutions.

III. Their works of travel—Their newspapers—In what sense can it be said that the Dutch reviews aided the birth of the cosmopolitan spirit in literature?—Bayle, Le Clerc, and Basnage—Multiplication of international reviews—Their hostility to antiquity—They pave the way for English literature—La Roche, La Chapelle, Maty—French imitators of the refugees: Dubos, Destouches, Desfontaines—Inferiority and unimportance of their work in comparison with that of Protestant criticism.

THE revocation of the Edict of Nantes was something more than a religious or political event of great importance in the history of France. It was productive also of far-reaching effects upon her intellectual destinies. For with the revocation began that movement of thought which opened the French mind to a comprehension of northern literature.

When Louis XIV. condemned four hundred thousand of his subjects, men of an active and enquiring turn of mind, to live beyond the confines of France, and principally in lands where Teutonic tongues were spoken, he did not suspect that his action would tend towards a thorough transformation of the national genius. It was, nevertheless, in consequence of the revocation

A

that French thought was brought in contact, first of all with England, and afterwards with Germany. As interpreters between the Germanic and Latin sections of Europe, the refugees were most industrious, and from the heart of the Low Countries, of Great Britain, of Brandenburg, and of Switzerland, Protestant criticism strove, for two centuries, to bring Frenchmen into communication with the mind of Europe.

Begun by the refugees, and carried on by Prévost and Voltaire, this propaganda on behalf, more particularly, of English literature, had important consequences. Its effects began to make themselves felt about the middle of the eighteenth century, that is to say, at the moment when Jean-Jacques Rousseau was revolutionizing French literature. As a critic of that age expressed it, "it had long been impossible to doubt that the intermixture of races improves every species, both animal and vegetable," and "the experiment which for thirty years had been made upon a neighbouring country, namely, England," had afforded a clear proof that "the crossing of minds, which have also their races," may result in fertility.[1]

It appears to me that Rousseau derived more benefit from this "crossing" between the French and English minds than has commonly been supposed. In briefly recalling the nature of the propaganda carried on by the refugees, and of that of their French imitators, we shall therefore be studying the very origins of the revolution which he effected.

I

In order to estimate its importance we must transport ourselves in spirit to the seventeenth century, and recall to mind the contempt professed by the more outspoken writers of that epoch for the literatures of the Northern countries, and especially for the people which Mme. de Staël described as "the most remarkable of the Germanic nations."

It was through England that France was brought into contact with non-Latin Europe. Now, of all European countries,

[1] Garat, *Mémoires sur Suard*, vol. i., p. 153.

England was the one with which Frenchmen of the *grand siècle* were least acquainted. They regarded it with suspicion on account of its religion, and with detestation on account of its political history. Attached as they were to Catholic and monarchical tradition, the "English tragedies," to use the expression of Descartes, had filled them with alarm. Mme. de Motteville speaks of Cromwell and his crew as "rebel savages." "Guilty nation," cried Bossuet, "more turbulent within its own borders and in its own havens than the ocean which washes its shores!" How could men who, according to Saumaise, were "more savage than their own dogs," and were still regarded by Frenchmen with the inveterate rancour engendered by the wars of the middle ages,[1] be thought capable of poetry or art?

But little acquainted with the English, the French despised them without scruple. Their contempt was returned with interest. Sir William Temple forbade his daughter to marry a Frenchman, "because he had always had a deep hatred of that nation on account of its proud and impetuous character, so little in harmony with the slavish dependence in which it is kept at home."[2] And if the English accuse the French of servility, they are in turn accused by the French of a savage disposition and senseless pride. "Pride and stupidity are their only manners; their least absurd caprices are full of extravagance," said Saint-Amant of the English, and he spoke *de visu*, having seen "the malignant Roundheads, to whom the very throne is an object of suspicion,"[3] at work in their own country.

Two migrations of English royalists, in 1649 and 1688, did not suffice to close this gulf between the two peoples. One would have thought it might have been bridged by the curiosity of travellers. But we have every reason to know that Frenchmen of the *grand siècle* were but little given to travel. Rare indeed were the writers who, like Malherbe or Descartes, had crossed the northern or eastern frontier. Italy was visited, and Spain;

---

[1] See M. Langlois's study on *Les Anglais au moyen âge* (*Revue historique*, 1894).

[2] A. Babeau, *Les voyageurs en France*, p. 99.

[3] *L'Albion* (*Œuvres*, ed. Livet, vol. ii., p. 439).

but no one ventured to cross the Channel. When, in 1654, Father Coulon, a Jesuit, published one of the earliest guides for travellers in England—possibly the first to appear in the French language [1]—this ancestor of Baedeker and Joanne did not disguise from his readers the difficulty of the undertaking, and had to appeal to the most celebrated instances in order to encourage them. "Once the dwelling-place of saints and angels, England is now the infernal abode of parricides and fiends. For all that, however, she has not changed her nature; she still remains where she was, and just as in the lower regions the justice of the Almighty is associated with pity, so in this hateful island you may observe at the same time the traces of ancient piety, and the commotions and disturbance caused by the brutality of a people excited, spite of their Northern stupidity (*sic*), to the verge of madness." Scarcely an attractive picture. Accordingly, Coulon feels the necessity of providing his reader with some consolation. "Since in former days Julius Cæsar had the courage and the curiosity to embark from the shore of Calais in order to seek a new world beyond our seas, and to add to his empire provinces which nature has separated from our dominions by another element, our traveller need not fear to cross over to England nor to entrust himself to the winds and to fortune, which formerly brought that ruler of the universe in safety to the port of Dover." He would therefore follow Julius Cæsar to England, but he would make no stay in the island. "I do not recommend any reader to penetrate very far into the country, for nature has subjected it to a very sorry climate, and placed it, as it were, at the extremity of the world, in order to forbid our entry. It would be better to set out once more for France." [2]

[1] *Le fidèle conducteur pour le voyage d'Angleterre*, by the sieur Coulon. Paris, Gervais Clouzier, 1654, 12mo. In the sixteenth century had appeared *Le guide des chemins d'Angleterre, fort nécessaire à ceux qui y voyagent* . . . [by Jean Bernard, Secretary of the King's Chamber]. Paris, Gervais Malot, 1579, 8vo.

[2] About the same time a certain sieur de la Boullaye Legoux published a few notes on England, which he had visited in 1643. He mentions as his friends: "Charles Stuart, first of the name, king of England," and "Mme. Cromwell, widow of the late Oliver Cromwell, of London." (See Rathery, *Des relations sociales et intellectuelles entre la France et l'Angleterre*, 4th part.)

Most men, in that day, held the same opinion as Coulon, and spared themselves the trouble of " setting out once more for France " by never crossing her frontier. The majority, like Guy Patin, regarded travelling as " a disturbance of body and mind to no purpose whatever."[1] Such writers as had visited England during the previous century—for instance, Brantôme, Ronsard, Monchrestien, Bodin, Henri Estienne, La Noue, and du Bartas—had commonly done so for diplomatic purposes, or in the train of a great personage.

The few men of letters who, in the seventeenth century, crossed the English Channel, were travellers almost in spite of themselves, and certainly had little curiosity concerning English literature. Such were Voiture,[2] Gabriel Naudé, who went to collect books for Mazarin's library, Puget de la Serre, whose duties as historiographer obliged him to follow Marie de Médicis,[3] Théophile de Viaud, who sought refuge in England for his own safety, Pavillon, d'Assoucy, Jean de Schelandre, Chappuzeau, almost all literary adventurers, upon whom, with the possible exception of Schelandre, English literature seems to have made no impression whatever. Saint-Amant, in some very inferior lines,[4] said of the Englishman, " he has nevertheless the audacity to boast of his own rhymesters; to his mind they are better than either Vergil or Horace. In comparison with a Janson [Ben Jonson], Seneca is but an insipid poet, destitute of either power or melody, and the famous Euripides has neither grace nor workmanship." And of some lines of English poetry he said : " Enough that they are in English; they shall be reduced to ashes." Pavillon expects to find England a wild region, covered with virgin forests, and is amazed to discover " never a

---

[1] From the way in which he mangles proper names it would appear doubtful whether Coulon himself ever crossed the straits. Exeter becomes *Excesse*, Bristol, *Brestel*, the Thames, *la Tamese*, etc

[2] *Cf.* Livet, *Précieux et Précieuses*, vol. i:, p. 191.

[3] See the account of Marie de Médicis' entry into London, by Puget de la Serre : the event occurred in 1639. (*Cf.* Edward Smith, *Foreign Visitors in England*, p. x.)

[4] *Cf. Albion, caprice héroï-comique*, dedicated to Mgr. le Marechal de Bassompierre, composed in 1644, and published by M. Livet in his edition of Saint-Amant, 1855, vol. ii

bridge or a gate to defend, not a single castle to storm, no
wrongs to redress nor robbers to chastize; in fact not the veriest
young spark to draw sword against." " But for the few young
ladies on palfreys whom one meets from time to time, I should
never have believed myself in the kingdom of Great Britain, so
changed seems everything in England since the days of King
Artus."[1] Le Pays—who received the nickname of "Voiture's
ape" and was so ill-treated by Boileau—remarks the ferocious
nature of English dramatic representations, but does not mention
any author or any piece by name.[2]

Nor were the French less ignorant of the language than of
the country. Who should have been at the pains to acquire it?
Europe spared them the trouble of speaking foreign languages
by using their own. Étienne Pasquier had already remarked
that there was not a nobleman's mansion in the whole of
Germany, England, and Scotland but had its French tutor.
French, in the seventeenth century, was, after Latin, the international language. It was in French that Bacon wrote to the
Marquis d'Effiat, and Hobbes to Gassendi. The foreign
languages taught in the schools of Port Royal were Spanish
and Italian.[3] In the scheme of studies drawn up by Richelieu
for the grammar school he intended to found in his native town,
we find no subjects represented beyond " the comparison of the

---

[1] Letter to Mme. de Pelissari. *Œuvres de M. Pavillon*, Paris, 1720, 12mo, p. 110.

[2] *Amitiez, amours et amourettes*, by M. Le Pays, 3rd edn., Paris, 1665, 12mo. p.
202. " You are aware, sir, that the rules of dramatic art, as we understand them,
will not allow the tragic events of a play to be enacted before the eyes of the spectator. Our poets understand the gentleness of our disposition, and never permit
blood to be spilt upon the stage. . . . Quite otherwise is it with English poets,
who, in order to pander to the humour and inclination of their audience, always introduce scenes of bloodshed, and never fail to embellish their pieces with the most
horrible catastrophes. In every play that is produced some one is either hung, torn
in pieces, or assassinated. And it is at such passages that their women clap their
hands and burst into laughter." As further instances of accounts of travel in the
seventeenth century, I may mention that of a journey by the Duc de Rohan: *Voyage
fait en l'an 1600 en Italie, Allemagne, Pays Bas, Angleterre et Écosse* (Amsterdam, 1646,
12mo), and the volume by Charles Patin entitled: *Relations historiques et curieuses de
voyages en Allemagne, Angleterre, Hollande, Bohême, Suisse, etc.*, by C. P. (Rouen, 1676,
12mo).

[3] Lantoine, *Histoire de l'enseignement secondaire en France au xviie siècle*, p. 181.

Greek, Latin, French, Italian, and Spanish languages." The writers of the day, Mme. de Sévigné, Racine, Corneille, La Fontaine, read Spanish or Italian, and sometimes both; but for the Teutonic languages they cared nothing whatever. La Bruyère and Saint-Simon are quoted as having known something of German. So late even as 1665 the *Journal des savants* was unable to find anyone who could contribute an account of the *Proceedings* of the Royal Society of London. "The English," wrote Le Clerc, "have many good works; it is a pity that authors in that country seldom write any language but their own."[1]

English was regarded as a barbarous jargon. Corneille used to show his friends, as a curiosity, an English translation of *Le Cid*, which he kept in a cabinet along with translations of the same work into Turkish and Sclavonian. Jean Doujat, the lawyer, who was believed to know all the languages of Europe; La Mothe le Vayer, who had married a Scotchwoman; Regnier Desmarais, who, in his grammar, introduces a few comparisons with English; the sieur de la Hoguette, who had visited England, had met Bacon, and was acquainted with some English novels,[2] were mentioned as having a knowledge of the language. Fénelon, Ramsay's friend, says vaguely: "I hear that the English do not mind what words they use, provided they suit their purpose. They borrow them from their neighbours wherever they find them."[3] Sorel, in his *Francion*, obtains a cheap success with a burlesque of the jargon spoken by an English lord.[4]

Nevertheless, even in the seventeenth century there existed works devoted to the teaching of English. From Gabriel Meurier, through Festeau and Miège, down to Louis Oursel and Boyer, various grammarians had turned their attention to the language.[5] One of them, Claude Mauger, in a grammar

---

[1] Rathery, part iii.
[2] *Ibid.*
[3] *Lettre à l'Académie*, iii.
[4] *Francion*, bk. ii., pp. 70-72.
[5] Gabriel Meurier's work (*Traité pour apprendre à parler françois et anglois*) dates from 1653. The *Alphabet anglois* of Louis Oursel is dated 1639 (Rouen, 8vo, 32 pp.). The same writer's *Grammere angloise* bears the same date (Rouen, 1639, 8vo, 205 pp.). Festeau's *Nouvelle grammaire anglaise* belongs to 1672. The *Dictionnaire anglais-français et français-anglais* of Miège is dated 1685.

which passed through thirteen editions, boasts, for the benefit
of his English readers, of having associated with some of the
best minds of Port Royal, who had placed his work in their
library.[1]

These works, however, were designed for the use of those
engaged in business. Boyer, in the grammar which he published
in 1700, was the first to proclaim that there is "something both
of Sophocles and of Aeschylus in Shakespeare." But Boyer was
a refugee, and his grammar, as well as his dictionary, belongs to
the eighteenth century. Adrien Baillet, as M. Jusserand has
pointed out, had already alluded to Shakespeare in his *Jugements
des Savants*, published at Paris in 1685-86, but he mentioned his name only, without giving any appreciation of his
work.[2]

Very few were the English books which found their way
into France before 1700; a few translations from Latin, More's
Utopia and Barclay's *Argenis*; certain historical works, such as
those of Burnet or Ricaut, the latter of whom, through the
medium of a translation, supplied Racine with the historical
materials of his *Bajazet*;[3] almost the whole of Bacon, whose
Essays were rendered into French in 1611 by a certain Jean
Baudouin,[4] and some of the writings of Hobbes; as regards
imaginative works, Godwin's *Man in the Moon*, and *The Discovery
of a New World*, by John Wilkins, both of them known to
Cyrano de Bergerac, and translated, the one by Jean Baudouin
in 1648, and the other by the sieur de la Montagne in 1655; a
novel by Greene, and Sidney's *Arcadia*—such were the principal

---

[1] " I assure you that there are no Words nor Phrases in my Grammar but are very
Modish, for I was every day with some of the ablest Gentlemen of Port Royal, who
assured me that my Grammar is in their Library." *Cf.* the notice at the end of
the *Grammaire angloise, expliquée par règles générales,* by Claude Mauger, professor
of languages, Bordeaux, not dated. The thirteenth edition bears the date
1689.

[2] See M. Jusserand's articles on *Shakespeare en France sous l'ancien regime* (*Cosmopolis,*
1896 and 1897).

[3] *Histoire de l'état present de l'empire ottoman,* trans. by Briot. Paris, 1670, 4to.

[4] See the list of these translations in Charles Adam's *Philosophie de Francois Bacon.*—
To M. Adam's list should be added the translation of the *De augmentis,* by the sieur
de Golefer, the royal historiographer. Paris, 1632, 4to.

English works which found their way across the Channel in the seventeenth century.[1]

The *Arcadia* alone became famous, on account of the reputation of its author. Two translators disputed the honour of introducing it to the French public. D'Urfé appears to have read it; Balzac praises the author; Sorel criticises it; while Boisrobert and Maréchal had recourse to it for the subjects of plays.

But all these translations, which we mention as curiosities merely, did not affect French literature to any appreciable extent. On the contrary, it was the French tragedies, romances and comedies that were finding their way abroad at this period, and were exerting a strong influence beyond the borders of France.[2] It would be difficult to name more than one or two seventeenth-century works, the subjects of which were taken from English books. Jean de Schelandre was possibly acquainted with Shakespeare; La Fosse, in his *Manlius*, has undoubtedly imitated Otway, and La Fontaine appears to have borrowed the subject of *Un Animal dans la lune* from *Hudibras*. Of English literature,

---

[1] *L'homme dans la lune*, an imaginary journey to the Moon, by Dominique Gonzalés [Jean Baudouin], Spanish adventurer. Paris, 1648, 8vo.

Découverte d'un nouveau monde, designed to show that there is an inhabitable world in the moon; and a discourse intended to make plain the possibility of getting there, together with a treatise on the planets. London, 1640, 8vo.

Le monde dans la lune, by the sieur de la Montagne. Rouen, 1655, 2 vols. 12mo.

Histoire tragique de Pandosto, roi de Bohême, et de Bellaria sa femme; together with the *Amours de Dorastus et de Favina*, translated from English into French by L. Regnault. Paris, 1615, 12mo (mentioned by Lenglet-Dufresnoy, *Bibliothèque des romans*, p. 44).

Mention is also made of certain *Memoires du chevalier Hazard, traduits de l'anglais sur l'original manuscrit*, Cologne, 1603, 12mo, which I have been unable to identify. (*Bibliothèque des romans*, March 1779.)

Le Blanc (*Lettres*, i., 33) speaks or a translation of J. Hall's *Quo vadis*, to which no date is assigned. Numerous translations of J. Hall's works were published at Geneva in the course of the seventeenth century.—Thomas Browne's *Religio Medici* was translated (from the Latin) by Nicolas le Febvre in 1668.—The *Eikon Basilikê*, translated by Porrée, appeared at Rouen in 1649.

With reference to translations of the *Arcadia*, see J. Jusserand, *The English Novel*, p. 282.—The *Arcadia* figured in the library of Fouquet.

[2] *Cf.* Beljame, *Le public et les hommes de lettres en Angleterre*, p 14 *et seq.*—J. Jusserand, *The English Novel*, chap. vii.

its general characteristics and essential features, cultivated minds
had no idea whatever, and it was from Addison that Boileau
heard of the existence of English poetry.

Saint-Évremond alone, among the critics of his time, has
spoken of it with a measure of understanding.   Obliged to live
in London, the friend of Waller, Buckingham, and D'Aubigny
succeeded at any rate in forming a fairly accurate idea of the
English genius, if he never obtained a knowledge of the
language.   He showed much acuteness in detecting the strong
and the weak points of the English drama.   He does not, it is
true, make mention of Shakespeare, or at any rate he alludes to
him only in a vague and cursory manner.[1]   But he names Ben
Jonson, whose *Catilina* and *Sejanus*, as also several of his comedies,
he had read or seen acted.   In the year which saw the production of *Phèdre*, he spoke in favourable terms of the English
drama, which "appeals too strongly to the senses," but possesses
fresh and vigorous beauties to which French tragedy cannot
attain.[2]   Above all, though the information he acquired was not
always very exact, his mind became broadened by contact with
a new literature so entirely different from the French.   Though
never more than a literary amateur, he was a man of an open
and comprehensive mind ; with Fontenelle he perceived that
"different varieties of ideas are like plants and flowers which
do not thrive equally well in every kind of climate,"[3] and like
him would have been ready to add : "Possibly our soil is
no better suited to the reasoning of the Egyptians than it is to
their palm-trees."[4]

But Saint-Évremond, like Fontenelle, is an isolated example.

---

[1] Letter to Mme. de Mazarin, 1682.   (*Œuvres mêlées* de Saint-Évremond, ed.
Giraud, vol. iii., p. 186).

[2] *Sur les tragédies*, 1677.—Ed. Giraud, vol. iii., p. 368.

[3] *Digression sur les anciens.*

[4] *Cf.* Saint-Évremond, *Dissertation sur Alexandre*, ed. Giraud, vol. i., p. 295 : "One
of the great faults of our nation is that we judge everything in reference to it, even
to the extent of calling those of our compatriots who have not the bearing and
manners characteristic of their country strangers in their own land ; hence we are
justly reproached with being unable to judge of things otherwise than by their relation to ourselves."—*Cf.* vol. i., p. 109, and vol. ii., p. 385.

Taken as a whole, seventeenth-century France remained closed
to the literatures of the Northern nations—or rather to the
only one of those literatures with which it might have formed
acquaintance.   For her, the map of intellectual Europe was
limited by the Alps, the Rhine, and the English Channel.
Beyond these boundaries was desert-land and darkness.   Away
yonder, in the regions of the North, dwelt a coarse-minded race
of men who led a sort of vegetable existence and were for ever
incapable of rising to the idea of an art stamped with their own
individuality or of independent thought.   "You must at least
confess," says one of Father Bouhours's characters, "that refinement of mind knows neither country nor race; that is to say
that, just as of old there were men of refined intellect among
the Greeks and Romans, so are there now among Frenchmen,
Italians, Spaniards, Englishmen, and even Germans and Musco-
vites."   His companion indignantly replies: "A strange phenomenon, forsooth, would that be—intellectual refinement in a
German or a Muscovite.   If there are such men in the world
they must be of those who never show their faces without
astonishing people.   Cardinal du Perron once said, speaking of
Gretser the Jesuit: "He has quite a refined mind for a German;
as though a cultured German were a prodigy."   "I acknowledge," Ariste interrupted, "that cultivated minds are somewhat
rarer in cold countries, because nature is there more languid and
mournful, so to speak."   "You should rather acknowledge,"
said Eugène, "that intellectual culture, as you have defined it,
is entirely incompatible with the coarse temperament and clumsy
frames of northern peoples."[1]
    What would Father Bouhours have said if he had been in-
formed that a day would come when those "clumsy frames"
and "coarse temperaments" would be the envy of French
writers, and when this "languid, mournful nature" would be
triumphantly contrasted with the bright sunshine of Italy?
"Our native prejudice," writes La Bruyère, "combined with
our national pride, makes us forget that reason belongs to all
climes alike, and that there is correct thinking wherever men

---

[1] *Les Entretiens d'Ariste et d'Eugène*, new edn., Amsterdam, 1671, pp. 231-232.

exist. We should not like to be similarly treated by those whom we call barbarians; and if there is any barbarism in us, it consists in our being amazed when we find other people reasoning as we do." In truth this " prejudice " was very strong, even in the nobler minds of that century. Not that the genius of the French nation was regarded as the highest manifestation of the genius of humanity; but that curiosity and admiration, instead of being attracted by works of foreign origin, were directed to those of antiquity. They were extended, if one may say so, not in space but in time. So powerful was the charm of antiquity that very few minds dreamed of breaking away from their time-honoured habit of fond veneration for it. Reverence for the humanities had become, as it were, the very substance of the French mind, and the history of human genius seemed to consist of but three stages : Athens, Rome, and Paris. Beyond these, beyond the three great epochs adorned by the brilliant names of Pericles, Augustus, and Louis XIV., classical criticism finds no age worthy of mention save that of Leo X., the glorious aftermath of the classical harvest. Across the periods of gloom these bright ages join hands and supplement each other. In the course of human progress they stand out like so many glittering beacons, which but render the dark intervals of the road still more obscure.

Are we then to make it a reproach to the men of the seventeenth century—to the genius of a Bossuet, to the open mind of a Fénelon, to the sober reason of a Boileau—that their conception of the world's intellectual history was what it was ? We should, indeed, be strangely simple if we did. Not only did historical circumstances beyond human control conceal from them the prodigious efflorescence of English literature in the sixteenth century, and the manner in which the German genius blossomed forth into poetry during the middle ages ; not only had Northern Europe, during their own time, produced nothing at all comparable to the literature of France, but the humanism with which they were imbued condemned them to remain strangers to everything that was not inspired by ancient models. Those even who revolted against the superstitious belief in antiquity,

such as Desmarets, Perrault, and Lamotte, did not dream of
setting up foreign, in opposition to classical, models. Whatever
they themselves may have thought, the works which they contrast
with those of antiquity are imitations of the antique; with the
Greek epic they compare the French, and, with ancient tragedy,
modern. The quarrel as to the ancients and the moderns is thus
a quarrel between Rome and Paris, and Perrault would have
been very much astonished if the name of Spenser or of Milton
had been introduced into the discussion. There was, in truth,
no question of replacing the established principles of art by fresh
ones; above all, none of substituting a new for an obsolete conception of man. It was merely a question of finding out whether
progress was still possible on the lines marked out by Homer,
Vergil and Sophocles, and whether or not mankind was condemned to remain subject to these masters. But to inquire
whether other models could not be set up in opposition to
these; whether, somewhere in the world, a different art had
not been realized by men of genius of another stamp, was a thing
of which no one dreamed; and to this, in the quarrel concerning
ancient and modern writers, which might have had beneficial
results, was due the weakness of those who supported the
moderns. In the works which they compare with the classics,
in the dramatic productions of Racine or Molière—works which,
though almost as perfect as their models, do not aim at throwing
them into oblivion, but glory, on the contrary, in carrying on
their tradition—antiquity itself is born again to a new life. The
purest element in the genius of these moderns is still the genius
of antiquity. Of a literature entirely free from classical contamination, a spontaneous growth—untainted by any germs of
foreign origin—in the heart of the national soil, Perrault could
have no idea, and could only have had, if for an antiquity apparently so little dissimilar from the age of Louis XIV. had been
substituted either the art of the middle ages or the literature
of the North. The cult of the humanities would have had to
be—indeed it actually needed to be—replaced or supplemented
by the cosmopolitan spirit.

Louis XIV. once had the curiosity to enquire whether there

were any writers and men of learning in England. The reply of his ambassador in London, the Comte de Comminges, was that "the arts and the sciences seem at times to forsake one country in order to do honour to another in its turn. At the present they have made their home in France, and if any vestiges of them are yet left in England, they are only to be found in the works of Bacon, Morus, and Bucanan, and coming to a later period, in those of a certain Miltonius, whose writings have made his name more infamous than those of the executioners and assassins of the English king."[1]

In the seventeenth century the whole of France, or very nearly the whole, held the same opinion as the Comte de Comminges. The nation was blinded by its literary supremacy. To use the vigorous language of a contemporary, it "was under the happy conviction that everything that was not French ate hay and walked on four legs," when a momentous historical event altered at once the political map and the intellectual frontiers of the continent, and prepared the way, in opposition to the Latin section of Europe, for the rise of the Germanic and Anglo-Saxon races.

II

The revocation of the Edict of Nantes had a two-fold effect. In the first place, it marked a pause in the diffusion of French influence abroad; England, a Protestant nation, and destined ere long to become to some extent Dutch and Calvinistic as well, assumed in consequence of the revocation an attitude of opposition to the group of Catholic states represented by France. In the second place, it established on the borders of France, and especially in Great Britain and the Low Countries, colonies of men whose liberal minds were embittered and sharpened by exile, and whose curiosity became increasingly attracted to their adoptive countries, to which they were already drawn by religious and political sympathy.

England, the uttermost territory of the old continent, "that

[1] *Cf.* J. Jusserand, *le Roman anglais*, p. 37.

heroic land," as Michelet [1] calls it, was the chief asylum of the refugees. Some estimate the number of those who came over at seventy thousand, others at eighty thousand [2]; and it may be safely asserted that they repaid British hospitality in a liberal manner, not only by the importation of their industrial skill, but also by their determined and fruitful efforts to spread abroad in France the science, the philosophy, and the literature of their adopted country.

Before 1688, the colony of refugees in London had been but small : Charles II. was not fond of them and did not make them welcome. But in 1688 they flocked to London. There they found an asylum, pensions, and places : Desmaizeaux received an Irish pension, Justel was appointed librarian to the king. They very soon became the defenders of the new government, and its advocates in opposition to the rest of Europe. Protected by the Whigs and zealously opposed to Sacheverell and the Tories, they took their share also in the internal politics of England, and were not long in forming a party. When, in 1709, their friends the Whigs introduced in parliament a bill for their naturalisation, harmony of disposition had already rendered it an accomplished fact. Why, however, should their British zeal have driven some of them to lend their financial support to their adoptive country against that which they had quitted ?

It is in this colony of Protestants in London—which flourished from 1688 to 1730, or thereabouts—that we must seek the original nucleus of that body of men whose limited but singularly restless and well-informed intelligence made them the most active agents of the cosmopolitan spirit in the world of science and of letters, and whose unwearying mediocrity peculiarly fitted them for the dissemination of knowledge in a popular form. Many of them became so far anglicised as to win for themselves a place in English literature. Among these were Pierre Antoine Motteux,

[1] Michelet, *Histoire de France*, vol. ii., p. 90.

[2] *Cf.* Weiss, *Histoire des réfugiés protestants de France*, vol. i., p. 272.—See also Sayous, *Histoire de la littérature française à l'étranger*, 1853, 2 vols. ; Rathery, 4th article, and an article in the *Revue Britannique* (May 1868).

who wrote plays in English which were produced with some success, and founded a monthly magazine called *The Gentleman* [1]; and Abel Boyer, who started a review named *The Postboy*, wrote an English tragedy, and compiled a dictionary of the language. Most of them spoke English, could write it if necessary, and were on familiar terms with the writers of the day.   In London they used to meet at the *The Rainbow Coffee-House* in the neighbourhood of Mary le Bone, and there they formed one of the earliest agencies in Europe for the supply of information on English affairs.   Doubtless Voltaire sat at their table during his stay in London, and profited by the experience of those who frequented *The Rainbow*.

The *doyen* of these gatherings, Pierre Daudé, a clerk of the Exchequer, was a fervent admirer of Bacon, had translated Chubb, and was looked upon as a sort of oracle on points of English philosophy and theology.[2]   Such another was " the celebrated M. de Moivre," the friend and disciple of Newton, no less well-informed, if we may believe one who had personal knowledge,[3] upon Corneille and Racine than upon Newton and Leibnitz, and " consulting grammarian to all the translators and critics of the place."   All had the encyclopædic spirit.   They discussed everything at *The Rainbow*, and kept abreast of all the knowledge of the day.   There, by the side of theologians like Colomiès or Misson, of an orientalist like de la Croze or a historian like Rapin de Thoyras, you might see Durand, historian, poet and authority on numismatics; César de Missy, preacher; Le Clerc, one of the leading journalists of the time; or the honest and excellent Coste, the translator of Locke.   In this grave and studious circle we can discern the dawn of the spirit of the eighteenth century, less inquisitive concerning literature than concerning science, but eager above all things to take in, with however superficial a glance, the whole field of human knowledge.   " It were much to be desired," wrote Le Clerc in

---

[1] *Cf.* Beljame, *Le public et es hommes de lettres*, Bibliographie.
[2] See the eulogium on Daudé in the *Bibliothèque Britannique*, 1733, vol. i., pp. 167-183.
[3] Le Blanc, *Lettres*, vol. i., pp. 77 and 142; vol. iii., p. 86.

1703,[1] "that, since the mind of man is very limited and the duration of life so short, each man would devote himself to one particular kind of reading and study. It must be confessed that by the opposite practice nothing is brought to perfection, and life is frittered away. . . . But how can it be helped ? The sciences, especially those which are concerned with facts, such as history and criticism, and all the others which are related to them, are so intimately connected together that we are compelled to study them in connection with one another, and that, do what we will, we find ourselves launched upon an inexhaustible ocean of reading. Besides, it is impossible to quench the natural curiosity of the human intellect, which, as a rule at any rate, desires instruction in every branch of knowledge."

These facts—namely, that they were industrious, inquiring and withal superficial—explain how it was that the refugees in England and in Holland were such excellent journalists. They compiled, translated and made excerpts. They were the most indefatigable translators and adapters the eighteenth century had seen: not even " the inevitable M. Eidous himself," as Grimm calls him, could compete with them. Armand de la Chapelle kept up the *Bibliothèque anglaise* for ten years, gave active assistance to the *Bibliothèque raisonnée des savants de l'Europe*—a sort of international tribune which, for five-and-twenty years was the organ of Protestant Europe—translated Ditton's *Discourse concerning the resurrection of Jesus Christ*, and, as a recreation, Steele's *Tatler*.

Desmaizeaux, the same who was the soul of the gatherings at *The Rainbow*, wrote biographies of Bayle, Boileau, and Saint-Évremond, contributed to all the newspapers in Holland and London, acted as the non-official correspondent of the *Journal des savants* and of Leibnitz, made translations for booksellers, wrote lives of Chillingworth and Hales in English, issued the unpublished works of Clarke, Newton, and Collins—and all without prejudice to an enormous private correspondence which lies buried in the archives of the British Museum. " He is the man who knows all the eminent persons : he writes to them, receives

[1] *Bibliothèque choisie*, introductory remarks.

letters from them, and is indefatigable in their service."[1]   He was a literary factotum.   Editor, translator, compiler and journalist, Desmaizeaux belonged to no one country; he was a citizen of learned and thinking Europe.[2]

There were many like him; some of them serious-minded men, fully convinced of the lofty nature of their task, others mere literary adventurers, like Thémiseul de Saint-Hyacinthe, the half-starved author of the *Chef-d'œuvre d'un inconnu*, who after having served, if we may believe Voltaire, as a dragoon during the persecution of the French Protestants, had crossed over to England, there had been converted, had translated *Robinson Crusoe*, and though always a destitute wanderer, had been nominated a member of the Royal Society of London.

It was English philosophy that the refugees, who were followers of Bacon and Locke, endeavoured first of all to render popular upon the Continent.   From the English colony in Amsterdam Locke met with an enthusiastic reception.   Several of his writings were published in the *Bibliothèques* of Le Clerc, and a certain "extract from an English work as yet unpublished, entitled *A philosophical essay concerning the understanding* . . . contributed by Mr Locke,"[3] appeared first of all in the *Bibliothèque Universelle*.   It was Pierre Coste, one of the refugees, who published the earliest translations of the master, in particular one of the *Essay on the Human Understanding*, in 1700, and who, as tutor in the house of Lady Masham, shared her admiration for the philosopher, attended him during his last moments, and closed his eyes.   The Dutch newspapers made the first undisguised attempt to disseminate Locke's principles in France, and attacked the philosophy of Descartes with the weapons of sarcasm.[4]   Lastly, it was Le Clerc who, upon the death of the master, printed a panegyric upon him in his paper, and wreathed his memory with respectful homage.[5]   Thus the refugees assumed the responsi-

---

[1] Sayous, *Le xviiie siècle à l'étranger*, vol. i., p. 16.

[2] See the article *Desmaizeaux* in *la France protestante*.

[3] *Bibliothèque universelle*, January 1688 : the abstract contains 92 pages.

[4] *Cf.* *Bibliothèque ancienne et moderne*, iv. 230 ; xiii. 225.

[5] This "historic eulogium of the late Mr Locke" will be found in the " *Œuvres diverses de M Locke*," Amsterdam, 1732, 2 vols. 12mo.

bility before Europe for the spread of "English philosophism." They made themselves its apostles, if not its martyrs, and it was not without good reason that after having made mention of Locke, Clarke and Newton, "the greatest philosophers and the best writers of their time," Voltaire associated with these illustrious names the now more modest name of Le Clerc.[1]

Liberals in philosophy, the refugees adhered also, and with zeal, perseverance and bitterness, to liberalism in politics.[2] Through their agency a knowledge of the English constitution was diffused throughout Europe. The English revolution had already given rise to a sort of theoretical republicanism in France. About 1650, a breath of liberty had passed over Europe. *Cælum ipsum respublicaturit*, it was said in Germany. "At that epoch," says a contemporary,[3] "there was more controversy concerning the right of kings than ever before, owing to the case of the English sovereign. Hence, both in private conversation and in public speeches, numberless tirades against kings, as though they were so many tyrants." It was said that Retz had even taken the trouble to have a narrative of the revolutions in Great Britain written by one of his own men, Salmonet the Scotchman, "in order to teach every one the proper method of procedure."[4] But the horror occasioned by the revolution of 1649 outweighed the sympathy it inspired, even among the opponents of royalty.

That of 1688, on the contrary, gave shape to these aspirations, and provided them with a programme, while at the same time it formed at the very doors of France, in London and at the Hague, two active centres for the diffusion of parliamentarian principles. In England the refugees openly acted as the champions of Liberalism in politics. Timid at times on theological questions,

[1] *Lettres anglaises*, vii.

[2] Le Blanc, *Lettres*, vol. iii., p. 243 : "We might condemn the satirical disposition which the refugees contracted among our neighbours, did not the misfortunes which embittered them render it in a manner excusable ; but we cannot excuse the English for judging us by what are merely idle declamations."

[3] Alexander Morus to Mestrezat, quoted by Rathery, *loc. cit.*

[4] *Cf.* a letter by Mazarin, Rathery, third part.

they were daring in their praises of the English government. On this point the *Journal Littéraire* published at the Hague is most instructive. The pulpit was no less loud in its praises of William III., nor did it deny itself either threats or the hope of revenge. " If ever," said César de Missy, in a sermon preached at the French chapel in the Savoy,[1] " we have been seen sitting together beside the waters of an unclean Babylon, that Babylon was France, our step-mother, and not England, which is for us a second fatherland, and worthy of that beautiful name, a Judæa, a Jerusalem, a Zion. . . . Happy banks watered by the Thames ! If ever the persecuted religion could compare you in any respect to Babylon, it would be because from you as from Babylon there might come forth a Cyrus or a Darius to restore the sanctuaries which a Nebuchadnezzar has pillaged and overthrown."

Accordingly the Protestant journalists openly lent their assistance to every scheme of reform which was mooted in France. They were in full sympathy with the *Polysynodie* of the Abbé de Saint-Pierre. Having neither a Republic nor a Parliament to which they might appeal, they aroused public opinion on political questions, and prepared it for the boldest solutions.

It was by them that the first history of English institutions was written. Gregorio Leti, Larrey, and especially Rapin de Thoyras obtained a knowledge of the facts from the English themselves. " But for the French, and for Rapin de Thoyras, the English would never have had a general history of their own nation." [2] In fact, Rapin's English history, which appeared, in eight volumes, at the Hague in 1724, marked an epoch, and long remained a classic. Rapin, who was a nephew of Pellisson, and had fought at the battle of the Boyne, had become, by aid of the royal favour, tutor to the sons of Lord Portland, and had turned his thankless office to account by observing aristocratic society in England from a near standpoint. His book, which is really the history of the growth of the power of Parliament, was in truth the first philosophical treatise on British institutions. Translated by Tindal, nephew of the deist, it aroused the liveliest curiosity

---

[1] Sayous, *op. cit.*, i. 24.
[2] Le Blanc, *Lettres*, vol. iii., p. 71.

in England. No book did more to make Europe acquainted with Great Britain.[1]

Little by little these efforts of the refugees produced their effect. The greatness of England, contrasted with the decline of France, attracted everyone's attention to the Government of William of Orange. It is true that by its politics and its religious tradition the bulk of the French nation still remained in sympathy with the Stuarts, and one only needs to glance through the novels of Prévost—through *Cléveland*, for example—to see that, as Michelet phrased it, " France kept a corner of her heart for little Joas, I mean the Pretender."[2]

Gradually, however, " the Jacobite spirit, that unhealthy passion for intrigue and gallantry," lost ground. Fénelon, who derived his knowledge of the English Constitution from the Scotchman Ramsay, was already dreaming of a form of Government which should leave " kings all-powerful for good, and powerless for evil,"[3] and Ramsay informs us that " the English Constitution, which he believed to possess this merit, pleased him better than any other."[4] With the arrival of the Regency and the conclusion of the English alliance this sympathetic influence grew stronger. Montesquieu says somewhere that in the days of his youth ministers " knew no more of England than a child six months old,"[5] but from 1715 this ceased to be true. Even the public began to follow English politics somewhat closely, and to make enquiries concerning the English theories of civil government which had been popularized by the refugees.[6] In certain minds the ideas of Locke were making their way. A few years later d'Argenson wrote : " Fifty years

[1] On Rapin de Thoyras, *cf.* the judgment of Voltaire; *Lettres anglaises*, end of Letter xxii. in the edition of 1734.

[2] *Histoire de France*, vol. xv., p. 46.

[3] It will be observed that the formula was appropriated word for word by Voltaire.—*Lettres anglaises*, viii.

[4] *Vie de Fénelon.*

[5] *Notes sur l'Angleterre* (*Œuvres complètes*, ed. Lefèvre, 1839, vol. ii., p. 484).

[6] In 1702, at the Hague, Samson translated Algernon Sidney's *Discourse on Civil Government* (3 vols. 8vo), which was afterwards read by Rousseau. Scheurléer and Rousset translated Mrs Manley's *Atlantis*, a satire upon the authors of the Revolution of 1688 (1714-16, 3 vols. 8vo), &c.

ago the public had no curiosity as to political news. . . . Now, however, English reasonings on politics and on liberty have crossed the sea, and are being adopted here: on all subjects we are growing more philosophical." [1] The Entresol Club was the meeting-place of anglomaniacs, " who like to discuss everything that goes on " ; there the Dutch gazettes and English newspapers could be read, and Bolingbroke was to be met. The attention of Frenchmen was aroused with regard to our neighbours. The propaganda of the refugees, aided by circumstances, was bearing fruit. [2]

III

But the Dutch, English, and Swiss Protestants did more than merely disseminate a knowledge of English philosophy and the principles of English politics ; they also made the French public acquainted with the manners, the science, and the literature of their neighbours. The earliest narratives of travel in England were the work of Protestants.

Even in the seventeenth century, so early as 1664, Samuel Sorbière had expressed himself frankly, indeed too much so, with regard to the English. The author of a version of More's *Utopia*, and the friend, correspondent and translator of Hobbes, Sorbière had offended the sensibilities of the English by a certain expression of opinion on the Comte d'Ulfeld, who had married an illegitimate daughter of the King of Denmark, and also by reproaching them " with not being so attached to their sovereigns as might be desired." In consequence of this imprudence, the book was suppressed and the author exiled to Nantes. It also brought upon him the severe censure of Voltaire. He speaks of "the late M. Sorbière, who, after

---

[1] *Remarques en lisant*, 1750. (Bibliothèque elzévirienne).

[2] On the influence of English political ideas in France, see especially Buckle's *History of Civilisation.*—Observe that English Freemasonry was introduced into France during the Regency, and that it rapidly became a centre for the dissemination of liberal and philosophic principles. The good Abbé Le Blanc mentions a society of drinkers and freethinkers as existing in 1745 : " Its orgies," he says, " are its principal mysteries."—(*Lettres*, vol. i., p. 35.) In 1738, moreover, they had been condemned by the Pope

spending no more than three months in London, and knowing
nothing of either the language or the customs of the country,
had thought proper to publish an account which was simply a
satire upon a nation of which he was entirely ignorant."[1]   Voltaire, however, was here no less unjust than inaccurate.[2]   The
Relation d'un voyage en Angleterre is in no sense a satire ; taking
into account the date of its publication, it was one of the earliest
properly grounded appreciations of the English mind to appear
in the French language.   For the most part, indeed, it was
a favourable one.   Sorbière is exceedingly courteous in his
remarks on the nobility of the English character, and finds it
"not unlike that of the ancient Romans."   He calls attention
to the wonderful prosperity of a country where "you never
see a countenance which excites your pity, nor a garment
which betrays destitution," and as he passes through the rural
districts "the hue of the grass seems to him brighter than
elsewhere."   He anticipates Taine in his enthusiasm for England's gardens and beds of flowers, her parks where "wander
great herds of deer," the luxuriance of her trees, and of the
hedges which intersect the landscape.

He cannot sufficiently admire English science.   He was most
faithful in attending the meetings of the Royal Society, and
describes its organisation in great detail.   He associated with
the most prominent physicists, and is loud in praise of the independence of their thought.   He cultivated the acquaintance
of Hobbes, and Wallis showed him over the Oxford colleges.

He passed, it is true, a somewhat hasty judgment upon
English books, "which contain," he said, "nothing but disconnected rhapsodies."   But he makes some exceptions, and
writes : "I have been very glad to let Frenchmen see that
wit, good sense, and eloquence are to be found everywhere."[3]
Of the English drama, in particular, and long before the oft-
quoted Saint-Évremond, he spoke with discrimination.   After

---

[1] Preface to the *Essai sur la poésie épique*, edn. of 1727.   *Cf.* Bengesco, *Bibliographie de Voltaire*, vol. ii., p. 5.

[2] *Cf.* on Sorbière's travels, the *Journal des Savants*, 1709, *Supplément*, p. 432.

[3] P. 172.

remarking the appearance of the stage, the "green cloth" which covers it, the lavishness of the decorations, and the music which is played in the intervals between the acts, he adds: "Their comedies would not be received in France with the same approbation as in England. Their poets pay no attention to uniformity of place, or to the rule that the action should be limited to twenty-four hours. They write comedies extending over five-and-twenty years, and after representing the marriage of a prince in the first act, they forthwith exhibit all the great deeds of his son, and take him to many different countries. They pride themselves especially on the accuracy with which they depict passion, vice, and virtue, and in this they succeed tolerably well. To portray a miser they make a man perform all the meanest actions characteristic of various ages, occasions and professions; it matters nothing to them that the result is a medley, because, say they, they only attend to one part at a time, and pay no attention to the total effect."

Sorbière acknowledges, however, that he does not understand English. But for one who spent no more than a few weeks on the farther side of the channel he did not waste his time, whatever Voltaire may say.

Sorbière's *Relation* dates from 1664, and was reprinted two years later. Misson's *Mémoires et observations faites par un voyageur en Angleterre* appeared in 1668, and *Remarques sur l'Angleterre faites par un voyageur*, by Le Sage de la Colombière, in 1715. These two authors were Protestants. The former, an ex-member of the Parlement de Paris and son-in-law of Mme. de la Sablière, was a refugee in London in 1688, and there occupied an important position in the religious world;[1] his work, though somewhat heavy, contained an abundance of information, and was translated into English.[2] The latter, a descendant of Agrippa D'Aubigné, after a ten years' residence in England as tutor, wrote the first French book in which the physical theories of Newton were pre-

---

[1] Sayous, *Dix-huitième siècle à l'étranger*, vol. i., p. 10.

[2] Mr Misson's *Memoirs and Observations in his travels over England* . . . translated by Mr Ozell. London, 1719, 8vo. *Cf.*, on Misson's book, *Journal des Savants*, 1699, p. 127.

sented in a connected fashion,[1] and collected in a slender volume
a certain number of observations, often trivial and sometimes
coarse, upon English manners.

But it is chiefly to the gazettes and newspapers of the refugees
that we must turn to find a real mine of information on all matters
relating to England.[2] In these delicately printed little volumes,
which may be reckoned by the hundred, and, as their title-pages
inform us, were published either at the Hague, at Amsterdam,
or in London ; in the reviews published by Le Clerc, La Chapelle
or Maty—the first imperfect patterns of our modern reviews—
are to be found the earliest studies of English, and also of
German, literature that were written in French.

Not, it is, true, in Bayle's *Nouvelles de la République des lettres* ;[3]
which is mainly a theological and scientific magazine, treating,
moreover, of few but French and Latin books. Nevertheless,
pursuing a practice destined to spread, the *Nouvelles* had already
their London correspondents, who contributed reports of scientific
events, of Boyle's experiments, of the meetings of the Royal
Society, and of the latest publications in astronomy, geography,
or medicine. One of these communications terminates as follows : " Whence it will be seen that England alone could furnish
sufficient material every month to fill a larger journal than ours
with notices of good books, of which however practically none
are to be seen in Holland. This is a case of negligence on the
part of our booksellers, which it is to be hoped they will
repair."[4]

Bayle's successors responded to this appeal. Le Clerc, a man

---

[1] *Le Mécanisme de l'esprit*, by Le Sage de la Colombière. Geneva, 1700 (*cf.* Sayous,
xviii *siècle*, vol. i., p. 103).

[2] In reference to the Dutch Gazettes, *cf.* Kœnen, *Histoire des réfugiés français aux
Pays-Bas*, Leyden, 1846 ; Ch. Weiss, *Histoire des réfugiés protestants de France ;* E.
Hatin, *Les Gazettes de Hollande*, 1865, 8vo, and *Histoire de la presse*, by the same
writer ; also the two works by Sayous, especially *La Littérature française à l'étranger*,
vol. ii., p. 27 *et seq.*

[3] *Nouvelles de la République des lettres*, by Bayle and others. Amsterdam, March
1684 to June 1718, 56 vols. 12mo. The portion written by Bayle ends with
February 1687, and has been reprinted in his *Œuvres complètes*. His successors
were La Roque, Jacques Bernard, Barrin, and Le Clerc.

[4] June 1685.

of prudence and of weight, who may be regarded as the second
founder of Protestant journalism, thought it his duty to do what
he could, in the *Bibliothèque universelle*, to remove the ignorance
of the public on the subject of England. " How few are the
people," he writes, " on this side the sea, who have a knowledge
of English. Yet the language contains a multitude of good
books, still untranslated, and apparently destined to remain so,
of which it would be highly beneficial to the public to have at
least some knowledge." [1]   Le Clerc therefore exerted himself to
supply the want. But literature was not his strong point ; he
had " too much calvinistic and socinian arrogance," as Boileau
roundly informed him, to concern himself with trivial matters.
Thus, when he speaks of English books, it is of scientific
treatises, books on history, or philosophical works like those of
Hobbes. Only by accident does he so far forget himself as to
speak of Addison's travels in Italy.[2]   On the other hand he never
wearies of praising, in his successive miscellanies,[3] the commercial,
maritime and political greatness of England.

More of a scholar than either Bayle or Le Clerc, Basnage de
Beauval, the third member of the triumvirate which laid the
foundations of international journalism, carried on the *Nouvelles
de la République des lettres*,[4] and, in an indiscriminate fashion,
devoted several numbers to Hobbes, Sherlock, Locke, Boyle, and
W. Temple,[5] to the dispute between Jeremy Collier and Dennis
on the moral condition of the stage, to Milton,[6] and to Milton's
later poems.[7] He possessed a more open mind than his famous
rivals. Above all, he had more zeal, and in opposition to
Father Bouhours warmly took up the defence of " Germany,
which had produced so many great men, and had invented so
many of the arts necessary to life." [8]

---

[1] *Bibliothèque universelle*, vol. xxvi., preface.   [2] *Bibliothèque choisie*, 1707, vol. xi., 198.
[3] *Bibliothèque universelle et historique*, Amsterdam, 1686-93, 26 vols. 12mo ; *Bibliothèque choisie*, Amsterdam, 1703-13, 27 vols. 12mo ; *Bibliothèque ancienne et moderne*,
Amsterdam, 1714-27, 26 vols. 12mo.   On England see, especially, vol. i. of the
Bibliothèque Universelle, pp. 118-120.
[4] In his *Histoire des ouvrages des savants*, Rotterdam, 1687-1709, 24 vols. 12mo.
[5] In reference to this, *cf.* a passage on the English character, June 1692.
[6] July 1698.   [7] February 1699.   [8] January 1700.

The success of these publications in Paris, and the relish with which they were read by La Fontaine, are well known.[1] Is it improbable that through them, at some time or other, the name of Milton caught the heedless eye of a Boileau or a Racine ? The more we learn of the history of these Dutch journals, the more of their space do we find allotted to studies of foreign, and especially of English, literature. " To a country so prolific of great men," we read in the *Histoire critique de la République des lettres*,[2] " we can but render all the justice that is her due. When a nation has made us acquainted with so many fine works as has Great Britain, we cannot allow them to remain for ever unknown to the rest of Europe." In short, certain men of letters in France became irritated at last by the anglomania of the Dutch journalists, and thought to correct public opinion by showing " that the French were not so degenerate as was pretended in Holland." With this object, the *Bibliothèque française* was founded by De Sauzet, Bernard, Camusat, Granet, and the abbé Goujet, but its duration was very brief.

The number of what may be called European reviews, on the contrary, continued to increase. All were due to the same spirit, and had the same end in view, namely, to break down the barriers between nations, and to prepare the way for a sort of international literature. It may, indeed, be doubted whether these efforts at dissemination were altogether disinterested ; too often love of Europe was, in reality, nothing more than hatred of France. But it cannot be denied that they were very active. From the *Bibliothèque raisonnée des ouvrages des savants de l'Europe*,[3] down to the *Nouvelle bibliothèque ou Histoire littéraire des principaux écrits qui se publient*,[4] and including among others *l'Europe savante*,[5] and *l'Histoire littéraire de l'Europe*,[6] the series of encyclopædic

---

[1] *Lettre à M. Simon de Troyes.*

[2] Utrecht, 1712, vol. i., preface.

[3] By La Chapelle, Desmaiseaux, Van Effen, Saint-Hyacinthe. Amsterdam, 1728-53, 52 vols. 12mo.

[4] By Chaix, Barbeyrac, d'Argens, La Chapelle, etc. The Hague, 1738-44, 19 vols. 12mo.

[5] By Saint-Hyacinthe, Van Effen and others. The Hague, 1718-20, 12 vols. 8vo.

[6] By Van Effen, 1726, 6 vols. 8vo.

miscellanies, the mere titles of which suffice to indicate their aim and scope, extended over more than fifty years.

Not one of these magazines will bear reading to-day. Their style is "Protestant" to the last degree; their criticism destitute of elegance; their humour ponderous. But their information is singularly copious and accurate.

When they indulge in satire, these journalists of Holland are terrible; their irony resembles a blow from a club. Of this type was their manifesto in the dispute concerning the ancients and the moderns, the once-famous *Chef d'œuvre d'un inconnu*, the idea of which they derived from Swift and from the *Spectator*. They wished to ridicule those would-be critics " who will not allow that any classical author ever thought incorrectly, or ever gave an inaccurate or trivial explanation." Swift, Pope, and Arbuthnot used to divert themselves at the expense of Bentley, the philologist, by supplying commentaries after their own fashion to lines of Vergil, *inter pocula*. The *Spectator* had published a skit of this sort—a slender shaft, and launched by no disrespectful hand—upon the partisans of the ancients. In the hands of Thémiseul de Saint-Hyacinthe and his friends this shaft becomes a paving-stone.

The passage to be explained being taken from a song sung by the daughter of a carpenter at the Hague :

> " L'autre jour Colin malade
> Dedans son lit,
> D'une grosse maladie
> Pensa mourir,"

the commentary is as follows : " ' Ill,' that is to say, ' not well,' or as the gentlemen of the French Academy observe, ' sensible of some derangement, some alteration in his health.' Colin therefore was ' ill '; not, however that his health was disordered by fever, or some other sickness which would demand the services of a doctor of medicine. He was exactly what is called in familiar language, *out of sorts*, or, in vulgar phrase, *uncommonly queer*. This complaint of Colin's brings to mind that of Seleucus Nicanor or Nicator " . . . and behold our explanatory note in a fair way to spread itself, as notes will, over twenty columns.

Such, when they try to be amusing, is the humour of the journalists of Holland—a third-rate imitation of Swift. As a rule, however, their tone is serious. Nothing of this sort is to be found in the whole series of the *Journal Littéraire*, which, founded at the Hague by Sallengre, Sgravesande, and Van Effen, attempted to take up the work relinquished by Basnage.[1] Here, by way of compensation, as in all these "gazettes," a great abundance of English literature is to be found. In metaphysics, the writers are followers of Locke, in science of Bacon and Newton, in politics of the Parliament. This is a truly cosmopolitan review; it has correspondents everywhere: at Brussels, at Leipzig, at Hamburg, at Cambridge, and in Italy. It is also—as the title promises—a literary review. It contains a lengthy comparison between English and French poetry,[2] and extracts from *The Spectator*, *The Tale of a Tub*, and *Gulliver*. Swift had an especial attraction for its writers. They delighted in his withering and somewhat unseemly jests, his sardonic laughter, his bitter mockery. Montaigne, likewise, they studied for the sake of his scepticism, Rabelais for his gaiety, Fontenelle for his irony. Like their contemporaries, they warmly espoused the side of the modern against the classical writers.

We have good grounds for believing that the English portion of these periodicals was responsible for their success, for magazines were shortly established which were especially devoted to England. "It is a country," said Michel de la Roche, the editor of the *Bibliothèque anglaise*,[3] "where the arts and sciences are as flourishing as in any other part of the world; in England they are cultivated in an atmosphere of liberty." La Roche had first of all attempted, in his *Memoirs of Literature*,[4] to introduce French productions to the English public. The scheme proving unsuccessful, he applied himself with great zest to the opposite

---

[1] The Hague, 1713-36 (with several interruptions), 24 vols. 12mo.
[2] Vol. ix.
[3] Or *Histoire littéraire de la Grande-Bretagne*, Amsterdam, 1717-28, 15 vols. 12mo.
[4] 1710-14, 4 vols. 4to.

task.   The *Bibliothèque anglaise*, however, bade fair to meet the same fate as the *Memoirs*, when it fell into the hands of the industrious Armand de la Chapelle, who extended its scope, while making, at the same time, his reservations with regard to English taste.   " There are perhaps few countries," he wrote, " where poetry is more deserving of public attention than it is in England, and if the English language were more common, foreigners would be surprised to find that it contains so many fine pieces of every description of poetry, with the possible exception of the dramatic, in which the taste of the English is still, to my mind, too singular."   The excellent La Chapelle's wits were as dull as his pen; nevertheless he died not unregretted.   De la Roche meanwhile had founded some new *Mémoires littéraires de la Grande Bretagne*—mainly scientific, in spite of their title,[1] while Desmaizeaux, Bernard, and others started the *Bibliothèque britannique*.   They professed a thorough knowledge of English and of English affairs.   Jordan, who happened to be in London when their magazine first appeared, declares that the authors are men of ability, and have a perfect acquaintance with the language.[2]   Their magazine, written in London and published at The Hague, affirms with justice that " England is more fertile than any other country in works distinguished by the freshness, the singularity and the boldness of their opinions; and that this is due to the fact that the English are free to examine everything and to refuse any court of appeal save that of reason."[3]

Repeatedly interrupted, the work of popularization undertaken by the refugees was resumed again and again with extraordinary tenacity.

The *Bibliothèque britannique* ceased to appear in 1747.   Three years later, a renewed attempt was made by one of the most interesting of all these journalists, Doctor Maty.   The son of a pastor at Utrecht, who had been excommunicated by the Synod

---

[1] 1720-24, The Hague, 16 vols. 12mo.

[2] *Histoire d'un voyage littéraire fait en* 1733, p. 159.

[3] *Bibliothèque Britannique ou histoire des ouvrages des savants de la Grande-Bretagne*, the Hague, 1733-47, 25 vols. 12mo.

of the Walloon Church of The Hague and had taken refuge in England, young Maty had lived in that country from the age of twenty-two years. Being a doctor, his aim in establishing a journal was chiefly to keep up with the work of English surgeons. But he included also " good English literature and well seasoned," as a critic of the time expressed it.[1] His *Journal britannique* extended to twenty-four volumes. He sought also, excellent man that he was, " to stimulate all men to a love of truth and virtue," and declared that " every thoughtful person was his friend." Fully master of his subject, and capable of writing English with facility, he nevertheless regretted that he had not been able to naturalise his tongue as well as his heart.[2] Gibbon, who speaks of him in most grateful terms,[3] asserts that "the author of the *Journal britannique* sometimes rises to the level of the poet and the philosopher." On obtaining a post at the British Museum he gave up his journal. But his son founded a review which was destined to make Englishmen acquainted with Europe. Cosmopolitanism was plainly a virtue common to the Maty family.

When Maty retired, several writers disputed the position he had vacated. De Joncourt established a *Nouvelle bibliothèque anglaise* ;[4] de Mauve resumed the *Journal britannique*, and continued it for two years;[5] while in 1767-1768 Gibbon and Deyverdun published two volumes of *Mémoires littéraires de la Grande Bretagne*,[6] in which Chesterfield and Hume manifested an interest, the latter even assisting it with his pen. Respecting Deyverdun, Gibbon bears witness that " his critical knowledge of our language and poetry was such as few foreigners have possessed."[7]

Not only, however, was Gibbon scarcely the man for so thank-

---

[1] Clément, *Les Cinq années littéraires*, vol. iii., p. 145.—*Cf. Mémoires de Trévoux*, December 1750 and February 1751.

[2] Letter to Gibbon, Hatin, *Histoire de la presse*, vol. ii., p. 435.

[3] *Mémoires*, vol. i. p. 126.

[4] The Hague, 1756-57, 3 vols. 12mo.

[5] I know nothing of this series beyond the mention made of it by Pictet in his own *Bibliothèque britannique* (vol. ii., 1796, pt. v.).

[6] *Cf. Memoirs of Edward Gibbon*, chap. xviii.

[7] *Ibid.*, vol. i., p. 102.

less a task, but the public—at the period we have reached—was
so fully informed on English matters, and by men of such
eminence, that an obscure compilation by two unknown men
had little chance of making its way. Here again the unwearying efforts made by journalists in Holland had led to important
results, and their patient labour during more than half-a-
century had opened up fresh vistas to the gaze of a curious
public.

Not content with giving accounts of English works in their
periodicals, the refugees devoted themselves with untiring zeal
to the work of translation. From the earliest years of the century the " demon translator," as Grimm called him, raged as
furiously as the " demon novelist." Every member of the clan
of refugees was engaged in the translation or adaptation of some
English book. The occupation provided a livelihood and gave
a kind of status in the world of letters. Justus Van Effen, who
rendered some dozens of volumes into prolix and inaccurate language, was mourned by his colleagues as though he had been a
French writer.[1] It is only fair, however, to say that to him
Frenchmen are indebted for the first version of *Robinson Crusoe*.

We have no intention of introducing here the tedious and interminable catalogue of translations by Van Effen and his colleagues, but shall be content to remark that the refugees very
soon acquired the habit of translating the more important works
produced in English as soon as they were published. Collins's
Discourse of Freethinking appeared in 1713, and was rendered into
French in 1714. Shaftesbury's *Letter concerning Enthusiasm*, published in 1708, was translated in the same year. Very few
works of note, especially of those on philosophical subjects,
escaped the attention of the refugees. Those which were not
immediately translated, such as Mandeville's *Fable of the Bees*,
were analysed at length.[2]

That Shakespeare and the great poets of the sixteenth century
received but rare and scanty notice need not surprise us. The

---

[1] See a panegyric on Van Effen in the *Bibliothèque française* of 1737.

[2] *Bibliothèque raisonnée des ouvrages des savants de l'Europe*, vol. iii., 1729, p. 402
et seq.

English themselves paid scarcely any attention to them.[1] But the whole of contemporary literature was conscientiously analysed, adapted, or translated. Addison and Steele were especially favoured: the *Spectator* was translated in 1714, the *Guardian* in 1725, the *Freeholder* in 1727, the *Tatler* in 1734. Boyer translated Addison's *Cato* in 1714, and the *Journal des Savants* contains a notice of it.[2] About the same period Pope's *Essay on Criticism* found two translators or imitators,[3] and both the book and its author were mentioned in the journals.[4] Swift's works crossed the channel scarcely less quickly. Several of them were advertised in the *Journal littéraire*[5] so early as 1713, and the same review printed portions of *Gulliver* and *The Tale of a Tub*. In 1720 the *Bibliothèque anglaise* translated the "Proposal for correcting, improving and ascertaining the English Tongue."[6] Van Effen's translation of *The Tale of a Tub* appeared at the Hague in the following year, and five years later, that of a satire on the practice of introducing dedications. In 1727 Desfontaines, following the example of the refugees, translated *Gulliver*, which had appeared in the preceding year. *Robinson Crusoe*, as has been seen already, was translated in 1720, the year after its publication.[7]

These examples suffice to show the activity of the refugees. It may be said without hesitation that they were familiar with the whole of contemporary English literature, and that through

---

[1] Boyer, however, as has been already observed, mentions Shakespeare in his grammar (1700) together with Ben Jonson, Dryden and Milton, and, moreover, he prefers Dryden. In 1716 the *Journal littéraire* (vol. ix.) devoted an article to Shakespeare, quoting *Hamlet*, *Richard III.*, *Henry VIII.*, and *Othello*.

[2] 1714, p. 448 *et seq.*

[3] *Essai sur la Critique*, imité de M. Pope [by Robeton, councillor and private secretary to the late King of England]. London and Amsterdam, 1717. (*Cf. Mémoires de Trévoux*, August 1717).—*Essai sur la critique*, imité de l'anglais de M. Pope, by J. Delage. London, 1717.

[4] *Cf. Bibliothèque ancienne et moderne*, vol. vii., part i.; *Journal des savants*, July 1717; *Bibliothèque anglaise*, 1719, part ii.

[5] May and June 1713.   [6] Vol. viii., part i.

[7] Lenglet Dufresnoy (*De l'usage des romans*) attributes this translation to Saint-Hyacinthe. The writer of the panegyric on Van Effen mentioned above, attributes it, from the middle of the first volume onwards, to the latter. The translation is, besides, anonymous.

them France was made acquainted with all its most important productions. Through them too this knowledge was spread far and wide. When the abbé Dubos visited London in 1698 and in 1702, he associated with the refugees, and particularly with Moivre,[1] and it was to them, doubtless, that he was indebted for that smattering of foreign literature which is discernible in his *Réflexions sur la poésie et la peinture.*

In his book Dubos quoted from a few English poets, among them Butler, the author of *Hudibras.*[2] He also translated, in a magazine published at the Hague, some scenes from Addison's *Cato.*[3] But his taste remained thoroughly French. " Though I often visit other countries," he wrote, " in order to become acquainted with their opinions, I do not surrender the opinions I hold as a Frenchman. Like Seneca I can say : *Soleo saepe in aliena castra transire non tanquam transfuga sed tanquam explorator.*"

A few years later than Dubos, Destouches visited London, whither he accompanied cardinal Dubois. He resided there from 1717 to 1723, and contracted a highly romantic marriage with a young Scotchwoman.[4]

Probably the refugees welcomed him no less warmly than they welcomed Dubos, and, a few years later, Voltaire. Destouches, who seems to have been acquainted with Addison, borrowed from him, as is well known, the subject of his *Tambour nocturne,* an adaptation of *The Drummer,* and, under the title of *Scènes anglaises,* translated several scenes from *The Tempest* of Dryden and Davenant. But the *Scènes anglaises* did not appear until 1745, and the *Tambour nocturne* was not played before 1762. Thus the part played by Destouches in bringing English works to the knowledge of the French public was insignificant.

It was otherwise with the abbé Desfontaines, the most active if not the most illustrious rival of the refugees in France before Voltaire and Prévost. Desfontaines' ambition, or one of the least of his ambitions, was to be, as it were, the recognised

---

[1] Le Blanc, *Lettres,* vol. i., p. 142.   [2] Part i., section 18.

[3] The first three; see *Nouvelles littéraires* (the Hague, October 1716); vol. viii., p. 285. *Cf.* in the same periodical (January 1717) two letters on *Cato* by Boyer.

[4] *Cf.* Desnoiresterres, *Voltaire et la société française,* vol. i., p. 215 Villemain, *Tableau de la littérature au xviiie siècle,* 12th lesson.

authority for introducing English works to the public notice. The translator of a pamphlet by Swift, *The Grand Mystery, or the Art of Meditating over an House of Office*, Desfontaines also (1727) either rendered *Gulliver* into French, or pretended to have done so; for there are fair grounds for believing that this version is by a certain Abbé Markan.[1] What is certain is that the irascible critic, for all his pretensions, had a very poor knowledge of English,[2] and Voltaire did not deny himself the pleasure of convicting him of it. This did not, however, prevent him from corresponding with Swift, nor even from writing a sequel to *Gulliver*,[3] which met with very little success. "Oh ! as to the new *Gulliver*," wrote Lenglet-Dufresnoy, "it is from beginning to end invented and manufactured by M. l'abbé Desfontaines."[4] Lastly, the abbé translated Fielding's *Joseph Andrews*, but the result is scarcely more creditable to his knowledge than is his *Gulliver*.

Thus, during the first thirty years of the century, the refugees remained the most industrious, the best informed and the most highly qualified of all those who devoted themselves to the task of popularizing English literature.

What they lacked was ability. They were compilers and abstractors, but not writers. Their part was to rough-hew the materials which have been worked up by more eminent men, and this is no contemptible function. They were the humble predecessors of a Voltaire and a Prévost. But it was necessary to say, since it has too often been forgotten, that the work of the latter was rendered possible only by the persevering labour of the former.

[1] E. Nisard, *Les ennemis de Voltaire*, p. 49.

[2] *Cf.* Clément, *Les cinq années littéraires*, vol. i., p. 61. Voltaire had commissioned Desfontaines to translate his *Essay on The Epic* from the English. Desfontaines made an error in every line (*cf.* the letters to d'Argens, 19th Nov. 1736, and to Thiériot, 14th June 1727). If we may believe Voltaire, he understood the language so little, that when required to give an account of Berkeley's *Alciphron*, which is an apology for Christianity, he took it for an atheistical production. (Letter to Cideville, 20th September 1735.)

[3] *Le Nouveau Gulliver ou Voyage de Jean Gulliver, fils du Capitaine Gulliver*, translated from an English manuscript by M. l'abbé D. F. Amsterdam, 1730, 2 vols. 12mo.

[4] *Bibliothèque des Romans*, p. 342.

Chapter II

I. Prévost and Voltaire were themselves preceded by the Swiss, Béat de Muralt, the author of the *Lettres sur les Anglais et les Français* (1725)—Muralt's character—Wherein he carried on the work of the refugees, wherein he went beyond them—His illusions—His opinions on English literature and the English intelligence—Great success of his book: Muralt and Desfontaines—His influence on Rousseau.

II. Admiration of the abbé Prévost for English ideas; he assists in diffusing them—His two journeys to England—His translations—His cosmopolitan novels: the *Mémoires d'un homme de qualité* and *l'Histoire de Cléveland*—His magazine, *La Pour et Contre* (1732-1740): the author's aim and method—England occupies a large share of its space.

III. Voltaire and the *Lettres anglaises* (1734)—Importance of the book in Voltaire's life—His intercourse with men of letters during his stay in London—Knowledge of the language—His efforts to awaken interest in English matters—Origin of the *Lettres philosophiques*: they consist of two books.

IV. Insufficiency of Voltaire's information; his wilful inaccuracy—The pamphleteer injurious to the critic—Why his book is nevertheless of the highest importance in the history of the influence of England—Voltaire encourages imitation of English works.

BETWEEN 1725 and 1740 three men were responsible, in varying degrees, for the work of directing the attention of the French public, aroused by Protestant criticism during the early part of the century, towards England.

One of them, now entirely forgotten, the author of a lively and agreeable collection of letters which made some stir in its day, was Béat de Muralt, a Protestant of Berne, who carried on, if he did not anticipate, the work of the refugees, and is very closely connected with them. Another, much more celebrated, became, through his novels, his journal, and certain famous translations, one of the warmest champions of the new literature

then being introduced into France.   This was the abbé Prévost.
The third, and by far the greatest, has given an account of his
work in the following words: " I was the first to make Frenchmen acquainted with Shakespeare ; I translated passages from
him forty years ago, as well as extracts from Milton, Waller,
Rochester, Dryden, and Pope.   I can assure you that before my
time there was not a man in France who had a knowledge of
English poetry, while Locke had scarcely been heard of." [1]
And certainly the author of the *Lettres anglaises* is entitled to
claim such credit as may be due to one who, by dint of his own
genius and notoriety, imbued Frenchmen with a veneration for
the philosophy, the political science and the literature of England.
But he has no excuse for forgetting or concealing what he owes
to those who preceded him.   For if the *Lettres anglaises* or
philosophiques were published in 1734, Muralt's *Lettres sur les
Anglais et les Français* had appeared in 1725, while the most
important of Prévost's novels, as well as the first volume, at any
rate, of *Le Pour et Contre* are likewise anterior to them.   Voltaire,
in short, provided " a brilliant summary," as Sainte-Beuve expressed it, of what had been said of England by other writers
before him.   But, besides drawing freely upon the works of
his predecessors, he neglects to mention that others had already
aroused the attention of the public and had prepared the way.

I

" Now that we are reprinting everything," wrote Sainte-
Beuve, " we certainly ought to reprint the letters of M. de
Muralt : they deserve it.   He was the first to say many things
which have since been repeated less plainly and less frankly." [2]

[1] Voltaire to Horace Walpole, 15th July 1768.
[2] On Muralt see the excellent monograph by M. de Greierz : *Béat Ludwig von
Muralt* (Frauenfeld, 1888, 8vo) ; an article by M. E. Ritter in the *Zeitschrift für
neufranzösische Sprache und Literatur* (1880), and various documents published by
same author, especially an account of Muralt's religious ideas, in the *Étrennes
chrétiennes* for 1894.   See also the histories of French literature in Switzerland
by M. Godet and M. Virgile Rossel (the latter of which contains a complete
bibliography).   Lastly, I may venture to refer the reader to an article in the

Plain, frank, and withal somewhat eccentric: such, in truth, was 'this atrabilious Swiss,' as he was called in his own day."

A Bernese of Protestant family, by education half French, half German, and born on the border line between two civilizations, he was well qualified thoroughly to understand them both. Employed as a soldier in the French service, he became tired of the military profession, and, crossing over to England, noted down his impression of the country, during 1694 and 1695, for the benefit of a friend. Returning to Switzerland he embraced pietistic ideas of a very exalted type, and having provoked his expulsion first from Berne and then from Geneva, took shelter at Colombier, where, after his mysticism had involved him in an extraordinary adventure, he died. " You read Muralt," St Preux writes to Julie: "remark his end, lament the extravagant errors of that sensible man." [1]

To these " extravagant errors " we owe certain religious works, now, deservedly it would seem, forgotten. [2]

Muralt's reputation, however, rests not on these works but on his *Lettres sur les Anglais et les Français et sur les voyages*, [3] frequently reprinted during the eighteenth century, and even under the Revolution. There are six letters on England and as many on France; both groups are written from a somewhat Protestant standpoint, but with a shrewd pen, and one a hundred times more vivid than those of Basnage de Beauval and Van Effen. When he wrote these charming pages, Muralt was not yet under the influence of the ideas which so entirely altered the course of his life during its later years, and almost

---

Revue d'histoire littéraire de la France (January 1894), in which I have spoken of Muralt more at length. Since the publication of the first edition of this book, two fresh editions of Muralt's *Lettres* have appeared (Berne and Paris, 1897), one with notes in French by M. E. Ritter, the other with notes in German by M. de Greierz.

[1] *Nouvelle Héloïse*, vi. 7. *Eloisa* (published by Hunter, Dublin, 1761), letter 159.

[2] *L'instinct divin recommandé aux hommes*, 1727; *Lettres sur l'esprit fort*, 1728; *Lettres fanatiques*, 1739. Muralt also left some fables, and collaborated with Marie Huber.

[3] (Geneva) 8vo. Possibly the book was on sale as early as 1724. (*Cf. Bibliothèque française*, vol. iv., part ii., pp. 70-82).

led him to withhold his book from publication for conscientious reasons.[1] He was fond of observing, and of recording what he saw with all the charm he could command. " Immediately a Frenchman enters another country," he writes, " he cannot contain himself for amazement at the spectacle of a whole nation differing from himself, and flees from the sight of so many horrors." Muralt endeavours not to be a Frenchman in that respect. He is no less distrustful of his countrymen's insatiable relish for intellectual smartness, whereby the nation is made " the perpetual subject of ridicule." He would have solidity, of the Bernese or even of the English type, without pedantry : " I think I had rather be a worthy Englishman than a worthy Frenchman ; but it would perhaps be less uncomfortable to be a worthless Frenchman than to be a worthless Englishman. I had also rather meet a deserving Frenchman than a deserving Englishman, just as it would give one more pleasure to find a treasure in gold pieces, which could be turned to immediate account, than to find it in ingots, which would first have to be converted into coin." [2] A discerning mind withal, keen and incisive, and strangely curious with regard to everything except " trifles "—by which must be understood whatever is merely a source of gratification, and does not contribute in any way to the inner life. If he happens to speak of comedy, it is to say that " grave people have even been seen, not only to derive amusement from it, but even to speak of it as seriously as though it were a matter of importance." Behold him therefore supported by excellent authority, and entitled to laugh without too many scruples. But it was because there was no French " levity " about him that he was able, in 1694, to form an admirable estimate of the English genius, such as had never before been formed in the French language.

It is true that he carried courtesy a little too far in his praise of English " liberty " and British " virtue "—those generous

---

[1] Muralt was sixty years old when the entreaties of his friends induced him to consent to its publication. But his letters had almost attained celebrity before they were printed, and one of them had appeared in the *Nouvelles littéraires* at the Hague (May 1718).

[2] Letter IV.

illusions of the eighteenth century.   "His mind is French,"
said the abbé Le Blanc, referring to him, "but his heart is
English." [1]   But whatever Le Blanc may say, it was because his
mind as well as his heart was somewhat English that Muralt
gave so flattering a definition of the moral and intellectual
temperament of Englishmen.   He gives a careful statement of
their origins—Saxon, Norman and Latin.   He observes their
manners, their sports and even their vices from a close standpoint, and as a man of caution and experience.   He investigates
their arts and manufactures.   He is captivated by their ingen-
uousness and their fidelity, and even by the savage element in
their character.   "May we not venture to say that a nation
requires some fierceness in order to guard itself against slavery,
just as one must be born a misanthrope in order to keep himself
an honest man ?   Reason alone cannot have great influence over
men ; it needs, I think, a touch of fierceness to sustain it." [2]
How attractive this "fierceness" and "misanthropy" were
shortly to appear to the frivolous French nature, and how far
Muralt is here in advance of his age, the age of Jean-Jacques,
who, moreover, was his convinced admirer !   The French spirit
"consists mainly in the art of making much of trifles."   The
English spirit is more precise, more solid, more free, and
more simple.[3]   "England is a country of reserve and composure."

Muralt, like the refugees, is a modern, though timid and of
narrow tastes.   He speaks cleverly of Boileau, and considers
that the French know scarcely anything of great poetry.   He
professes to despise "genius of an inferior order," and believes
that to clothe common thoughts in beautiful language is to give
us the semblance of poetry, but not poetry itself."   Unfortunately
he has not made it sufficiently clear that the English are more

[1] *Lettres*, vol. i., p. 87.   [2] Edition of 1725, p. 55.
[3] *Cf.* p. 65.   "The epithet 'good man' is never taken in bad part among the
English, whatever the tone in which it is pronounced : so far from it that when they
wish to praise their own nation highly they mention their 'good-natured people,'
people of a pleasant disposition, of whom they maintain that neither the name nor the
reality is to be met with elsewhere."   Rousseau appropriated this observation from
Muralt (*Émile*, l. ii. note 26).

truly poets than the classical writers of France.[1] Like Saint-
Évremond he does not go back to the fountain-heads, to Shakespeare—though he makes casual mention of him—or to Spenser.
He confines himself to Ben Jonson, whom he compares and finds
inferior to Molière, "though a truly great poet in certain
respects." One of the reasons which he gives for the inferiority
of the English as regards comedy is, however, of considerable
weight : "In France characters belong to general types, and
comprise each a whole species of men, whereas in England,
where every one lives as he pleases, the poet finds scarcely any
but individual characters, which are extremely numerous, but
cannot produce any striking effect."[2] A sound and fruitful
idea ; it is to be regretted that the author did not follow it
further.

But, to tell the truth, he was not sufficiently well acquainted
with English dramatic literature. He judges it as a moralist, and
a severe one. It offends his good sense and his conscience.
"Humour," or, as he calls it, "*houmour*," is merely the faculty of
"turning our ideas of things topsy-turvy, and thereby rendering
virtue ridiculous and vice attractive." His judgment of Shadwell
and Congreve is precisely that which would have been passed
upon them by Rousseau.

Of English tragedy he has spoken to better purpose, revealing
to his reader, or at any rate perceiving for himself, its savage
grandeur. "England is a country of passions and catastrophes.
. . . Moreover, the genius of the nation is for the serious ; its
language is powerful and concise." What a pity that they fall
into the same errors as the French, and present us with a
be-ribboned Achilles and a Hannibal in powdered wig ! No

[1] Further, it is essential to remember that Muralt was in England in 1694 or
1695. He represented England, as Sainte-Beuve said, "in all its crudeness under
William, and before it had time to become refined under Queen Anne." He does not
mention either Pope or Addison, nor did he put any finishing touches to his book
before it was published.

[2] Edn. of 1725, p. 23. Saint-Évremond had already remarked that English
comedy is not "a mere love-intrigue, full of adventures and amorous conversation, as
in Spain or in France ; it is a representation of ordinary life with all the variety of
temper and the differences of character which are to be found in men." *De la
comédie anglaise.*

historical colour, no sustained solemnity; an offensive mixture
of the comic and the tragic, and spectacles which only excite
disgust : " It appears to me that poets who possess true genius,
and are capable of rousing the feelings, ought not to have
recourse to instruments of torture." Such instruments are too
much in evidence upon the English stage.

Muralt's extremely well-expressed *résumé* of his own estimate of
the English intelligence was widely appreciated during the eighteenth century. " I must not forget to tell you," he says, " that the
English prosecute the sciences with much success, and that there
are many good writers among them on every kind of subject.
This does not seem to me surprising ; they feel themselves free ;
they do as they like ; they are fond of using their reason ; they
do not observe that urbanity in conversation and that attention
to manners by which the intellect may be squandered and im-
poverished. . . . *There are people among the English who think more
deeply and entertain more of these profound thoughts than intelligent men
of other nations.* But it appears to me that as a rule they lack
both refinement and simplicity, and I think you would find their
imaginative works over-weighted with thought." Does it therefore follow that they are wanting in imagination ? " Most of
them possess it, but its fire resembles that of their coke ; it is
powerful, but yields little light." [1] Here again, why has he not
explained what he meant by means of examples ? Certainly
no one, in 1694, could have given the French nation a more
complete and well-founded opinion on a subject still so new.

Muralt's intention was merely to give a sketch. Incomplete
as it was however, his sketch achieved a brilliant success. The
book was translated into English [2] and read in Germany.[3] But it
was in France, more especially, that the collection of letters
made its way. Never, before Muralt suggested it, had the
question of the intellectual supremacy of England been brought
before the public as a whole. His presumption in doing so was

---

[1] First letter.
[2] *Letters describing the Character and Customs of the English and French nations* . . . by
M. de Muralt, a gentleman of Switzerland.   Second edition, London, 1726, 8vo.
[3] See Hirzel's edition of Haller's poems (Frauenfeld, 1882).

great, and was thought extreme. His criticism of French
" politeness " gave offence. " Our author is guilty of a paradox," says the *Bibliothèque française*,[1] " when he refuses to hear
of anything but good sense, as though good sense were incompatible with politeness." The *Journal des savants* devoted two
long articles to an abstract of the book.[2] The majority of the
author's critics, while fully recognising his originality, held that
his position was indefensible. A Jesuit, the reverend father de
la Sante, professor of rhetoric at the college of Louis-le-Grand,
felt it his duty to refute it in a public oration.[3] Desfontaines
caught the infection and published an *Apologie du caractère des
Anglais et des Français*,[4] in which he sharply criticised the author's
errors and disputed his conclusions, while, at the same time,
he acknowledged his merit in somewhat singular terms : " I was
very pleased to find a thinking Swiss. With regard to certain
nations we have, it must be confessed, ridiculous prejudices. So
I am beginning to conceive of philosophers on the summits of
the Alps, just as I have for some time been imagining poets from
Astrakhan or Norway. This Swiss, who has thoughts in his
head, is not, if you please, a Frenchman in disguise, nor a Swiss
' spectator '[5]; he is a Swiss, a real Swiss, but a Swiss who is
at once both an Englishman and a Frenchman, that is to say, his
mind has been formed by intercourse with these two nations.
As a Swiss he has both good sense and simplicity; as an Englishman plenty of depth and penetration ; as a Frenchman animation
and a certain amount of subtlety." The merit of Muralt's mind,

---

[1] Vol. iv., part ii., pp. 70-82, and vol. vi., part i., pp. 102-123.

[2] August 1726. *Cf. Bibliothèque des livres nouveaux* (September, October, and
December 1726); *Journal littéraire de la Haye*, 1731, vol. xviii., pp. 50 and 240;
Mercure Suisse, March 1733, November and December 1736 ; *Lettres juives* of d'Argens,
letter 68 or 72—according to the edition referred to ; Clément, *Les cinq années
littéraires*, 1st March 1751, and 30th December 1752.

[3] 28th January 1728 (*Mercure de France*, May 1728). It is clear that, three
years after its publication, the excitement aroused by Muralt's book had not
yet subsided.

[4] *Ou observations sur le livre intitulé : Lettres sur les Anglais et les Français et sur les
voyages, avec la défense de la sixième satire de Despréaux et la justification du bel esprit
français* [the last two pieces are by Brumoy]. Paris, 1726, 12mo.

[5] An allusion to the imitations of Addison which were so numerous at that time.

namely its cosmopolitan character, a rare quality at that period, was thus discerned by Desfontaines with considerable accuracy.

Nevertheless, he is foolish enough to reproach Muralt with certain supposed errors; and incurs in consequence a smart rebuke from Voltaire. " Is there a fresh edition of a wise and clever book by M. de Muralt, who does so much honour to Switzerland . . . forthwith the abbé Desfontaines takes his pen, abuses M. de Muralt, whom he does not know, and pronounces a sweeping judgment upon England, which he has never seen." [1]

Voltaire was an admirer of Muralt—" the wise and clever M. de Muralt," as he calls him once more in the *Lettres anglaises*.[2] He certainly made him his guide in his first studies in English. " M. de Muralt's letters," wrote one who knew,[3] " are highly appreciated here by all sensible people. Those who inveigh against the depravity of taste and style in France delight to extol this book as a model of beauty, vigour and simplicity." Jean-Jacques, in his turn, praised that " wise man," " the sober Muralt," and borrowed from him, as we shall see, on more than one occasion.

Thus Muralt, in company with the refugees, to whom he is closely allied, was among the first in France to institute a comparison between the French and the English intellect, and to show a preference for the latter. And since he was in addition a writer of talent, the success of his *Lettres*, published nearly ten years earlier than the *Lettres anglaises*, should be noted as a symptom.

II

Stimulated by Muralt, public curiosity with regard to England soon found fresh nourishment in the cosmopolitan novels of the abbé Prévost.

The abbé had twice sought refuge in England; the first time

---

[1] *Mémoire du sieur de Voltaire*: Works, published by Moland, vol. xxiii., p. 32. It will be observed that the passage was written in 1739, subsequently to the *Lettres anglaises*, and to Voltaire's residence in England.

[2] Beginning of letter xix. (suppressed in later editions).

[3] A letter from Jacob Vernet to Turrettini, dated Paris, 7th March 1726; quoted by M. E. Ritter.

in 1728, after his rupture with the Benedictines of Saint-Germaine des Prés. On that occasion he remained there until 1731,[1] and appears to have enjoyed the delights of his first residence to the full, as well as the intoxication of recovered freedom. Employed as secretary or tutor in the house of an English peer, he seems to have been obliged through a " love affair " to leave both his " agreeable position " and the country he had found so attractive.[2]

He returned thither in 1733, this time in the society of a young lady who had accompanied him from Holland. He has complained of the cold manner in which, on account of this circumstance, he was received by the refugees, who, on the occasion of his first visit, had probably welcomed the unfrocked Benedictine, so restless-minded and inquisitive, with open arms.[3] " He is a shrewd man," wrote Jordan, who saw him in London in 1733, " and has a knowledge not only of polite literature but also of theology, history and philosophy. . . . I will say nothing of his conduct, nor of a criminal action of which he has been guilty in London. . . . It is no business of mine."[4] Whatever this mysterious crime may have been, Prévost, who was obliged to live in England and to earn his own living, became more completely anglicised than any other writer of the eighteenth century. He acquired a thorough knowledge of the language, and henceforth worked as a salaried translator of English books. Not to mention in this place his celebrated versions of Richardson, he rendered into French Van Loon's *History of the Low Countries as illustrated by their Coinage*, the *Travels of Robert Lade*, Middleton's *History of the Life of Cicero*, Hume's *History of the House of Stuart*, Dryden's tragedy *All for Love*. His *Histoire des voyages* is itself nothing more than an adaptation of a book by Green,[5] just as his

---

[1] The exact date of his return is unknown. One of his letters, dated 10th November 1731, was written from the Hague. See the book upon *L'abbé Prévost*, by M. H. Harrisse, p. 150. On the 20th June 1731, Prévost witnessed the first performance of Lillo's *London Merchant* in London.

[2] See M. Brunetière's fine study of Prévost : *Études critiques*, vol. iii., p. 195.

[3] Prévost translated Van Loon's *History* in conjunction with Van Effen.

[4] Jordan, *Histoire d'un voyage littéraire fait en* 1733, p. 148.

[5] *A new general collection of voyages and travels*, London, 1745-47.

novel *Almoran et Hamet* is merely an adaptation from J. Hawkesworth.

Thus Prévost made abundant use of his knowledge of the English language, which he seems to have written and spoken with facility.[1]

But, above all, he took a keen interest in the country, in its customs, laws and literature. Naturally inquisitive with regard to foreign nations, he endeavoured to introduce in his earlier novels almost every country in Europe. The originality of the *Mémoires d'un homme de qualité*, written during his first residence in England, consists not so much in their romantic but disconnected thread of action, which is constantly hindered by unexpected incidents, as in the representation of foreign manners—German, Spanish or Italian, as well as Turkish, Dutch, and English. It is all very well for him to write contemptuously : " I leave to geographers, and to those who only travel from curiosity, the task of supplying the public with descriptions of the countries they have traversed. The narrative I write consists only of actions and feelings."[2] The real novelty of the book consists, if not in the physical, at any rate in the moral geography, if I may say so, of the countries traversed by its hero.

But if there was nothing very new in making a few rough, and moreover conventional, sketches of Spain in the manner of Lesage, or in venturing, like Montesquieu, to describe the manners of a harem, assuredly there was considerable novelty in aspiring to give us " an idea of German pleasures and Teutonic gallantry," or, better still—since here Prévost was drawing from life—of the character and manners of the English. In this respect, these *Mémoires d'un homme de qualité*, which obtained so great a success in their day, are quite peculiarly instructive. Few books have done so much to create among Frenchmen a knowledge, to quote the author's own words, of " a country which other European nations esteem less highly than it deserves, because they are not sufficiently acquainted with it."[3] And few

---

[1] There is an English letter from Prévost to Thiériot extant (*Œuvres de Voltaire*, vol. xxxiii., p. 467).

[2] *Mémoires d'un homme de qualité* (*Œuvres choisies*, vol. i., p. 330).

[3] Vol. ii., p. 237.

writers have laboured so earnestly to remove " certain childish prejudices, common to most men, but especially to the French, which lead them to arrogate to themselves a superiority over every other nation in the world." [1]

England occupies an important place in the *Mémoires*. First of all, we have some attractive pictures of manners and customs ; a masquerade in the Haymarket, an English ball, a description of London, a " gladiatorial contest," or, more precisely, a boxing-match, followed by a bout with sabres, " a kind of school where," according to the indulgent narrator, " youths are trained to be courageous, and to despise death and wounds." [2] Here, again, is a full account of a journey through England, full of shrewd and accurate observations, [3] and vivid as a picture. The description of Tunbridge Wells is a historical document : we learn from it that a cup of coffee costs threepence, chocolate the same ; there are balls where " lively shopgirls rub elbows with duchesses," and where love-adventures are plentiful. " If this enchanting place had existed in the times of the ancients, they would never have said that Venus and the Graces dwelt in Cythera." The work is almost a guide-book, more especially for those who are in search of adventures of a certain kind.

But Prévost does not forget to inquire about more serious matters. He acquires information concerning the poets, quotes Milton, Spenser, Addison and Thomson, and remarks the prosperity of the drama : " I have seen several of their plays, which appeared to me not inferior to those of Greece or France. I will even go so far as to say that they would surpass them, if their poets paid more attention to the rules of construction ; but as regards beauty of sentiment, whether tender or sublime, and that tragic power which stirs the heart to its depths and never fails to arouse the passions of the most torpid soul ; in respect also of the power of expression, and the art of conducting events or contriving situations, I have read nothing, either in Greek or in French, superior to the English drama." [4] He mentions Shakespeare's *Hamlet*, Dryden's *Don Sebastian*, Otway's *Venice*

[1] Vol. ii., p. 251.
[2] *Cf.* vol. ii., pp. 281, 288, 289, 326.
[3] Book xi.
[4] Vol. ii., pp. 270-71.

Preserved, and a few comedies by Congreve and Farquhar—the very examples afterwards employed by Voltaire in his *Lettres*, and possibly suggested to him by Prévost's novel. It will also be observed that Prévost saw all these plays acted, and derived "infinite satisfaction" from their representation.

His freshest and most enthusiastic pages have reference to the national character. Considering that Muralt does not belong to France, Prévost was really the first French writer to become fascinated with that free, wise, philosophical and in other respects quite ideal England which was the Salentum of the eighteenth century. Everything connected with the country delighted him—its air of liberty to begin with. "What a lesson to see a lord or two, a baronet, a shoemaker, a tailor, a wine-merchant and a few others of the same stamp," all seated together round the same table in a coffee-house and chatting familiarly, pipe in mouth, on matters of public interest ! Verily, "the coffee-houses are, as it were, the seat of English liberty." [1] It is true that the common people are somewhat coarse. But it is also true that "there is no country where one finds such integrity, such humanity, and such sound notions of honour, prudence and happiness as among the English. Love of the public weal, a taste for practical science, and a horror of dependence and of flattery, are virtues which are almost innate in these fortunate people ; they descend from father to son like an inheritance." The English, in short, are "one of the first nations in the universe."

Then follows a comparison between English, French and Spaniards. It is worth noting that Spain is very harshly treated by Prévost : she was gradually sinking in public estimation, and had to pay dearly for the long spell of good fortune she had enjoyed in France [2] from Corneille to Lesage. The Frenchman, fascinating as he is on first acquaintance, does not improve as he becomes better known. The Englishman, though somewhat rough, is the only one who promises much to observant eyes.

---

[1] Vol. i., p. 293.

[2] See M. Morel Fatio's curious study of the vicissitudes of Spanish influence in France. (*Études sur l'Espagne.*)

" His is a wholesome exterior and we feel at once that there is no hidden depravity beneath it. When we get to know him as he is within, we find nothing but robust and perfect parts equally satisfactory to the eye and for use. . . . In short, the English virtues are as a rule lasting ones, because they are founded on principles; and those principles are the product of a happy disposition and an uncorrupted reason." [1]

But if such be the case, whence this people's evil reputation? It is due, in the first place, to their bloody and terrible history; yet does it greatly differ, in this respect, from that of other nations? In the next place, being separated from the rest of the world by "a dangerous sea"—*toto divisos orbe Britannos*—they are less known, because less seen. "People seldom travel in England," or so at least Prévost assures us, and consequently they form incorrect conceptions of its inhabitants. You must know them in their own country. Then perhaps, like the author of Manon Lescaut, you will desire to see "all who are dear to you" resemble the English.

Here the author's feelings are aroused. He is carried away by enthusiasm, and he too exclaims, O *fortunatos nimium!* "Happy isle, and happy, too happy inhabitants, if they are truly conscious of all their advantages of climate and situation! What do they lack of all that can render life comfortable and enjoyable? As regards the aspect of nature, their summer is not excessive in point of heat, nor is the cold of their winter extreme. Their soil produces in abundance everything they require for their own use. They can do without the goods of their neighbours; nevertheless they add to their own possessions all the rarest and most precious productions of every country in the world. . . . Are they less fortunate in the moral sphere? They have successfully defended their liberty against all the assaults of tyranny. To all appearance it is established upon impregnable foundations. Their laws are wise and easy to understand. There is not one of them but ministers to the public weal; nor is the public weal in England a mere name which serves to disguise the injustice and violence of those who hold the reins

[1] Vol. ii., pp. 247-252.

D

of power : every citizen is fully acquainted with his own rights ; the people have theirs, the limits of which they never transgress, just as the power of the great is defined by bounds they dare not overstep. Nor do the English enjoy less freedom in religious matters. They have recognised that every form of compulsion is a violation of the spirit of the Gospel. They know that the human heart is the kingdom of God. . . . Accordingly, virtue with them never consists in cant and affectation. . . . Religion in England, in the towns and even the humblest villages, finds its expression in hospitals for the sick, homes of refuge for the aged of both sexes, schools for the education of children, in short, in a thousand tokens of piety and of zeal both for country and religion. Would not any sensible man prefer these wise and religious institutions to our convents and monasteries where, as is only too well known, an idle and useless life is sometimes honoured with the name of hatred of the world and of contemplation of heavenly truths ? " [1]

But for the last sentence—in which the malignity of the unfrocked monk is too clearly apparent—should we not think we were reading a page from Fénelon or Bernardin de Saint-Pierre, describing some Salentum or marvellous Ile-de-France ? And is it not true that in 1729, in a book which was favourably received by the public, England was represented as an *Ultima Thule* where the happiness of the race was realised in love and fellowship through the free play of the human faculties ?

His vein once discovered, Prévost worked it freely in his other novels.[2] In particular, the *Philosophe anglais, ou Histoire de Monsieur Cléveland, fils naturel de Cromwell*, which was published from 1732 to 1739, is simply an exaltation of British virtue. Having extolled the virtues of the people, he deemed it needful to exhibit them in action, and this is the main object of these six large volumes, wherein a whole chapter of the history of England under Cromwell and Charles II. is in a manner

---

[1] Vol. ii., pp. 379-381.
[2] *Cf.* The *Lettres de Mentor à un jeune seigneur.* London [Paris], 1764, 12mo. The author inquired into the condition of poetry in England and in France, into the progress of education in the two countries, etc.

novelized. The hero of the book, the philosopher Cleveland, is a sort of romantic Montesquieu, with a fondness for travel. Never for a moment, as he crosses continent or sea, does his philosophy fail him. In the depths of misfortune, in the heart of American solitudes, among savages who murder his dearest friends, and devour—or so, at least, he supposes—his own daughter, Cleveland, unmoved, meditates, observes and enacts laws. Nothing can be more curious than his profession of faith, in which there has been remarked a foretaste, as it were, of that of the Savoyard vicar.[1]

Nor can anything be more singular than the methods he employs in order to civilize the savages and turn them into so many philosophers. Cleveland has but one weakness, and that a thoroughly English one. He is haunted by the idea of suicide; he has the *spleen*: "a kind of wild frenzy more common among the English than among other European nations. . . . The most dangerous and terrible of diseases." Nevertheless, after a fearful struggle Cleveland gets the better even of the *spleen.* How else could he be worthy of the names of philosopher and Englishman?

At the very moment when he was publishing *Cléveland,* Prévost had plunged into a new enterprise, the sole and acknowledged aim of which was the diffusion of English thought in France: he had founded *Le Pour et Contre.*[2] There was novelty in the undertaking; in the words of Prévost's biographer, it "bore no resemblance to the journals of the period."[3] Accordingly it achieved a great success. But the author took it into his head to endanger the success of the magazine by employing Le Fèvre de Saint-Marc, a second-rate compiler, as his assistant.[4] The public, whom Prévost had intended to mislead, was not to be deceived. He was obliged to resume the pen,[5] and did

[1] Book vii. *Cf.* Brunetière, *Étude sur Prévost.*

[2] *Le Pour et Contre* was issued from 1733 to 1740, and comprises 20 volumes.

[3] *Cf.* The *Essai sur la vie de l'abbé Prévost,* prefixed to the *Œuvres choisies.*

[4] Editor of Boileau, Chaulieu and Malherbe, and author of an *Abrégé chronologique de l'Histoire de L'Italie.*

[5] To satisfy his readers Prévost himself says, "The greater part of the second volume and the whole of the eighteenth are not by me" (vol. xx., p. 335).

not again lay it down until the journal reached its seventeenth
volume.   At this point he once more became weary of his task,
and did not return to it until the beginning of the nineteenth
volume.

Of the twenty volumes of which the entire series of his
journal consists, only the first four were composed in London.
Prévost had, in fact, returned to France, and, thanks to the
protection of the Prince de Conti, obtained the right to resume
the dress of a secular priest.   Employed as chaplain to the
prince, he continued to edit his journal, with the assistance of
his literary correspondents in London, but, it was said, in a less
independent manner than formerly through his inability to withstand the influence of his fellow-journalists.[1]

However this may have been, the success of his miscellany
was beyond doubt.   Spurious copies were issued in Holland,
"without my knowledge," says Prévost, "and with additions
of which some are extremely ridiculous."   His competitors grew
angry when they saw themselves left behind: and the hot-
tempered Desfontaines—supplanted by Prévost in the coveted
work of popularising English information, and unable to deny
the attractiveness of the magazine — contested the author's
veracity.   He accused him more especially of speaking about
England not *de visu*, but according to the reports of travellers,
such as Camden and others.[2]   This treacherous insinuation was
apparently without foundation.[3]   The public remained faithful
to Prévost.[4]

In *Le Pour et Contre* it discovered an encyclopædic review,
more varied, amusing, and genuinely literary than the Dutch
journals upon which it had been modelled.   In truth, if the art
of arousing public attention by every manner of means is one

---

[1] *Bibliothèque française*, vol. xxix., p. 155.

[2] *Observations sur les écrits modernes*, vol. i., p. 328.

[3] Prévost seems to have travelled about England a good deal; in vol. vii. of
Le Pour et Contre (p. 241) he informs his readers that he has just returned from a nine
months' journey through the provinces of the United Kingdom, and promises an
account of it in two volumes, which never appeared.   However, he made use of his
reminiscences in his novels (*cf. Mémoires d'un homme de qualité*, book xi.).

[4] *Cf.* the *Mercure* for December 1733, October 1735, etc.

of the journalist's professional virtues, Prévost may claim an honoured place in the annals of modern periodical literature. The information accumulated in his magazine is of the utmost variety. He forgets neither fashions, sports, theatres, nor wit and humour; not even "medical chat" and the "correspondence column." As its title promises, his journal really is a "periodical publication of a novel character in which all matters of interest to public curiosity are fully treated." He gratified the taste for exact, varied, copious and up-to-date information which was growing up in France at that period. No less than twelve objects does he set before himself, among which the character of "ladies distinguished by their merit," and "well-established facts which appear to transcend the power of nature," are among those of first importance. He supplies items of current information and chronicles of the day. Prescriptions for the small-pox or apoplexy, volcanic eruptions, Egyptian mummies, gigantic aloes, "love-intrigues" and erotic verses, tittle-tattle, and "echoes from the fashionable world," are all alike grist for his mill. "Why should I prefer one reader to another? If you *publish* a work do you not thereby declare that you write to please everybody?"[1] A candid confession. Still more frank— and characteristic even of another age—is the modesty of the editor, who is obliged to speak of everything when he knows nothing.

"*Though by no means versed in the writings of metaphysicians*, any more than in geometry and algebra, *of which I confess I understand practically nothing*, I venture to-day to impart to my readers a few reflections on the divisibility of matter and its existence, and on the nature of the souls of the lower animals, of man, and of superior intelligences."[2] His courage as a reviewer is such that he does not shrink either from the abbé Nollet's experiments on phosphorus, from Newton's physics, or from equally abstruse problems in algebra.

But though Prévost pays considerable attention, perhaps too much, to matters of trifling interest, he does not lose sight of his main object. "An entirely original feature of this paper

[1] Vol. ii., p. 38. [2] Vol. xiii., p. 169.

will be the publication, in each issue, of some special fact respecting the genius of the English, the curiosities of London and of other parts of the island, the progress they are every day making in science and in art, and even at times of translations of the finest scenes from their plays."[1] Is not London, in fact, "a point of convergence, as it were, for all the wonders and curiosities the world contains"[2]—a sort of intellectual capital of the universe ? Nor does he intend in any sense to vindicate the English; he speaks "simply as a historian who wishes to make them known."[3] The method proved highly effective. He himself states that he has an advantage over his competitors "in being able to give to the subject of his articles, and even to a single thought, a novelty of expression, an English colouring, if the words be allowed, which cannot fail to hit the taste of the French."[4] In fact he hits it so truly that he is overwhelmed with letters and questions, some on art, some on science, some on the fashions; he is unable to cope with them, and is fairly inundated.

On manners, customs, and anecdotes of private and public life, he is inexhaustible. He mentions the popular singers of the day, and the dancers, Farinelli and Mlle. Sallé. He retails the petty rumours of the political world. "A thousand times" he is entreated to give an exact translation of the official report of a parliamentary debate. He resolves to do so, translates the report of a sitting, and makes quite a hit. On other occasions he has to give an account of the English fauna and flora, scenery, natural curiosities, the fluctuations of public opinion, the differences of scientific men, and the controversies of theologians.

But his most brilliant successes were the "short pieces or fragments of foreign literature." These were the rarest specimens in the collection, as the author, who was well aware of the fact, informs his readers.

He knows that the French have everything to learn. While Molière is being played in London, and also *Brutus* and *Zaïre*; while French novels are being read and plundered, Frenchmen

---

[1] Vol. i., pp. 10-11.   [2] Vol. iii., p. 50.
[3] Vol. viii., p. 325.   [4] Vol. iii., p. 50.

are scarcely acquainted with a single English production. Yet in London, "ten thousand copies of a good book are easily sold in a month. . . . A book of which four hundred copies are bought creates a sensation in Paris."[1] What could be more convincing? What is one to think of a nation which in three months, from December 1st to March 1st, turns out "a hundred and fourteen works of various sizes?"

Too often, it is true, neither "grace nor subtlety" can be discovered in this mass of books. Yet how numerous are their original beauties! The ancient poets, such as Chaucer and Gower, who are little read even by the English themselves, receive no more than a passing allusion, as curiosities. But in compensation he makes all the more of *Shakespear* (*sic.*).[1] This great writer, the son of "a woollen manufacturer," possessed true genius. Of ancient writers he knew very little, certainly, but what of that? Had it been otherwise he would doubtless have lost some of "the vehemence, the impetuosity, the fine frenzy, if the expression be allowed, which flash forth even from his least striking productions." He is a very great poet. Then follows an examination of *The Tempest*, which in France would be considered a ridiculous play, of *The Merry Wives of Windsor*, of *Othello*, and, lastly, of *Hamlet*. Here Prévost's taste revolts; "an extraordinary rhapsody," he exclaims, "in which it is impossible to distinguish either form or probability." Yet he had read it and had detected the author's genius.

Elsewhere Prévost deals with the life of Milton,[2] not without inaccuracies, the most serious of which occurs when he makes it a reproach against the author of *Paradise Lost*, that he died "free from all religious ties." His treatment of Dryden is better, and shows more knowledge. Translations are given of *Alexander's Feast* and *Cleopatra*, the latter, to the despair, it should be said, of certain readers, filling several numbers of the journal.[3] Doubtless they preferred the anecdotes of living writers—Addison, Dennis, Tindal, Bentley, Berkeley, and others—with which Prévost enlivens his pages. A translation of Steele's comedy, *The Conscious Lovers*, or, according to Prévost's version,

---

[1] Vol. ii., p. 272.　　[2] Vol. xii., p. 128.　　[3] Nos. 62, 82, and 96-101.

L'amour confident de lui-même[1]; a review of Pope's letters; an abstract of Glover's *Leonidas*, a " masterpiece of English poetry," which was shortly afterwards translated; some scenes from Fielding's *Miser*; a few short pieces by Swift, such as *Martinus Scriblerus Peri Bathos*[2]—all was novel, stimulating, and gratifying to the curiosity.

Prévost was thus very conscientious in the pursuit of his calling as literary chronicler. He kept opinion in a state of healthy activity. He established a connection between Paris and London. When his journal ceased to appear it was keenly regretted. If Prévost ever mapped out a programme of life—and this is extremely doubtful—he could say, when he laid down his pen, that the first part of his task was accomplished. Following Muralt, and anticipating, by a brief interval, Voltaire, he had naturalized the taste for English literature in France. But in thus making himself its champion he had contracted towards his readers a debt of honour, which he discharged—as is well known—with the greatest talent and success, by translating Richardson.

III

In the year which witnessed the publication of *Pour et Contre* there had appeared in London, in its earliest form, the famous book which, by modifying its character, had definitely impressed the influence of the English genius upon France, namely, the *Lettres philosophiques* of Voltaire.

In every respect the *Lettres philosophiques* or *anglaises*—for Voltaire made use of both titles—is a work of the first importance. From its publication dates the commencement of that open campaign against the Christian religion which was destined to occupy the whole of the century; thence, too, the attack upon political institutions; thence, also, and above all, the rise of that new spirit, contemptuous of questions of art, critical, eager for reform, combative and practical, which concerned itself rather with political and natural science than with poetry and elo-

---

[1] Nos. 109 *et seq.*   [2] Vol. xiii.

quence, and was interested, before all things, in literature dealing with the active side of life and the diffusion of knowledge. The *Lettres anglaises* are the patent of majority of the eighteenth century.

They mark, also, a decisive advance in the growth of English influence. On this point we may trust to contemporary evidence. "This work," says Condorcet, "was, with us, the starting-point of a revolution; it began to call into existence the taste for English philosophy and literature, to give us an interest in the manners, the politics and the commercial knowledge of the English people, and to spread their language among us."[1] Voltaire may at least be credited with having added a seasoning of wit, animation and cynicism to certain truths scattered among the writings of his predecessors, but up to that time not familiar to the public. This is why, however strongly he may have repudiated it later, Voltaire was largely responsible for the anglomania of his epoch.

He had come to England at thirty-two, the age of intellectual maturity, and under the best conditions for deriving the utmost profit from his enforced residence there; prepared already to understand the English mind by his previous relations with several Englishmen of worth—Lord Stair, Bishop Atterbury, the merchant Falkener, and particularly Bolingbroke, in close acquaintanceship with whom he had, as he himself expressed it,[2] "learned to think"; and, above all, prepared by the deadly affront put upon him by M. de Rohan-Chabot and by his momentary scorn for France to welcome with enthusiasm anything which did not remind him of his ungrateful country. His visit to England was a turning-point in his life. Hitherto a poet and nothing else, his exile and misfortune now sealed him a philosopher. "It is M. de Voltaire's good fortune," wrote a contemporary, "that he has visited England. . . . The poetic gift of this author has long been apparent to every one. But no

[1] *Vie de Voltaire.*
[2] To Thiériot, 12th August 1737. *Cf.* also his letter of 2nd January 1723 to the same person. He had been introduced to Bolingbroke in 1719, and had visited him, and Mme. de Villette as well, at *La Source.*

one had thought of classing him among the thinkers and the reasoners." [1]

The remark is of the greatest importance. For it renders it beside the point to maintain that in reality the genius of Voltaire owed less to England than has been supposed; to observe, with Michelet,[2] that all the scepticism of the English was already to be found in Bayle, in Fontenelle, in Chaulieu or in La Fare; and to recall, with M. Brunetière, the "impiety" of Voltaire's early life, his first associations, his early reading, his maiden verses, the Society of the Temple, the patronage of Ninon, the *Épitre à Uranie*, and many other unanswerable arguments which show clearly that even before 1726 Voltaire was no longer a believer. It will never be proved that his residence in England did not broaden, stimulate and temper his intelligence, nor that it did not endow him with that authority which was still wanting to the author of *Mariamne* and *l'Indiscret*. Certainly it was not from the English that Voltaire learned to doubt all religious truth. Before ever he read Tindal or Collins he had written: "Our priests are not what a foolish populace supposes; their learning rests on the foundation of our credulity."[3] "Let us trust in ourselves alone," was his conclusion; "let us view everything with our own eyes; 'tis they are our tripods, our oracles, our gods."[4] Before ever he set foot in England he had breathed in France the atmosphere of a country already destitute of religion, and of a capital concerning which Madame wrote: "I do not believe there are a hundred people in Paris, even if we take into account ecclesiastics as well as men of the world, who possess a sincere faith in Christianity or have any belief in our Saviour: the thought makes one shudder."[5] Finally, before he fled from M. de Rohan-Chabot, he had already found mental

---

[1] *Bibliothèque française*, on Histoire littéraire de la France, voL xx., 1735, p. 190.

[2] *Histoire de France*, vol. xvi., p. 70: "What does he owe to the English deists? Less in reality than has been supposed. He is far more dependent on our own free-thinkers of the seventeenth century, on the doctrines of the Gassendists and of Bernier, Molière, Hesnault, Boulainvilliers, &c." The same view is maintained by Lanfrey (*L'Église et les philosophes au xviiie siècle*).

[3] *Œdipe*, iv. i.   [4] *Ibid.*, ii. 1.

[5] Quoted by M. Brunetière, *Revue des Deux Mondes*, 1st November 1890.

sustenance in Bayle's "incomparable dictionary," as Locke calls it,[1] the arsenal whence all the sceptics of the eighteenth century, English and French alike, had taken their weapons. The *Dictionnaire critique* had twice been translated into English, and even sold in parts to encourage its circulation,[2] and Toland, Collins, Tindal and others, not to mention Bernard de Mandeville, had borrowed unsparingly from "the greatest dialectician who ever wrote."[3]

But if the English deists are undoubtedly the disciples of the French free-thinkers of the seventeenth century and of Bayle, does it therefore follow that they merely imitated them ? Because Locke had recourse to Bayle, shall we conclude that he invented nothing himself ? And, to speak more generally, because public opinion in France between 1700 and 1730 was gradually throwing off the fetters of Catholicism, are we therefore to conclude that in point of religious belief it had arrived at the same independence as England ? Such an idea would be strangely paradoxical. "There is no religion in England," wrote Montesquieu, in the record of his travels. "If any one mentions religion, everybody begins to laugh. Someone having said, during my own stay there, 'I hold that as an article of faith,' everybody began laughing." Montesquieu evidently exaggerates. But there is truth in Muralt's statement that there was a certain indefinable air of finality, composure and resolution in the scepticism of the cultured classes among the English which was wanting in the frivolous unbelief of the French : "In point of religion, you would almost say that every Englishman has made up his mind either to have it in earnest or to have none at all, and that

---

[1] *Cf.* Le Clerc, in the *Bibliothèque ancienne et moderne*, vol. xiii., p. 458.

[2] Desfontaines, *Lettre d'une dame anglaise*, at the end of the translation of Fielding's *Joseph Andrews*. Concerning English translations of Bayle, *cf. Histoire des ouvrages des savants*, June 1709, p. 284 ; *Bibliothèque britannique*, vol. iv., p. 176, and vol. i., p. 460. The earlier of the two translations was of an inferior order. The second, enlarged and more accurate, began to appear in 1734 under the title: A General Dictionary, Historical and Critical, in which a New and Accurate Translation of that of the celebrated Mr Bayle is included. . . . London, 1734, folio. The authors of the adaptation are John Peter Barnard, Thomas Birch, John Lockman, George Sale. A life of Bayle by Desmaizeaux is prefixed.

[3] Voltaire, *Poème sur Lisbonne*, Preface.

England, in distinction from other countries, contains no hypocrites." [1] In France, liberty of thought, however widely spread, was not, as in England, a part of the national spirit; it shrank from displaying itself openly and did not adopt the same aggressive attitude. In this respect, therefore, Voltaire found England in advance of his native country. Similarly, he discovered in English books a new and complete philosophy, very positive and precise, of which only the germ was to be found in Bayle. This philosophy Voltaire rendered popular in France. It is true that the refugees had already published translations or abstracts of Herbert, Blount, Shaftesbury, Toland, Tindal and Collins. Not only, however, were these translations done in that harsh and inaccurate style which the refugees had contracted in a foreign land,[2] but they were not read beyond the limits of a very small circle. Voltaire absorbed the substance of them, and transmitted it to the public in general. We find the author of *Œdipe* and the *Henriade* writing a *Traité de métaphysique*, which is an abridgment of Locke, and publishing *Éléments de la philosophie de Newton*. In this sense, then, England gave Voltaire, the wisely and worldly-minded sceptic, an entirely fresh character—that of a philosopher. His unbelief derived substance from English philosophy. In the phrase of Mr John Morley, " Voltaire left France a poet, he returned to it a sage." [3]

What is certain is that during the three years, or thereabouts, which he spent in England, he gave evidence of remarkable activity of mind.[4] Through the agency of Bolingbroke, the first to receive him as his guest, and also of Bubb Doding-

---

[1] *Lettre sur les Anglais et les Français*, p. 16.

[2] Tabaraud, *Histoire du philosophisme anglais*, vol. ii., p. 338.

[3] *Voltaire*, p. 58.   See Taine, *Littérature anglaise*, vol. iv., p. 215: " The entire arsenal of the sceptics and materialists was built and furnished in England before the French arrived : Voltaire merely selected his arrows there and fitted them to the string." All his contemporaries were of the same opinion ; see especially Condorcet, *Vie de Voltaire*; Garat, *Mémoires sur Suard*, vol. ii. ; Tabaraud, *Histoire du philosophisme anglais*; and the unknown author of the *Préservatif contre l'anglomanie* (1757).

[4] On his residence in England, see Churton Collins, *Bolingbroke and Voltaire in England*, and Mr A. Ballantyne's recent book, *Voltaire's visit to England*, which does not add much to the foregoing. Voltaire's stay seems to have extended from 30th May 1726 to February or March 1729.

ton and Falkener, the doors alike of Tory, Whig and middle-class society were at once opened to admit him. Of the English political world—which treated him, moreover, in princely fashion by subscribing £2000 towards the *Henriade*[1]—he obtained a close view—too close, indeed, if slanderers be credited.[2] The king granted him a private audience, and Queen Caroline gave him permission to dedicate the famous epic to herself.

Petted by the official world, Voltaire also associated much with men of science. He attended Newton's funeral in March 1727, made the acquaintance of the great man's niece, Mrs Conduit, questioned his medical adviser, and, in short, made a close investigation of Newtonianism, the most important of all English novelties. Meanwhile he attended the meetings of the Royal Society, of which he was afterwards elected a member, and acquired a knowledge of the latest advances in science. He rendered himself familiar with religious and philosophical controversies, obtained information concerning the Quakers, and visited Andrew Pitt at Hampstead. He read the philosophers, ransacked, or glanced through, Locke, " the sagacious Locke," Bacon, of whose works he never obtained an adequate knowledge, Chubb, Tillotson, Berkeley, Woolston and Tindal. With these, and with Clarke, whose " metaphysical imagination " appalled him, he became friendly. In the society of " these intrepid defenders of natural law " he contracted new and fruitful habits of thought.

He knew almost all the great English writers, concerning whom Desmaizeaux and the starveling Saint-Hyacinthe — whose relations with him very soon became somewhat strained —had doubtless given him more than one piece of useful information. He visited Pope at Twickenham, and owing to his still imperfect knowledge of English, their interview was rather an awkward one; this, however, did not prevent them

---

[1] Michelet errs in stating that Voltaire only received " a few guineas from the queen " (vol. xvi., p. 69). Longchamp and Wagnère (*Mémoires sur Voltaire*, vol. ii., p. 492) even speak of £6000 as the proceeds of the subscription and the sale.

[2] He was accused of having played the spy. (See a letter from Bolingbroke to Mme. de Terriole, in Churton Collins.)

from afterwards becoming intimate.[1]   He knew Swift fairly
well, and spent three months with him at Lord Peterborough's
house : when Swift thought of visiting France, Voltaire offered
him a letter of introduction to M. de Morville, while Swift, on
his part, wrote a preface for Voltaire's *Essai sur la poésie épique*.[2]

At Dodington's house he met Young, not yet the author of
the *Night Thoughts*, and Thomson, who charmed him with " the
grandeur of his genius and his noble simplicity."[3]   He went
much to the theatre, witnessed performances of Shakespeare,
which filled him " with ecstasy,"[4] became friendly with Colley
Cibber, met Gay, who showed him *The Beggar's Opera* before
it was produced, and paid to Congreve a visit which has ever
since remained famous, though to Voltaire it was disappointing
by reason of the affectation which led the old dramatist to insist
on being treated as a gentleman rather than as a poet.[5]

In short, there was scarcely a single distinguished writer of
the period with whom circumstances did not bring him into
contact.   If he took no pains to make the acquaintance of Daniel
de Foe, it was because de Foe avoided even his own countrymen[6]
and friends, and possessed, moreover, an evil reputation.   But
he sought information both with regard to famous writers of the
past, such as Addison and Dryden, and to living authors of less
celebrity, such as Garth and Parnell.[7]

And, lastly, he made himself familiar with the language.   He

---

[1] Villemain (*Tableau de la littérature du xviiie siècle,* 7th lesson) echoes a very
doubtful anecdote in reference to this subject.   Voltaire having uttered some coarse
jest at the expense of the catholic religion, Pope rose abruptly and left the room in
indignation.   Owen Ruffhead (*Life of Pope,* p. 156) repeats the story.   Goldsmith
(*Miscellaneous Works,* vol. iv., p. 24) maintains, on the contrary, that the interview
was a cordial one.   It seems safest to admit, with Duvernet, that owing to the
inability of Voltaire to speak English, and of Pope to speak French, the interview
was slightly embarrassed.   On the other hand Voltaire asserts that he has " lived a
good deal " with Pope.   Voltaire continued to correspond with him after his return
to France (*cf.* A Ballantyne, *op. cit.,* pp. 86-90).

[2] Bengesco, *Bibliographie de Voltaire,* vol. ii., p. 4.

[3] Ballantyne, p. 99.   [4] *Discours sur la tragédie.*

[5] *Lettres anglaises,* edn. of 1734, letter xix.   *Cf.* Johnson, *Life of Congreve.*

[6] Minto, *Daniel de Foe,* p. 165.

[7] From Parnell Voltaire borrowed the story of the hermit in *Zadig.*   He translated the earlier part of Garth's *Dispensary.*

had already, when confined in the Bastille, devoted himself to mastering its elements, and Thiériot had sent him English books. While in England he applied himself to it with ardour, and attended the theatre assiduously, the book of the play in his hand.[1] He very soon managed to read English and to write it, but he had more difficulty in speaking the language ; after eighteen months' residence he still understood it very imperfectly in conversation.[2] At a later period he confessed to Sherlock that although he was perfectly sensible of its harmony, he had never been able to master it thoroughly.[3] On the other hand he wrote letters in English to his friends, especially to Thiériot, and composed verses in the language.[4]

It was in English that he wrote the first act of *Brutus* [5] and *Charles XII.*[6] He became so accustomed to think in English that, if we may believe him, he found it difficult to think in his mother-tongue. He even undertook the work of an English writer : it was in that language that he published his *Essai sur les guerres civiles de France* and the *Essai sur la poésie épique*, " a mis-shapen English embryo" which he afterwards recast in a French form,[7]—both pieces being so correct and even elegantly written that a good judge has proposed to include Voltaire among the number of English classics.[8]

Throughout his life Voltaire retained his liking for the language, which he never altogether mastered, though he was always ready to use it. At Cirey, which he jocosely called *Cireyshire*, he wrangled in English with Mme. de Graffigny, so

[1] A. Ballantyne, pp. 48-49.

[2] *Cf. Avis au lecteur*, prefixed to the *Essai sur la poésie épique*, reprinted by Bengesco (vol. ii., p. 5).

[3] *Lettres d'un voyageur anglais*, xxv.

[4] These will be found in Ballantyne, pp. 68-69.

[5] Goldsmith gives a fragment of this earliest version (*Works*, ed. Cunningham, vol. iv., p. 20).

[6] Some of these notes are in the Bibliothèque Nationale.

[7] *An Essay upon the civil Wars of France. Extracted from curious Manuscripts. And also upon the Epick poetry of the European nations from Homer down to Milton*, by M. de Voltaire. London, 1727, 8vo. The copy given by Voltaire to Sir Hans Sloane is in the British Museum, and contains a dedication.

[8] M. Churton Collins, p. 265. Spence, it is true, asserts that Voltaire was assisted by Young (Ballantyne, p. 53).

that the servants might not understand.   He talked English with Franklin, and said to Mme. Denis, when she complained that she could not follow him : "I confess I am proud of being able to speak Franklin's language."   He was acquainted even with its least becoming expressions : Pennant the naturalist, who visited him at Ferney in 1765, found him perfectly familiar with English oaths.[1]

The accusation brought against him by Desfontaines, and later by Mme. de Genlis, of being absolutely ignorant of the language of Shakespeare, is therefore unjust.[2]   Though his knowledge of it became less accurate as he grew old, he always had as thorough a mastery of it as any French writer of the eighteenth century.   And considering that ignorance of the English idiom had previously been almost universal, and with some even a source of pride, Voltaire's knowledge of it, when he returned to France in 1729, was no small testimony to his originality.

Nor did his pre-occupation with London and with England cease upon his return to France.   He corresponded with Bolingbroke, Pope, Gay, Lord Hervey, Falkener, Pitt and Lord Lyttelton.   The link was formed, never again to be broken. Throughout his life Voltaire remained deeply and sincerely grateful to the country which had welcomed him during his exile.   Even when he was concerned and irritated at the influence of England upon literature, he continued to receive Fox, Beckford, Boswell, Sherlock, Wilkes and as many more, at Ferney, with an affability no less untiring than their curiosity.   Ferney, as Voltaire delighted to prove, was one of the most hospitable houses in Europe to all who bore an English name.   When Sherlock visited him, Voltaire enjoyed pointing out upon the shelves of his library the works of Shakespeare, Milton, Congreve, Rochester, Shaftesbury, Bolingbroke and others as well —objects of his youthful admiration to which he had remained faithful in maturer years.

The zeal with which, after 1729, he devoted himself to praising the English is only too well known.   His efforts, it is

---

[1] *Cf.* A. Ballantyne, p. 50 *et seq.*
[2] *Voltairomanie*, pp. 26, 27 and 46. *Mémoires*, vol. iii., p. 362. *Cf.* also Baretti, in his letter to Voltaire concerning Shakespeare.

true, were not entirely disinterested: "What! Is England the only land in which mortals dare to think? O London, rival of Athens! O happy land! As you have expelled your tyrants, so too have you driven out the shameful prejudices which warred against you. England is the country where everything may be said and every deed be rewarded as it deserves."[1]

Nevertheless, interested as it was, Voltaire's admiration was perfectly sincere. Even to Thiériot, an intimate friend, he wrote: "I add my weak voice to all the voices of England in order to create some impression of the difference there is between their liberty and our bondage, between their enlightened security and our foolish superstition, between the encouragement which the arts receive in London and the shameful oppression beneath which they languish in Paris."[2]

It was just at this time that he dedicated *Brutus* to Bolingbroke, and *Zaïre* to Falkener, using, in the latter case, terms so enthusiastic that the public took offence. But his boldest stroke was the publication of the *Lettres anglaises*.

The project had been formed long before. Some of the letters seem to go back to the early days of his exile. The greater part of them had been written between the close of 1728 and that of 1732.[3] So early as 1727 he publicly announced his intention of writing an account of his journey, and, in view of this undertaking, invited communications concerning Newton, Locke, Tillotson, Milton, Boyle and others.[4] It was not, however, until he had returned to France that he carried out his design. The framework was ready to hand, in the letters he had addressed to Thiériot, at the latter's request, concerning the manners and customs of the country.[5] They were simply modified, completed, and arranged in strict sequence.

[1] *Lines on the death of Mlle. Le Couvreur*, 1731.   [2] 1st May 1731.

[3] The book was almost finished in September, and was completed in November (Letters to Formont, September and November 1732). In December he submitted the letters on Newton to the criticism of Maupertuis.

[4] Notice to the reader in the English edition of the *Essai sur la poésie épique*: M. Bengesco has translated this curious fragment, which Voltaire suppressed in subsequent editions (*Bibliographie*, vol. ii., p. 5).

[5] *Cf.* Bengesco, vol. ii., p. 12, and Voltaire to Cideville, 15th December 1732.

The reader will be familiar with the difficulties placed by the censor in the way of printing the book. Voltaire then sent his manuscript to Thiériot, who happened to be in London, and he had the work translated by a man named Lockman. The English edition was brought out in London, during August 1733. Prévost assures us that it met with great success.[1] However that may be, it was reprinted in the same and the following years in Dublin, Glasgow and London.

The French edition did not appear until the next year, when it was published by Jore, and placed on sale in April.[2] In spite of what Voltaire has said, it does not materially differ from the English one.[3]

It is needless to recall here the scandal created by this famous work, and the decree of 10th June 1734 condemning it to be burnt, as " calculated to encourage licence of a kind most dangerous to religion and to the order of civil society." No single book, of all Voltaire's writings, caused a more lively agitation or provoked more controversy.

The *Lettres anglaises* contain, in fact, two works : a pamphlet —philosophical, political and religious, and a study of England. With the pamphlet we are not here concerned—except in so far as it distorts the study which the author intended to write.

IV

It would be a waste of time to attempt to prove that Voltaire's ill-feeling perverted his judgment. The whole of the earlier part of his book is simply a satire. The four letters on the Quakers are a coarse attack upon religion, and do not pretend to be anything else. Elsewhere, however, the author is either careless, or ill-informed, or deliberately inaccurate.

---

[1] *Pour et Contre*, vol. i., p. 242. *Cf.* Voltaire to Formont, letter 359 in Moland's edition, and to the abbé de Sade, 29th August 1733.

[2] Beuchot wrongly asserts the existence of an edition published in 1731.

[3] To Cideville, 4th January 1732.

His commonest error is that of exaggerating characteristics. He is well enough aware that he is writing a panegyric and not drawing a portrait.

Just as Tacitus had his Germany, so Voltaire has his England, too beautiful to be true—as, indeed, his contemporaries assured him. To one it seemed that Voltaire was not master of his subject,[1] and to another that, while the *Lettres* might be " amusing " reading, " it was a question whether the facts were always accurate, the reflexions always true, the criticism always just."[2] Such was the opinion of Prévost, who was one of the first to read the book. Such too is our verdict upon it to-day.

On the subject of the religious condition of England, and upon toleration and liberty of thought, there are palpable and deliberate exaggerations. But there are exaggerations also on less burning topics : on commerce, for instance, and the circumstances of men of letters.

If we may believe Voltaire, there is nothing more enviable than the condition of literary men in this land of freedom. A sweet spirit of brotherhood reigns between the poet and the peer. The surest way to attain any lofty position is to write an ode or a treatise on moral philosophy. Did not Addison become a Secretary of State ? Newton, Warden of the Mint ? Prior, an ambassador ? Swift, an Irish dean ? Did not Pope make £8000 by a translation of Homer ? And the lesson becomes still more instructive if it be added that Prior was a "waiter at a tavern," and that he owed his good fortune to the Earl of Dorset, himself a " good poet and a bit of a drunkard," who discovered him in his tavern reading Horace. Lastly, were not actresses, provided they had genius, buried at Westminster by the side of such as Newton ?

But Voltaire makes no mention of the facts, which he might have witnessed with his own eyes, that a poet like Thomson had to sell his verses for a mere trifle in order to buy shoes ; that Savage, without a roof to shelter him, was forced to spend the

---

[1] Jordan, *Histoire d'un voyage littéraire fait en* 1733, p. 186.
[2] *Pour et Contre*, Nos. xi., xii., and xiii.

night in the streets; that Johnson, at the beginning of his career, once went forty-eight hours without food; in short that the poet painted by Hogarth, living in a miserable lodging, forced to wear his dressing-gown while his wife mends his only pair of breeches, was a figure not unknown to reality.[1]   In the years between 1726 and 1729, the good times when Priors were ambassadors and Addisons ministers were past and done with. This Voltaire knew, yet he has not mentioned it.

The reasons are that he is before all things a pamphleteer, and that he is writing a satire.   A good critic[2] has reproached him with having spoken very unjustly of English institutions, with having made no effort to understand the machinery of English government, and with having failed to perceive the relation between that government and the genius of the race.   This is to forget that Voltaire is rather satirizing his own country than writing a historical study.

He was neither very accurate nor very scrupulous in speaking of English literature.   But since he was better acquainted with it than with English politics, and not only had a very sincere admiration for it, but keenly appreciated the pleasure of making it known to his fellow-countrymen, it happens that the literary portion of the book is the best even to-day.

It is certainly too discursive.   Voltaire was a rapid writer. He says that Shakespeare was living two centuries before 1734. He takes a scene in *Venice Preserved*, which is a satire upon Shaftesbury, for a simple piece of comedy—merely from want of careful reading.   In a picture of contemporary literature he forgets to mention *The Spectator*, which first appeared in 1711, *Robinson Crusoe*, which belongs to 1719, and Thomson's *Seasons*, the first canto of which appeared in the year of his arrival in England.   He scarcely mentions *Gulliver*, and, in the first edition, he did not even make any allusion to the *Essay on Man*, which was published in 1731.

Hence it follows that the picture is seriously incomplete. Worse still, it is also seriously and wilfully inaccurate.   What

---

[1] Beljame, *Le public et les hommes de lettres*, pp. 364-377.
[2] Mr John Morley in his fine study on Voltaire.

are we to say, for example, of this pretended translation—this
thoroughly " philosophical " version of *Hamlet's* soliloquy :

> On *nous menace*, on dit que cette courte vie
> De *tourments éternels* est aussitôt suivie.
> O mort ! moment fatal ! *affreuse éternité !*
> Tout cœur à ton nom seul se glace épouvanté.
> Eh ! qui pourrait sans toi supporter cette vie,
> De *nos prêtres menteurs bénir l'hypocrisie ?* [1]

Really, who ever thought of finding Shakespeare in this
predicament ?

Would the reader like to know why the English, who have
appropriated so freely from Molière, have never imitated or
translated *Tartuffe* ?   " The subject of it could not possibly be
a success in London : the reason being that men derive very
little enjoyment from portraits of people they do not know."
The remark is smart, but is it legitimate criticism ?

There is an art of quotation which is itself a process of satire ;
and of this art Voltaire was a master.   If he desires to prove
that English noblemen cultivate letters, there falls from his pen
a quotation from Lord Hervey, which happens to be a picture of
ecclesiastical life in Italy.

> Les monsignor, soi-disant grands,
> Seuls dans leurs palais magnifiques,
> Y sont d'illustres fainéants
> Sans argent et sans domestiques.

This is slightly impertinent.   Still, it was necessary to give an
idea of the " somewhat lusty " imaginations of these English.
But Voltaire goes further, and places his own friends in uncomfortable positions.   Take his appreciation of Swift's *Tale of a Tub* :
" In this country, which certain other European countries find so
odd, it is not considered at all strange that, in his *Tale of a Tub*,
the reverend Swift, dean of a cathedral, should have ridiculed
Catholicism, Lutheranism, and Calvinism; he claims in excuse that
he has not meddled with Christianity itself.   *He pretends that if he
has given a hundred birch-strokes to the children, he has respected their
father ; but certain very fastidious people thought the rods must have been*

[1] *Œuvres*, ed. Moland, vol. xxii., p. 151.

so long that they reached even the father."[1]   If this is not treachery,
what is it?   And what is to be said of an insinuation which
ranks Swift among the philosophers whose very name threw him
into a rage?   But Voltaire, as a friend of Swift, felt no stings of
conscience, and in his letter "on the English authors who have
written against religion," does not scruple to place both Jeremy
Taylor, one of the glories of Anglicanism, and Dean Swift, who
would certainly have felt little flattered to find himself in such
company,[2] by the side of theologians like Warburton and
Tillotson.

If, therefore, we set aside such of Voltaire's opinions on
English literature as may have been prompted by wilful mis-
conception and bad faith, the residue of impartial and comprehensive criticism is of small extent.   It should be said, however, that this part at any rate is interesting and, in certain
respects, distinctly novel.   If literary criticism is the art of
understanding foreign works in themselves and for themselves,
there are in the *Lettres anglaises* two or three chapters in which
Voltaire's keen and enquiring mind was genuinely critical.

His early taste in English literature was for the poets of the
Restoration: Rochester, Waller, Dorset, and Roscommon, all of
whom he quotes.   Though very French in flavour, they were
almost unknown in France.   In a translation of an extract from
one of Rochester's satires, Voltaire seeks to give his reader some
idea of "the impetuous freedom of English style."   His success
is open to question, but his intention, at any rate, was good.

With one of the strangest and certainly one of the most
characteristically English productions of the same period, namely,
Butler's *Hudibras*, he was more fortunate.   Butler's ponderous
raillery, the ferocious insolence of his sneering laughter, his
art of cutting up history and life into colossal caricatures—an
art which implies much individuality, however inferior it may
be in type—had evidently a great attraction for Voltaire.   He
comes very near to putting Butler above Milton.   In the ability

---

[1] Vol. xxii., p. 175.

[2] On Swift, see the fifth of the *Lettres, a S. A. le prince de* . . . (vol. xxvi., p.
489), and the letter to Mme. du Deffand, 13th October 1759.

to excite laughter the author of *Hudibras* is unrivalled: " A man whose imagination contained the tenth part of the comic spirit, good or bad, which reigns in this work, would still be very amusing." [1]   In comparison with such a masterpiece the French *Menippean Satire* is " of very indifferent quality." The platitudes of the poem; the obscenity, the strange combination of frivolity and ponderous buffoonery, the musty odours of kitchen and stable, which render Butler's work, considered as a poem, odd and almost monstrous—nothing of all this repelled Voltaire. He chuckled without scruple at Butler's noisy puppets, disporting himself with all the menials and applauding Hudibras, who

> Tout rempli d'une sainte bile,
> Suivi de son grand écuyer,
> S'échappa de son poulailler,
> Avec son sabre et l'Évangile. [2]

In the same way he relished the spicy and cynical English comedy of the Restoration. He liked its blunt naturalness, and the almost impudent fidelity with which it depicted every-day life. True, its naturalness was not altogether free from coarseness, nor its portraiture from vulgarity. Yet coarseness and vulgarity were after all characteristics of English manners, and it was upon their manners that the English had founded their comedy. Their climate was productive of misanthropy, and so, by means of Wycherley's pen, they placed misanthropes upon the stage. This implied, no doubt, a lack of " delicacy " and " propriety." It was a little too " daring for French manners," and the English drama was no school of all the virtues. It had to be acknowledged, however, that it was " the school of wit and of good comedy." Classical by the higher side of his mind, Voltaire always had a secret fondness for coarse pleasantry,

---

[1] Letter xxii.

[2] A paraphrase of two lines in *Hudibras* (canto i.):

> Then did Sir Knight abandon dwelling,
> And out he rode a colonelling. (Bohn's Library edn., p. 4.)

Voltaire was always fond of *Hudibras*; *cf.* Nichols, *Illustrations of the eighteenth century*, vol. iii., p. 722.

which found abundant satisfaction in the plays of Wycherley, in
Congreve—or in Swift, the "Rabelais of England," whose
works had "a strange and inimitable flavour," and whose *humour*
Voltaire was one of the few Frenchmen to appreciate to the full.
"One who has read classical authors only," he wrote, "despises
everything written in a living language; and the man who knows
no language save his own is like those who, never having left
the French court, pretend that the rest of the world is of little
consequence, and that anyone who has seen Versailles has seen
everything." [1]   Voltaire—at the time when he was writing the
Lettres anglaises—made a very sincere effort to see, and to see
correctly, something beside Versailles.

There is therefore no occasion to congratulate him on having
understood Pope, whose "subjects, for the most part, are
general and appeal to all nationalities"; we may rather praise
his concise, but significant, appreciation of the tragic poets of
England, who, "barbarous" as they are, exhibit nevertheless
"surprising flashes in the midst of their darkness." He has
well observed that if the language or the imagination of
Shakespeare appears to us "unnatural," it is because his style
is "too close an imitation of the Hebrew writers, who are full
of Asiatic inflation." Voltaire was undoubtedly the first French
critic to point out this affinity between the British genius and
the genius of the Bible—the chief of English books. He was
vaguely aware how foreign was the poetry of England to the
French spirit, and how closely it was bound to the soil which
had witnessed its birth: "The poetic genius of the English has
hitherto resembled a thickly-growing tree of nature's own plant-
ing, which puts forth a thousand branches at random, and grows
vigorously, yet irregularly. If you attempt to do violence to
nature, and to trim it after the fashion of the trees in the garden
at Marly, it will die." This is rather to suggest a clue than to
prove by evidence. To tell the truth, Voltaire says scarcely
anything definite concerning English poetic literature, least of
all anything which had not been said before. The few pages
of Shakespeare which he translates are very inadequate speci-

[1] *Essai sur la poésie épique*, chap. i.

mens. The *Lettres philosophiques*, we must repeat, are not a synopsis of English literature : any one who looked to find in them a sketch of that literature in 1730 would be greatly disappointed. But by way of compensation they created the desire to be acquainted with it, and that was the main thing. Partly out of spite and partly from genuine admiration, Voltaire not only introduced English taste, but also constituted himself its apologist, though a few years later he atoned for his action by opposing that taste and retracting his own declarations. What was better, he praised with warmth, and was easily aroused to ardour. " M. de Voltaire," said the Dutch gazettes,[1] " is not of those cold judges who have intellect and nothing else, and are rendered insensible to the delights of admiring, and of having their feelings aroused, by the pleasure they take in criticizing. He praises the fine pieces of which he speaks, as a man, and a man of genius."

And this is why the *Lettres anglaises* remain an epoch in the history of criticism. Prepared by the refugees, and unsettled by Muralt and Prévost, opinion was definitely won over by Voltaire. The ten years which followed the publication of the *Lettres* assured the success of English literature in France. Four years later, J. B. Rousseau recognised with regret the progress of " this miserable English spirit, which has insinuated itself into our midst during the past twenty years."[2] About the same time the abbé du Resnel, the translator of Pope, shows clearly that the study of English is gaining ground in France, and that the most famous English writers are no longer unknown to Frenchmen. He adds, it is true, that " this *liaison*, as it may be called, is still too recent " to convince him " that the two nations are really ready to harmonize with one another," and regrets the discredit into which Italian books are falling.[3] Five years later, however, Goujet declares that " English poetry is scarcely less known to-day than that of

---

[1] *Bibliothèque britannique*, 1733, vol. ii., pp. 121-2.
[2] Letter to Louis Racine, Brussels, 18th May 1738.
[3] *Les principes de la morale et du goût*, translated from the English of Mr Pope. Paris, 1737, 8vo, p. xxiii.

the. Italians or the Spaniards."[1]   The *Mémoires de Trévoux*
state that France had become "a very good friend to English
literature," and express concern at the fact.[2]   The *Correspondance
littéraire* remarks that the vogue of translations from English "is
lasting longer than such fashions usually last in this country."[3]
In 1755 Fréron writes: "Barely forty years ago a man who
ventured to speak of English tragedy and comedy would
have been hissed in fashionable society. . . . It has been a
great surprise to us to find that this nation is the equal
of ours in genius, its superior in power, and its inferior only
in subtlety and elegance."[4]   I may be excused for quoting
so much evidence of a revolution of such importance in French
taste.

There was still, according to the point of view which we
adopt, either one more step to be taken, or one more error to
be committed.   Now that curiosity with regard to English
works had been thoroughly aroused, it remained to recommend
them for imitation.   From this consequence Voltaire did not
shrink.

Of what does the history of literature consist but of imitation
and borrowing?   Montesquieu borrows from Mariana, Boiardo
from Pulci, Ariosto from Boiardo.   The English have frequently
pilfered from the French without making any acknowledgment.
Books are like "the fire on our hearths."   We obtain kindling
from our neighbours, light our own fire with it, hand it on
to others, and it becomes common property.   The fortunate ones
are those who manage to borrow in season!   Since therefore the

---

[1] *Bibliothèque française*, vol. vii., p. 189.   "Our intercourse with the English, our
study of their language, the eagerness of our writers to translate their works, are so
many different ways in which a knowledge of the style and genius of their poetry
has been rendered easier for us."   *Cf.* Silhouette, Introduction to the translation of
Pope's *Essay on Man*.   London, 1741, 4to.

[2] October 1749.   *Cf. L'Esprit des journalistes de Trévoux*.   Paris, 1771, vol. ii.,
p. 491: "It may be said that the productions of this country are sowing among
us the germs of all the unbridled opinions which have made as many ungodly
Christians in England as bad citizens."

[3] 1st August 1753.

[4] *Journal étranger*, September 1755, p. 4.   See also La Harpe, *Cours de littérature*,
vol. iii., p. 208.

English have profited largely by works in the French language,
" we, who have lent to them, ought to borrow from them in our
turn."[1]

Coming, as it did, at the right moment, this advice was
followed.

[1] Vol. xxii., p. 177, note. In 1756, Voltaire suppressed this passage, feeling,
doubtless, that his advice had been followed too faithfully.

Chapter III

I. Circumstances which contributed to the diffusion of the cosmopolitan spirit during the first half of the century—Decline of the patriotic idea—Exhausted state of the national literature.

II. Spread of the scientific spirit, and its literary results. `

III. The work of Jean-Jacques Rousseau in its relation to the influence of England ; in him the Latin genius is combined with the Germanic.

I

THE refugees and Muralt, Voltaire and the abbé Prévost had prepared opinion in France for the influence of English literature, and by means of this influence, for that also of other Northern literatures. They all contributed, some with full consciousness and intention, others from simple intellectual curiosity and without any calculation of the consequences their action might entail, to impair the venerable prestige of classical literature by affording the French mind a glimpse of a literature which to all appearance at any rate was absolutely indigenous, was profoundly original, and, instead of being founded on tradition, tended exclusively in the direction of progress.

"It seems," wrote Gottsched in 1739, "that the English are setting themselves to drive the French out of Germany."[1] In France the invasion of English literature took place more slowly. Nevertheless, between 1700 and 1760, approximately speaking, a few of those who aspired to educate the masses were promoting

[1] Manuscript letter preserved in the Zurich Library and quoted by M. de Greierz, in his *Muralt.*

the cross-fertilization of the two literatures. Many circumstances assisted them in their endeavour.

In the first place, it must be admitted, the decay of the patriotic idea. " The eighteenth century," it has been justly said, " was neither Christian nor French." [1] That is why, no less in literature than in everything else, it failed to maintain what for two centuries had been regarded as the national tradition. It is curious that the periods of the recrudescence of anglomania should coincide exactly with our most painful defeats or most disastrous treaties. Our admiration of England was never more lively than in 1748 and 1763, or thereabouts, and during the war with America. During the seven years war, it reached fever-heat. In vain did a few patriots raise their voices in denunciation of " that detestable country, the horrible resort of the savages of Europe, where reason, humanity and nature are unable to make their voices heard." [2] In vain did the press pour forth its pamphlets and satires. We read in a poem issued in 1762 : " Blood-nurtured tigers ! Your Lockes and Newtons never taught you such barbarous lessons as these. From them arose your imperishable renown ; they have absolved you from a Cromwell's crimes." [3]

The author of a *Petit catéchisme politique des Anglais, par demandes et par réponses,* [4] endeavours to rouse the national sentiment over the Port Mahon affair : " How do we define the science of government ? " the English are supposed to be asked. " It is the practical knowledge of everything that is unjust and dishonest.—What is ' natural right ' ?—It is an ancient code of law implanted in the human heart, which we have just

[1] E. Faguet, *xviii* siècle*, preface.

[2] *Les Sauvages de l'Europe.* Berlin, 1750. (See the *Journal encyclopédique,* 1st June 1764.)

[3] D'Arnauld, *A la Nation,* 1762.

[4] 1756. (*Journal encyclopédique,* September 1756). See also the *Adresse à la nation anglaise,* a patriotic poem, by a citizen, Paris, 1757; 12mo : " It has been thought permissible," says the author, in language which is highly significant, " to tell the truth boldly to a nation which tells it so frankly to its own kings " ; and *La différence du patriotisme national chez les Français et chez les Anglais* (by Basset de la Marelle. Paris, 1766) in which the author calls attention very decidedly to the decline of the patriotic sentiment.

amended in accordance with patterns only to be found in Barbary. . . .—What is a treaty ?—The thing for which we care less than for anything else in the world.—What are boundaries ?—We have not the slightest desire to know.— What are friends ?—What we shall never possess."

Friends they possessed, nevertheless, and very warm ones. Gibbon, who visited Paris in 1763, writes: "Our opinions, our manners, and even our dress were adopted in France; a ray of his nation's glory illumined every Englishman, and he was always supposed to be a patriot and a philosopher born."[1] "What did you think of the French ?" Voltaire once asked Sherlock. " I found them agreeable, intelligent and refined," his guest replied. " I only noticed one fault in them : they imitate the English too much."[2]   Immediately after the conclusion of the disastrous peace which deprived France of her fairest colonies, Favart celebrated the union of the two peoples in his *Anglais à Bordeaux*: "Courage and honour knit nations together, and two peoples equal in virtue and intelligence throw down the barriers their decrees have raised, that they may be for ever friends."[3]   So strangely feeble was the national sentiment that these lines were applauded to the skies, and their author dragged on to the stage and loudly cheered.

We must therefore note, as one of the causes which assisted the diffusion of anglomania, the decline of the patriotic idea.

By a strange inconsistency, the virtues which the French admired in their neighbours were just those in which they themselves were most deficient. They envied the patriotism of the English, with all its fierceness and brutality.[4] Even in 1728, Marivaux expressed his astonishment at these inconsistencies in a

---

[1] *Mémoires*, ch. xv.   [2] *Lettres d'un voyageur anglais*, p. 135.

[3] The treaty of Paris was concluded in February. The play was produced in March 1763. The author submitted it to the English ambassador, who altered its title, and caused the performance to be preceded by that of *Brutus*, "a patriotic tragedy in the English style." In consequence of this disgraceful success, the *Journal encyclopédique* says : "The author formulates the charge that at Paris the English are represented as a great and generous nation which seeks to rival the French in talent and in virtue, an accusation which the public endorses by its applause." (1st March 1763.)

[4] *Cf.* Bolingbroke's *Letters on Patriotism*, translated by the Comte de Bissy.

delightful passage : " It is an amusing nation—ours ; its vanity is not like the vanity of other peoples ; they are vain in a perfectly natural fashion ; they don't strive to be subtle with it as well ; they think a hundred times more of what is made in their own country than of anything made anywhere else on earth ; there is not a trifle they possess but is superior to everything we have, no matter how beautiful ; they speak of it with a respect they dare not fully express for fear of spoiling it ; and they believe they are quite right, or, if ever there are times when they do not believe it, they are careful not to say so, for, if they did, where would be the honour of their country ? There is some sincerity in vanity of this sort. . . . But as for us Frenchmen, we cannot let well alone, and have altered all that ; *our* vanity, forsooth, is of a much more ingenious sort, we are infinitely more cunning in our self-conceit. Think highly of anything made in our own country ! Why, whatever should we come to if we had to praise our fellow-countrymen ? They would get too conceited, and we should be too much humiliated. No, no ! It will never do to give such an advantage to men we spend all our lives with, and may meet wherever we go. Let us praise foreigners, by all means ; *they* will never be rendered vain by it. . . . Behold your portrait, *Messieurs les Français.* One would never believe how a Frenchman enjoys despising our best works, and preferring the silly nonsense which comes from a distance. ' Those people think more than we do,' says he, speaking of foreigners : and at heart he doesn't believe it, and if he thinks he does I assure him he is mistaken. Why, what *does* he believe then ? Nothing ; but the fact is men's self-conceit must be kept alive. . . . When he ranks foreigners above his own country, however, *Monsieur* is no longer a native of it, he is the man of every nation" [1]—the cosmopolitan.

To be a citizen " of every nation," not to belong to one's " native country "—this was the dream of French writers in the eighteenth century, and that is why " the silly nonsense which comes from a distance " met with such success. Is it not a mark of the " philosopher " to possess just this absolute de-

[1] *L'Indigent philosophe*, 5th No. (1728).

tachment from that national bond which may very well be one of the most absurd prejudices handed down from early ages ? Where Marivaux was mistaken was in seeing in it nothing more than a fashion. It was one of the most profound tendencies of the age, one of its essential characteristics. Now that which distinguishes nations from one another, that which differentiates races, is, strictly, literature or art, that is to say, the expression of their manners and inherent genius. What unites them, on the other hand, is the philosophical or scientific spirit. Art is infinitely various, philosophy is one. The relativity of the former is opposed to the universality of the latter. And, by a natural consequence, as the influence of science increases, the power of art wanes.

These two results were verified in the earlier half of the eighteenth century.

Its first twenty years were, in a literary sense, barren. They witnessed little more than the liquidation of the *grand siècle.* One by one the survivors of the great epoch passed away ; in 1704 Bossuet and Bourdaloue, in 1706 Bayle, in 1707 Vauban and Mabillon, in 1711 Boileau, and in 1715 Fénelon and Malebranche, as well as Louis XIV. The prominent writers of the eighteenth century, on the other hand, were but just coming into existence : Duclos was born in 1704, Buffon in 1707, Gresset and Mably in 1709, Rousseau in 1712, Diderot and Raynal in 1713, Helvétius, Vauvenargues and Condillac in 1715, d'Alembert in 1717, Fréron in 1718, Marmontel, d'Holbach and Grimm in 1723. Fontenelle alone—and herein lies his originality—formed, with Lesage, a connecting link between the two centuries. Montesquieu, Voltaire, Marivaux and Prévost were just taking the field, and indeed already opening fire.

But if the period witnessed the disappearance of many figures in the literary world, it was marked also by the publication of many posthumous works ; Bourdaloue's sermons, in 1707 ; the *Politique tirée de l'Écriture Sainte,* in 1709 ; the *Mémoires* of Retz, in 1717 ; the *Dialogues sur l'éloquence de la chaire,* in 1718 ; followed by the *Traité de la connaissance de Dieu et de soi-même* (1722), the *Mémoires* of Mme. de Motteville (1723), the *Lettres* of Mme. de Sévigné (1726), the *Élévations sur les Mystères* and the *Traité de la concupiscence* (1727 and 1731). The contempt with which these belated works were received by those harbingers of the century, the Dutch journals, was worth seeing. Obviously the years of waiting seemed tedious and empty. Opinion was wavering between a slowly dying admiration and a vague and as yet unsatisfied need of something fresh; there was an anxious expectation of the advent of a new literature for which the works of Englishmen provided a timely satisfaction.

For if, by a sort of posthumous vitality, the seventeenth century was being lengthened out into the early years of the eighteenth, the new spirit did not as yet assert itself in any decisive work. *Œdipe* did not make its appearance until 1718, nor the *Lettres persanes* until 1721. Old and effete types of literature still dragged out a painful existence. It is impossible, without the indulgent spirit of their contemporaries, to become warmly interested in the tragedies of Crébillon and Lagrange-Chancel. In comedy the protracted influence of Molière was wearing itself out in the last works of Boursault and Regnard and in the earlier ones of Dufresny and Destouches. *Turcaret* afforded a solitary exception in 1709, and even this piece, so far as form was concerned, remained entirely in accordance with tradition.

In history likewise, as also in moral and political philosophy, these years were unproductive. A few of Massillon's sermons gave a foretaste of a new eloquence, one better adapted to the age, savouring more of the present world, less solid also, and less religious than those of Bossuet's school and Bourdaloue's. Imaginative literature was in a languid condition: the one exception, *Gil Blas*, began to appear in 1715. The *Mémoires du chevalier de Gramont*, one of the very few works of importance belonging to this unfruitful period, were written by a foreigner, and were, moreover, among the books which did most to spread a knowledge of England among the French.

I have shown how the refugees endeavoured to turn the sterility of French literature to account in their effort to compel Frenchmen to admire the literature of a neighbouring country, and how they succeeded, if not in naturalising it in France, at any rate in arousing attention with respect to it.   That literature was destined gradually to become the refuge of all who were disgusted with the barrenness of the classical art of France ; and all that the latter was to lose the literature of England was destined to gain.

II

Another influence which prepared the way for the success of English works in France was the scientific and philosophical spirit.

Even in the seventeenth century England had seemed to be the home of experimental science.   So early as 1665 the *Journal des savants* declared that "fair philosophy was more flourishing there than anywhere else in the world."[1]   Chapelain, speaking of the English, wrote to Vossius : "They are learned, inquiring and open-minded, and you need scarcely expect anything of them but what is good."[2]   "The English," wrote Father Rapin a few years later, " by virtue of that penetrative genius which is common among them, are fond of methods which are deep, abstruse and far-fetched ; and by reason of their inveterate liking for work, are still more devoted than other nations to the observation of nature."[3]   So, La Fontaine : " The English are deep thinkers : in this respect their intellect corresponds with their temperament ; given to examine every subject thoroughly, and skilful in experiment, they extend the empire of science in every direction."[4]

The great name of the man of whom it has been said that he was "in a sense the type, or the proof-engraving, of the English genius"[5]—the name of Bacon, symbolized all the aspirations then beginning to be aroused by the empirical sciences, and afterwards so magnificently realised by Newton.   Is it any wonder that the man who spoke so eloquently of progress, and so contemptuously

[1] 30th March 1665.
[2] *Lettres de Chapelain*, ed. Tamizey de Larroque, vol. ii., p. 393.
[3] *Œuvres*, 1725, vol. ii., p. 365.   The passage was written in 1676.
[4] *Le Renard anglais*, published in 1694.
[5] Garat, *Mémoires sur Suard*, vol. ii., p. 45.

of tradition, who considered that "we ought to look, not to the darkness of antiquity, but to the light of nature, for our discoveries," should have been in the eyes of a d'Alembert, "the greatest, the most universal, and the most eloquent of philosophers."[1] And the hopes of Bacon were realised by Newton. In Voltaire's phrase, the heavens declared the glory of the author of the *Principia* and the *Optics*. English science, every day more glorious, appeared to the contemporaries of Voltaire and Maupertuis as the greatest revival of the human intellect since ancient times. It did more for the glory of the English genius than all the Addisons and the Popes together. The experimental or Baconian method triumphantly resisted the distinctively French method of Descartes. "I believe," wrote Le Clerc, "that the world is beginning to abandon that positive manner with which Descartes, who is responsible for it, used to set forth his conjectures in place of demonstrations; you do not find a single man of learning who is such a systematiser, so to speak, as he was. The English, in particular, are more averse to it than any other people."[2]

Henceforth—from 1700 to 1740—the whole "English party" gathered themselves together under the name of Newton, from Maupertuis, the first Frenchman to become an avowed "Newtonian,"[3] to Voltaire, who spread the new physics with so much eloquence.[4] "Many of our learned men," writes a witness in 1745, "have ranged themselves already beneath the English banner. . . . How pompously they extol everything which comes to us from that country! How eagerly they seek to make proselytes! To hear fanatics of this sort there are no real men except the English: not a step can be taken in philosophy or in letters without a knowledge of their tongue: according to them it is the key to all the sciences; they look

---

1 *Discours préliminaire de l'Encyclopédie.*
2 Letter to Louis Tronchin, Sayous, *La littérature française à l'étranger*, vol. ii., p. 41.
3 *Discours sur la Figure des astres*, 1732. *Cf.* d'Alembert, *Discours préliminaire.*
4 The *Optics* was translated by Coste in 1722. The *Éloge* of Newton, by Fontenelle, dates from 1727. The *Éléments de la philosophie de Newton*, by Voltaire, from 1738. The *Épitre LI.*, to Mme. du Châtelet, written in 1736, appeared in the same year.

upon it as the only rich language, upon English methods of thought as the only correct ones, and on the English manner of life as the only one that is reasonable." [1]

And so the homage paid to English science, by turning all eyes upon the country of Newton, preceded and prepared the way for the worship of Shakespeare and Richardson. It is less difficult to bring men together upon the ground of science, which knows no country, than upon that of art, which cannot so easily become universal and human.

But this evolution of the spirit of the age had still other results, even upon literature. It was in the school of Bacon, Locke and Newton that the French mind, up to that time full of respect for ancient models, and, under their influence, convinced of the superiority of art to science, forgot both its admiration for the ancients and its respect for art itself.

" Poetry is ingenious nonsense," said Newton. " All speculations on this subject," Locke had written, " however curious or refined or seeming profound and solid, if they teach not their followers to do something either better or in a shorter and easier way than otherwise they could, or else lead them to the discovery of some new and useful invention, deserve not the name of knowledge (or so much as the vast time of our idle hours to be thrown away upon such an empty idle philosophy). They that are studiously busy in the cultivating and adorning such dry barren notions are vigorously employed to little purpose, and might with as much reason have retained, now they are men, the babies they made when they were children." [2] This is exactly the spirit of the eighteenth century: contempt for all needless speculation, absolute indifference to problems, the solution of which does not directly affect our happiness in this world, exclusive concern with physical or moral comfort. Our business in this world, in Locke's opinion, is not to know all things, but to know those alone which concern the management of our own lives. To French thinkers of the seventeenth century, to Pascal and Descartes, it had seemed that the object

---

[1] Le Blanc, *Lettres*, vol. i., p. 63.
[2] Locke, *De Arte Medica*, Shaftesbury papers, series viii., No. 2.

of life was something outside of life itself, that human thought found its dignity in projecting itself, if one may say so, without limit. *Baconism* confined thought and science to the present existence. It maintained that there were ingenious yet useless truths which, like stars " too remote from our sphere, afford us no light."[1] The one solid fact was the necessity to which we are subjected of improving our present condition, of obtaining control over matter, of rendering it our docile and useful slave. Beyond that, all was idle fantasy. "When a man employs himself," writes Johnson, "upon remote and unnecessary subjects, and wastes his life upon questions which cannot be resolved, of which the solution would conduce very little to the advancement of happiness; when he lavishes his hours in calculating the weight of the terraqueous globe, or in adjusting successive systems of worlds beyond the reach of the telescope ; he may be very properly recalled from his excursions by this precept [Be acquainted with thyself], and reminded that there is a nearer Being with which it is his duty to be more acquainted ; and from which his attention has hitherto been withheld by studies to which he has no other motive than vanity or curiosity."[2]

Such a conception as this carries with it a contempt for everything in the nature of mere amusement, intellectual diversion, or superfluous thought. Poetry becomes "ingenious nonsense." The rationalism of a Locke will tolerate literature only as a modest clothing for ideas. The anglomaniacs, who, according to Voltaire, profess a great respect for "the four rules of arithmetic, and good sense," contrast that "rough ingenuity" which makes the English the Michael Angelos, as it were, of literary art, with the "easy elegance" of the French, who may be described more modestly as its Raphaels.[3] Casting aside all respect for models, they hold with Bacon that it is an "idle and useless thing to make the thoughts of man our principal study." Locke never studied books; he endeavoured to establish "the experimental physics of the

---

[1] *Lettres anglaises*, xxiv.   [2] *The Rambler*, No. xxiv.
[3] Garat, *Mémoires sur Suard*, vol. ii., p. 48.

soul," [1] and thus provided a notable example of what modern thought, independent of all tradition, should be.

In 1740, however, Locke and the English notwithstanding, the French public was still amusing itself with its tragedies, operas and frivolous verses. It applauded those who amused it, and was even yet the gayest and most volatile people in the world, the " whipped cream of Europe," to use the words of Voltaire. But, little by little, it began to feel a sense of shame, and to compare itself with the inhabitants of neighbouring countries. A Frenchman of this type would find himself a giddy-brained creature when weighed against a Bacon, a Newton, or even the " sagacious Addison" or the "respectable dean Swift." He would consider that " purity of language " and a " polished style " can only " serve to set one off in the world, and give one the reputation of a scholar," [2] ends which are of very little consequence. At any rate, many men of sound intelligence were soon to acquire a conviction that the bounds of literature were but narrow, and that the " imitation of nature in her beauty seems confined to certain limits which one or two generations at most very quickly attain." [3]

France, in short, to borrow once more the actual language of contemporary writers, " *owes to England the great revolution which has taken place in her literature.* . . . How many excellent works, in place of the ingenious trifles which have come at last to be valued at no more that their true worth, have appeared in recent years upon the useful arts—upon agriculture, the most indispensable and therefore the first of all, upon commerce, finance, manufactures, navigation, and the colonies, in short upon

---

[1] D'Alembert, *Discours préliminaire.*

[2] Locke's Journals, as quoted in *The Life of John Locke, with extracts from his Correspondence, Journals, and Commonplace Book,* by Lord King, 2 vols. 8vo, 1830. " Purity of language, a polished style, or exact criticism in foreign languages—thus I think Greek and Latin may be called, as well as French and Italian—and to spend much time in these may perhaps serve to set one off in the world, and give one the reputation of a scholar; but if that be all, methinks it is labouring for an outside ; it is at best but a handsome dress of truth or falsehood that one busies oneself about, and makes most of those who lay out their time this way rather as fashionable gentlemen than as wise or useful men." Vol. ii., p. 176.

[3] D'Alembert, *Discours préliminaire.*

everything which can contribute to render peoples more happy and States more flourishing."[1]

Thus did the French spirit join hands with the English upon the ground of a common ideal. Before the two nations adopted identical modes of feeling and imagination, the regularity of their scientific and philosophical intercourse had accustomed them to a kind of intellectual alliance. Whilst Voltaire and Prévost were striving to acclimatize English literature among the French, France was learning to look more and more towards the North for inspiration and guidance. "From the English," wrote Voltaire to Helvetius, "we have adopted annuities, Consolidated Funds, depreciation funds, the construction and management of vessels, attraction, the differential calculus, the seven primitive colours, and inoculation. Insensibly we shall adopt their noble freedom of thought, and their profound contempt for the twaddle of the schools."[2]

III

Such was the negative influence, if one may say so, of the English mind upon France, at the time immediately following the publication of the *Lettres philosophiques*. No great literary work had as yet achieved a decisive conquest of the public taste. But the public asked nothing better than to be taken captive. By mere force of attachment to tradition, it remained faithful to ancient models, but its attachment was without zeal and without conviction. "The productions of a healthy antiquity," wrote Fréron sadly, "are no longer consulted. The finest geniuses of Rome and Athens are scarcely known by name."[3] The abbé Le Blanc complained that a contempt, for which there was no

[1] *Journal encyclopédique*, April 1758. *Cf.* the *Journal étranger*, April 1754: "A day will come when custom will demand that a man shall be well-informed, observant, capable of reasoning, and of appropriate discussion upon a natural phenomenon, just as the tone of to-day leads us to speak with discernment on any subject connected with the agreeable arts, to pronounce a subtle yet ready opinion upon a poetical work, or to criticise a dramatic production."

[2] 15th September 1763. *Cf.* to Mme. du Deffand, 17th September 1757.

[3] *Lettres sur quelques écrits de ce temps*, vol. ii., p. 234.

justification, had given place to a "blind prepossession," and having given evidence of the advance of anglomania, he expressed the hope that the worship of new gods might not cause the old ones to be forgotten.[1]

France having thus become acquainted with England—the two nations having been brought into contact, it merely remained to infuse the French mind with all that was best in the minds of Englishmen, or, if the expression be preferred, to unite the first of the Latin with the greatest of the Germanic nations of Europe —a task which was accomplished by the Swiss, Jean-Jacques Rousseau.

[1] *Lettres*, vol. ii., p. 234.   *Cf.* vol. iii., p. 227.

Book II

JEAN-JACQUES ROUSSEAU AND ENGLISH LITERATURE

Chapter I

ROUSSEAU AND ENGLAND

I. Origins of Rousseau's genius: what it owes to Geneva, and through Geneva to England—Its exotic character.

II. Rousseau, like his contemporaries, an admirer of England—Freedom of the English intellect—Respect felt by Frenchmen of the eighteenth century for English virtue.

III. How these features come to be found also in Rousseau—Whence did he derive his notions concerning England?—Muralt's influence over him—English manners in *La Nouvelle Héloïse*—Milord Bomston, or the Englishman—Rousseau's work reflects the anglomania of the age.

I

No writer of his age was better, fitted by the circumstances of his origin to effect a union between the Germanic and the Latin sections of Europe.

"There is something English," said Doudan, "in the Genevan nature." However just the remark may be, one would hesitate to apply it to Rousseau—swept by the current of life, as he was in early youth, far away from his native town— had he not himself dwelt upon the idea with satisfaction. Voltaire irreverently said of Geneva that it imitated England as the frog imitated the ox: it was the Gille of the English nation.[1] What seems absurd to him is for Rousseau a ground of national pride. "The manners of the English," he says, "have reached even so far as this country ; and the men, living

[1] Quoted by Ballantyne, *op. cit.*, p. 283. Letter to George Keate.

more separate from the women than with us "—Saint-Preux is
the speaker—" contract among themselves a graver turn, and
have more solidity in their discourse." [1] Some part, therefore,
of their gravity, their *Gründlichkeit*, came to the Genevans from
beyond the Channel. Hence, as Jean-Jacques has said, that
" dogmatical and frigid air " which conceals ardent passions.
Hence too, in conversation, " their habits of speaking at a most
inordinate length, of introducing preliminary statements, or
exordiums, of indulging in affectation and stilted phrases ; and
hence, also, their want of facility, and their entire lack of that
artless simplicity which expresses the feeling before the thought,
and so enhances the value of what is said." How many of their
characteristics, if Rousseau's portrait of the Genevans be studied
afresh, will be seen to be either English or such as one would
expect of the English people !

The truth is, as he observes, that the relations between the
two nations had always been most intimate. A religious community was formed at Geneva in the sixteenth century by the
Englishmen who were persecuted and banished by Mary Tudor,
and John Knox was a disciple of Calvin. Great Britain, on her
part, protected the little republic in better days, gave a welcome
to distinguished Genevans, and readily entrusted them with positions in the army and the church. [2] Founded on similarity of
genius and religion, this intercourse became, in the eighteenth
century, still more close. Debating clubs were formed at
Geneva, with a membership half Genevan, half English. [3]
Sismondi informs us that the Genevans wrote in French, but
" read and thought in English," and Napoleon found fault with
them for knowing the latter language " too well." At no
period was the intercourse between Great Britain and Rousseau's
native country more intimate than during the eighteenth century.

---

[1] *Nouvelle Héloïse*, vi. 5.

[2] Two Casaubons became church dignitaries, while four men of the name of
Prévost distinguished themselves, among others, as superior officers in the English
army, &c. (*Cf.* A. Bouvier, *Le protestantisme à Genève*. Paris, 1884.)

[3] *Cf.* M. Pictet's book, *Pictet de Rochemont*, p. 61. See also Sismondi, *Considérations sur Genève dans ses rapports avec l'Angleterre et les États protestants*. London,
1814.

Many Genevan pastors officiated in the churches of the refugees. Several Genevan scholars became members of the Royal Society of London, and Newton corresponded with Abauzit. Delolme, Francis d'Ivernois and Mallet du Pan made it their business to propagate a knowledge of the British constitution in Europe. Many prominent Genevans, such as Alphonse Turretin, Tronchin, André de Luc, de Saussure, and before their time the renowned and "venerable Abauzit," whose wisdom and genius Rousseau extolled in such extravagant language, had studied at English universities. The first book of the eighteenth century on the subject of England was by a Genevan, Le Sage de la Colombière. And it was from Geneva, also, the centre of cosmopolitan tendencies in Europe, that Marie-Auguste and Charles Pictet first issued the *Bibliothèque britannique*, the true successor to the cosmopolitan reviews established by the refugees, and designed, according to the intention of its original editors, to spread English ideas wherever the French tongue was spoken.[1]

Those, therefore, who were prejudiced in favour of things English had always a partiality for Geneva, and without attributing to this fact any direct influence on the formation of the genius of Rousseau, we may nevertheless point out—seeing that he himself so loudly proclaimed his Genevan origin—how far his country was herself indebted to the English genius.

Geneva's debt to the genius of England, however, was but a part of her total debt to the Teutonic genius. "To be born a Frenchwoman," wrote Mme. de Staël, "with a foreign character, *with French tastes and habits, and the ideas and feelings of the North*, is a contrast which ruins one's life." Now this contrast—or alloy—is the very basis of the Genevan mind, the intellectual portion of which is Latin, while the soul is Germanic ; and hence it is that between France and Geneva there have arisen the strangest and, at times, most painful misunderstandings. The

[1] Concerning the establishment of this periodical see M. Pictet's book, *Pictet de Rochemont* (Georg, 1892, 8vo, p. 53 *et seq.*). Pictet's design was to "commend England to public notice, and to suggest her as a model for her neighbours." He hopes to make his review "an oasis for English ideas."

defect which, in the words of the subtlest and most ingenious of her writers, Geneva can never pardon in the French mind is its absolute inability to recognise " personal dignity and the majesty of conscience," or to conceive of " personality as supreme and conscious of itself." [1] It is worth while to recall the strange and incautious parallel he draws between the Germanic and the Latin mind : " The thirst for truth is not a French passion. In everything appearance is preferred to reality, the outside to the inside, the fashion to the material, that which shines to that which profits, opinion to conscience. . . . All this is probably the result of an exaggerated sociability, which weakens the soul's forces of resistance, destroys its capacity for investigation and personal conviction, and kills in it the worship of the ideal." [2] Too sociable and trained to too strict a uniformity, the French mind is mistrustful of the individual. It looks with suspicion on isolated convictions, and insists that the stamp of the whole community shall be affixed to every idea entertained by its separate members. It has a veneration for "the current coin of the intellectual realm."

The expression is severe and profoundly unjust, but it might have been used by Jean-Jacques. Like Muralt, like Rousseau, like Benjamin Constant, Amiel was following the pure Germanic tradition. And what more has Rousseau said, on many and many an admirable page, than Amiel says here ? In contrast to a France which he deemed too thoroughly Latin, too deeply Catholic, he determined to be Protestant and Genevan to the core. He too aspired to exalt the dignity of the individual. It was to the individual consciousness that he made appeal. He destroyed, so far as he was able to do so, the moral and intellectual currency.

I am not forgetting that through one of his ancestors he was of French family, and by blood, therefore, half a Frenchman. But was he French by virtue of the influences to which he was

---

[1] Amiel, *Journal intime*, vol. ii., p. 92 ; vol. i., p. 87. (Mrs Humphry Ward's translation, p. 172.)

[2] Amiel, *Journal intime*, vol. ii., p. 186. (Mrs Humphry Ward's translation, p. 220.)

subjected in childhood and youth?   The Gallic stock from which he sprang had been " re-tempered by the Reformation."[1] If we are to believe one of those who know him best, he had been infused with the purest essence of Germanic protestantism. Through Mme. de Warens, a disciple of the pietist Magny, he would acquire the main principles of Spener and the German pietists.   Romanic pietism, Magny and Mme. de Warens would thus prove to be " three links uniting Germanic thought and piety with Rousseau's religious ideas."   A sentiment of profound and habitual devoutness, great independence in the face of traditional authority, signal indifference to disputes on points of dogma, an ever-present sense of the Deity and of an eternal future, the practice of religious meditation—such were the characteristics of this sort of protestant quietism,[2] which would form a direct link between the spiritualism of Rousseau and the religious traditions of Germany.   Of this, however, I do not feel confident ; I cannot forget a certain disturbing phrase employed by Jean-Jacques.[3]

But it is none the less true that Rousseau, though of French extraction, only half belongs to France.   Foreign critics commonly look upon him as the most German of Frenchmen, if not indeed as the most English.   He was, at any rate, a cosmopolitan.   Looking at the question broadly, it will readily be granted that he was the embodiment of all the depth, the variety and the individuality with which protestantism, when it was no longer confined to France, was able to imbue the French mind.   Contrasted with the classical literature of the French, a literature not only essentially sociable in character, but finding in society at once the bond of

---

[1] See H. F. Amiel, in the interesting volume entitled *Rousseau jugé par les Genevois d'aujourd'hui*, p. 30, and, on Rousseau's ancestors, M. E. Ritter (*La famille et la jeunesse de J. J. Rousseau*, 1896).

[2] E. Ritter, *Magny et le piétisme romand*, Lausanne, 1894, and *Revue des Deux Mondes*, 15th March 1895.

[3] *Nouvelle Héloïse*, vi. 7.   Saint-Preux laments the " aberrations " of Muralt, who had become a pietist and persuades Julie not to read the *Instinct divin*.   Rousseau adds the following note concerning the pietists : " A class of crazy people who conceived the notion of living as Christians and following the Gospel to the letter, closely resembling the Methodists in England, the Moravians in Germany, the Jansenists in France, at the present day."

connection between its branches, and its principal and almost its only theme, Rousseau seems to be a paradox. One marvels that he should have comprehended it; one doubts whether he loved it. " Egotism," he said, " is excluded as scrupulously from the French drama as from the writings of Messieurs de Port-Royal; and the passions of the human heart never speak, but with all the modesty of Christian humility, in the third person." [1]

Now it is the first person that Rousseau employs, never the third. No genius was ever more individual, more lyrical, and therefore less French—in the sense in which the classic authors of the language understood the word. The *Nouvelle Héloïse*, as was justly remarked by Mme. de Staël, " sets forth the characteristics of a man's genius, not those of a nation's manners." [2] The same might be said of most of his books : they depart entirely from the French classical tradition. The work of a foreigner, they are singularly at variance with the practice of French classical art. They are its absolute antithesis : its very negation even. They have deprived those who have sought inspiration from them of the power of comprehending it.

How easily one pictures him on the other hand as taking his place in the genealogy of English literary art ! How thoroughly he belongs to it by his deep sense of "inward dignity," by his love of detail and his close observation of trifles, by his love of that " home " which he so passionately extolled, and by his yearnings after nature—the nature which Thomson had discovered thirty years before him ! Prone to morbid revelation of the self, is he not the compatriot of Swift ? Is he not, in virtue of the richness and abundance of the poetic element in his nature, of the school of Milton or of Gray ? Fond of melancholy reverie, how closely akin he would have been, had the spirit of his age permitted it, to Shakespeare ! True, these racial problems are obscure, and words can but faintly express the complexity of what we dimly perceive. But if it is true that Romanticism was " a kind of rebellion against the spirit of a race steeped in the Latin tradition," [3] who was it that added to it not only the fer-

---

[1] *Nouvelle Héloïse*, ii. 17.   [2] *De la littérature*, i. 15.
[3] F. Brunetière, *L'évolution de la poésie lyrique*, vol. i., p. 178.

ment of revolt, but also this germ of exoticism, if not the man of whom it has been said that though French by language he was a foreigner by genius, because he had derived his talent entirely " from the depths of his own soul ? " [1]

What is certain is that in the history of the growth of cosmopolitan tendencies, Rousseau occupies the first place. Between Europe of the North and Europe of the South he was the mighty link that bound the genius of the one to that of the other. Rousseau accomplished what neither the refugees, nor Prévost, nor Voltaire had succeeded in doing ; he inoculated the French mind, by the unaided power of his own genius, with a full comprehension of these new beauties. He transformed not French taste only, but even French conceptions of art ; and it happened that this new notion of art, as distinguished and set forth by him for all to see, corresponded exactly with the idea which the endeavours of English writers had been tending to realise since the beginning of the century. What Richardson and Pope, Thomson and Macpherson had attempted, and to some extent accomplished, was by him perfected and completed with all the power of a genius superior to theirs. From them he derives, and with them, in the history of European literature, he is allied. If it cannot be said that he is a disciple of each one of them, he at least carried on their labours. He completed and crowned their work. Like them he was sensitive and profoundly religious, deeply poetic and intensely lyrical.

In like manner it was England next to Geneva that he loved the best. To his contemporaries it seemed that the *Nouvelle Héloïse*, in which England occupies such an important place, was coloured, as it were, with an English tint. Before considering how far Rousseau was indebted to certain English writers, and wherein his thought ran parallel to that of others, we must therefore inquire what he thought of England, and whether he shared, in respect to her, the infatuation of his contemporaries.

---

[1] Mme. de Staël, *De l'Allemagne*, v. 1.

II

It is not in its literature only that the influence of one nation over another makes itself manifest, nor in the mere imitation of works that literary influence finds its expression. Such influence consists also, and principally, of those currents of opinion, those mysterious trains of thought and feeling, which at certain periods impel one people towards another people, France of the sixteenth century towards Italy—the land of beauty, France of the seventeenth towards Spain — the land of heroism, France of the early part of the present century towards Germany—" the land of thought," as it was called by Mme. de Staël. Nor is it merely, in such cases of international influence, some particular book or writer that commands admiration; it is an aggregate of works, a particular literary or moral aspiration, a certain ideal of life, a collective soul, the heart and the mind of a nation. It is not enough, therefore, to ask, in respect of these influences : what did Frenchmen know of Italy in 1550 ? Of Spain in 1630 ? Of Germany in 1815 ? Of England in 1760 ? What they knew of these nations was not always what they liked in them. And what they liked in them did not always accord with the reality. A certain idea of the Greek genius, true enough no doubt, inspired Racine, and gave him a love for Greece; a very different, though by no means false, conception of the same genius inspired André Chénier, and gave him an affection for another Greece, no less real than the first, yet appreciably different. To be influenced by a foreign nation, therefore, certainly implies a knowledge of it, but usually also a knowledge which is maimed and incomplete. Captivated by a few striking and essential features, admiration overlooks what seems to be either inconsistent with them or of less importance. Such was the case of those who lived in the eighteenth century with regard to England. They admired an ideal England, because they resolved that she should correspond with their dream.

" English," said La Harpe, " was introduced among us with the taste for philosophy, which was then beginning to develop;

and we were acquainted with Bacon, Locke, Addison and Shaftesbury before we had read Pope and Milton."[1] Accordingly, the first characteristic in English works to strike the attention of men in the eighteenth century was the boldness of thought and the profound genius they revealed. " Those people think more than we do," said Marivaux ironically. But Voltaire, quite seriously, wrote : " Everything proves that the English are bolder and more philosophical than we are ";[2] Diderot, in one of his early works represents England as " the country of philosophers, systematisers and men of inquiring mind."[3] Buffon is never weary of expressing his admiration for " this sensible and profoundly thoughtful nation," and even goes so far as to say that " Fénelon, Voltaire and Jean-Jacques would not make a furrow one line in depth on a head so massive with thought as that of Bacon, that of Newton, or—happily for us—that of Montesquieu."[4]

Such was the verdict passed by the great minds of the age. But public opinion had forestalled them. " The English," wrote the translator of *The Tale of a Tub*, " are extremely deficient in restraint and moderation not only as regards conduct and manners, but also in their turn of mind : their wanton imagination entirely exhausts itself in comparisons and metaphors "; and he makes it a reproach to them that by their singularity they depart from the " noble simplicity " of the ancients.[5] This quality of independence in English thought sometimes sheds a vague perfume of heresy over English works : in one of Prévost's novels we find the English philosophers, Hobbes and Toland, relegated to one particular corner in a library, along with " curious " and prohibited volumes, such as

---

[1] *Cours de littérature*, vol. iii., p. 224.

[2] *Lettres anglaises*, xi.—*Cf.* to Helvetius, 26th June 1765 : " We in France are not made to be first in the race for knowledge : we get our truths from elsewhere." See also the letters to Mme. du Deffand, 13th October 1759 ; to Helvetius, 25th August 1763, and to Marmontel, 1st August 1769.

[3] *Lettre sur les aveugles*, ed. Tourneux, vol. i., p. 312.

[4] Letter to Mme. Necker, 2nd January 1777.

[5] *Le Conte du Tonneau*, by Jonathan Swift. Translated from the English, the Hague, 1732, vol i., preface.

G

those of Vanini, Cardan and Paracelsus.[1] But the depth of the
English genius was also becoming a commonplace of criticism,
and even of conversation. In a pleasing comedy by Boissy,
produced immediately after the publication of Muralt's *Lettres
sur les Anglais et les Français* and seven years earlier than that of
the *Lettres philosophiques*, the author—who, by the way, has
manifestly borrowed from Muralt's work—puts the following
declaration into the mouth of one of his characters: " ' Good
sense is simply the common sense which is possessed by the man
in the street, and belongs to all countries alike. But intellectual
refinement is found only in France. France, so to speak, is its
native soil, whence we supply it to all the other nations of
Europe. The refined intelligence hovers gracefully above its
subject, culling only its bloom. It is wit that makes a man
agreeable, sprightly, gay, merry, amusing, the charm of a party,
a good talker, full of pleasant banter—in fine, a Frenchman.
Good sense, on the other hand, weighs down the matter it deals
with under the impression that it is sounding it thoroughly ; it
handles everything in a tedious, methodical manner. It is good
sense which makes a man dull, pedantic, melancholy, taciturn, a
bore, the plague of a party, a moraliser, a dreamer—in short,
an . . .' — ' An Englishman, you mean ? ' — ' Good manners
forbade me to put it quite so plainly, but you have hit it.'—' In
fact, according to you an Englishman has good sense, but no
wit.'—' Very good '—' And a Frenchman wit, without common
sense.'—' Capital.' " Whence it follows " that the English
are profound without being brilliant." [2]

From the moment when the hare-brained de Polinville
expressed this idea on the French stage, down to the period
when Rousseau began to write, respect for English depth and
seriousness had been steadily growing in France. One does not
wonder that a second-rate critic should be amazed at " reasonings
so vast that one would take them for the operations of a super-
human intelligence." [3] But one cannot, without surprise, read

---

[1] *Mémoires d'un homme de qualité*, vol. iii., p. 11.
[2] *Le Français à Londres* (1727), scene xvi.
[3] The Abbé Millot, introduction to a translation of the *Essay on Man*.

in d'Argenson's *Journal* that " the English nation is philosophical,
it consists of men who think much and constantly ; we may see
it in their books."[1] These books, it is true, are destitute of
art ; their matter is disconnected, *ex abrupto*. But they contain
" fresh ideas and great penetration," and they are " free from the
commonplace." D'Argenson adds that the only men of real
originality and individuality that he knew in France were those
men of letters who had frequently visited England : namely,
Voltaire—which is perhaps correct, and the abbé Le Blanc—
which is paradoxical, to say the least.

But if the English were applauded for the independence of
their thought, and if there was already a disposition to admit
that " the English mind is a mind of a different stamp, created
by itself,"[2] they were no less admired for their high spirit.

From England, the land of freedom, there blew, as d'Argenson
said, " the breath of liberty." Voltaire had greatly admired
the strength of the English middle class, Montesquieu the
excellence of the constitution and of public morals. In *Le
Français à Londres* the merchant Jacques Rosbif, puffed up with
his own importance, assumed the character of a philosophising
rustic who speaks his mind to the ruling classes : " What do I
care for an imaginary nobility ? The honest folk are the true
nobles ; nothing is really plebeian except vice." The terrible
irony with which Voltaire handled the subject in his *Lettres
anglaises* is only too well-known. He satirizes the country
squires who come up from the depths of their province, a name
ending in *ac* or *ille* their only fortune, and play the part of slaves
in a minister's antechamber. He extols the honest merchant who,
in the seclusion of his office, gives orders on Surat or Cairo and
contributes to the happiness of the world.[3] He does more ; he
dedicates *Zaïre* " to Mr Falkener, an English merchant." The
idea seemed funny, and the Comédie Italienne put upon the
stage " Mr Falkener, or the honest merchant." Voltaire took
up the challenge, and, in a second dedication which, to his satisfaction, he was able to address to " M. le Chevalier Falkener,

---

[1] *Journal et mémoires*, October 1747 (ed. Jannet, v. 232).

[2] Garat, *Mémoires sur Suard*, vol. i., p. 70.   [3] Letter x., *Sur le commerce*.

English Ambassador to the Ottoman Porte," had the pleasure of once more humbling the national pride, which could not conceive how a merchant could become a legislator, a good officer, or a public minister. Could the reader possibly find any difficulty in believing that the Royal Exchange in London was "a more respectable place than many courts?" Or could he really be so blind as not to acknowledge that the occupation of wool-merchant was the highest of all professions?

Voltaire's assertions, in which he possibly had no very strong belief, were substantiated by Montesquieu.—Imagine a nation of an unusual character,—unambitious of conquest, thinking nothing of military men, and a great deal of "civil titles"; imagine this people invested with the empire of the sea, situated in the centre of the commercial world of Europe, and bringing to its transactions a good faith and integrity never exhibited by others; imagine it blessed with a virtuous nobility, an active and charitable clergy, a well-informed and industrious populace; attribute to it further an ingrained habit of judging men solely by their real qualities, and of neglecting the false splendour of idleness in favour of solid worth; conceive, lastly, in the intellectual products of this nation—the work of men of meditation, "*who have thought in solitude*"—a "bold and original spirit of discovery," the fruit of a certain fierce integrity of disposition—and would not such a nation be the happiest of all? In short, and here the author throws off the mask, "this is the nation which, more than any other, has succeeded in making the best use of three great possessions: religion, commerce and freedom."[1]

So magnificent a panegyric from such a pen set the seal decisively upon English virtue, which became one of the idols of the age. In vain a few obscure voices were raised in protest against the "astounding metamorphosis" which was turning every one's head. What! a nation formerly regarded as the incarnation of arrogance, jealousy, selfishness, and cruelty—the modern Carthage—was now represented as all that was generous, magnanimous and humane! "What a reckoning that great man, the renowned, the illustrious Voltaire will have to pay before

[1] *Esprit des lois*, book xix., ch. xxvii., and book xx., ch. viii.

God for the vast host of those whose heads he has turned!"[1]
But the infatuation was too strong: a journalist of the day, criti-
cising one of Jean-Jacques' expressions, wrote: "As an untamed
courser erects his mane, paws the ground, and struggles violently
at the mere approach of the bit, whereas a horse that has been
broken in patiently endures both switch and spur, so the Englishman refuses to bow his head beneath a yoke which the greater
part of mankind endure without a murmur, and prefers the most
stormy liberty to peaceful subjection."[2]

The illusion was a gross one, or, to say the very least, the
exaggeration was palpable. Looked at closely, eighteenth-century England appears anything but the privileged home of virtue
and honour. Its nobility is brutal and dissolute, its clergy ignorant, its justice venal: Fielding's novels abound in characteristic
and only too faithful touches which give us but a sorry idea of
the upper classes at that time.[3] Montesquieu himself observed
that in England "money was held in sovereign estimation, while
virtue was scarcely esteemed at all."[4] Yet he too gave way
before the general enthusiasm, which amazed even the English
themselves. "We may be dupes to French follies," wrote
Horace Walpole, "but they are ten times greater fools to be
the dupes of our virtue."[5]

In truth, admiration magnified and transformed everything.
The brutality of the English was a matter of common repute,
but it was regarded as a sign of energy; "*nature in England
seems to be more vigorous and straightforward than among the
French*."[6] "It is there that you will find true love of duty and
respect, tender reverence for parents, unqualified submission to
their will. . . . An English village maiden is a kind of celestial
being."[7] This is the tone taken by novels of the period. A
certain survival of barbarism was not displeasing. Lord Carlisle

---

[1] *Préservatif contre l'anglomanie*, Minorca and Paris, 1757.

[2] *Journal encyclopédique*, April 1758.

[3] An English critic, Mr Forsyth, has composed an entire picture of the period out
of material supplied by its novels alone (*Cf.* Forsyth, *Novels and Novelists*).—See also
Lecky.

[4] *Notes sur l'Angleterre*.   [5] *Letters*, vol. iv., p. 119.

[6] D'Arnaud, *Œuvres*, vol. i., pp. xv.-xvi.   [7] *Ibid.*

wrote from France : "They think we are very little altered since the days of Julius Cæsar ; that we leave our clothes at Calais, having no further occasion for them," and that every Englishman conceals his nakedness by means of a sunflower, "like the prints in Clarke's Cæsar."[1] This touch of barbarism gave additional flavour to insular virtue, and the Danubian peasant only preached the better for being a Danubian. The French were under the spell of the English sensitiveness, of that virginity of heart and senses by which the source of great emotions, exhausted in the gay youths of France by scepticism and pleasure, is kept unimpaired. "However vivid," it was said, "the colours in which Southern passions are painted, neither Italy nor Spain can produce examples as grand and tragic as those of England."[2]

Philosophical, contemplative, passionate : such was the impression of the English produced on the mind of a French reader towards the middle of the century. Such too was the conception gathered of English literature : a literature produced by men of discernment and sombre disposition, dialecticians by nature and in the highest degree philosophical. All these features may be summed up in a single characteristic : individualism. In contrast to a people in whom all native originality has been obliterated by over-sociability, and all relief worn down by constant friction, England presented the spectacle of a lusty and vigorous nation, whose genius, like a freshly struck medal, still retained all its brilliant distinctness of outline.

III

ROUSSEAU shared the admiration of his contemporaries, and gave expression to it in the most eloquent form.

At Les Charmettes he had read the *Lettres philosophiques* with deep interest. There, too, he had discovered a few English books—the *Essay on the Understanding* and the *Spectator*,[3]—and

---

[1] G. *Selwyn and his contemporaries*, by J. Heneage Jesse, vol. ii., p. 202.

[2] *Journal étranger*, June 1755, p. 237.

[3] See the *Confessions* : Œuvres, ed. Hachette, vol. viii., p. 78.

had begun to study the English language. Mme. de Warens had taught him to love Bayle and Saint-Évremond: "Her taste, if I may say so, was of a somewhat Protestant character; she talked of no one but Bayle, and thought very highly of Saint-Évremond, who had died long before in France." From the latter Rousseau, too, may have derived a few ideas concerning England. He had certainly read the novels of Prévost, and especially *Cleveland*, with passionate interest.

At Paris, in 1744, he was brought into contact with all the literary men who were interested in English matters: Marivaux; Desfontaines, who assisted him with his counsel[1]; Saurin, the future author of a drama called *Beverley*, an imitation of Edward Moore; Grimm, a man of open mind and inquisitive with regard to foreign topics; Prévost, "a most amiable and simple character, the author of writings inspired by a warm disposition and well worthy of immortality,"[2] who was introduced to him in the house of Mussard, a fellow-countryman, at Passy; above all, Diderot, the anglophile, whose mind was already turned, as it remained throughout his life, to England, the land of his dreams. An atmosphere so propitious to everything that came from beyond the Channel did much to strengthen in Rousseau the sympathies which he afterwards expressed with such warmth.

He read the *Esprit des Lois* on its first appearance, and, in 1756, the *Lettres sur les Anglais et les Français* of Muralt, who was not only his fellow-countryman, but in more than one respect his precursor. The book was sent him by Deleyre;[3] he had a great admiration for it and borrowed from it extensively; indeed most of his ideas concerning England were derived from Muralt. But he was also indebted to him for several reflexions in the *Lettre sur les spectacles*. "Virtue," Muralt had written, speaking of comedy, "is held up as a spectacle for popular curiosity; men relegate it to the theatre as its only appropriate sphere, and all these fine feelings seem to them as remote from ordinary life as

---

[1] *Cf.* H. Beaudoin, *Jean-Jacques Rousseau*, vol. i., p. 154.   [2] *Confessions*, ii., 8.
[3] Letter of 2nd November 1756 (*cf.* Streckeisen Moultou; *Jean-Jacques Rousseau, ses amis et ses ennemis*).

the dresses and postures of the theatre are from those they see in their own homes."[1] "The theatre," said Rousseau, "has its own rules, maxims and morality, as well as the dress and diction which are peculiar to it. These things, it is said, would not do for us at all, and we should think it just as absurd to adopt our hero's virtues as to speak in verse and put on a Roman toga." Nor does he make the least attempt to disguise the fact that he has borrowed; indeed he refers to his author on the following page.[2]

Rousseau borrowed largely from Muralt in the *Nouvelle Héloïse*, where he frequently mentions him by name.[3] He kept Muralt's book before him when writing his descriptions of Parisian manners. Sometimes it is an opinion on French conversation that he appropriates, sometimes a criticism on the French intellect. "You read Muralt," Saint-Preux writes to Julie; "I indeed read him, too; but I make choice of his letters, you of his *Divine instinct*. But remark his end, lament the extravagant errors of that sensible man."[4] It was this "sensible man" who suggested certain of Rousseau's reservations concerning the English character : "I know," he wrote, "the English are very boastful of their humanity and of the kindly disposition of their nation, calling themselves '*good-natured people*'; but, shout this as loud as they will, no one repeats it after them."[5] The expression, as we have seen, is taken from Muralt.[6]

It is Muralt again who often suggests to him the very terms in which to express his fervent admiration. "I have taken a liberty with the English nation," he wrote to Mme. de Boufflers, "which it never forgives in any one, least of

[1] Letter v.

[2] See M. L. Fontaine's excellent edition of the *Lettre sur les spectacles*, pp. 135 and 136. "It is a mistake, said the solemn Muralt, to expect an author to represent the actual relations of things upon the stage," &c. : an allusion to a passage in Muralt's fifth letter.

[3] *Cf.* the passages quoted above, and vi., 7.

[4] *Nouvelle Héloïse*, vi., 3.   [5] *Émile*, book ii.

[6] Letter iv.—He also borrows from Muralt (letter v.), a few ideas upon English juries which he expresses in the letter of 4th October 1761, to M. d'Offreville; and a passage in the *Lettres écrites de la Montagne*, letter v. (*Cf.* letter iv. of Muralt).

all in foreigners, namely, that of saying the worst of them as well as the best."[1] To tell the truth, however, he had spoken well of them much more frequently than he had spoken ill.

He liked the fierce patriotism of the English. "The only nation of *men*," he calls them, " which remains among the various herds that are scattered over the face of the earth."[2] Rousseau's Swiss are proud of their nationality: they lead the life of the Genevan or of the peasant of the Valais, and live it with pride. " It is a fine thing to have a native-land; God help those who think they possess one, but in reality have nothing more than a land to dwell in ! "[3] Now the English have the faults of their nationality : they are Genevans hailing from beyond the Channel, reserved and unapproachable, neither hospitable nor frank. ". We must agree in their favour, however, that an Englishman is never obliged to any person for that hospitality he churlishly refuses others. *Where, except in London, is there to be seen any of these insolent islanders servilely cringing at court ?* In what country, except their own, do they seek to make their fortunes ? They are churlish, it is true, but their churlishness does not displease me, while it is consistent with justice. *I think it is very well they should be nothing but Englishmen, since they have no occasion to be men.*"[4]

It is interesting to note that Muralt had felt obliged to make a few reservations concerning the brutality of English vices. Rousseau extenuated them, if he did not actually make them a subject of commendation. A comparison of the two passages is instructive. "Their women," Muralt had written, " easily give way to tender feelings, they make no great effort to conceal them, and . . . are capable of the greatest firmness for the sake of a lover; in spite of this they are gentle, almost entirely without

[1] August 1762. On the English constitution, see the *Contrat Social* and the *Gouvernement de Pologne*, ch. x.

[2] *Nouvelle Héloïse*, vi.—This and many other of the quotations from *La Nouvelle Héloïse* are taken from a translation published by Hunter, Dublin, 1761.

[3] *Ibid.*, vi., 5.

[4] *Nouvelle Héloïse*, ii., 9. Rousseau returns to the same idea and the same expressions in *Émile*, book v.: " Englishmen never try to get on with other nations. . . . *they are too proud to go begging beyond their own borders*, &c.

cunning and artifice, natural in conversation, and little spoiled by the flattery of the men, who only devote to them a very small portion of their time. Most Englishmen, in fact, prefer wine and gaming. . . . It is quite true that when they fall in love their passion is violent: with them, love is no weakness to be ashamed of, but a serious and important matter, in which the alternative to success is often enough the loss of reason or of life." [1] " English women," says Rousseau, "are gentle and timid ; English men, harsh and ferocious. . . . With this exception, the two sexes are closely similar. Each likes living apart from the other ; and each sets great store by the pleasures of the table. . . . They both indulge in play, *but without extravagance, and both make a merit of it rather than a passion* : both have a great respect for honourable conduct ; *both esteem conjugal fidelity* [Muralt had not said so much] ; . . . both are silent and reserved, difficult to arouse, yet violent in their passions : for both of them love is a terrible and tragic affair, *involving, said Muralt, no less than the loss of reason or of life*. . . . Thus both sexes are more self-collected, less given to indulge in frivolous imitation, have more relish for the true pleasures of life, and think less of appearing happy than of being so." [2]

In writing his novel, Rousseau was careful to place certain scenes in an English setting, and was complimented thereon by all his contemporaries.

In the *Héloïse* there is a "morning spent in the English fashion," with which he was undoubtedly very well satisfied. What is the English fashion of spending a morning ? Rousseau describes it as a state of contemplation, a silent communion, " a

[1] Letter lii.

[2] *Lettre sur les spectacles.*—It will be observed that the severe expression which occurs in the *Confessions* : " I never liked either England or the English," was written subsequently to Rousseau's residence in England, and, consequently to the persecution to which he thought he was subjected there. It is not a sober opinion, but an outburst of ill-humour. Moreover, Rousseau himself makes a formal recantation of the expression in *Rousseau juge de Jean-Jacques (Premier dialogue*, note). Speaking of the English nation, he writes : " It has been too often misled concerning me for me not to have been sometimes mistaken concerning it," and he speaks of choosing an Englishman as confidant, in order " to repair in a properly attested manner the evil I may have thought or said of his nation." See also the *Third Dialogue* (vol. ix., p. 280).

motionless ecstasy," which the light French temperament would find unendurable. Here again his account is merely an amplification of a passage from Muralt : " The English," the philosopher of Berne had said, " have seen plainly enough that people who speak for the sake of speaking seldom fail to talk nonsense, and that conversation should be an exchange of sentiments, not of words; and since, on this assumption, matter for conversation is not always forthcoming, it sometimes happens that they are silent for a long time together." [1] This is precisely the way of spending the morning described by Rousseau. Madame de Wolmar's friends find it delightful to hold their peace for two hours at a time, passing the morning " in company and in silence; tasting at once the pleasure of being together, and the sweetness of self-recollection." [2] Rousseau had been greatly impressed by this picture, and accordingly selected it as the subject of one of the engravings executed for his book by Gravelot : the persons represented are taking tea and reading the newspapers—or at anyrate holding them in their hands. Observe the " air of sweet and dreamy contemplation " in the three onlookers : Julie in particular " is evidently in a delicious ecstasy." [3]

To-day this strikes us as somewhat trivial. Such, however, was not the opinion of Rousseau's contemporaries. They had a lively appreciation of the " morning spent in the English fashion " just as they delighted in Julie's English garden. " The men who have produced the grand and colossal scenes of Shakespeare and the whimsical figures of *Hudibras* show the effects of the same spirit in their gardens, just as they do in morals, medicine and philosophy." The whole of the eighteenth century agreed with the opinion here expressed by the Prince de Ligne.[4] Grimm declared that whenever he left an English garden he felt as deep an emotion as on coming away from the theatre after

[1] i., 4.   [2] v., 1.   [3] Œuvres, vol. v., p. 97.
[4] *Coup d'œil sur les jardins.—Cf.* the same author's *Coup d'œil sur Bel-Œil ;* Le Blanc, *Lettres,* vol. ii., p. 63 (which Rousseau appears to have read); de Chabanon, *Épitre sur la manie des jardins anglais,* 1775 ; Masson, *Le jardin anglais,* a poem in four cantos, translated into French, 1789; Delille, &c.—See also Vitet, *Études sur les beaux-arts,* vol. ii.

seeing a tragedy.[1] Julie's *Élysée*, conceived in the "English style" invented by Kent, the landscape-gardener, was immensely popular, and for long enough there was not a good sentimental novel published which had not its grove, its avenue of trees and its "arbour."—Therein none of man's handiwork was to be seen; everything was the work of nature. The garden was a simple orchard; not a foreign plant within it. Here was a thick and verdant carpet of turf, wild and garden thyme, marjoram, "thickets of rose-trees," and "masses of lilac," festoons thrown carelessly from tree to tree, wild yet delicious fruits, a background of verdure which produced the effect of a forest, yet consisted merely of creepers and parasitic plants, and a stream which displayed its meanderings to the best advantage. The birds, "inseparable mates," encouraged the mind to yield itself to the sweetest sentiment in nature. Everywhere there was moss, and Lord Edward had sent from England the secret of making it grow. Symmetry there was none, for it is nature's enemy, nor fine prospects, for "the taste for views and distances arises from the propensity of most men to find enjoyment only in places where they are not."—Muralt had repeated the story that Le Nôtre, when summoned to London by Charles II. in order to beautify St James's Park, declared that all his art could not rival its simplicity.[2] Rousseau, who borrows from him this anecdote, also found in the English garden the realisation of the ideal he had conceived.[3]

Nor is it the manners and the setting only, that have something English about them; what is more significant, the most sympathetic character in the story is Lord Edward, "or the Englishman," as he is called in the brief description the author wrote for the engravings.

About his person you observe "an air of grandeur which

[1] Ed. Scherer, *Melchior Grimm*, p. 254.

[2] Letter vi.—See all the concluding portion of the letter, on English scenery.—Observe that in Rousseau's chapter (*Nouvelle Héloïse*, iv., 11) Lord Cobham's garden at Staw, which he criticises, is a "Chinese," not an English, garden.

[3] Garat, in his *Mémoires sur Suard*, speaks of England "where so many landscapes resemble those of the *Héloïse*, though they have not the same May sunshine" (vol. ii., p. 157). A fine specimen of the nonsense a man may write under the influence of a preconceived idea.

proceeds rather from the soul than from rank"; the stamp of a somewhat fierce courage and of a virtue not free from austerity, and a " grave and stoical " bearing beneath which " he conceals with difficulty an extreme sensibility; he wears the dress of an English lord without ostentation, and carries himself with just a touch of swagger. Mentally, Lord Edward is sensitive and philosophical, a worthy countryman of both Richardson and Locke.[1] His conversation is sensible, racy and animated. He betrays more energy than grace, and to Julie it seems at first that there is " something harsh about him."[2] He is quick-tempered, and avoids like the plague " the reserved and cautious politeness which our young officers bring us from France." He provokes Saint-Preux to a duel brutally enough; but when he has perceived his fault he is sufficiently generous to ask pardon on his knees before witnesses. For after all, as Muralt said, is it not well-known that English bravery " never descends to duelling," and that in that " sensible country " men have a loftier idea of honour?[3] Besides " in this honest Englishman natural humanity is not impaired by the philosophical lack of feeling common to his nation."

When in Italy Lord Edward had fallen passionately in love, and in the most romantic manner: deprived of the friendship of Saint-Preux, he was not proof against a sudden assault upon his senses and his heart.[4] He falls a victim to the charms of Julie at first sight, and prides himself on his sensibility : " it was by way of the passions " he says artlessly, " that I was led to philosophy." At the same time he is greatly interested in painting and music, especially, like Jean-Jacques himself, in Italian music.

---

[1] Many features of Lord Edward's character are reminiscences of the portrait of Cleveland. Prévost's novel was read by Jean-Jacques with passionate interest. (*Confessions*, i., 5.)

[2] *Nouvelle Héloïse*, i., 44.   [3] *Lettres*, p. 4.

[4] See the short novel entitled *Les Amours de Milord Édouard*, which forms a sequel to the *Héloïse*. Contemporaries were much engrossed with Rousseau's story. See *Les Aventures d'Édouard Bomston, pour servir de suite à la Nouvelle Héloïse*, Lausanne, 1789, and the *Lettres d'un jeune lord à une religieuse italienne*, imitated from the English [by Mme. Suard], Paris, 1788.—See also *Letters of an Italian Nun and an English gentleman*, *translated from the French of J. J. Rousseau*, London, 1781, 12mo, which, in spite of dates, seems to be a translation of the preceding.

But to mention the more dignified aspects of this figure, drawn by Rousseau with so much partiality.

A " veneer of stoicism " is thrown over all Bomston's actions. He can be solemn when confronted with serious events : to Saint-Preux, who sacrifices everything to love, he says, " Throw off your childhood, my friend, awake ! Surrender not your entire existence to the long lethargy of reason " ; and, rallying him upon his weakness : " Your heart, my dear fellow, has long deceived us as to your intelligence ! " [1] Ah, Bomston ! Is this the tone of a philosopher ? Can wisdom consistently express itself in language at once so turgid and so bitter ? Again, would a prudent man advise a young girl, as you do, to fly from her father's roof in company with her tutor ? This spoils Lord Edward for me. I prefer him in the famous letter on suicide, even if he does, to some extent, presume upon his privilege of being English : " Mine is a steadfast soul ; I am an Englishman. I know how to die, because I know how to live, and to suffer as a man." It is a good thing to have a native land, but not quite such a good thing to sing its praises so loudly. " We are not the slaves of our monarch, but his friends ; not the tyrants of the people, but their leaders. . . . We allow none to say : *God and my sword*, but simply *God and my right*." We may excuse Bomston, since it is Jean-Jacques who is speaking through his mouth, and making him say all these fine things. Lord Edward, happily for Rousseau, is not a real Englishman.

Yes, Bomston, " generous soul, noble friend," you were but the sincerest and most artless expression of the anglomania of Jean-Jacques Rousseau !

[1] *N. H.*, v., i.

Chapter II

I. Rousseau's early associations in Paris: Diderot and the admirers of England.
II. His first studies in English: Pope, and his popularity—Influence of his commonplace philosophy upon his age and upon Rousseau—Daniel Defoe: success of *Robinson Crusoe*.
III. Rousseau's admiration for English literature is directed mainly to the bourgeois variety—Why? Because of his literary tendencies—His admiration for the English drama; translation of *The London Merchant* (1748).

I

Rousseau's early studies in English were those of the majority of his contemporaries : the authors he had read at Les Charmettes were Locke and Addison. Pope, Milton, Richardson's novels, *Robinson Crusoe*, and a few other works of less importance, were probably read during his second residence in Paris. We may believe, though without positively asserting so much, that he was among the earliest French admirers of some of these masterpieces. Knowing how greatly he appreciated it, we cannot help believing that he read *Pamela*, immediately after its first appearance in Paris, in 1742. Just at that moment he was very intimate with Desfontaines, and we know that *Pamela* involved Desfontaines in a very unpleasant affair.[1] And what is more probable than that Prévost, whom he frequently met during 1751, talked to him of *Clarissa Harlowe*, which had appeared in the original in 1748, and had just been translated into French— with what enthusiasm, the reader will recollect—by Prévost himself? Finally, we cannot doubt that Diderot, Diderot the anglophile, with whom Rousseau became intimate immediately he arrived in Paris, drew his attention to some of the English

[1] See below, p. 209.

works which at that time were beginning to make a great sensation.

It is important here to remember that Diderot, whose acquaintance Rousseau had made in 1741, when he first came to Paris, remained his literary confidant for sixteen years—the decisive years of Jean-Jacques' life, and those which witnessed the elaboration of his greatest works. There were similarities between them in point of age, taste and fortune: Diderot, like Rousseau, was poor and of humble birth; like him, of a sensitive disposition and musical. Diderot had his Nanette, Rousseau had his Thérèse, and intercourse between the two households was frequent. It will be remembered how the two proposed to take a walking tour in Italy with Grimm. The reader knows how they conceived the plan of starting a newspaper together, to be edited by each alternately, called the *Persifleur*, which, however, did not survive its first number. And every one will recollect the friendship which Rousseau manifested for Diderot when the latter was imprisoned at Vincennes. I believe, he says, that if his captivity had lasted, "I should have died from despair at the gate of that miserable dungeon."[1] This was the golden age of their friendship. It was also the period when they were working in concert. Rousseau showed his friend his *Discours sur les sciences*, and accepted his good advice. He consulted him likewise on the *Discours de l'inégalité*, and on the *Nouvelle Héloïse*. In return Rousseau assisted, at any rate by his suggestions, in the composition of the *Entretiens sur le Fils Naturel*; Diderot entrusted him with the secret of his dramatic attempts, and made him acquainted with the outline of the *Père de famille*.

Now of all the eighteenth-century writers, Diderot—the fact has perhaps scarcely received sufficient attention—is the most inquisitive concerning foreign and particularly English literature.[2] He is "quite English," as M. Brunetière has well said.[3] No

[1] *Confessions*, ii., 8.

[2] See the works of Rosenkrantz and Mr. John Morley, where this point of view is cogently presented. M. L. Ducros has likewise adopted it in his book on *Diderot, l'homme et l'écrivain*. (Paris, 1894, 12mo.)

[3] *Les époques du théâtre français*, p. 295.

one " went begging " more freely, as Crébillon forcibly put it, from neighbouring peoples, who moreover rewarded him with fervent admiration. The German anglophiles found their opinions almost as well represented in his works as in those of Rousseau. Lessing declares that " no writer of a more philosophical mind had concerned himself with the theatre " since Aristotle. Herder calls him " a true German," and drew Goethe's attention to his works. Goethe became fascinated by him. " Diderot—is Diderot," he wrote to Zelter even so late as March 9, 1831, shortly before his death, " a unique individuality. The man who turns up his nose at him and his works is a Philistine." [1]

By the extremely modern character of his genius, no less than by his essentially cosmopolitan taste, Diderot stands by himself in the history of eighteenth century criticism. He had learned English thoroughly, and Mr. John Morley testifies that his knowledge of it was remarkable.[2] He turned his knowledge to account during the early years of his career—at the very time when he became intimate with Jean-Jacques—by translating several works from the English [3] : Stanyan's *History of Greece*, in 1743 ; Shaftesbury's *Essay on merit and virtue*, in 1745 ; and in 1746, with the assistance of Eidous and Toussaint, James's *Dictionary of Medicine*, the introduction to which was useful to him later on in his own *Encyclopédie*. At the same time he enriched his mind by studying Bacon, from whom he borrowed the essential portions of the *Pensées philosophiques*, and Bernard de Mandeville, whose *Fable of the Bees* supplied him with the greater part of the ideas subsequently developed in the famous *Supplément au voyage de Bougainville*. Again, it was to an English work, Chambers' *Dictionary*, that he was indebted for the plan and the idea of the *Encyclopédie*. Throughout his life, Diderot counselled admiration of England, the land, as he wrote in 1749, " of philosophers, systematisers and men of enquiring mind." All his life,

[1] See C. Joret, *Herder*, pp. 101, 372, &c., and Gandar's essay on *Diderot et la critique allemande* in *Souvenirs d'enseignement*.

[2] On his method of learning it see the article *Encyclopédie*.

[3] Observe that Diderot had also got together the materials for a history of Charles I. (*Life of Sir Samuel Romilly*, vol. i., p. 46).

too, we see him surrounded by Englishmen, such as Hume, Garrick, Wilkes and "father Hoop," or friends of the English, like Toussaint, Suard, and Deleyre the "Baconian." His house was a kind of rendezvous for all the anglophiles of Paris.

From the literary point of view, it is scarcely necessary to remind the reader that he claims, as regards his plays, to belong to the school of Lillo and Moore, and, as regards his novels, to that of Richardson and Sterne. No man, in point of taste if not of intellect, could be less French than he ; no man was more ready to look beyond the borders of his native country; none cut himself off so completely and with such determination "from the Latin tradition." All his disciples, too, cultivated and developed with the utmost care the taste for what was exotic. "How greatly," says Geoffroy, "the taste of French authors had been led astray by anglomania since 1765!" The principal author of the error deplored by Geoffroy is Diderot; it was he who taught Sébastien Mercier to extol the genius of Richardson and Fielding,[1] and Baculard d'Arnaud to praise Germany, the land "where the wings of genius are not clipped by the timid shears of fine wit."[2] He it was who constituted himself the patron of Lessing's *Sara Sampson* on its appearance in France, who wrote a preface to the French version, and declared that in Germany "genius had taken the high-road of nature."[3] He, too, it was who compared the *London Merchant* to Sophocles, and himself

---

[1] *Essai sur l'art dramatique*, p. 326. "Let yourselves revel, ye fresh and sensitive souls, in the reading of *Pamela, Clarissa, and Grandison* ; of Fielding, with all his variety . . . &c." Elsewhere he praises "the immortal Richardson, who (says the narrative of his life) spent twelve years in society almost without opening his lips, so bent was he upon catching what passed around him." Mercier also admires the Germans: "The foundation of their dramatic art is excellent. . . . If they improve upon it, as they give promise of doing, it will not be long before they excel us."

[2] *Cf. Liebman, anecdote allemande.* He says, further, of Germany, where he had spent some years : "There is no country where more real men are to be found. . . . These towns are the home of truth and of simplicity, of what the English have called *good nature.* . . . The moment the Germans subject themselves to the slavery of imitation they will take the first step towards decadence." See Gottsched's letters to Baculard, edited by M. Th. Süpfle (*Zeitschrift für vergleichende Literaturgeschichte*, vol. i., p. 146 *et seq.*).

[3] *Journal étranger*, December 1761. It is highly probable that the article is by Diderot.—See Crouslé : *Lessing et le goût français en Allemagne*, p. 376.

translated *The Gamester*, a work which he considered the masterpiece of the modern drama.

Such was the man in intimacy with whom Jean-Jacques spent the most fruitful years of his life ; the man of whom it could be said, now that he was the most German of Frenchmen, and now that he was the most English ; the one man, at anyrate, of all the great writers of the age, whose taste was most thoroughly alive to the productions of other countries.

The influence of Diderot, sufficiently evident in its effect upon Rousseau's literary ideas, was no less apparent in his selection of models.

II

IN addition to Richardson, whose decisive influence on Rousseau's genius must be studied by itself, the writers whom Jean-Jacques seems to have chiefly admired were Pope, Addison and the author of *Robinson Crusoe*.[1]

Translated by the refugees, praised by Voltaire, celebrated, from the very commencement of the century, in Germany, Italy, Sweden, Holland, and throughout reading and thinking Europe,[2] Pope, in his day, was the representative of all that was most attractive in English moral philosophy and metaphysics. The *Essay on Man*, the first part of which appeared in 1732, had made him the popular poet of deism. It had been immediately translated by the abbé du Resnel.[3] Other versions, by Silhouette, de Seré, de Schleinitz, the abbé Millot, and de Saint-Simon, had

---

[1] We must add the name of Milton, thus eloquently apostrophized in *Émile*: " Divine Milton, teach my clumsy pen to describe the pleasures of love," &c. (book vii.). Dupré de Saint-Maur's translation (1729) did not succeed in naturalizing Milton's works in France. For the eighteenth century Milton is no more than a great name.

[2] Translations of the *Essay on Criticism* and the *Rape of the Lock* are very numerous. The principal translators of the former were Robeton, Delage, and de la Pilonière in 1717, and du Resnel in 1730. The famous *Epistle from Eloisa to Abelard* was also translated and imitated.

[3] On du Resnel's translation (1736), see *Mémoires de Trévoux*, June 1736; *Journal des savants*, April 1736; *Observations sur les écrits modernes*, vol. iv., letter 47.—See also La Harpe, *Cours de littérature*, vol. iii.

followed, pending the appearance of those by Fontanes and Delille.[1] The *Essay on Man* may be said to have been truly *gallicized*. A dispute broke out concerning Pope's doctrines : de Crouzas attacked him, Warburton, Silhouette and others defended him. " I am sure," writes Jean-Jacques, "that M. de Crouzas' book will never inspire a good action, and that there is nothing good which one might not be induced to attempt after reading the poem of Pope." [2]

For Rousseau, the *Essay on Man*, as has been excellently said, was a kind of sacred volume, a " metrical gospel," wherein the men of his day delighted to find their most flattering illusions and their loftiest hopes vindicated in beautiful verse.[3] Pope " carries the torch into the abysses of man's being. With him alone does man attain to self-knowledge." [4]

Pope's teaching involves, in the first place, a contempt for all futile investigation of insoluble problems. We must commune with our own selves, and within ourselves seek that rule of conduct which no metaphysic can ever give us, the rule which nature herself supplies. She speaks loudly within us ; she cries out that our duty is to be happy, in so far as we may without prejudice to the happiness of others. Now happiness—and here we see the dawn of that sensibility which was destined to become the actual moral principle of the age—happiness consists mainly in the satisfaction of our passions, and this the various religions unjustly condemn. Pope believes in the moral excellence and the original purity of our instincts :

> These mix'd with art, and to due bounds confin'd,
> Make and maintain the balance of the mind :
> The lights and shades, whose well-accorded strife
> Gives all the strength and colour of our life.[5]

In this harmony lies not happiness only, but also the actual personality of man. Reason is one ; passion, on the contrary, infinitely diverse. It is, in truth, that which differentiates one

[1] On these translations see Goujet, *Bibliothèque française*, vol. vii., pp. 227-267.
[2] *Nouvelle Héloïse*.
[3] See M. Émile Montégut's remarkable study on Pope.
[4] Voltaire, *Poème sur la loi naturelle*.   [5] *Essay on Man*, Ep. ii., ll. 119-122.

man from another, and consequently the satisfaction of the passions, which constitute the sole real basis of the self, is the one nutriment which our craving for happiness demands. Yes, said Voltaire, the interpreter of Pope, " God in his goodness has given us the passions, that he may raise us to the height of noble deeds." To the exuberance of the passions, Voltaire, like Pope, opposes the restraint of social obligations. But this restraint is lax and feeble, and Pope still remains one of the inaugurators of the movement which led the age of Rousseau to magnify passion, regarded as the true end of man. Further, he never had anything but pity for that philosophy of the humble-minded which pretends " to chasten man under the pretence of exalting him." [1] For Pope the passionate man alone is complete. He venerates passion as the ruling power in man, not so much because it is moral, as because it is beautiful and renders man more great. That is as much as to say that in certain pages of the *Essay on Man* there is, as it were, a foretaste of Rousseau. Above all, the author makes a complacent parade of that vague and maudlin spirit of benevolence so dear to the whole period. If Pope does not actually cause our tears to flow, he at least excites a certain tender feeling and a certain melting mood, which he regards as creditable to man. Sensitiveness, if it is not virtue, is at least the beginning of virtue :

> Wide, and more wide, th' o'erflowings of the mind
> Take every creature in, of every kind ;
> Earth smiles around, with boundless bounty blessed,
> And heaven beholds its image in his breast,[2]

or, if Voltaire be preferred to Pope,[3] let the reader peruse once more the sentimental tirade on benevolence, at the end of the *Discours sur la vraie vertu ;* the subject is the same, and the expressions are almost identical.

The *Essay on Man* did more to spread English deism in France

---

[1] Voltaire, *Cinquième discours en vers.*   [2] *Essay on Man*, Ep. iv., ll. 369-372.

[3] We may observe, in passing, that Voltaire owns to having written one half of the lines in du Resnel's translation. (To Thibouville, 2nd February 1769.) The fact does not add to his reputation.

than all the works of Shaftesbury. At bottom the doctrine is Shaftesbury's, but it is shorn of his aggressiveness, purified from all leaven of scepticism and pantheism, rendered more vague and indefinite, and therefore more poetical. Can we wonder either that Rousseau read Pope's poem or that he wrote to Voltaire: " The poem of Pope alleviates my troubles and encourages me to be patient ? "[1] What the author of the *Profession de foi du Vicaire Savoyard* discovered in Pope was himself.

It was a system of morals again, a homely, *bourgeois* system, that he sought in the *Spectator*, one of the most popular books of the century.

Through the refugees the names of the " sagacious Mr Addison" and the " virtuous Mr Steele" had become well known. In 1719 the *Journal des savants* had reviewed the *Letters from Italy*. Ten years later the author received a biographical notice in the *Bibliothèque anglaise*.[2] Like Pope, he attained a European reputation at a very early age. His *Cato* was accounted a great work in the eighteenth century ; an adaptation of it, made by a certain Deschamps two years after its production, was highly successful, and Voltaire frequently compares Addison's one tragedy with the whole of Shakespeare's plays.[3]

But his great title to celebrity was undoubtedly the publication, in collaboration with Steele, of his magazines dealing with moral subjects. Of these the *Spectator* was alike the most original and the most highly appreciated. A daily paper, non-political, concerned before all things with homely, practical philosophy, resolutely refusing to make any allusion to the scandals of the day or in any way to provoke the unhealthy curiosity of its readers, the *Spectator* caused a revolution in the English press, and thereby throughout Europe.

" His manner of writing," said Voltaire, speaking of the author of the *Spectator*, " would be an excellent model in any

---

[1] 18th August 1756.   [2] Vol. vi., pp. 213-220.

[3] *Caton d'Utique*, a tragedy dedicated to the Duke of Orleans (by M. C. Deschamps, Paris, 1715, 12mo).—Gottsched imitated Addison's *Cato* in his *Death of Cato*, and his drama was translated by Riccoboni in his *Recherches historiques sur les théâtres de l'Europe*, Paris, 1738, 8vo.—*La prétendue veuve ou l'époux magicien*, a comedy in five acts, Paris, 1737, 8vo, was also a translation from Addison.

country."[1] Now he acquired this manner, to a large extent, from his French models. The accomplished intellect of Addison had no difficulty in appropriating not only ancient philosophy, but whatever was best in the French moralists of the seventeenth century as well.[2] Therewith also—and herein he displayed the most accurate knowledge of his country's manners—he associated an amiable and unassuming *bourgeois* philosophy which won over all those who were dismayed by the subtlety of a La Bruyère. Beneath the most classical forms, Addison remains at heart thoroughly English. It should be remarked that at the commencement of the century he was, for foreigners, the personification of the *bourgeois* element in the English intelligence. " My heart was Addison's," writes Breitinger at Zurich ; " with him I left my humble retreat, and took my first steps in the society of men." Bodmer started his *Discourse der Mahlern* (1721) in imitation of the *Spectator*, and dedicated them " to the august Spectator of the English nation."[3] Improving magazines were published also by Gottsched, Klopstock, and many others. It has been computed that more than one hundred and eighty imitations of the *Spectator* were published in Germany before 1760,[4] and the *Journal Étranger*, mentioning a great many of them, called the attention of French readers to this astonishing proof of Addison's success. His good fortune soon spread to Holland, which had its *Spectateur hollandais*, having already had its *Babillard* and its *Contrôleuse spirituelle* ;[5] to Italy, where Gozzi established his *Osservatore* ; and even to Russia, where the first review patronised by Catherine II. was an imitation of the English journals of moral teaching.[6]

In France their popularity was equally great. " There is not a person but has read the *Spectator*," writes Tabaraud ; "its success has been prodigious."[7] In 1716 the *Mémoires de Trévoux*,

---

[1] *Siècle de Louis XIV.*, ch. xxxiv.   [2] *Cf.* Voltaire, *Lettre à Milord Harvey*, 1740.

[3] *Cf.* Joret, *Herder*, and an interesting pamphlet by Th. Vetter : *Zürich als Vermittlerin englischer Literatur im achtzehnten Jahrhundert*, Zurich, 1891, 8vo. See the same writer's edition of Bodmer's *Discourse* (Frauenfeld, 1891, 8vo).

[4] Perry, *English Literature in the Eighteenth Century*, Fr. trans., p. 166.

[5] Hatin, *Les Gazettes de Hollande*, p. 200.   [6] *Cf. The Academy*, 25th March 1882.

[7] *Histoire du philosophisme anglais*, vol. i., p. 66. *Cf.* 1st, with regard to the *Spectator* ; *Le Spectateur ou le Socrate moderne où l'on voit un portrait naïf des mœurs de ce siècle;*

which were, however, very unfavourable to English productions, declare "the English Socrates" to be greatly superior to the "French Theophrastus." Camusat finds in him certain new and remarkable ideas which cannot but enhance "the good opinion at present entertained of English books."[1] Its success astonished Voltaire at first; but during his stay in England he came to understand Addison's originality, and expressed his admiration in the warmest terms.[2] D'Argenson considered that no one could read anything "more agreeable or better done."[3] In short, its success was general, and imitations of it innumerable; some, and the greater portion, absolutely forgotten to-day, others, such as Marivaux's *Spectateur français*, having been preserved from total oblivion by the names of their authors. There were a *Misanthrope*, a *Censeur*, an *Inquisiteur*, *Spectators* Swiss and American, as well as Dutch and Danish, not to mention a *Radoteur*, a *Bagatelle*, and a *Fantasque*. Addison had discovered a form of literature really adapted to the needs of contemporary readers, and all Europe adopted his idea.[4] But none of these productions obscured the recollection of the original. Marivaux himself did not succeed in striking the full and copious vein of his model, or in acquiring the same wealth of information on moral topics, and the same interest in problems suggested by every-day life.

Amsterdam, 1714, 12mo, 456 pp. The other volumes follow in order, to the number of seven, down to 1754. The translator of the first six is unknown; the translation of the last two is attributed by some to Elie de Joncourt, by others to J. P. Moet (*Cf.* Quérard and Barbier).—The *Spectator* was reprinted in three quarto volumes.— 2nd, with regard to the *Tatler*: *Le Babillard ou le Nouvelliste philosophe, traduit de l'anglais de Steele* by A. D. L. C. [Armand de la Chapelle], Amsterdam, 1723, 12mo.—This is only the first volume; the second appeared at Amsterdam in 1735.—3rd, concerning the *Guardian*: *Le Mentor moderne, ou Discours sur les mœurs du siècle*, translated . . . [by Van Effen], The Hague, 1724, 3 vols. 12mo.—In bibliographical lists there are many erroneous details.

[1] Camusat's *Bibliothèque française* (vol. vii., 1726, p. 193).
[2] *Cf.* Ballantyne, p. 309, and see Sharpe, *Letters from Italy*.
[3] *Mémoires*, ed. Jannet, vol. v., p. 164.
[4] See in Hatin's *Histoire de la presse* a long though incomplete list of these imitations. In Caylus (*Œuvres badines*, 1787, vol. vi.) there is a satirical letter on the *Spectators*: "An Englishman writes several disconnected articles, puts them together, and gives them the name of *Spectator*: his book succeeds, and its success is deserved: forthwith there spring up *Spectators* called French, Unknown, Swiss, &c."

After the literature of the day Addison was a relief: in his broad stream of morality, at once so simple and so pure, the readers of a Fontenelle—as often happens in an era of scepticism—loved to plunge themselves as though in a bath of virtue. Marivaux, with his cold and over-refined intellect, entirely failed to produce the same effect.[1]

In the moral philosophy of the *Spectator*, robust as it was and respectable, though, to our modern taste, somewhat commonplace and unaspiring, there was that which, by its very faults, proved attractive to those whose wearied palates were beginning to demand simple fare. " The English are easier to please than we are," it was said, " with regard to works on morality : they do not mind what is commonplace, provided only it be useful, and presented in popular form ; with us, moralizing only goes down when it is clever and pointed."[2] Their very lack of refinement and style constituted the charm of these lay sermons. They occasioned no regret for the incomparable subtlety of La Bruyère, the profound philosophy of La Rochefoucauld, the mild and gentle spirit of Nicole,[3] or the vigorous dialectic of Bourdaloue, the master of Addison. There was something pleasant in that flameless warmth, that radiance which to us seems so pallid. " Virtue," the reader thought, " as represented here, has nothing chilling, harsh, burdensome or dismal, about it ; . . . this is a pleasing sort of virtue, made for man, responsive to all his natural faculties . . . and capable of affording them the most exquisite sensations :"[4] a virtue, in short, adapted to the requirements of the eighteenth century. The English moralist's narrow horizon, his profoundly *bourgeois* character, his moderation and amiable tolerance, all seemed fresh and original. In the early part of the present century Cardinal Maury, who had witnessed the persistence of this fashion, was unable to comprehend how anyone could ever have preferred Addison to La

[1] *Cf.* G. Larroumet, *Marivaux*, p. 394.
[2] *Gazette littéraire de l'Europe*, vol. vi., p. 354.
[3] Locke had translated the *Essais* of Nicole for Lord Shaftesbury: his translation was published by Thomas Hancock in 1828 (*Cf.* H. Marion, *Locke*, p. 147).
[4] Preface to the *Mentor moderne* (The Hague, 1724, vol. i.).

Bruyère ;[1] and we, too, prefer the latter. But those who were contemporary with the *Lettres Persanes*—the idea for which Montesquieu was accused of having taken from the *Spectator*—relished the ethics which appealed to heart rather than to mind —the moral teaching not of a scholar but of a moralist. " Use, but do not abuse—such is the wise man's advice. I avoid alike Epictetus and Petronius. Neither abstinence nor excess ever made a happy man."[2] Here we have the substance of the sermon preached by Addison under two or three hundred heads, and addressed to the commonplace souls of his contemporaries as their morning viaticum.—Did he not recommend his reflections to all well-regulated families who, with their breakfast of tea and bread-and-butter, would have his paper served up to them as an accompaniment to the spoons and the tray ? The sermon is not new, but everything can be renovated, even platitudes—they, indeed, above all. The reader will be familiar with the agreeable background Addison contrived to give to his sermonizing ; how, in the " Club " to which we are introduced, the good Sir Roger de Coverley, Freeport the merchant, the veteran warrior Captain Sentry, and the amiable dandy Will Honeycomb enable him to present his moral teaching, in the pleasantest manner in the world, in a concrete form. There, the questions of marriage, of religion, of education, of the best form of government are discussed. But there also are treated, seriously or lightly, as becomes the occasion, such trifling problems as a La Bruyère would have deemed beneath his notice : what ladies should wear indoors, the impropriety of talking freely in public vehicles, dancing, the deportment of married couples in society, belief in the existence of ghosts, how one should behave in church, and a thousand questions relating to good-breeding or to hygiene. Addison considers the question of the suckling of children ; enquires whether or not it is well to indulge the fancies of women with child, and humorously recounts the vexations of a husband ; he discusses, with a smile, the use of chocolate, and recommends becoming methods whereby women may enhance their beauty.

[1] *Lettres et opuscules* of J. de Maistre, vol. ii., p. 177.
[2] Voltaire, fifth *Discours en vers sur l'homme.*

He constitutes himself adviser, confessor, and family doctor. No question is too mean for him, provided it affects, either directly or remotely, the moral or physical health of man.

French readers found this solicitude no less charming than amusing : Addison and Steele were compared to Socrates, and it was considered that " these truly wise men " had brought heaven's philosophy down to earth, " the phantoms of the study upon the stage of the world." [1] Prévost too, in his *Pour et Contre*, played the part of Addison and Steele. He inquired " whether high rank or official position are incompatible with certain talents ; " he gave rules for conversation ; portrayed the effects produced upon the character by the fierce emotions of love ; lavished counsel upon the fair, consolation upon the ill-favoured, and learned advice upon those who are on the wane : he even discussed the practice of tea-drinking, and concluded that by the use of this " liquor," which relaxes the fibres of the stomach, " the brave man becomes cowardly, the strong workman weak, and women become sterile." [2] The work of Addison was drawn upon to an unlimited extent ; sometimes for simple tales, sometimes for philosophical allegories, [3] sometimes, and most frequently, for the subjects of plays. For Addison is not a moralist only, he is also rich in pictures of middle-class life, in pathetic scenes, in dramatic adventures. Baculard d'Arnaud takes from him the subject of a tragedy, [4] Boissy the plot for a comedy, [5] La Chaussée several ideas and more than one entire situation. [6] And with the advance of the century his celebrity increases, at the expense of that of the French moralists : " It is difficult," wrote Saint-Lambert, " to read much of the *Spectator* without becoming a better man ; he reconciles you with human nature, while La Bruyère makes you dread it." [7]

Rousseau read it at Chambéry, on his return from Turin, and

---

[1] *Journal étranger*, February 1762. [2] Vol. xii., p. 207.

[3] Raynal borrows from the *Spectator* an anecdote for the *Histoire philosophique des deux Indes* (J. Morley, *Diderot*, vol. ii., p. 226) ; Voltaire an allegory for the article *Religion* in the *Dictionnaire philosophique*, &c. The moral journals also provided Berquin with the materials for his *Tableaux anglais* (Paris, 1775, 8vo).

[4] *Euphémie.* [5] *Les Valets maîtres.*

[6] Lanson, *Nivelle de la Chaussée*, p. 133. [7] *Essai sur la vie de Bolingbroke* (1796).

appreciated it highly. "The *Spectator*," he says, "pleased me greatly, and did me good."[1] Like his contemporaries he loved its *bourgeois* moralizing, so simple, so appropriate to the family circle. It is Addison whom he advises Sophie to read in order to learn the duties of an honest woman.[2] From him, doubtless, he took the idea of the *Persifleur*, which he afterwards established in conjunction with Diderot, and did not carry beyond a single number.[3] From him, too, he appears to have borrowed what he says in the *Lettre sur les spectacles* concerning the clubs and societies of London, a few touches, also, in the description of the English garden in the *Nouvelle Héloïse*, and some of the ideas in *Émile* on the advantage of inuring children to the endurance of cold. These little obligations, however, are not of much importance.[4] The point of interest to us is that Rousseau understood and loved an Addison whose genius, in common with his own, possessed a rare and precious quality of moral elevation, and who, in more than one respect, may perhaps be considered a champion of the same causes.[5]

Lastly, among the English books with which he was familiar there was one upon which he pronounced a magnificent eulogy, namely, *The Life and Strange Surprising Adventures of Robinson Crusoe, of York, Mariner, who lived Eight-and-twenty Years all alone in an uninhabited Island on the Coast of America, near the Mouth of the great River of Oronoque. . . . Written by Himself.*

Published in 1719 and 1720, Defoe's novel, as we have seen, had been translated by the refugees in 1720 and 1721, and had since then been reprinted over and over again. The edition read by Rousseau was undoubtedly the inaccurate translation by Saint-Hyacinthe and Van Effen. The work was already famous;

---

[1] *Confessions*, i., 3.   [2] *Émile*, book v.   [3] *Confessions*, ii., 7.

[4] *Cf.* L. Mézières, *Histoire de la littérature anglaise*, vol. i., p. 145.

[5] *Cf.* particularly what Addison says of the morality of the theatre. — On this question Rousseau, also, perhaps read *La critique du théâtre anglais comparé au théâtre d'Athènes, de Rome, et de France* . . . [translated from Jeremy Collier by de Courbeville], Paris, 1715, 12mo. Several French writers appear to have gained a knowledge of the English stage from this book. (*Cf. Mémoires de Trévoux*, April 1704; *Journal des savants*, 1715, p. 219; *Mémoires de Trévoux*, July 1716, and May, June, July and August 1732.—See also a letter from Brossette to J. B. Rousseau, 25th December 1715.

the attention of the newspapers had been attracted to it immediately it appeared,[1] and Lesage, assisted by d'Orneval, had founded upon it the story of a comic opera for the *théâtre de la Foire*.[2] Very early too the book became launched upon the great stream of European literature : there had appeared a *Robinson allemand*, a *Robinson italien*, a *Robinson de Silésie*, and Robinsons of which the hero was either a priest, a doctor, a Jew, a poet, a bookseller, or even a woman.[3] It has been computed that by 1760 forty *Robinsonades* had already made their appearance in Germany,[4] not to mention those published in Holland and Austria.[5]

In spite of its popularity it does not appear that the success of the book was in the first instance due to its true merits : the author's marvellous gift of observation, which, as he himself says, enabled him to present a " statement of facts," passed almost unnoticed. Though one of the great books of the century, the work did not at once create a school, either in its native country or in France.

The translators of the book, it is true, assert that most of its readers feel that they are actually living with Robinson, so great is the power of the author's art to create illusion.[6] "With him they seemed to be spending whole years in building a hut, in hollowing out a cave, in erecting a palisade ; they fancied themselves occupied for months together in helping him to polish a single plank, and felt themselves as much imprisoned in their reading as Robinson in his solitude."[7] Many of the details, indeed, seemed minute or unworthy of notice. A few years earlier Mari-

[1] *Cf. Journal des savants*, 1720, p. 503 *et seq.*
[2] This comic opera is lost. (See Barberet: *Lesage et le théâtre de la Foire*, p. 222).
[3] Perry, *English Literature in the Eighteenth Century*, p. 264.
[4] *Cf.* Kippenberg, *Robinson in Deutschland bis zur Insel Felsenburg* (1713-43), Hanover, 1892, 8vo.
[5] H. F. Wagner: *Robinson in Österreich*, Salzburg, 1886, 8vo. A list of Dutch imitations will be found in the *Annales typographiques*, 1759, vol. i., p. 58.
[6] See M. J. Jusserand's remarkable study *Le roman anglais et la réforme littéraire de Daniel de Foe*, Brussels, 1887. We may justly object that the author exaggerates, not the greatness of Defoe's work, but its immediate influence: Defoe was truly enough the creator of realistic fiction in England, but for more than twenty years he had not a single disciple.
[7] Preface to vol. ii.

vaux also, in a now forgotten novel, had described the island-life of a recluse; but how much "nobler" was his recital! Marivaux's hero wants some broth; but what of that! He kills some birds with his bow and arrows. But he has no vessel for cooking purposes. " How ingenious we become when we have to live by our wits! Taking some earth and kneading it with water, I fashioned a pot from it as best I could, and set it out in the sun to dry." In an hour's time the pot is finished and the broth prepared: what could be more expeditious? The same skill, the same ingenuity, when he has to make some bread. " As heaven has distributed its gifts to every spot on earth,[1] I perceived that there was a kind of grain growing wild in the island, which the natives did not use because they were unacquainted with it. I had a quantity of it cut . . . and dried. Finally I managed to discover the secret of extracting the flour, from which I kneaded several small loaves." Nothing can be simpler, as we see; nor can anything give us a better idea of the difference between two separate types of genius, and even between two races, than a comparison of Marivaux's Robinson with that of Defoe. The savages of the one are real savages; those of the other dwell together as in one great family, and feel " innocence and peace steal into their hearts." " They called me their father." What a contrast to the practical, bargain-driving, thoroughly English Robinson who sells his slave Xury for a few pistoles.

Now the readers of Saint-Hyacinthe and Van Effen—I will not say of Defoe—do not seem to have fully perceived the originality of this acute observation of detail, this perfect veri-similitude of the least little fact, this seizing of reality, which gives the English novel all the relief of an authentic narrative—a *statement of facts*. What they enjoyed in *Robinson Crusoe* was a curious story of travel, which readers of the *Thousand and one nights*, the *Aventures de Beauchêne* or the *Histoire des voyages* found gratifying to that appetite for tales of adventure and of expeditions to remote regions which was so widely spread in that day.[2] The

---

[1] See *Les Effets surprenants de la sympathie* (1713), part ii.
[2] On this taste for travel see L. Claretie, *Lesage romancier*, p. 60 *et seq.*—English critics

romantic isolation of the hero produced a lively impression. It was almost traditional with eighteenth-century novelists to make their heroes pass some time on an island. Prévost, in his *Histoire de Cléveland*, imagines a philosophical recluse and misanthrope, of whom Cléveland, as is proper, makes a friend.[1] Fielding inflicts the ordeal of solitude upon Mrs Heartfree, and Jean-Jacques upon Saint-Preux. Rousseau's hero even dwells in two islands successively: " I was perhaps the only soul," he says, " to whom so pleasant an exile was in no way alarming. . . . In this fearsome yet delightful abode, I have seen what human ingenuity will attempt in order to extricate civilized man from a solitude where he lacks nothing, and to plunge him afresh into a vortex of new wants."[2] They all remained subject to the spell of the marvellous adventure related by Defoe, and Bernardin de Saint-Pierre, reading *Robinson Crusoe* on the shores of the English Channel in the closing days of the century, felt the yearning for unknown lands awake within him.[3]

Rousseau, however, was the first to point out the wide philosophic import of the book. It "constituted a very able treatise on natural philosophy," and was to be the one and only volume in the library of Émile. The author, it is true, he does not name: the men of that century did not know who he was; Fréron, speaking of *Robinson Crusoe* in 1768, thought it necessary to remind the reader in a note that the author was "a certain Daniel de Foe";[4] while another translator attributes it to Steele.[5] Nothing whatever was known of the writer's personality and talent. But Jean-Jacques pronounced a splendid eulogy upon the educational qualities of the work, preferring its author

have remarked certain similarities between *Robinson Crusoe* and Lesage's novel *Les Aventures de Beauchêne* (*Cf.* Saintsbury, *A short history of French literature*); I do not think, however, that there are any grounds for inferring that there was imitation.

[1] See the solitary's curious discourse when he set foot on his island (vol. iv., p. 70). The episode pleased Prévost's readers, for fifty years later de la Chabeaussière took from it the subject for his *Nouveau Robinson*, a comedy in three acts with music by Dalayrac (1786).

[2] *Nouvelle Héloïse*, iv., 3. [3] Maury, *Bernardin de St Pierre*, p. 6.

[4] *Année littéraire*, 1768, vol. i., p. 235.

[5] *Les avantures ou la vie et les voyages de Robinson Crusoé, traduction de l'ouvrage anglais attribué au célèbre Richard Steele*, Francfort, 1769, 2 vols., 12mo.

to Aristotle, Pliny and Buffon.[1] " I want Émile," he said, " to examine his hero's behaviour, to try and find out whether he omitted anything, and whether anything better could have been done." He saw quite clearly how closely the author of *Robinson Crusoe* had adhered to life, and perceived the lofty teaching he had managed to extract from it. Rousseau raised to its proper position what had been regarded as nothing more than a novel, when in reality it was a moral treatise. It was his testimony to its qualities that gave Daniel Defoe's work a place in the philosophical heritage of humanity.[2]

III

For English literature of the more common and popular type Rousseau had an even greater admiration than for the *Spectator* or for *Robinson Crusoe*. Therein he found his own literary aspirations realized.

There is no doubt that between 1745 and 1758 the subjects of Rousseau's admiration were those admired by Diderot. During the early days of their intimacy, their thoughts were turned more especially towards the theatre, Rousseau's even more than Diderot's. Both were enthusiastic playgoers. Jean-Jacques had a free seat at the Opéra and the Comédie : he boasts of having faithfully witnessed every play produced during ten years, especially those of Molière. During his residence at Chambéry he had written a tragic opera, *Iphis et Anaxarète*. While tutor in M. de Mably's household at Lyon he wrote his *Découverte du Nouveau Monde*. It is needless to enumerate here the operas for which he provided the libretti. But *Narcisse, Les Prisonniers de guerre, L'Engagement téméraire*, and all the other attempts, which, after all, add nothing to his fame, afford ample proof of the

---

[1] *Émile*, book iii.

[2] Further translations of Defoe's masterpiece followed the publication of *Émile*. See *Robinson Crusoé*, a new imitation of the English work, by M. Feutry, Amsterdam, 1765, 2 vols. 12mo, and *L'Île de Robinson Crusoé*, adapted from the English by M. de Montreille, Paris, 1767, 12mo.—See also La Harpe's estimate, which is a mere echo of Rousseau's (*Cours de littérature*, vol. iii., p. 190).

strength of his predilection for the theatre. Three years after the appearance of the *Discours sur les sciences et les arts* he had not yet abjured it, and produced his *Narcisse ou l'amant de lui-même* : the piece was a failure, but he published it nevertheless, abusing his public in the preface. At Geneva, two years afterwards, he began *Lucrèce*, a tragedy in prose. His *Pygmalion* was written later still. All his life long Rousseau loved the theatre— Rousseau, the writer of the *Lettre sur les spectacles*. Men impugn nothing so savagely as what they have greatly loved.

Not only, however, was the theatre the subject of his thoughts and aspirations; there is no doubt that he took a lively interest in the dramatic reform contemplated by his friend. Among the ideas expressed in his *Lettre sur les spectacles* and in the literary chapters of the *Nouvelle Héloïse* there are some which he undoubtedly acquired from Diderot, or held in common with him.

Like Diderot, he is of opinion that tragedy has had its day, and that Corneille and Racine, for all their genius, " are but speech-makers."[1] Many of their pieces, tragic as they are, have no power to move the feelings, and above all—a point on which Diderot insisted more than upon any other—they " give no sort of information on the manners characteristic of those whom they amuse." They contain no simple and natural sentiments, but merely " smart things " which catch the ear of the crowd.[2] Like Diderot, he thinks that the drama should be formed upon the social ideal, which is constantly changing ; do we not know that there are " five or six hundred thousand souls in Paris of whom the stage takes no heed whatever ? "[3] Like him, he holds that taste varies with the age, and that after all it is nothing more than " the faculty of judging what is pleasing or displeasing to the greatest number."[4] Hence it follows " that the true models for taste are to be found in nature," which always leaves something to be revealed, and is a thousand times richer than French poets have supposed. If the ancients are superior to us, it is simply because they were first in the field, and therefore at closer quarters with eternal nature. Yet how much is still left to be

---

[1] *Nouvelle Héloïse*, ii. 17.   With this passage *cf.* ch. xxxviii. of *Bijoux indiscrets*.
[2] *Lettre sur les spectacles*.   [3] *N. H.*, ii. 17.   [4] *Émile*, book iv.

I

discovered.   The matter of the drama has, as it were, become congealed in antiquated moulds.   It remains for us " to keep close to life," to reveal the provincial world—that is to say, the whole universe outside of Paris,—to find again the true man beneath the polished and unnatural man of society.   In the circle of which Diderot and Jean-Jacques were members it was considered that in France " all ranks and conditions had become fused together for social purposes ": *seigneurs*, magistrates, financiers, men of letters and soldiers were all alike, and only one condition of life remained, that of man of the world.   "*The English, on the contrary, have preserved, with their liberty, the privilege of being each individually exactly what nature has made him*, of not concealing his opinions, nor the prejudices and manners of the profession he follows : that is why their novels of domestic interest are such pleasant reading."[1]   And that, also, is one of the reasons why Rousseau was so attracted towards " this proud and intrepid people, who despise sorrow and death, and fear nothing in the world but hunger and *ennui*."[2]   He likes them because they are still capable of great passions, because " no famous deed was ever achieved by cold reason," and because in the Englishman man recognises his own best possible type.

Like Diderot also, though with deeper conviction than he, Rousseau found in English writers his own interest in questions of moral philosophy.   With the majority of Protestant writers he regarded the beautiful as in its essence nothing but a form of the good.   " If the moral system is corrupt," his friend wrote, " it follows of necessity that the taste is false."[3]   Rousseau goes further and expressly declares that " the good is nothing more than the beautiful put into practice," that the one is closely bound up with the other, that they have a common source in a perfectly regulated nature, that " taste may be brought to perfection by the same methods as wisdom"—which is paradoxical —and " that a soul thoroughly alive to the charms of virtue ought to be proportionately sensitive to every other kind of beauty"—which is false, but extremely English.   Let us,

[1] *Correspondance littéraire*, August 1753.   [2] *N. H.*, iv. 3.
[3] *De la poésie dramatique*, xxii.

therefore, have tragedies which breathe patriotism and the love of freedom, and they will be fine tragedies. Let us have dramas which call forth our tears on behalf of virtue, and those dramas will be true to nature.

Now it is still more true of the English people, as Suard observed, than of the Roman people, that it "breathes tragedy,"[1] and it is to the English drama that we must look for the revival of pathos. Very early in the century La Motte called for "action that is impressive," such as was introduced by English playwrights,[2] and a few years later Montesquieu compared their dramatic pieces not to the ordinary products of nature so much as to the sports in which she has developed what was originally only a happy accident.[3] In the very year in which Rousseau definitely took up his residence in Paris, appeared the first volume of the too famous *Théâtre anglais* of La Place, with which he was undoubtedly acquainted. Therein one might learn that "readers who do not believe that the French mind must of necessity be the type of all others will be qualified to enjoy reading Shakespeare, not only because they will thereby discover how the English genius differs from the French, but because they will find in his works flashes of power and new and original beauties which, in spite of their foreign appearance, seem all the more effective to those who did not expect to meet with them."

Among those who did expect to meet with them must be reckoned Diderot and Rousseau. Shakespeare, however—the Shakespeare of La Place—does not seem to have made a very vivid impression upon them. Diderot, though capable of consulting the original text, had but scant praise for the author of

---

[1] Garat, *Mémoires sur Suard*, vol. ii., p. 127.

[2] *Discours sur la tragédie*, prefixed to *Romulus*.

[3] *Pensées diverses*. In the *Mémoires de Trévoux*, April 1704, we read: "The English, who for more than a century have paid much attention to dramatic poetry, have at last brought it to a degree of perfection which most of their neighbours cannot but admire. Their national genius, the bent of their language, the liberty of criticism which is assumed in England, all contribute to this result."—*Cf.* also Riccoboni : *Réflexions historiques et critiques sur les différents théâtres de l'Europe* (1738).

Othello, and has expressed it in the vaguest terms. For it is no very high praise to compare him to that "shapeless, roughly carved colossus," [1] St. Christopher of Notre-Dame, if it is added that there is not one of his scenes "of which, *with a little talent*, something great might not be made." [2] Diderot seems in fact to admire Shakespeare because he is English, and, although he belongs to the past, extremely modern. He is always inaccurate when he speaks of him, and his expressions have none of that warmth which sincerity of feeling imparts to admiration. As for Rousseau, he commends Voltaire, somewhere or other, for having ventured to follow the example of the English, and put some life into the drama. [3] This, if we please, we may call an indirect way of praising Shakespeare—and we know, moreover, that Rousseau thought highly of him, though that was all. [4] Must we condemn Rousseau or Diderot for not having had a better understanding of Shakespeare as interpreted by La Place ? Verily, they would have required the eyes of a lynx to do so. Besides, their ideal, it must be confessed, was to be found elsewhere. What they were dreaming of was the *bourgeois* drama, invented, with such a flourish of trumpets, by Diderot; "tragedies rendered interesting by patriotism and love of liberty;" [5] in short, *The London Merchant* and *The Gamester*.

In reality, it was La Chaussée who had produced the earliest specimens of pathetic comedy, but him they did not greatly appreciate. Diderot cared little for him because he merely heralded a new type, and because, moreover, he was but an indifferent herald. [6] Rousseau, on his part, confessed that if the plays of La Chaussée or Destouches are "refined," they are also, however instructive they may be, still more tedious, and that one might just as well go to hear a sermon. [7] Moreover, as Prévost had

[1] *Paradoxe sur le comédien*, ed. Moland, vol. viii., p. 384.

[2] Letter to Voltaire, 29th September 1762.   [3] *N. H.*, ii. 17.

[4] Bernardin de Saint-Pierre: *Fragments sur Jean-Jacques Rousseau.*

[5] *N. H.*, ii. 17.

[6] *Œuvres de Diderot*, vol. xix., p. 314. After a performance of the *Père de famille* he writes : "Duclos said, as we came out, that three pieces like that in one year would kill tragedy. Let them get used to emotions of this sort, and *after that endure Destouches and La Chaussée if they can.*"

[7] *Lettre sur les spectacles*, ed. Fontaine, p. 165.

observed, La Chaussée himself was merely a disciple, though perhaps an involuntary one, of the English. " I cannot abstain from informing," he said, " the public that they [the writers of pathetic comedy] are not the first who have formed this project, and that if the example of a sensible nation is of any value they may justify themselves by that of our neighbours." And he proceeded to quote some instances of the English drama of pathos,[1] and introduced the *London Merchant* to his readers' notice.

The author of this once famous play, which impressed Rousseau as a master-piece, was George Lillo, born, in 1693, of a Dutch father and an English mother, both of them dissenters. Like Richardson, Sedaine, Jean-Jacques, and many members of the lower middle class who, in the eighteenth century, tried their hands at fiction and the drama, he at first pursued a handicraft, and was somewhat late in entering upon his literary career. After a fruitless attempt at opera he produced *George Barnwell* or the *London Merchant* in 1731. In spite of the season—the height of summer—the piece had a run of twenty nights. In vain the author's enemies conspired against him, and had several thousand copies of the old ballad on which the play was founded sold in the streets. Those who sold them, says a witness, were overcome by their feelings, and dropped the ballads in order to get at their pocket handkerchiefs. Pope, who was then living, thought the plot of the piece well-managed and the style natural without being vulgar.[2] Queen Caroline wished to possess the manuscript of the work, and the city merchants, proud of a sermon which reflected so much honour upon them, praised it to the skies. It continued to hold the stage, though apparently less on account of its literary qualities than because it was an edifying play. The Theatre Royal at Manchester was long accustomed to present *George Barnwell* once a year, on Shrove Tuesday, for the instruction of the apprentices of the town. When Ross, the actor,

---

[1] *Pour et contre*, vol. xii., p. 145. It may moreover be observed that La Chaussée was himself imitated in England : his *Préjugé à la mode* furnished the theme of Murphy's *The Way to keep him* (1761). (See *Le nouveau théâtre anglais*, Paris, 1769, vol. i.). Paul Lacroix mentions *Mélanide* as having been reprinted in Dublin (1749). (*Catalogue de Soleinne*, vol. ii., p. 91.)

[2] Perry, *Littérature anglaise au xviiie siècle*, p. 277.

played Barnwell, in 1752, a young apprentice, who, like the
hero of the piece, had robbed his employer in order to keep his
mistress, was so smitten with remorse while watching the performance, that he lost his reason.   A doctor was called in, inter-
ceded with the father, and by pacifying him managed to restore
the senses of the sick youth, who became an honest merchant.
Ross, in his memoirs, declares that he thenceforth received
every year a sum of ten guineas, with the words : " A tribute
of gratitude from one who was highly obliged, and saved from
ruin, by seeing Mr Ross's performance of *Barnwell*." [1]   What a
pity that Diderot was unacquainted with this incident.   What
a tirade we have lost !

Thus the *London Merchant* worked miracles.   Lillo's other
pieces, the *Christian Hero* or *Fatal Curiosity*, *Marina* or *Elmerick*
had a less brilliant success.[2]   But when he died, their author was
widely regretted.   Fielding praised him for his " perfect knowledge of the human heart," his noble character, his philosophy,
which was that of a happy man, and his generous repugnance to
depending on others.   " He had the spirit of an old Roman,
joined to the innocence of a primitive Christian." [3]   Significant
praise, from such an authority.

Read again to-day, the " master-piece " of this remarkable
character seems less sublime.   It is a melodrama of a decidedly
sombre type, highly moral, and in parts, but in parts only, full
of pathos.   It must not be forgotten that the story of a young
apprentice, who is beguiled by a woman of loose life and led
on to commit robbery and murder, was a subject almost new to
the stage.   Writers of comedy had been lavish in the presentation of dissipated young fellows who had to reap the fruits of
their youthful follies ; but those follies merely occasioned laughter, and their retribution was never severe.   Such scatterbrains
got off with nothing worse than a matrimonial fiasco—a pretty
piece of business !—or, more cheaply still, with a paternal lec-

[1] *Biographia Dramatica (The London Merchant)*.
[2] None of them were known in France. (*Cf.* Grimm, *Correspondance littéraire*
April 1764).
[3] *The Champion*, in *Biographia Dramatica*.   See the article on Lillo in the *Dictionary
of National Biography*, where a detailed bibliography is given.

ture.   But to depict the tumult occasioned in a lad's soul by base
desires, to study the slow and irretrievable descent of a feeble will
towards vice, severely yet sorrowfully to elicit the moral conveyed by a life thus maimed and spoiled, was, in 1731, something quite new.   *Manon* was as yet unwritten, and who shall say
that Lillo's play, which Prévost saw performed in London, and
spoke of with such enthusiasm, did not count for something in
the creation of his romance ?   However this may be, there is a
touch of the rogue about Des Grieux, and Manon is too lovable ;
the lesson conveyed is less direct and less tragic.   The manner
in which the humble dissenter George Lillo determined to pro-
ceed was very different.   He aimed at producing a more forcible
impression, and wrote, not a dramatic work, but a sermon in the
form of a play.

The character of Barnwell, it is true, is but slightly studied ;
he is a puppet.   He cannot take his pleasure without preaching
and lecturing.   Observe him in the hour of his fall : he is speaking
to the courtesan : " To hear you talk, though in the cause of
vice ; to gaze upon your beauty, press your hand, and see your
snow-white bosom heave and fall, inflame my wishes ; my pulse
beats high, my senses all are in a hurry, and I am on the rock of
wild desire.—Yet, for a moment's guilty pleasure, shall I lose my
innocence, my piece of mind, and hopes of solid happiness ?—
MILLWOOD : Chimeras all ! . . . Along with me, and prove no
joys like woman-kind, no Heav'n like love." [1]   This is really
too simple and abrupt ; the reader is amazed and stupefied.
But even so long ago as 1731 an author could acquire a
reputation for being very profound by slurring over transi-
tions, destroying gradations, and boldly skipping problems in
psychology.

The courtesan, Millwood, is not a woman, but an idea—the
beast of the Apocalypse, which has declared war against humanity.
By ruining Barnwell she avenges herself on all the male sex.
Like certain heroines of the modern drama, like the stranger

[1] *George Barnwell*, Act i. sc. iii. (*Modern British Drama*, vol. ii.).

of Dumas *fils*, she is a blind force, a living enigma, a pest with a symbolic meaning. Her ill-will is directed against society. "I would have my conquest complete, like those of the Spaniards in the new world; who first plundered the natives of all the wealth they had, and then condemned the wretches to the mines for life, to work for more."[1] She is an enemy of law, religion, the clergy, the machinery of justice, and all established order. For you must know that such as these only live by ruined reputations and perverted innocence, "as the inhospitable natives of Cornwall do by shipwrecks."[2] Millwood's strange confession of faith, which ranks her with Ibsen's heroines as a rebel against society, is omitted by the French translator, Clément de Genève, as offensive and out of place. "What are your laws, of which you make your boast, but the fool's wisdom, and the coward's valour, the instrument and screen of all your villanies? By them you punish in others what you act yourselves, or would have acted, had you been in their circumstances. The judge, who condemns the poor man for being a thief, had been a thief himself had he been poor."[3] From a woman such a declaration of war against society was doubtless something fresh; and she, too, was no doubt a new dramatic type—woman as the embodiment of fatality. She glances for one moment at young Barnwell as she meets him in the street, and that one look is enough; thereby she condemns an innocent youth to robbery, murder, and the gallows. If this is not "the despotism of woman incarnate,"[4] what is it?

Observe the rapidity of his fall. From the hour when he yields, the apprentice is a lost man: the next day he commits robbery; the day after, murder. The scene in which the crime is enacted lacks neither vigour nor sombre beauty. It is as simple as a scene in Marlowe's *Faustus*, but from the complicity of the elements it gains a certain savage grandeur which must assuredly have impressed Rousseau. Standing beneath the open sky, and appealing to nature, Barnwell is about to kill the uncle

[1] Act i. sc. ii.
[2] Act iv. sc. ii.
[3] Act iv. sc. ii.
[4] Dumas *fils*, Preface to *L'Étrangère*.

by whom he has been educated and treated as a son, but whom he is nevertheless compelled to rob. And as he slays him, he philosophizes concerning his crime:

Scene : A Walk at some distance from a Country Seat.

BARNWELL (*alone*).—A dismal gloom obscures the face of day. Either the sun has slipped behind a cloud, or journeys down the west of heaven with more than common speed, to avoid the sight of what I am doomed to act. Since I set forth on this accursed design, where'er I tread, methinks the solid earth trembles beneath my feet. Murder my uncle!—Yonder limpid stream, whose hoary fall has made a natural cascade, as I passed by, in doleful accents seemed to murmur—Murder! The earth, the air, and water seemed concerned. But that is not strange: the world is punished, and nature feels a shock, when Providence permits a good man's fall. Just heaven! then what should I feel for him that was my father's only brother, and since his death has been to me a father; that took me up an infant and an orphan, reared me with tenderest care, and still indulged me with most paternal fondness! Yet here I stand his destined murderer—I stiffen with horror at my own impiety.—It is yet unperformed.— What if I quit my bloody purpose, and fly the place? [*Going, then stops.*] But whither, oh, whither shall I fly? My master's once friendly doors are ever shut against me; and without money, Millwood will never see me more; and she has got such firm possession of my heart, and governs there with such despotic sway, that life is not to be endured without her. Ay, there is the cause of all my sin and sorrow! it is more than love, it is the fever of the soul, and madness of desire. . . .

[*His uncle appears, in a walk. Barnwell puts on a vizor, and draws a pistol, unperceived.*

BARNWELL'S UNCLE.—Oh, death! thou strange mysterious power, seen every day, yet never understood, but by the incommunicative dead, what art thou? The extensive mind of man, that with a thought circles the earth's vast globe, sinks to the centre, or ascends above the stars; that worlds exotic finds, or thinks it finds, thy thick clouds attempt to pass in vain; lost, and bewildered in the horrid gloom, defeated, she returns more doubtful than before, of nothing certain but of labour lost.

[*During this speech, Barnwell sometimes presents the pistol, but draws it back again.*
BARNWELL.—Oh! 'tis impossible.

[*Throwing down the pistol. Uncle starts, and attempts to draw his sword.*
UNCLE.—A man so near me! Armed and masked—
BARNWELL.—Nay, then, there's no retreat.

[*Plucks a poignard from his bosom, and stabs him.*
UNCLE.—Oh! I am slain. All gracious Heaven, regard the prayer of thy dying servant! Bless, with thy choicest blessings, my dearest nephew! forgive my murderer, and take my fleeting soul to endless mercy!

[*Barnwell throws off his mask, runs to him, and, kneeling by him, raises and chafes him.*
BARNWELL.—Expiring saint! Oh, murdered martyred uncle! lift up your dying eyes, and view your nephew in your murderer. Oh, do not look so tenderly upon me!—Let indignation lighten from your eyes, and blast me, ere you

die.—By heaven, he weeps, in pity of my woes.—Tears, tears for blood!—The murdered in the agonies of death, weeps for his murderer.—Oh, speak your pious purpose; pronounce my pardon then, and take me with you.—He would, but cannot.—Oh, why, with such fond affection, do you press my murdering hand?—[*Uncle sighs and dies.*]—What, will you kiss me?—Life, that hovered on his lips but till he had sealed my pardon, in that sigh expired.—He is gone for ever, and oh! I follow.—[*Swoons away upon his uncle's dead body.*]

Artless as it is, the scene is full of pathos; a certain lyrical inspiration finds its way into Lillo's awkward yet poetic style, so ill rendered by his translator.

As the drama closes, the gallows is to be seen—in that day a very daring effect, before which the author himself had hesitated. The translator suppressed the scene, but added it afterwards, with an apology for doing so. Pompous in form, this swift and tragic drama nevertheless contains something suggestive of those rude yet powerful old plays *Arden of Feversham* and *A Yorkshire Tragedy*, in which Shakespeare, of whom they are scarcely unworthy, may possibly have had some share. We must regard Lillo as related, not so much to Southerne and Rowe, his immediate predecessors, as to Ford, Dekker, Heywood, and perhaps Shakespeare.[1] The brutal clumsiness of a beginner, the scorn for customary methods of procedure, and the contempt for convention, by which his imitation of these models was supplemented, gave his work the effect of originality.

George Barnwell, which in England was regarded as a common and rather vulgar drama of some merit, produced on the Continent the impression of a work of genius, and gave the theatre a new lease of life. The Germans became as enthusiastic over Lillo as over Shakespeare; Gottsched and Lessing extolled him to the skies, and the latter imitated him in *Sara Sampson*. He became one of the classics of the modern drama.[2] Yet, strange as it may seem, even to the Germans he appeared too brutal, and Sébastien Mercier's *Jenneval*, a modified but inferior adaptation,

---

[1] On these "assize-court dramas," see Mézières, *Prédécesseurs et contemporains de Shakespeare*, and, especially, J. A. Symonds, *Shakespeare's predecessors in the English drama*, p. 418 *et seq.* Observe that Lillo, at his death, left an adaptation of that fine piece, *Arden of Feversham*.

[2] *Cf.* Hettner, *Das moderne Drama*, Brunswick, 1852.

was played in preference. The name of Lillo was none the less famous, and we must turn to W. Schlegel to find the *London Merchant* regarded as a " regular assize-court story, scarcely less absurd than trivial." [1] Many were the tears shed over this " assize-court story," before it was relegated from the tragic stage to the boards of the *foire*.

Prévost, in *Pour et Contre*, led the chorus in praise of the new master-piece in France. " A tragedy which has been acted thirty-eight times consecutively at Drury Lane, amidst unflagging applause from a constantly crowded house ; which has met with similar success wherever it has been performed ; which has been printed and published to the number of many thousand copies, and is read with no less interest and pleasure than it is witnessed upon the stage—a tragedy which has called forth so many marks of approbation and esteem must occasion in those who hear it spoken of one or other of two thoughts : either that it is one of those master-pieces the perfect beauty of which is perceived by all ; or that it is so well adapted to the particular taste of the nation which thus delights in it that it may be considered as a certain indication of the present state of that nation's taste." [2] Of these two explanations Prévost accepted the former. The *London Merchant* was, in his eyes, a master-piece, and in support of his verdict he translated a scene from the play.

A few years later *George Barnwell* found a translator, who was attracted by the warm praise of Prévost. Formerly a minister, and also tutor to the children of Lord Waldegrave, the English ambassador, Clément de Genève [3] was an avowed admirer of England. The writer of a " hyperdrama," *Les Frimaçons*, and for that reason expelled from the society of Genevan pastors, Clément was also the author of a literary journal, no less caustic than spirited, which makes anglomania an article of faith. Therein the French are reproached for their ignorance " of the beauty of the unstudied, the vast, the fantastic, the gloomy, the

[1] W. Schlegel, *Littérature dramatique*, 34th lesson.

[2] *Pour et Contre*, vol. iii., p. 337. Prévost translates the scene in which Mill-wood hands her lover over to justice.

[3] Born at Geneva, 1707, Clément de Genève died at Charenton in 1767. (Senebier, *Histoire littéraire de Genève*.)

terrible," and of romantic beauty in every form. "Come to London," he concludes, "we will enlarge your imagination."[1]— So Clément, who knew English, translated the *London Merchant*, shed tears as he corrected the proofs of his translation, and exclaimed in his preface : " Avaunt, ye small wits, whose quality is not so much delicacy as subtlety and frivolity ; ye thankless, hardened hearts, wrecked by excess and overmuch thinking ! You are not made for the sweetness of shedding tears ! "[2]

A select public yielded to persuasion and, following Clément's advice, " plunged with delight into the deepest and most poignant distress." Lillo seemed more pathetic than Shakespeare, and the *London Merchant* more terrible than the *Merchant of Venice*.[3] The piece, to tell the truth, was an appeal to " the irresponsive and vulgar souls of a barbarous people," but who could resist its pathos ? " Every act, every scene, as the play progresses, excites more pity, more horror, more heart-rending anguish." What art in the employment of contrast ! What a " climax of terror ! "[4] The slanderer Collé, who declared the translator a fool, in the same breath confessed himself moved to tears ; he too exclaimed : " What truth ! What vehemence ! What intensity of interest ! " The workmanship is not good ; but there is " genius in abundance," which covers a multitude of faults.[5] In a *Lettre de Barnevelt* (sic) *dans la prison à Truman, son ami*,[6] Dorat, also, poured out his soul in whining verse. Lillo's drama furnished Mme. de Beaumont with a theme for a novel,[7] Anseaume with the subject of a comedy, and Sébastien Mercier

---

[1] *Les cinq années littéraires*, 15th March 1752.

[2] *Le Marchand de Londres ou l'histoire de George Barnwell, tragédie bourgeoise en cinq actes, traduite de l'anglais de Lillo*, by M . . ., 1748, 12mo, 139 pp. In the edition of 1751, the hanging scene is also included. A further edition was issued in 1767.

[3] *Journal encyclopédique*, 15th June 1768.

[4] *Journal étranger*, February 1760. *Journal encyclopédique*, March 1764.

[5] Collé, *Journal*, ed. H. Bonhomme, vol. i., p. 21.

[6] Paris, 1764. *Cf.* Fréron, *Année littéraire*, 1764, vol. i., and *Journal Encyclopédique*, 1st March 1764.

[7] *Lettres du marquis de Roselle*.

with the idea for a drama.[1] For a moment the *Comédie* thought
of producing this remarkable work, but finally recoiled before its
English uncouthness.[2] The play was said to have touched even
Voltaire, but it appealed to Diderot most of all. He believed
he had at last discovered the long-sought dramatic masterpiece.
" Call the *London Merchant* what you will, so long as you admit
that the play scintillates with flashes of beauty and splendour." [3]
Throughout his life he meditated publishing an annotated edition
of the work, together with one of the *Gamester*.[4]

Was it Diderot who introduced it to the notice of Rousseau,
or Clément de Genève, his fellow-countryman, or Prévost, his
friend ? It does not signify. The important point is that he
shared the admiration of all his circle. " An admirable piece of
work," we read in a note to the *Lettre sur les spectacles*, " with a
moral which goes more straight to the point than that of any
French play I am acquainted with." [5] The man who thought it
needful to teach the young " to distrust the illusions of love," and
" to beware at times of surrendering a virtuous heart to an object
unworthy of its solicitude," confessed that nowhere but in Lillo,
except in the *Misanthrope*, had he found that which corresponded
to this ideal.

The testimony is brief but significant, and justifies the stress
I have laid upon a drama which excited the fervent admiration of
Rousseau and of his time.

But neither Addison, nor Defoe, nor Lillo himself, well worth
attention as he considered them to be, fully realised his own ideal
of *bourgeois* literature ; and the author of the *Nouvelle Héloïse*, who,
after all, was rather a novelist than a dramatist, could only feel
at home, if I may say so, in English fiction.

[1] *L'école de la jeunesse ou le Barnevelt français*, a comedy in verse in three acts by
M. Anseaume, played at the *Italiens*, 24th January 1765. *Jenneval ou le Barnevelt
français*, Paris, 1769, 8vo. A singular fact is that Mercier, though an uncompromising reformer of the drama, did not dare to kill his Jenneval, but married
him to the daughter of the man he had robbed.

[2] " *L'ostrogothie anglaise.*" [3] Article *Encyclopédie.*

[4] To Mlle. Voland, vol. ii., p. 87 and p. 140.

[5] This note does not occur in the first edition, but was printed in the edition of
1781.

Chapter III

I

OF all the creations of English literature during the eighteenth century, the most original was certainly the novel of middle-class manners, or, as Taine calls it, the *roman antiromanesque*. Very few revolutions in European literature can be compared to that effected at this period by Defoe, Richardson and Fielding, whose positive and observant minds led them boldly to substitute the accurate study of contemporary society for narratives of adventure of the French or Spanish type. And, assuredly, very few have had such far-reaching consequences. It is not too much to say, of this " austere middle-class thought," that as it developed it produced the effect of " the voice of a nation buried beneath the earth."[1] This voice was heard in every country. In Germany, in France, in the northern countries, and even in Italy, the English novel gave the impression of work which was entirely fresh, similar to nothing else, untrammelled in its glorious flight by any classic models, and absolutely free from any taint of traditional influence. The Harlowes and the Joneses seemed to usurp in the wearied imagination of mankind the place held

[1] Taine, *Littérature anglaise*, vol. iv., p. 84.

142

for centuries by the heroes of Greece and Italy, or by the knights-errant of epic poetry. The novel—a form of literature almost unknown to the ancients—became with the English the epic of the modern world.

"They are the first," says Mme. de Staël with justice, "who have ventured to believe that a representation of the private affections is enough to interest the human mind and heart ; that neither celebrated characters nor marvellous events are necessary in order to captivate the imagination, and that in the power of love there is that which can renew scenes and situations without limit, and without ever blunting the edge of curiosity. And it is in the hands of the English also that the novel has become a work with a moral purpose, wherein obscure virtues and humble destinies may discover motives to moral enthusiasm, and may invent a form of heroism of their own."[1] Fiction, a type of literature previously regarded as inferior, was thereby revolutionized. Thereby also, the English became the models of every novelist now wielding a pen. "Where shall we find the progenitors of our own novels," said Goethe to Eckermann, "if not in Goldsmith and Fielding ? " In truth the English novelists rendered this frivolous branch of literature capable of conveying ideas and passions ; they shewed that, instead of being, in the words of Voltaire, "the work of feeble-minded creatures whose facile productions are unworthy the attention of serious people," it was something better ; and from the humble position in which it had languished they raised it to the highest level of all, from which it has never again descended.

Thereby also, unintentionally no doubt, and perhaps unconsciously, they dealt an effective blow at the long domination of classical literature. Here was a fresh arrival, entirely apart from all recognized modes, from those classified by Boileau—from those which a writer of consequence could cultivate without prejudice to his reputation or loss of prestige—springing up in a single day, or at any rate quite suddenly elevated to such high honour, and at a single step assuming in men's minds the position hitherto claimed by dramatic literature alone, or by poetry of

[1] *De la littérature*, i. 15.

the highest order. In works of this description the modern man recognized himself, not under ancient features, or beneath the form of a type which was conventional simply by reason of its generality, but with his faults, his vices, his absurdities, and his passing fancies—everything in short which *dates* a portrait. *Bourgeois* literature, that is to say nearly all the literature of modern times, has its root in the English novel.

Of the two greatest novelists of the eighteenth century, excluding Defoe, one, Fielding, was a man of cultivated mind, was an ardent admirer of antiquity, and had been educated at Eton, where, however, the process of classical training had not destroyed his vigorous native originality. The other, the son of a carpenter named Richardson, was devoid of literary culture, or possessed at any rate no more than a smattering which he had acquired himself,—just enough to enable him to play the pedant if necessary. "A self-made man," and too thoroughly Christian to appreciate the beauty of pagan works, he was also too thorough an Englishman—and an Englishman of the people— to feel that desire for refinement which classical culture bestows. Both were, in their own line, great innovators, and, though rivals, laboured at the same task.[1] Both proved the truth of Montesquieu's saying concerning the English : "They admire the ancients, but will not even imitate them."[2] Thanks to them, and to a few less brilliant lights, the English novel, freed at last from the ancient domination of heroic fiction,[3] shed abroad an incomparable lustre.

In the first place there was the group of works consisting of *Pamela* (1740), its parody *Joseph Andrews* (1742)—the first of Fielding's novels—and *Jonathan Wild*, his second; the earliest specimens of an art as yet imperfect and uncertain. Then— after five years' silence—the series of master-pieces was in-

---

[1] Fielding was eighteen years younger than Richardson, and always spoke of him with deference. He was loud in praise of his "profound knowledge of human nature" and his "command of pathos." Richardson did not do equal justice to Fielding (Barbauld, vol. v., p. 275).

[2] *Pensées diverses.*

[3] On the prolonged popularity of the French novel in England, see Beljame, p. 14 *et seq*, and J. Jusserand, *The English Novel*, ch. vii.

augurated by the famous *Clarissa* (1748). One after the other came Smollett's *Roderick Random* (1748) and *Peregrine Pickle* (1751), reviving the picaresque tradition; Fielding's masterpiece *Tom Jones* (1749), and shortly afterwards that delightful novel *Amelia* (1751); the series coming to an end in 1754 with *Sir Charles Grandison*, the last of the three novels of Richardson. The same year witnessed the death of Fielding, that of Richardson occurring seven years later.

Next we have a fresh generation of novelists taking up and carrying on the work of the masters : Sterne, who in 1759 made his first appearance with the first part of *Tristram Shandy*; Goldsmith, who produced the *Vicar of Wakefield* in 1766; while Smollett, five years later, reappeared with *Humphrey Clinker*. Then it seemed as though the genius of English fiction was reduced to silence for half a century, a silence broken only by the sentimental works of Miss Burney and Henry Mackenzie, and lasting until 1811, when the first of Miss Austen's novels—followed shortly afterwards by *Waverley*—ushered in a new era.

The success these various novelists met with beyond the limits of their own country was very diverse.

Smollett was too essentially English to be generally understood. Goldsmith, more popular in Germany than in France, found the way to many hearts, but was not regarded as a very great writer. Fielding, the most original of all, attained celebrity, but in France, at any rate, was not understood; in Germany his name was associated with that of Richardson. He was imitated by Wieland, for whom he had a great fascination; Musæus also copied him, and free-thinkers triumphantly contrasted him with Richardson the preacher.[1] In France his name was in every mouth, but the full significance of his work was not perceived. Some took him for a coarse and trivial exponent of the " picaresque " school, others for a disciple of the author of *Clarissa*, to whom, however, he bears very little resemblance.

---

[1] See Mr. Erich Schmidt's book : *Richardson, Rousseau und Goethe*, Jena, 1875, 8vo, p. 68 *et seq.*

K

Who was to blame for this ? In the first place the translators, Desfontaines and La Place, who defaced and burlesqued him. Who could have recognised in the crude version of La Place the novel of which Stendhal said that it was to other novels what the *Iliad* is to other epics ?[1] It is impossible, without close examination, to credit the extent to which the translator of *Tom Jones* has misrepresented his author.[2] In the next place, Fielding seemed too exclusively English; it was remarked that Richardson's novels, which were less national, were on that account more interesting to readers of all nationalities.[3] Lastly, and this is the main reason, Fielding, like Smollett, with whom, indeed, he was confused, appeared too " picaresque." France had had enough of her Lesage, the very writer whose "infinite humour and sagacity" attracted Smollett's praise. Why then should she have accepted his imitators, or those whom she regarded as such? " The talent of these men consists in the fidelity with which they report the jests and gossip of the lower classes."[4] What do we find in their books? " Tavern-scenes, brawls on the high road, innumerable assaults with fist or stick " — fine subjects forsooth![5] In truth it was scarcely to be expected that readers of *Cléveland* and *Marianne* would appreciate the scene in which a certain rude fellow pulled away good Parson Adams' chair just as he was going to sit down, while another tipped a plateful of soup over his

---

[1] *Mémoires d'un touriste*, vol. i., p. 39.

[2] See *Les Aventures de Joseph Andrews et du ministre Abraham Adams*, translated into French [by Desfontaines], London, 1743, 2 vols. 12mo, frequently reprinted; *Histoire de Jonathan Wild le Grand*, translated from the English of Mr Fielding, London and Paris, 1763, 2 vols. 12mo [this translation is by Charles Picquet]; *Amélie, histoire anglaise*, a free translation from the English [by De Puisieux], Paris, 1762, 4 vols. 12mo; the same work was also adapted by Mme. Riccoboni; *Histoire de Tom Jones ou l'Enfant trouvé*, translated from the English by M. D. L. P. [de la Place], London (Paris), 1750, 4 vols. 12mo. The following works have also been attributed to Fielding : *Mémoires du chevalier de Kilpar* (Paris, 1768, 2 vols. 12mo), really by Montagnac; *Les malheurs du sentiment* (1789, 12mo); *Julien l'Apostat* (1765, 12mo), &c. These frauds prove at any rate the popularity of Fielding's name.

[3] *Journal étranger*, February 1760.

[4] *Correspondance littéraire*, September 1761.

[5] *Lettres sur quelques écrits de ce temps*, vol. x., p. 226.

breeches, and as if this were not enough, a third tied a cracker to his cassock, and a fourth adroitly placed behind him a tub of water, in which he could not help taking a bath. A scene like this simply carries us back to Furetière or Scarron.

This, however, was the least important side of Fielding's robust genius. The other side, the valiant and healthy realism of a great and candid mind, was not appreciated. *Tom Jones* was turned into comic-operas and comedies: Poinsinet made a laughable vaudeville out of it, and Desforges more than one pathetic play.[1] But Fréron could not forgive its "low comedy,"[2] and Voltaire declares that he could see nothing even passable in it, except the story of a barber.[3] In vain Mme. du Deffand praised "the true lessons in morality" and the "infinite truth"[4] it conveyed; in vain La Harpe wrote bravely: "For me the first novel in the whole world is *Tom Jones.*" The general public did not perceive its importance. It praised its "truth and joviality,"[5] and pronounced it sometimes "agreeable" and sometimes "sublime," but did not understand it. Its simple, unsentimental moralizing no longer satisfied an audience familiar with *Clarissa*, and Fielding possessed the defect of lacking sensibility. Was it not he who apostrophised Love in this irreverent fashion: "O love! what monstrous tricks dost thou play with thy votaries of both sexes! . . . Thou puttest out our eyes, stoppest up our ears, and takest away the power of our nostrils. . . . When thou pleasest, thou canst make a mole-hill appear as a mountain,

---

[1] Poinsinet's *Tom Jones* was played at the Comédie Italienne on the 27th February 1765, with music by Philidor (*cf. Journal encyclopédique*, 15th April 1765). Desforges produced his *Tom Jones à Londres*, five acts in verse, at the Italiens, on the 22nd October 1782, and his *Fellamar et Tom Jones*, at the same theatre, on the 17th April 1787. (*Cf. Correspondance littéraire*, November 1782 and May 1787.)

[2] *Lettres sur quelques écrits*, 1751, vol. v., p. 3.

[3] To Mme. du Deffand, 13th October 1759.

[4] 14th July and 8th August 1773, to Walpole.

[5] An article by Voltaire in the *Gazette littéraire*, May 1764. *Cf.* Clément, *Les cinq années littéraires*, vol. ii., p. 56 *et seq*; Horace Walpole, *Letters to Mme. du Deffand*; Geoffroy, *Cours de littérature dramatique*, vol. iii., p. 262.

a Jew's harp sound like a trumpet, and a daisy smell like a violet. . . . In short, thou turnest the heart of man inside out, as a juggler doth a petticoat."[1] The heart of the reader of Jean-Jacques declined to be taken for a juggler's " petticoat."

The fame of Richardson, on the other hand, was spreading throughout the length and breadth of Europe, and carrying the reputation of English fiction into every country.   In Holland he was translated by Pastor Stinstra.   In Italy *Pamela* was dramatised by Goldoni.[2]   But it was in Germany, above all, that his works obtained unprecedented favour: as a German critic has remarked, Richardson belongs just as much to German as to English literature, and so profound has been his influence that his genius has become incorporated with the very fabric of Germanic fiction.[3] The *Discourse der Mahlern* were fascinated by *Pamela*, from the very first appearance of that pious tale; *Pamela* and *Grandison* were translated by Gellert, who also copied their author in his *Leben der schwedischen Gräfin*;[4] Klopstock went into raptures over Clarissa, and applied for permission to leave Copenhagen in the hope of being appointed Danish *chargé d'affaires* in London, his sole object being that of living with or near Richardson; and failing to achieve his object, he sought consolation in corresponding with him and in writing an ode on the death of Clarissa.   Some idea of the pitch which enthusiasm had reached in Klopstock's circle may be obtained from the following note written by his wife to the author of *Grandison*: "Having finished your Clarissa (Oh! the heavenly

---

[1] *Joseph Andrews*, bk. i., ch. vii.

[2] See the *Journal étranger*, February 1755. The play was translated: *Paméla*, a prose comedy by Charles Goldoni, advocate, of Venice; performed at Mantua in 1750; translated into French by D. B. D. V. [de Bonnel de Valguier], Paris, 1759, 8vo.

[3] See Erich Schmidt: *Richardson, Rousseau und Goethe*, which gives a number of details in reference to this subject; and an article in the *Zeitschrift für vergleichende Literaturgeschichte*, new series, Berlin, 1887-88, vol. i., p. 217 *et seq*.

[4] *Das Leben der schwedischen Gräfin von G . . .*, 1746, translated by Formey under the title *La comtesse suédoise ou Mémoires de Mme. de G . . .*, Berlin, 1754, two parts, 8vo.

book !), I would have pray'd you to write the history of a *manly* Clarissa, but I had not courage enough at that time. . . . You have since written the manly Clarissa, without my prayer; oh, you have done it, to the great joy and thanks of all your happy readers ! Now you can write no more, you must write the history of an Angel." [1] Wieland read and re-read *Clarissa*, contemplated writing some letters from Grandison to his pupil, and composed a drama called *Clementina von Porretta*. Lessing proclaimed Richardson the creator of middle-class literature, and drew from him the inspiration for his own plays. Imitations and panegyrics were alike innumerable. Futile were the protests of a more dispassionate critic against what he called the *furor anglicanus* : he himself, when it came to the point, ranked Lovelace among the heroes, together with Alexander, Charles XII., Richelieu and Masaniello. [2] In vain did Musæus write his *Grandison II.*, a gentle satire on Richardson, wherein he ridiculed the deluge of angelic creatures which had burst over his country like a water-spout. In vain did Wieland, after reading Fielding, renounce his blind admiration for Fielding's rival. In vain did the free-thinking party point in triumph to the robust author of Joseph Andrews as the superior of the pious and finikin eulogist of Pamela. The charm of Richardson's heroines proved the stronger. Numbers of travellers in England went to visit Hampstead and the Flask Walk, just as others at a later period made the pilgrimage to Clarens. One of them, in a transport of enthusiasm, kissed the great man's bench and inkstand. [3]

In the opinion of one of his worshippers, Richardson takes rank with the first of Greek poets. " This is that creative soul, who, through his deeply instructive works, renders us sensitive to the charm of virtue, and whose Grandison wrings from the heart of the vilest his first yearnings after righteousness. The works he has created shall not suffer from the ravages of time. They are very nature, true taste, and religion itself. More

[1] See Mrs Barbauld, vol. iii., pp. 139-159.
[2] Knigge, *Die Verwirrungen des Philosophen.*
[3] Mrs Barbauld, vol. i., p. clxv.

immortal than the immortality of Homer is the fame among Christians of the Englishman Richardson." [1]

II

Such, too, was the opinion, or rather the feeling of the French public, when once it had become acquainted with *Clarissa Harlowe.*

The main thing to be observed here is that in comparison with English novels *Gil Blas*, *La Vie de Marianne*, and *Cléveland* appeared to the French equally insipid.   Since then, Lesage, Marivaux and Prévost have been restored to their rightful place.   In one has been seen the master of Fielding and Smollett, in another the predecessor of Richardson, while all have been recognized as emulators and rivals of the English novelists.   But their contemporaries were far from placing them in the same rank—and nothing affords a more striking proof of the progress of English influence.   For anglomania had very soon ceased to be regarded as a passing fashion of no special significance : Richardson's success was European, and it is unreasonable to suppose that minds like those of Diderot, Rousseau, Goethe, André Chénier, and Mme. de Staël were merely the dupes of a feverish and absurd infatuation.   And if these writers were unanimous in placing *Clarissa* and *Grandison* far above *Gil Blas* and the *Paysan Parvenu*, is not that a sign of a profound alteration in the public disposition ?   Does it not also show that they found in the English novelist something which neither Lesage

---

[1] Gellert, *Ueber Richardson's Bildniss :—*

Dies ist der schöpferische Geist,
Der uns durch lehrende Gedichte
Den Reiz der Tugend fühlen heisst,
Der durch den Grandison selbst einem Bösewichte
Den ersten Wunsch, auch fromm zu sein, entreisst.
Die Werke, die er schuf, wird keine Zeit verwüsten,
Sie sind Natur, Geschmack, Religion.
Unsterblich ist Homer, unsterblicher bei Christen
Der Britte Richardson.

nor Prévost nor Crébillon *fils* had as yet given them? To ask the reason for this contempt is to ask why Richardson, and Rousseau after him, met with such success in France.

As concerns Lesage, readers were no longer satisfied either with the form of his novels, with the kind of characters he affected, or with the moral of his work. Not only did he follow Spanish models,—from which opinion now turned with aversion,—but he still held to the artificial form of the novel "in episodes," which renders the story a mere series of disconnected adventures, quite incompatible with the coherent analysis of a single character—except perhaps in the case of the character of Gil Blas. Undoubtedly Lesage comes very near to being a great writer, as much in virtue of the perspicuity of his observation as of the charm of a supple and witty style. But at bottom he belongs distinctly to the "picaresque" school; in other words, he is a writer of comedy. The contemporaries of Richardson and Rousseau refused to regard *Gil Blas* as anything else than a humorous novel. They thought with Joubert that the book must be the work of a man who plays dominoes and does his writing after leaving the theatre. Their eyes were closed to that description of middle-class life, and that painstaking study of a certain social atmosphere which we do not hesitate to admire. It was a witty work, they thought, but lacking any deep meaning. They would have been amazed at any attempt to extract a moral or a "conception of life" from such a tissue of roguery and double-dealing. The central character, who is by turns brigand, lackey, physician, and agent or secretary to a minister, is certainly an amusing creation, but is rather too much of an epitome to be quite true. Not only is there a superabundance of crude romance, robbers' caves, captive beauties, disguises, and unexpected encounters, but this world of thieves and sharpers is a very monotonous one. The souls here revealed—if the characters have any—are essentially those of profligates, brawlers, and petty rhymesters. The picture is a vulgar one, because it was drawn from vulgar models.

Above all there is nothing *bourgeois* about it ; the world of Gil Blas is the *demi-monde* ; its heroes all have more or less of a gallows-bird air ; beneath their embroidered clothes and under the lace of their brilliant doublets a fragment of halter hangs round their necks. A world of adventurers and blacklegs, starveling barbers and medical assassins, unscrupulous priests and shameless parsons—could this be the commonplace world of middle-class life, the world of mild virtues and moderate vices, of which after all the age was awaiting the representation ? I am afraid that the society frequented by Gil Blas is as remote from it as is the world of fashion inhabited by Marianne and Artamène. Between the heroic and the picaresque types of fiction, the average humanity to which I belong, and of which I seek the representation, still remained undiscovered, a humanity doubtless very different from the society described by Lesage, which is decidedly lower and more shameless than the generality of mankind.

The best proof is that among those with whom Gil Blas associated love was unknown. The author even seems to take a mischievous delight in belittling love. One of his characters[1] calls it "a malady to which we are subject just as animals are to madness." Even when it is not positively grotesque, love, as here represented, has something laughable and ridiculous about it. It is derangement, or sickness, but not passion in the higher sense of the word. Lesage's women, when they are enamoured, are either adventuresses who love from interest, or women of the town who love with the senses only—unless they happen to be princesses who love to distraction, and because that is the part they are cast for. Too often they are *bourgeoises* with a passion for barbers' assistants, such as Mergeline had for Diego. Love of this type never soars to any empyrean. As the lover who has been breathing a serenade beneath some grated window leaves his post, he finds himself capped at the next corner "with a perfuming pan which by no means gratifies his sense of smell." The madrigal ends in a burlesque adventure and the dawning romance in coarse satire.

[1] Book ii., ch. vii.

Hence it follows that since Lesage only studied the lowest and most superficial of the feelings which go to make up human nature, and deliberately turned aside from those which are at once the noblest and most profound, the moral he conveys is merely trite and commonplace. In vain shall we seek beneath the stone the soul of Pedro Garcias, the licentiate : all we shall find is a bag of money. Such a moral is purely negative ; what it teaches is the art of buttoning up one's pockets and stowing away one's pocket-book. We close the last of these four volumes fully convinced that the world contains many different varieties of cut-purse. But seek the least information in reply to the hundred and one problems of. every-day life and of man's inward experience which hourly suggest themselves—and you will find nothing but an arid waste of satire. It is impossible to be more completely detached from love, from family life, from the thought of death, than Lesage. In truth, fiction in this form is as yet nothing more than a means of gratifying the imagination, which likes to keep to the highway and deal with what it can find ; it is not in any degree a revelation of the soul ; its ambition is mean and un-aspiring. And this was what was felt by the contemporaries of Lesage. Desfontaines praised him for the "ingenuity" of his novels ; Voltaire, in the *Siècle de Louis XV.*, coldly congratulated him on his "naturalness" ; Marmontel, who classed him as a satirist, reproached him for his limited knowledge of the world. The majority, with much justice, praised the ease and purity of his style.[1] As Sainte-Beuve remarked, Lesage was but sparingly praised by the critics, even after he had been writing for a quarter of a century. How are we to account for this ? By the fact that he no longer satisfied the needs of the age. His work did not appear sufficiently serious. To the reader of English novels it seemed to be simply the dramatic work of Regnard divided up into chapters.

To Prévost, opinion has been more indulgent. Of all the novelists of the eighteenth century his name has been most fre-

[1] See Sainte-Beuve's curious article, *Jugements et témoignages sur Le Sage* (*Causeries*, volume containing list of contents). Observe that Lesage had no literary influence whatever. He had not a single disciple (Lintilhac, *Lesage*, p. 189).

quently associated with those of English writers—not only because he translated them, but because he was regarded as the
only one worthy to be compared with them.   To begin with, in
contrast to Lesage, he is always serious, and even gloomy.   His
biographer praises him for having brought the terrors of tragedy
within the scope of fiction.[1]   The encomium was but too well
merited.   In the next place, he lacks artistic skill—no bad recommendation from the reader's point of view, in 1750 or thereabouts.   Lastly, he is as full of passion and feeling as could be
desired.   Many a reader must have been able to say with Jean-
Jacques :   " The reading of Cléveland's imaginary misfortunes
had, I think, made me create more bad blood than have my own
troubles." [2]

Prévost's art, on the other hand, except in *Manon Lescaut*, is
inferior.   He is unable either " to keep to his design, or to regulate his progress." [3]   He accumulates episodes and incidents,
in volume after volume, without ever creating a firm connection
between the heterogeneous parts of his narrative by means of the
unity of his characters.   In short, he wrote too quickly ; to quote
the words of a contemporary, he was " content with a rapid success, and never, either in good or evil fortune, had any other
object than to be read with avidity, and by the multitude." [4]

What was worse, he was so simple as to acknowledge the fact.
How can a man be taken seriously when he writes thus concerning his own works :   " The *Mémoires d'un homme de qualité* and
their sequel, *Cléveland* and the *Doyen de Killerine* are entirely *useless
for historical purposes ; their sole merit lies in the fact that they afford
a suitable and amusing piece of reading.*" [5]   This unpretentiousness
disarms criticism, it is true, but admiration, forestalled by so ingenuous a confession, is weakened by it.   For all his ability,
Prévost has no ambition beyond that of being " interesting " and
" pathetic " :   " he appears to have forgotten that the object of
the novel is the reformation of conduct," [6]—and at certain periods

---

[1] *Essai sur la vie de Prévost*, introductory to the *Œuvres choisies*.   This point has
been developed by M. Brunetière in his study on Prévost.

[2] *Confessions*, i. 5.   [3] La Harpe, *Cours de littérature*, vol. iii., p. 186.

[4] Marmontel, *Essai sur les romans*.   [5] *Pour et Contre*, vol. vi., p. 353.

[6] Marmontel, *ibid.*

it is an inexcusable fault to be simply a novelist and nothing more. The success of Richardson, as also of Rousseau, was due to the fact that both were moralists, educators, spiritual directors in the first place,—and novelists only in the second. Prévost, excellent man, reforms nothing, not even the novel. Until he read Richardson, he still held the same conception of fiction as the author of *Cassandre* and *Cléopâtre*—capital books, he called them, and very much maligned. Let us be faithful, thought Prévost, to our father's love for gallantry and romance : " If we try to draw men as they are, we make their faults appear too attractive, . . . whereas in romantic fiction nothing is called virtue unless it deserves to be." [1]

But when he came to read *Pamela* and *Clarissa* he changed his mind, and, with equal frankness, placed English novels above the romances whose ascendancy they had destroyed. When translating *Clarissa Harlowe* he wrote : " I begin by a confession which ought to do some credit to my honesty because it might do little honour to my discernment. Of all the imaginative works I have read, and my self-conceit does not lead me to except my own, none have given me greater pleasure than the one now submitted to the public." [2] Sheltering himself therefore in this manner behind the English, from that day forward he strove to walk in their footsteps. [3] In truth it would have been discourteous to protest, and the public was careful not to do so.

Of all the French novelists of the eighteenth century, Marivaux is the one who bears most resemblance to the English ; he has the best claim to be regarded as their predecessor, if not their master.

He was the introducer of a simpler form in fiction, one less loaded with worn-out ornaments. He discarded the low adventures in which Lesage delighted, and the easy style of romance which Prévost handled with such success. He deliberately set himself to depict the soul of average humanity in his own day,

[1] *Mémoires d'un homme de qualité*, vol. i., p. 406.
[2] Preface to the French version of *Clarissa*.
[3] Compare with *Clarissa* the *Mémoires pour servir à l'histoire de la vertu*, in Prévost's translation.

" the heart, not of the puppet of an author's fancy, but of a man and a Frenchman, one who has actually existed in our own times."[1] He aimed at being the Chardin of lower middle-class life. Now that he has received so much and such warm commendation, it is needless to show that, before ever Fielding or Richardson did so, Marivaux contrived to enrich the art of fiction with those imperceptible touches which resemble the strokes of a miniature painter; that like them he is tedious and prolix ; that, like them, he reduces action to a minimum and puts " the metaphysics of the heart " in the foreground ;[2] that he preaches and moralizes as they do, and that he is sensitive and even sensual as they are. Like them, above all, he has the true realist's consciousness of the complexity of his models, and his anxiety to reveal them in all the richness and variability of their nature. " No one," as he says, " can present people altogether as they are,"[3] and " the human soul has many more modes of behaviour than we have words wherewith to describe them."[4] This almost morbid desire to be true and to be modern renders Marivaux unique in his generation.

In spite of these conspicuous merits, Marivaux's greatness as a novelist has only become apparent in our own day. What stood in his way at first was his idleness. Who could feel any interest in novels which were never completed by their author, which were in a manner interwoven one with another, and of which the chapters led to no issue and took, as in the case of *La Vie de Marianne*, ten whole years to appear ?[5] *Pamela* was already

[1] *Vie de Marianne*, 8th part.

[2] The similarity was detected by his contemporaries: "If any of our writers could be suspected of understanding them, we should be tempted to believe that it is from them [the English] that they have learnt to use the most extraordinary words as ordinary expressions, to be extremely subtle in dealing with the feelings of the heart, to attribute imperceptible differences to all its impulses, and to compose from all this a jargon almost as metaphysical and quite as incomprehensible as that of the schools." (Du Resnel, *Les principes de la morale et du goût*, 1737, p. xxiii.)

[3] *Marianne*, 4th part.

[4] *Paysan parvenu*, 5th part. *Cf.* in the 3rd part of the same novel: "Can any-one describe all his feelings? Those who think they can are devoid of feeling, and apparently only see half of what there is to be seen."

[5] 1731-1741.

translated before *Marianne* was completed. May it not have
been the dazzling success of the English novel that discouraged
Marivaux from finishing his own ?

Again, Marivaux, charming writer as he is, makes what is a
serious error for a painter of every-day life; he writes too well,
and never loses his self-consciousness. His subtle mind is for
ever mocking at itself, and that such a master of delightful
chatter should have aimed at being the artist of the masses is
simply paradoxical. He lacks both the robust coarseness of
Fielding and the fearless prolixity of Richardson. How could
he paint a picture of contemporary manners with the bold strokes
of a vigorous brush, when he could also indulge in affectation
of this sort : " I must have a little leisure in order to come
to an understanding with my heart ; I find it disputatious,
and to-day I shall try to break it in to hard work." [1]   No
wonder Desfontaines wrote : " What a tissue of insipidity and
emptiness is *La Vie de Marianne* ! " [2]—La Harpe : " Everything
is portrayed with a sincerity of language which is intended to
appear simple, but only betrays artifice " ; [3]—Marmontel : " He
scarcely ever allows himself a chance to use a vigorous,
masculine touch ; he is the Girardon of fiction " ; [4]—and Buffon,
in regard to *Marianne* : " The small-minded, and those who
are fond of affectation, will admire both thought and style." [5]
That is exactly the verdict of the age, and it is well to
recall it. Because his work was too highly finished, too
polished in form, because he had too much wit for a period
that would have nothing but genius, Marivaux did not acquire
a reputation at all equal to his merits. Richardson was admired
by his contemporaries because he wrote badly. Where Marivaux
failed was in not writing worse.

Lastly, for the very reasons that he wrote too well and that
his perceptions were too subtle, his pictures, which were merely
true, appeared trivial. The contrast between the choice of

---

[1] *Paysan parvenu*, part i.
[2] Translation of *Joseph Andrews*, vol. ii., p. 326.
[3] *Cours de littérature*, vol. iii., p. 186.
[4] *Essai sur les romans*.   [5] Letter to President Bouhier, 8th February 1739.

models and the method of treatment caused offence. What
he gives us is a very nice imitation of a vulgar reality. To
quote a highly appropriate metaphor of Sainte-Beuve's, he
paints masquers and grotesque figures on porcelain ; hence a
certain annoying effect not unlike that of glazing, which " makes
everything glitter as we read." [1]   This also explains why contemporary writers ˙bitterly reproached him for the very quality
which they praised in English novelists—the audacity of some of
his descriptions.[2]   It seems strange to find the future translator
of *Pamela* blaming Marivaux for the scene with the coachman
which we admire so much to-day, or condemning the description of Mme. Dufour's shop as " unworthy of a well-bred man,
and most disgusting in a printed book." [3]   A few years, and " disgusting " features were to be the making of Richardson's reputation.   English writers would have had to supply very much
bolder and more uncompromising models before Frenchmen
could endure the realism of Marivaux without being shocked.[4]

For all these reasons, Marivaux was not, in his own day,
estimated at his true worth as a novelist.   His place, Sainte-
Beuve has justly said, was at that time merely beside and a
little above Crébillon *fils*.

England and Germany treated him with greater justice.   " Of
all French authors," wrote Diderot, " M. de Marivaux is the one
whom the English like the best," [5] and Gray declared that he
desired no other paradise than to read the novels of Marivaux
and Crébillon *fils* for ever and ever.[6]   Foreigners appreciated his
concern for the moral, his application of a subtle analysis to
cases of conscience, his respect for honesty and his affectation of
sensibility.   In translation, Marivaux loses some of his preciosity,

[1] *Causeries*, vol. ix., p. 358.   [2] G. Larroumet, *Marivaux*, p. 334.
[3] *Pour et Contre*, vol. ii., p. 346.
[4] It is amusing to find that the first English novels were considered vulgar in
comparison with Spanish fiction of the picaresque school: " The characters of
people of humble station in England," said Desfontaines, " are not interesting,
but the strapping girls, the muleteers, the shepherds and the goatherds of
Spain are delightful." (*Observations sur les écrits modernes*, vol. xxxiii., p. 313.)
[5] *Lettre sur les aveugles*, ed. Tourneux, vol. i., p. 301.
[6] Gray's *Works*, ed. Gosse, vol. ii., p. 107.

his form is less prejudicial to the real soundness of his matter ; so
that there has been found an English reader who could pronounce
Marianne, in an English version, the finest novel in the world.[1]

Must we go a step further ? Are we to reckon Richardson
as one of those who read him and derived inspiration from him,
and did *Marianne* suggest *Pamela* ? Such was the general opinion
in the eighteenth century. Diderot maintains it,[2] and Mme. Du
Boccage wrote from England in 1750 : " When dining with
people of literary taste, we did not fail to praise the clever
authors of *Tom Jones* and *Clarissa*. I was asked for news of the
creator of *Marianne* and the *Paysan parvenu, which has possibly
been the model for these new stories.*"[3] On the appearance of
Clarissa, English journals compared the author to Marivaux.[4]

In spite of this tradition—generally adopted by critics [5]—it
seems to me doubtful whether Richardson imitated the author of
Marianne. It is not certain that Marivaux's novel had been
translated into English when he wrote *Pamela*, and it is well
known that Richardson was absolutely ignorant of French. So
far, therefore, as this argument is concerned, the supposed
influence of *Marianne* upon *Pamela* is, to say the least, doubtful.[6]
May not Richardson, nevertheless, have had *Marianne* in mind
when he wrote *Clarissa* ? But in his *Postscriptum* he quotes and
appears to endorse the verdict of a French critic, who declares
that " Marivaux's novels are absolutely improbable." This

[1] Macaulay's opinion.

[2] " *Pamela, Clarissa* and *Grandison* were inspired by the novels of M. de Marivaux." (Rough draft of a preface, ed. Tourneux, vol. v., p. 434.)

[3] Larroumet, p. 348.

[4] *Gentleman's Magazine* (June 1749, vol. xix., p. 245). Observe, however, that
the article is a translation from the French.

[5] M. Larroumet writes : " It is evident that Richardson took both the idea and
the principal character of *Pamela* from *Marianne*."

[6] From M. Jusserand I hear of *The Life of Marianne, or the adventures of the
Countess of . . .*, by M. de Marivaux, translated from the French, the second
edition revised and corrected, London, Charles Davis, 1743, 12mo, vol. ii. The
edition to which this volume belongs is therefore a reprint. What is the date of
the first edition ? If Richardson made use of the work, it must have been 1738
or 1739. There is also another and much later English version : *The Virtuous
Orphan, or the Life of Marianne, Countess of . . .*, London, 1784, 4 vols. 8vo. No
mention is made of the above-mentioned edition.

consideration is of great importance. Throughout his copious correspondence the English novelist makes no mention of his supposed model. Moreover, *Clarissa* has practically nothing in common with *Marianne*, nor has *Pamela*, whatever may be said to the contrary. Reperuse the two books as we will, we detect nothing but disparity ; Marianne, the accomplished and sprightly coquette, is totally different from the humble and simple Pamela ; the story of one bears scarcely the least resemblance to that of the other ; and lastly, Richardson, as we need hardly repeat, is just as careless with regard to art as Marivaux is over-careful. It appears, therefore, that the debt of one towards the other, if it exists at all, is insignificant.[1] In the history of European literature Marivaux anticipated Richardson, but it does not appear that we can regard him as his master.[2]

However this may be, native fiction in France was quite eclipsed by the splendour of the art supposed to be imitated from it : " If it is true," said Grimm, " that Marivaux's novels have served Richardson and Fielding as models, it may be said that for the first time a poor original has given rise to admirable copies." The fame of the " master " never equalled that of the disciple, and, if Richardson was to find rivals and competitors in France, the author of *Marianne* was not among them.

III

While the fame of Lesage and Marivaux was increasing in England, English fiction was, as La Harpe says, " being transplanted to French soil, and naturalised " ; and if his biographer is to be believed, Richardson's novels did more in France for the reputation of their translator than they had done in England for

---

[1] We possess a very detailed knowledge of the circumstances which inspired Richardson to write *Pamela*. He owes the story to one of his friends, as he himself tells us. (*Cf.* Mrs Barbauld, *Life and Correspondence of Samuel Richardson*, vol. i. p. 52.) The origin of the novel contains no trace of literary imitation.

[2] M. J. Jusserand (*Les grandes écoles du roman anglais*, p. 49) is of the same opinion. I have consulted him on the present occasion, and he maintains his conclusions : Marivaux, current opinion notwithstanding, is not the teacher of Richardson.

that of their author."[1]   This, though a palpable exaggeration, is not so monstrous as one might suppose.   The eighteenth century was just as grateful to Prévost for his adaptations of *Clarissa* and *Grandison* as for his own novels, *Cléveland* and *Manon*, and he himself frequently spoke with pride of what he regarded as an important part of his work.   Seldom indeed has a more eminent translator devoted himself to spreading the fame of a more illustrious model.   Even during the last century it was remarked[2] that " for the greatest master of pathos among English novelists it was a piece of rare good fortune to find such a translator as the author of *Cléveland*."   No one, in fact, was better qualified for such an undertaking as this than the man who alike in his novels and in his journal had acted as the earnest and persistent eulogist of the English genius.

The translation of *Pamela* appeared in 1741 and 1742.   Engrossed just then with other occupations, Prévost seems to have employed the services of a collaborator.[3]   It is, further, certain that on this occasion he entered into communication with Richardson, who sent him a number of additions and corrections, and furnished him with previously unpublished portraits of some of the characters for insertion in the French edition.[4]

Clarissa Harlowe, published in 1748, was translated in 1751, just at the time when Prévost became friendly with Rousseau.[5] Prévost's version was incomplete, and thereby gave offence to Richardson.   Ten years later Diderot also complained of it in his celebrated *Éloge*,[6] and at the same time the *Journal étranger*

[1] *Œuvres choisies*, vol. i., p. 24.   [2] Marmontel, *Essai sur les romans*.

[3] Aubert de la Chesnaye-Desbois, a most prolific writer on a great variety of subjects, and author more especially of *Lettres amusantes et critiques sur les romans* (1743), where English fiction is dealt with at considerable length. (See *Biographie générale*, and Hauréau, *Histoire littéraire du Maine*, 1870, vol. i., p. 114.)

[4] See Prévost's preface. *Pamela, ou la vertu récompensée*, translated from the English, London, 1742, 4 parts, 12mo ; frequently reprinted.

[5] *Lettres anglaises ou Histoire de Clarisse Harlowe*, translated from the English, Paris, 1751, 4 vols. 12mo. (The *Nouvelles littéraires* announce the appearance of the first part in January 1751.)

[6] Mrs. Barbauld, vol. vi., p. 244: "This gentleman has thought fit to omit some of the most afflicting parts. . . . He treats the story as a true one, and says, in one place, that the English editor has often sacrificed his story to moral instructions, warnings, &c.—the very motive with me of the story being written at all."

published a translation, by Suard, of the account of Clarissa's funeral, the principal portion omitted, for the benefit of readers whose hearts were not "too weak to endure a succession of deep and powerful emotions."[1] This translation, with a few other fragments, found a place in subsequent editions.

At a later period the worshippers of the English novelist were no longer satisfied with Prévost's "elegant" but by no means faithful translation; and a more complete version of the masterpiece was issued by Letourneur.[2]

Finally, in 1754, appeared Prévost's version of *Grandison*,[3] which was followed by a more complete and more painstaking translation, published in Germany.[4] The author was a Protestant minister, Gaspard Joël Monod, and, according to Prévost, his translation is "one of the most extraordinary monuments ever issued from the press."

While Monod's is a clumsy and literal version, Prévost's is by no means open to the same reproach. The very method of translation adopted by Prévost is in itself a mine of evidence concerning French taste in the eighteenth century.

"The taste of Prévost," says his biographer, "was so

[1] *Journal étranger* (March 1762). See *Supplément aux lettres de Miss Clarisse Harlowe*, translated from the English, with a panegyric on the author.

[2] *Clarisse Harlowe*, new and only complete translation, by M. Letourneur. . . . Dedicated to Monsieur, the king's brother, Geneva and Paris, 1785-87, 10 vols. 8vo, or 14 vols. 18mo, illustrated by Chodowiecki. *Clarissa* was once more translated, by Barré (1845-46, 2 vols. 8vo), and abridged by J. Janin (1846, 2 vols. 12mo).—The chevalier de Champigny published two vols. of *Lettres anglaises* at St Petersburg and Frankfort, in 1774, as a sequel to *Clarissa*.

[3] *Nouvelles lettres anglaises ou histoire du chevalier Grandisson*, by the author of *Pamela* and *Clarissa*, Amsterdam, 8 parts in 4 vols. 12mo. The original edition of this translation bears the date of 1755 on vols. i., ii., and the first part of vol. iii.; the second half of vol. iii., and vol. iv., are dated 1756. This second part of the novel does not appear to have been on sale before 1758, for at that date Grimm and Fréron speak of it as a new work. See H. Harrisse, *L'abbé Prévost*, p. 379. As Prévost translated *Grandison* in 1753, M. Harrisse concludes that he translated either from one of the spurious versions which were in circulation so early as 1753, or from a manuscript copy supplied by Richardson himself.

[4] *Histoire de sir Charles Grandisson*, a complete version of the original English edition, Gottingen and Leyden, 1756, 7 vols. 12mo. (With regard to this translation, see *Correspondance littéraire*, August 1748; and upon the author, Senebier, *Histoire littéraire de Genève*, vol. iii., p. 251).

unerring as to make it impossible for him to confine himself to merely translating his original." He himself loudly maintained "the supreme right of every author who employs his mother-tongue for the purpose of giving pleasure,"[1]— and in virtue of this right made many alterations and suppressions. The reasons he assigns are most curious. "I have no fear," he says, "that I shall be accused of treating my author with severity. Now that English literature has been known in France for twenty years," Prévost writes in 1751, "readers are aware that it often requires these little emendations before it can become naturalized." Still, he does consider himself bound to retain the "national colouring" of manners and customs, for the rights of a translator do not include that of "transforming the substance of a book," and besides, "a foreign air is no bad recommendation in France." But there was nothing absolute, it seems, even in this principle, since elsewhere he prides himself on having reduced to the common practice of Europe everything in English customs which might give offence to French taste.[2]

Since Prévost's translations form an integral part of the history of the French novel, and since it was through them that Rousseau became acquainted with Richardson, it is important also to observe that mistaken renderings are by no means infrequent ; that there are traces of haste and carelessness ; that a great number of letters are curtailed or blended together, and that some are simply analysed, while others are entirely suppressed. In certain cases these suppressions are due to the translator's delicacy : they are sacrifices "to the taste of the French nation." In others they arise from scruples of one kind or another : the letters of Leman the servant, with their colloquial expressions, disappear as being "too low"; the same fate

[1] Preface to *Clarisse*.
[2] Preface to *Grandison* : "I have suppressed or reduced to the common practice of Europe whatever in English customs might give offence to other nations. It has seemed to me that these remnants of the rude manners of ancient Britain, to which nothing but familiarity can still keep the English blind, would bring discredit upon a book in which good-breeding ought to go hand in hand with nobility and virtue."

befalls several "indecent" passages; and the story of the sham licence granted to Lovelace by the Bishop of London is omitted as irreverent. On other occasions it is the realism of certain details which disturbs Prévost: the incarceration of Clarissa is a "very long and very English" episode; the anguish of her death would not be tolerated in its entirety, and her posthumous letters do not appear in the translation. Some of Lovelace's forgeries seem really too "revolting" to be transcribed; and if after all the translator decides to include them, it is "in order to prove that the work is founded on reality." The same squeamishness caused the omission of the death-scene of the libertine Belton, in *Clarissa*, and also of the descriptions of Sinclair's death and of Clarissa's funeral. In *Grandison*, Prévost went so far as to alter the *dénouement*.[1]

Thus the contemporaries of Diderot and Rousseau did not read Richardson "in the crude state," but Richardson refined by Prévost, relieved of a certain amount of dross and reduced by almost a third. But the English novelist suffered less from these changes than might be supposed. In reality he is destitute of style; and even writes incorrectly. His whole merit lies in his wealth of moral observation and his mastery of pathos. And in the "charming infidelities" of Prévost there remained enough of observation to prevent the French taste from finding any very great cause of offence in this overwhelming mass of analysis. In the more passionate scenes what is essential has been left intact: the author of *Cléveland* was not likely to clip the wings of the author of *Clarissa* in such passages as these. Where Prévost has been false to his author is in giving us less moralizing, less of trivial detail, and a more ornate and elegant form. And in compensation for this infidelity he has left the pathos of the work and the distinctness of the characters unimpaired. In spite of Prévost's pruning, Richardson's work seemed very fresh to French readers.

[1] *Cf.* the edition of 1784, vol. iv., p. 401.

Chapter IV

I

To-DAY the works of Richardson are entirely forgotten. Of these once famous novels the public no longer knows anything beyond the titles. Even the critics scarcely pay any attention to the man who was considered the greatest of all English writers in point of pathos,[1] and if *Tom Jones*, the *Vicar of Wakefield* and *Robinson Crusoe* are still read, *Clarissa Harlowe* is read no more than *Clélie* or *Le Grand Cyrus*. This neglect may be explained, but it cannot be justified. Richardson's work must always be of the highest importance in the history of fiction, by reason of the magnitude of the revolution he effected.

His very faults even, obvious as they are, stamp him with originality.

We can imagine the shock it would give, not Voltaire or

[1] No satisfactory monograph on Richardson exists. The principal source of information concerning him is Mrs Barbauld's collection : *Life and Correspondence of Samuel Richardson*, 1806, 6 vols. 8vo. The best study of his work as a whole is that by Mr Leslie Stephen, in his *Hours in a Library*. Sir Walter Scott's study should also be consulted.

Marivaux only, but also Addison and Pope, when, on opening
Pamela, they found such compliments as this : A suitor, putting
his hands on a young lady's shoulders, says to her, playfully :
" Let me see, let me see, . . . where do your wings grow ?
for I never saw anybody fly like you." So happy does this
touch appear to the author that he employs it again in another
of his novels, where Lovelace, speaking of Clarissa, says :
" Surely, Belford, this is an angel. And yet, had she not
been known to be a female, they would not from *babyhood*
have dressed her as such, nor would she, but upon that
conviction, have continued the dress."[1]   So much for the
language of gallantry.   When the characters talk naturally
they speak in the following manner : " Tost to and fro by
the high winds of passionate controul (and, as I think, un-
seasonable severity), I behold the desired port, the *single state*,
into which I would fain steer ; but am kept off by the foaming
billows of a brother's and sister's envy, and by the raging winds
of a supposed invaded authority ; while I see in Lovelace, the
rocks on the one hand, and in Solmes, the sands on the other ;
and tremble lest I should split upon the former, or strike upon
the latter."[2]   Such is the language of that affected little provincial, the immortal Clarissa.

But affectation goes hand and hand with coarseness.   A certain Lady Davers—intended as a portrait of a lady of quality—
has an inexhaustible flow of fishwife's pleasantries, and such expressions as " wench," " chastity," " insolent creature," fall thick
as hail on poor Pamela's head.   On another occasion, a gentleman,
speaking to a young lady, delicately alludes to his intention of
perpetuating with her at once his happiness and his race.

Not only is the author both vulgar and affected, but he is a
pedant as well.   When Clarissa is dying, Lovelace exclaims :
" She is very ill ! " and adds sententiously : " What a fine subject for tragedy would the injuries of this lady and her behaviour
under them . . . make."[3]   Then follow ten or twelve pages in

[1] *The novels of Samuel Richardson* (*Ballantyne's Novelists' Library*), vol. ii., p. 197.
[2] *Ibid.*, vol. i., p. 669.
[3] Vol. ii., p. 565.   Observe the curious footnote.

which the author sketches the plot of this tragedy, and favours the reader with his reflections on the state of the drama, and on the causes of its decadence—a digression which refreshes our interest, nevertheless.

When he intends to be impressive, he is bombastic. Lovelace, in a passion, threatens Clarissa, and she exclaims, "For your own sake, leave me !—My soul is above thee, man ! . . . Urge me not to tell thee, how sincerely I think my soul above thee." [1] This pathetic passage—if they read it—must have delighted the readers of *La Vie de Marianne*, but the translators were careful to tone down everything of this sort.

The romantic element is commonplace to the last degree, or else it is the lowest of low comedy. On one occasion Lovelace, in a frightful dream, foresees his own destiny ; he beholds Clarissa ascending to heaven amid a chorus of angels, and himself falling into a bottomless abyss. On another, in the very crisis of his sufferings, he occupies himself with selling gloves and soap-balls in order to pass the time, installing himself behind a counter and—for no reason perceptible to the reader—mystifying the passers by.

But assuming that the French reader has become used to Richardson's peculiarities of form, his want of taste, his coarseness, his pedantry and affectation, how, if he has studied good novels, can he tolerate the perpetual intrusion of the author's personality, that preaching *I* which buttonholes you on every page and shouts into your ears : "Whatever you do, mark the moral of this tale !" The mere title of one of his novels takes up a whole page—so that we may be in no doubt as to its object : " *Pamela*, or virtue rewarded, in a series of Familiar Letters from a Beautiful Young Damsel to her Parents. Now first published in order to cultivate the principles of virtue and religion in the minds of the youth of both sexes. A narrative which has its foundation in truth and nature ; [2] and at the same time that it agreeably

---

[1] Vol. i., p. 200.

[2] A friend of Richardson's had told him the story of a servant-girl whom her master had attempted to seduce, but whose innocence had so touched him that he had married her. (*Cf.* Walter Scott, *Lives of the Novelists*, vol. ii., p. 30.)

entertains, by a variety of curious and affecting incidents is entirely divested of all those images, which, in too many pieces
calculated for amusement only, tend to inflame the minds they
should instruct." But not to dwell longer upon the title, which
is a programme in itself, let us resign ourselves to a rapid perusal
of this singular book. Just as we are beginning to get an idea of
the characters, to take an interest in the progress of events, the
author assails us with the following reflection : " The whole [of
this history] will show the base acts of designing men to gain
their wicked ends, and how much it behoves the fair sex to stand
upon their guard against artful contrivances, especially when
riches and power conspire against innocence and a low estate."[1]
A strange novel, forsooth, is this sermon !

Not only is the moralizing cumbersome, but the narrative
is simply crowded with matter. Richardson gives us not so
much novels by means of letters, as letters developed and spun
out into the form of novels. In *Clarissa* eight volumes are
devoted to a story which extends over less than twelve months—
from January 10th to December 8th of the same year. We feel
as we read these substantial volumes that life is spent in writing
letters. In the light of this constant interchange of notes and
epistles, it seems to take the appearance of a vast game of chess,
in which the players are for ever seated before a writing-desk,
thinking out to-morrow's move. An incredible and truly
paradoxical abuse of the inkstand ! Miss Byron, in *Grandison*,
writes, on March 22nd, a letter which occupies fourteen pages of
a closely-printed edition. On the same day she writes two
others, one ten, the other twelve pages long ; on the 23rd, two
others of eighteen and ten pages ; and on the 24th, two which
together fill thirty pages. She remarks at last that she must
lay down her pen, but allows herself nevertheless a postscript of
six pages. Thus in three days she writes nearly one hundred
and fifty pages of an ordinary-sized volume.—And all the
characters are alike. Not a moment but two or three couriers
are on the road. Nor is this all : this world of scribblers makes
it a practice to preserve a duplicate of the most trifling note.

[1] Ballantyne, vol. vi., p. 52.

Clarissa dockets all her missives, and, as she herself acknowledges, collects documents for the use of her future biographer.
On her deathbed she writes a long will, besides eleven letters
for various people, and copies of those letters as well.   " No
wonder," says her executor, " that she was always writing."
But how did she find the time to live ?

This is the *documentary* novel with a vengeance.   Everything
is in the form of a report or a draft of minutes.   Every letter is
a memorandum, containing references, *errata*, *corrigenda*, and
addenda. On every page we find *résumés* of previous *résumés*,
and analyses of analyses. Some of these letters are of the nature
of an *official statement* ; reasons are classified, numbered, docketed,
and have their preambles and their vouchers. Everything is
described, nothing omitted : a word, a frown, the position of a
chair—everything is set down. The author is a shorthand-
reporter of the most diffuse and scrupulous type. In fact, in
the most important scenes, a corner is found for a clerk, who
writes from dictation. When Pollexfen resolves to fight
Grandison and has it out with him, he takes care to have a
" writer " in a recess, who is instructed to note down every little
word. Grandison's declarations of love, even, are duly formulated and initialled. When Clementina is reconciled to her
family, Grandison draws up an agreement in six clauses which
gives rise to an elaborate interchange of comments.[1] It is the
triumph of the scribbling habit : everything possible is said, and
everything that is said is put on paper ; one after the other the
characters make their appearance, each with his or her missive,
and resembling, to use Victor Hugo's amusing simile, the foreign
actors who, unable to appear except in succession, and not being
permitted to speak upon the boards, come forward one after
another, each bearing above his head a great placard whereon the
public may read the part he has to play.[2]

How remote are these heavy, formal novels from the light and
airy little books of the earlier part of the century, such as the
Lettres persanes or *Manon* ! What a difference there is between

---

[1] See Prévost's translation, vol. iv., pp. 208 and 236.
[2] *Littérature et philosophie mêlées :* on Walter Scott.

Grandison and *Cleveland* even ! Those who regard Richardson
as a feeble imitator of Marivaux have never read Richardson.
With his pedantry and affectation the printer makes one think
involuntarily of Walpole's neat description of the Baron de
Gleichen as bewildering himself with definitions of things which
do not need defining, and drowning himself in a spoonful of
water from sheer determination to get to the bottom. Richardson
drowns himself in an ocean of documentary evidence.[1]

When taken to task for his prolixity, he replied that it was
merely his novel method of writing ; of substituting for the
picture of events taken from a distance a patient, minute, and
laborious narrative which records the progress of events from
day to day, from hour to hour, and almost from minute to
minute. It would seem indeed that such records must be
improbable ; that, further, when a writer makes use of so
monotonous a form he limits himself to the portrayal of one
kind of heroes only, those who have leisure and are also given
to contemplation, who have the time and the inclination to keep
a journal of their lives ; lastly, that it must weaken the effect to
give two or three successive versions of the same fact. But all
these objections, in Richardson's view, could not outweigh the
necessity of representing life in its infinite complexity.—Most
novels, he said, are highly improbable, because they simplify
and abbreviate everything. They only give us one aspect of
things. I mean to show you their whole reality. I shall be
long, and certainly tedious. But I do not write to divert you ;
I merely desire to instruct you. Are you fond of watching the
drama of a human life ? If so you will like my books.[2]

II

Richardson's art, in fact, is as different as possible from the
classical art of France.

But here it is important to know what we mean. Richard-

---

[1] And even then he sacrificed half of each of his MSS. (W. Scott, *ibid.*, vol. ii.,
p. 74.)

[2] See the *Postscriptum* to *Clarissa*, a regular declaration of literary faith.

son's novels, besides being improbable in form, are often also
romantic in point of matter. While it may be said that he
" keeps close to life " in his selection of characters and in his
lavish—and indeed extravagant—use of trifling details, he cannot
be said to keep equally near to it, if his plot alone be considered.
It is doubtless true that events which might happen in the
eighteenth century have in many cases become impossible at the
present day : we may admit that in eighteenth-century England
so audacious a fellow as Lovelace might have kidnapped a girl
of such moral courage as Clarissa ; that he might have kept
her in confinement for whole months together, have introduced her to his family, have imprisoned her—without rousing her suspicions—in a house of ill-fame, have violated
her during sleep, and finally have brought about her death
by privation and suffering. All this, though extraordinary
enough, is not impossible. But what is not, and never can be,
admissible is the means employed by the author to render such
an intrigue probable ; the interception of letters, the forgery or
imitation of messages, the transcription of bundles of letters in a
single night, the compliance of courtesans who play the great
lady when required, and of the keeper of a disorderly house in
passing for a lady of noble birth, the versatility of servants in
being made up to represent gentlemen of rank and consequence
—of Joseph Leman and Donald Patrick, who play every variety
of part—their compliance in lending themselves to every whim,
the feats of Lovelace in overhearing conversations and noting
them down upon his tablets, the simplicity of Clarissa in never
for a moment conceiving the idea of putting herself under the
protection of a magistrate. What manifestly exceeds possibility
is all this paraphernalia of tricks, machinations and stratagems,
this perfect arsenal of snares, pitfalls, places of confinement, and
traps, which are of the very essence of the novel of adventure.
We must resign ourselves to finding these remnants of
the old novel of cape and sword in the work of the founder
of modern fiction. This defect, it is true, gave less offence
to eighteenth century readers, accustomed as they were to
find accurate observation enshrined in a purely imaginary

setting,[1] and moreover still full of their reading of seventeenth century novelists and of Prévost. The contrast between the author's avowed intention of painting contemporary life and his manifest incapacity to combine his picture with a simple and probable intrigue, is none the less striking. Richardson, the painter of middle-class life, like Rousseau in the *Nouvelle Héloïse*, remains faithful, in this respect, to the old conception of this branch of literature. And this perhaps, as in the case of Rousseau, was not the least among the causes of his success.

This reservation being made, we find in Richardson an art which is absolutely new.

It is a minute, a patient, a laborious art; what he gives us is a mosaic of delicate impressions, not one of them worth reporting in itself, but which, accumulated, produce the effect of life. Nothing could be less French, nothing less classic. The French like to find art in the smallest things; they like every phrase to be well-balanced, and also every thought, however ordinary, to be clothed in the choicest language. Now this polished art to which the masters attain—the precision of idea and expression which indicates that the thinking capacity is well regulated and under complete control; the perfect adjustment of thought and language; the maintenance of perfect symmetry between the clauses of a sentence, the paragraphs of a chapter, the parts of a book; the anxiety to avoid repetition, or, in so far as it is unavoidable, to relieve it with a touch of satire or of pathos; the sense which requires that effects shall be graduated and interest guided in the same manner as one would conduct an intrigue in real life, by making the most of surprises, guarding against inconvenient questions, and gradually supplying curiosity with nourishment, in a definite and skilfully ordered sequence, so that it progresses from situation to situation and from one gratification to another,—to all this Richardson is a complete stranger. He is destitute of art, or, if he has any, it is nature's own. His usual, or rather his only, method is one of repetition or accumulation: that of the single drop which slowly and surely wears a hole in the rock whereon it drips. Of the arts of transition,

[1] The *Lettres persanes*, and, later, the novels of Voltaire, *Candide* or *Zadig*.

composition, and adjustment of parts he knows nothing. He has not the slightest fear of wearying the reader, but there is a rare audacity in his art of wearing out the attention. Twenty times, a hundred times, you lay the book aside in vexation, and twenty or a hundred times you take it up again. For, long and heavy as the story may be, the writer has passion, and the picture obtained by the painter from a sorry and vulgar model glows with colour and with life. Nothing is more beautiful than a pot or a kettle if only it be painted by Chardin. So, also, it is true that nothing is so vulgar as the Harlowe circle, and nothing so pretentious as the writer who tells us of it : no one is more completely representative of what (in the almost un-translatable words of an English critic) may be called *our common English clumsiness*.[1] But, awkward and embarrassed as is his utterance, this man has nevertheless the gift of deep emotion before the spectacle of life. He was born with the necessity for observing the world, and for giving expression to what he sees with all the accuracy of which he is capable. He could not, in fact, have written eight volumes on the history of a group of squalid and cross-grained *bourgeois*, had it not inspired him with some deep emotion.

And we, if we divest ourselves of such refinement, such delicacy, and such love of the graceful and the elegant as may have been instilled into us by two or three centuries of classical culture, shall feel it too. "Imagination," said Voltaire, "can fulfil its office only when supplemented by profound judgment : it is for ever combining its own pictures, correcting its mistakes, erecting all its edifices in due order. . . . It is by his imagination that the poet creates his personages, endows them with character and passion, invents his plot, presents it in narrative form, com-plicates the intrigue and provides for the catastrophe : a work which demands, further, that the author's judgment shall be not only most profound but also most acute. In all these products of the creative imagination, and even in novels, the greatest art is required. Those who are incapable of it are objects of con-tempt to people of sound judgment."[2] Such is the classical

[1] Mr Leslie Stephen, *Hours in a Library*, 1st series. [2] *Dictionnaire philosophique*.

critic's conception of the creative imagination. But let "right-minded people" take warning. They have no business here. In Richardson's novels they will find neither ingenuity of plot, nor skilful "complication" of the intrigue, nor cleverly prepared catastrophe, but simply a bundle of letters none too well arranged, which require to be read not as a work of art but as a collection of curious yet deeply moving documents.

In a forgotten drawer you find a bundle of yellow papers. You glance carelessly over one page, then over another, then over a third. Then, in spite of yourself, your curiosity is aroused. They deal with an old—a very old—love-story. You do not know the people concerned in it; their names tell you nothing, and the events take place in a distant country. Yet the story takes hold of your attention: a touch of passion, like a half-faded perfume, still lingers among these faded leaves; the names acquire some meaning, the phantoms start into life, the old souvenirs live and move beneath your eyes. Hours pass, yet you are reading still, softly stirred and, as it were, lulled by the rhythm of a life long since extinct. At a certain point the story becomes extremely pathetic: the anguish becomes heart-rending; a cry of despair arises from the depths of the past. . . . You check yourself. "What is this story to me?" you say, and at the same moment you brush aside a tear. . . . Such is the experience of every reader of *Clarissa Harlowe*. If realism is the art of giving the impression of life, Richardson is the greatest of realists.

But between his method and that of the French classical writers, though the result may be the same, there is nothing in common. With him, as with the Dutch painters, there is, as regards subject, neither trivial nor sublime. The fact had already been remarked by contemporary writers: "Every picture which gives a faithful presentation of nature, whatever it may be, is always beautiful; nothing is excluded from our works save the filthy and the loathsome, which is banished also by the painter. Do we not hold the pictures of Heemskirk and other Dutch painters in high esteem, although their subjects are of the lowest? . . . If you are so prejudiced by your lofty

French ideas as to find something contemptible in certain of the images in this book, *I beg you to reflect that among us nothing which represents nature is ever despised.*[1] This was, or seemed to be, something new. " It was part of the destiny of Holland," an eminent critic has said, " to love a good likeness."[2] Nothing, it would seem, could be more common than such a destiny; in reality, nothing is more rare. There have been very few genuine realists in France, such, I mean, as plunge boldly and unhesitatingly into the heart of reality, without the least anxiety as to whether they will find it tedious, monotonous, and barren. Lesage, the most realistic of all French eighteenth-century novelists, is at the same time a most subtle artist—too subtle, in fact—and too self-controlled ; he does not let himself go ; he is afraid of making his subject tedious or ridiculous ; it is no part of his destiny irrevocably and with all his heart to love " a good likeness."

Richardson, like a true Englishman, has no such scruples. In describing Grandison's wedding he spares us neither a costume nor a bow nor a curtsy ; we know the exact number of carriages, the occupants of each, and how everyone was dressed on the occasion ; we are not left in ignorance with regard to the amount of money distributed by the good Sir Charles to the village girls who had strewn his path with flowers. Verbiage, you call it ? Then you have no passion for " the good likeness."

When a person of consequence enters a room we are told his gestures, his attitude, and the number of steps he takes. " The description of movements is what pleases, especially in novels of domestic interest. See how complacently the author of *Pamela*, *Grandison* and *Clarissa* lingers over it ! See how forcible, how

---

[1] Desfontaines, *Lettre d'une dame anglaise*, printed at the end of his translation of *Joseph Andrews*, vol. ii. Similarly du Resnel, in the remarks preliminary to his translation of the *Essay on Man* : " They [the English] are exceedingly happy in their imitation of nature ; but, like the Flemish painters, they are *not in the least particular about choosing what is beautiful in nature*, everything which truly represents it gives them pleasure ; whereas we require selection from what nature offers, and blame the workman, however delicate and faithful his touch, if he has not chosen a sublime and elevated subject."

[2] E. Fromentin, *Les maîtres d'autrefois*, p. 165.

significant, how pathetic it renders his language! I see the character; I see him whether he speaks or is silent . . ."[1]   I see Colbrand, the Swiss, in *Pamela*, with "his frightful long hair," and the "something on his throat, that sticks out . . . like a wen," beneath his neck cloth.   I see Mrs Jewkes, "a broad, squat, pursy *fat thing*," with her "huge hands," her "flat and crook'd" nose, her "spiteful, grey, goggling eye," and a complexion that makes her face look "as if it had been pickled a month in salt-petre."   I see Solmes, Clarissa Harlowe's poor suitor, with his "splay feet," always seeming to count his steps when he walks, and stupidly "gnawing the head of his hazel; a carved head almost as ugly as his own."[2]   And if they speak the smallest inflexion of voice is noted, and dots and dashes are used without stint.   "See how many pauses, full stops and interruptions there are, how many speeches are broken off,"—and how scrupulous the author is about truth of detail!

Just as certain facts formerly considered insignificant are now placed in a prominent position, so certain characters also, hitherto restricted to the narrow limits of the ridiculous, step boldly forth into the sunlight.   The characters belonging to the inferior classes are not, in this case, as with Marivaux, merely a coach-man or a little seamstress, introduced as pleasing subjects for vignettes; the whole action of the story passes between servants, and a waiting-maid is its heroine.   Excluding the squire, who attempts the seduction of Pamela, and is odious in other respects, what are the characters in this story?   The gardener Arthur, the coachman Robert, Isaac the lackey, and even Tommy, "the poor little scullion-boy."   May not all these people be as worthy of your interest as the *comtes* and *marquises* in your comedies?   Away with your Mascarilles, Frontins, Scapins, and Lisettes, crafty, designing and depraved, every one of them, and utterly conventional in type.   See our good steward here, weeping because his beloved Pamela is so ill-treated: "Was ever the like heard!   'Tis too much, too much; I can't bear it.   As I hope to live I am quite melted.   Dear sir, forgive her!"[3]   Truly, the

[1] Diderot, *Éloge de Richardson*.   [2] Ballantyne, vi., p. 559.   [3] Letter xxviii.

best of men. Pamela, too, is the best-behaved of housemaids. You will not be surprised, therefore, to find quite a volume devoted to the question as to whether or not she shall be dismissed. Is she to leave or not? Is she to be driven or to walk? Is she to hire a carriage, or will some one allow her the use of one? If she goes on horseback, will it be proper for her to ride behind a servant on the same horse. Shall she take one, two, or three bundles? Shall she carry away her old clothes or leave them behind her? Shall she wear her best Sunday gown or her working-day dress? Never, said Keats, was any one so conscientiously devoted to " making mountains out of mole-hills."[1] Nor was any one ever so passionately fond of " a good likeness." Here, again, for your amusement, is a correct inventory of our waiting-maid's dresses, petticoats, stockings, collars, cuffs, hats and mittens. No milliner would give a better description of the calico night-gown, the " quilted calimanco coat," the pair of pockets, the new flannel coat. In her exile Pamela provides herself with " forty sheets of note-paper, a dozen pens, a small bottle of ink," some wax and wafers. Like her biographer, she has a practical mind. You are told how she makes tea, the number of nubs of sugar she puts in, and the kind of cakes she provides. You are taken to the kitchen and shown how to clean the pots and pans. " I, t'other day, tried, when Rachel's back was turned, if I could not scour a pewter plate; . . . it only blistered my hand in two places. . . . I hope to make my hands as red as a blood-pudding and as hard as a beechen trencher. . . ."[2] I dare not attempt to reckon up the number of tea-drinking scenes in Richardson's three novels : the consumption is appalling, but nothing can weary the author.

The conversation of the characters is correspondingly insipid. The servants talk the queerest jargon. Leman, in *Clarissa*, writes letters containing the most amusing spelling. If some women and coachmen are talking around the kitchen table the author takes his seat in a corner, records what they say—sparing us

[1] Keats, *Works*, ed. Buxton Forman, vol. iv., p. 15.
[2] Ballantyne, vi., p. 46.

M

neither blunders nor scurrility—and revels in dragging his reader through a morass of vulgarity and platitude.

It is of the essence of all true realism, not only to bring us into actual contact with the vulgar side of things, but also to show us their brutality and hideousness. For in those by-places of existence, where every form of distress that life can inflict seems to be accumulated, the poverty of human nature is fully revealed. When a man lies stretched on the hospital bed in the agonies of death, everything in him that savours of the beast forces its way out. The mask thrown over his face by social convention falls, and nothing is left but a naked shivering figure, trembling with fever and with terror. There is no better way of stripping a man of all prestige, as of a vesture in which he has wrapped himself, than that of bringing him face to face with anguish and death; nor is there any subject which lays such a fierce hold upon the interest of the reader, certain as he is, in this case at any rate, that he is reading his own history.

In *Clarissa* Richardson introduced descriptions of the pangs of death, and of the preparations for it, to an even unjustifiable extent. Clarissa buys her coffin beforehand, has it placed in her bedroom, uses it as a kind of desk, and gives precise orders concerning the manner in which her body is to be placed in it as soon as cold. She dies a lingering death before our eyes. The libertine, Belton, too, is ten or fifteen pages in dying. Elsewhere, again, we have the never to be forgotten picture—marvellous and horrible in its power—of the death agony of the woman Sinclair. Here Prévost's resolution failed him. " This scene," he writes, " is essentially English; in other words it is depicted in colours so vivid and, unfortunately, so repugnant to our national taste that however toned down it would be intolerable in French. Suffice it to add that the subject of this remarkable picture is everything that is infamous and terrible."[1] But the curious, among whom was Diderot, read the original, which was rendered in full by other translators.[2]

In a house of ill-fame an old woman, abandoned by the doctors, lies dying, the women of the establishment, fresh from

Vol. iv., p. 480.   [2] Ballantyne's edn., vol. ii., letter ccccvi.

the arms of their last night's lovers, gathered around her. The paint has run on their wasted faces, " discovering coarse wrinkled skins "; their hair is black only where the black-lead comb had left its trace. " They were all slip-shod; stockingless some; only under-petticoated all; their gowns, made to cover straddling hoops, hanging trollopy, and tangling about their heels." Some, " unpadded," their eyes heavy with sleep, yawned and stretched themselves. The room was filled with the odour of plasters, liniments, and spirituous liquors.[1]

Meanwhile the dying woman struggles with death, " spreading the whole troubled bed with her huge quaggy carcase, clenching her broad hands, and rolling her great red eye-balls." " Her matted grizzly hair, made irreverend by her wickedness (her clouted head-dress being half off, spread about her fat ears and brawny neck); her livid lips parched and working violently; her broad chin in convulsive motion; her wide mouth, by reason of the contraction of her forehead (which seemed to be half lost in its own frightful furrows) splitting her face, as it were, into two parts; and her huge tongue hideously rolling in it; heaving, puffing as if for breath; her bellows-shaped and various-coloured breasts ascending by turns to her chin, and descending out of sight, with the violence of her gaspings."

Her end being spoken of: " *Die*, did you say, sir ? "—she exclaims,—" ' *Die !*—I *will not*, I *cannot* die !—I know not *how* to die ! *Die*, sir !—And *must* I then die ?—Leave this world ?—I cannot bear it !—And who brought you hither, sir ? [her eyes striking fire at me] who brought you here to tell me I must *die*, sir ?—I cannot, I will not leave this world. Let others die, who wish for another ! who expect a better ! I have had my plagues in this; but would compound for all future hopes, so as I may be nothing after this !' And then she howled and bellowed by turns. By my faith, Lovelace, I trembled in every joint. . . . 'Sally !—Polly !—Sister Carter ! said she, did you not tell me I might *recover* ? Did not the *surgeon* tell me I might ?'"

The surgeons appear, and carry on a long discussion with

[1] Vol. ii., p. 687.

regard to *tibia, fibula* and *patella.*   Finally they give her up, and she is told of their verdict.

> " Then did the poor wretch set up an inarticulate frightful howl, such a one as I never before heard uttered, as if already pangs infernal had taken hold of her; and seeing every one half-frighted, and me motioning to withdraw, O pity me, pity me, Mr Belford, cried she, her words interrupted by groans—I find you think I shall die!   And *what* I may be, and *where,* in a very few hours—who can tell?
> " I told her it was in vain to flatter her: it was my opinion she would not recover.
> " I was going to re-advise her to calm her spirits, and endeavour to resign herself, and to make the best of the opportunity yet left her; but this declaration set her into a most outrageous raving.   She would have torn her hair, and beaten her breast, had not some of the wretches held her hands by force. . . ."[1]

III

Minute, tedious, and sometimes repulsive as a painter of human suffering, Richardson excelled in the delineation of character, but of one particular type of character only—the very type, in fact, which, up to that time, had been most neglected by French novelists.

When he meant to reflect upon the habits of the fashionable world, his work was not even second-rate.   This was only to be expected.   The carpenter's son who had taken to printing failed in depicting aristocratic society, not only because he had seen very little of it, but also because certain delicate shades of difference can only be caught by an art more subtle and flexible than his.   Like Rousseau, Richardson had a great fear of intruding upon persons of rank, and at the same time a great desire to enjoy their favour; like him, in spite of his own humble origin, he had a profound respect for birth and rank.   But Grandison and Clementina are no more genuine aristocrats than Julie d'Étanges or M. de Wolmar.

Grandison, the model man of the world, is a splendid specimen of physique without a soul.   His figure is " rather slender than full," " his face in shape a fine oval," his complexion clear, his clothes of the best cut, and his morals above reproach.

[1] Vol. ii., p. 691.

" What a man is this, so to act ! " cries the unreserved Miss Byron. She can find but one fault in him : " What I think seems a little to savour of singularity, his horses are not docked ; their tails are only tied up when they are on the road. . . . I want, methinks, my dear, to find some fault in his outward appearance." [1]   To such trivialities can Samuel Richardson descend when he attempts to depict the manners of fashionable society. His Grandison, whose face seems always radiant with the pleasure of having practised all his virtues, is a lay figure. The world in which he moves is an assemblage of grimacing puppets. They neither cry nor walk nor live but according to sound principles and well-established rules. When they love, it is in the most exalted fashion : Grandison avows his feeling for Henrietta " with all the truth and plainness which [he thinks] are required in treaties of this nature, equally with those set on foot between nation and nation," [2] and is scrupulous in his observance of the prescribed formalities. His courtly and sonorous verbiage intoxicates all these pompous creatures, each puffed up with his own per-fection. The desire to think generous thoughts and to do noble deeds is contagious. This insufferable Celadon keeps a school for instruction in the sublime as regards both sentiment and behaviour.

Richardson, poor man, thought he was drawing a picture of society. At most he merely depicted its exterior, and even of that his portrait is, in places, a caricature. His aristocrats are upstarts ; some of the Lombard Street mud still clings to their heels. The source and origin of their elegance is a life as regular as though it were spent in a business office. Clarissa sleeps six hours, reads and writes for three, devotes two to domestic tasks and household accounts, five to drawing, music, needlework, and conversation with the clergyman of the parish ; the two morning meals occupy two hours ; one is spent in visit-ing the poor ; and four are left for supper and chatting—the very apotheosis of method. So, too, Grandison sleeps, eats, and makes his bow according to rigorous rules. When, on entering

[1] Vol. iii., p. 91.   [2] Ballantyne, viii., p. 585.

church, he sees some ladies of his acquaintance, and among them the object of his affections, does he turn to greet them? By no means! Sir Charles knows too well that his respects are due in the first place to the Deity. Reverently he bows his head, then, raising himself, accords his second bow to Miss Byron, and follows it with successive salutations of the other ladies. His behaviour is most elaborately thought out, and the author is careful to draw our attention to the fact. A figure like Grandison, who constantly acts in accordance with certain formulas by which his life is regulated down to the smallest detail—a " man-machine," whose gestures we can anticipate as we can those of an automaton—scarcely comes within the pale of real human nature, and in so far as he does so is an intolerable moral pedant. How greatly inferior is Richardson in work of this sort to the classical writers of France! They write for an aristocratic public; the souls they portray are of the finest temper; they penetrate the innermost recesses of the human heart, and distinguish the most delicate shades of feeling.

Richardson succeeds only when he portrays simple natures. Whatever the social plane from which they are taken—and it is worth noting that with the exception of Grandison and his circle his characters belong at best to the upper strata of provincial middle-class society—they are all, if one may say so, people of the common herd, whose natures are made up of two or three elementary feelings, and whose moral life derives a unity from the clear and easily discernible aim it has set before it.

We need make no exception in favour of the much discussed character of Lovelace, though mistaken attempts have been made to hold him up as a kind of hero of vice, an impossible monster, " an almost fantastic mixture of qualities intended to fit him for the difficult part he has to play." [1]

Lovelace was certainly never drawn from life. It is doubtful whether, as has been maintained, he represents the Duke of Wharton, or any other famous libertine. [2] If he does, it is unquestionable that the portrait is not in every respect a faithful

[1] Leslie Stephen, *Hours in a Library*, vol. i., p. 105.
[2] Villemain, *xviiie siècle*, 27th lesson.

one. For, if Richardson conceived the idea of drawing from a living model, his acquaintance with polite society was too imperfect to admit of his fully succeeding. Taking this fact into consideration, everything which belongs to the exterior of the character, everything in the portrait of Lovelace which describes the gentleman, will be found conventional. Lovelace, like Grandison, is only a make-believe aristocrat.

Moreover, since he required to paint a criminal, Richardson, good, pious man, evidently strained certain features in order to increase the horror his character inspired. In particular, he surrounded him with a crew of myrmidons, sharpers, and thieves, who make him appear at certain moments a regular hero of melodrama. In order to magnify him, the honest printer's imagination invested Lovelace with the halo of a famous criminal— after the fashion of Cartouche or Robert Macaire. Like them, he writes letters in cypher, assumes false names, and dreams of conspiracies, arson and ambush.[1] On one occasion he disguises his followers as men of fortune and family, that he may take them to dine with his mistress, and commits his instructions to them with the strictest formality. "Instructions to be observed by John Belford, Richard Mowbray, Thomas Belton and James Tourville, Esquires of the body to General Robert Lovelace, on their admission to the presence of his goddess." And, his orders once given, he cries, like Mephistopheles addressing the spirits of the air : " Here's a first faint sketch of my plot. Stand by, varlets, tanta-ra-ra-ra ! Veil your bonnets and confess your master ! "[2]   He is choked with his own pride : " Now, Belford," he writes to his friend, "for the narrative of narratives." He has anticipated everything, arranged everything, contrived everything. Success is certain, and posterity will do justice to him as a consummate artist in vice : what a figure he will cut in the annals of profligacy ! This is puerile, and the character of a man like Lovelace rather suggests the hero of the

---

[1] " Had I been a military hero, I should have made gunpowder useless ; for I should have blown up all my adversaries by dint of stratagem, turning their own devices upon them " (vol. ii., p. 48).

[2] Ballantyne, vii., p. 124.

travelling booth, fashioned out of the coarse materials of legend, than an eighteenth-century Englishman of rank.

Stripped of these trappings, however, Lovelace is thoroughly representative both of his country and of his time. He is one of the most living of all the characters in Richardson's gallery.

Like Don Juan he is an atheist, and glories in the fact. But while he allows himself the broadest jokes on certain subjects, outwardly he professes to respect things sacred. He is a consummate master of *cant*. He declares to Clarissa that he has always preserved "a great admiration for religion," appears at church, and grants reductions of rent to such of his tenants as also attend it. This he does in the gravest manner in the world, with a suppressed irony which finds vent in his letters to his bosom friend Belford,—"diabolical" letters, essentially English in their clumsy fervour, and full of droll and sentimental pathos, at which we do not know whether to laugh or to cry.

His failing is not so much debauchery as pride—and this is characteristic of his age. Was it not the eighteenth century which produced the peculiar type of man who is a seducer only from motives of vanity; who is cruel and cold, and sacrifices everything not so much to sensuality as to the pride of conquest and of reckoning up his victims? This "species of perverted Quixotry,"[1] to use Scott's phrase, is not so well understood at the present day. Nowhere can the thoughts and ideals of an epoch concerning love and gallantry be seen more clearly than in its fiction : Lovelace, like Valmont in the *Liaisons dangereuses*, is the personification of the type of gallantry peculiar to the eighteenth century, the age of Richelieu and Lord Baltimore. Love of this sort demands intrigue, strife and bloodshed; it intoxicates man like a chase which excites his self-conceit before it inflames his senses. Of this type is Lovelace, a profligate who boasts of his profligacy. He lusts after every woman the possession of whom would enhance his reputation. He desires Clarissa, but he also desires her friend Miss Howe. "*One* man cannot have every woman worth having. — Pity though — when the man is such a *very* clever fellow!"[2] In the tavern

---

[1] *Lives of the novelists*, vol. ii., p. 39.   [2] Ballantyne, vii., p. 31.

to which he carries his victim he becomes enamoured of
the landlord's daughters, as soon as he perceives that their
mother is suspicious of him.   His difficulty is to find an
adequate stimulus.   The virtue, social position, and moral
worth of Clarissa Harlowe are so many spurs to his desire.
When she kisses him he considers this simple favour more
delicious than complete possession of any other woman, such is
the value which it derives from respect, timidity and the fear of
scandal.   It depends entirely on him, observe, whether he will
marry her or not.   He thinks of doing so, and is ready to yield
to the temptation, but suddenly pride obtains the mastery, the
blood of the Lovelaces forbids the last of their stock to ".lick
the dust for a wife."[1]   " To carry off such a girl as this, in
spite of all her watchful and implacable friends : and in spite of
a prudence that I never met with in any of her sex :—what a
triumph !—What a triumph over the whole sex !—And then
such a revenge to gratify ! "   A revenge upon love, which
he hates because he is consumed by it : " Love, which I hate,
heartily hate, because 'tis my master ! "   Truly these are, as
Diderot said, " the sentiments of a cannibal, the cries of a wild
beast," maddened and intoxicated by the sight of blood.   Is
Lovelace happy when his victim is once within his power ?   By
no means.   He is seized with a fresh desire to torture her.   In
his letters to Belford he loads her with insult and contempt: he
would have her for his mistress, but he would also have her
ruined, polluted in the eyes of men, and absolutely at the mercy
of his " own imperial will."[2]   He even laughs with satanic
merriment : " Hah, hah, hah, hah !—I must here—I must here
lay down my pen, to hold my sides ; for I must have my laugh
out, now the fit is upon me."   What ?   She expects some
mischief from me ?   " I don't care to disappoint anybody I have
a value for."

His punishment is that at last he comes to believe what he
says.   " The modest ones and I are pretty much upon a par.
The difference between us is only, what they *think*, *I act*."[3]
The man who has come to this has shut himself off from real

<hr>

[1] Vol. ii., p. 39.   [2] II., 23.   [3] II., 48.

love. Thus when Lovelace endeavours to love Clarissa with a pure passion, it is no longer within his power. Suspicion, paltry jealousy and withering doubt are too strong: "Is virtue to be established by common bruit only? Has her virtue ever been proved?"[1] With cogent and mischievous logic he convinces himself that no woman is honest. All his mistress's vernal bloom and grace is nothing but trickery and falsehood. This it is which constitutes the profound truth of Lovelace's character: that there is a fatality which imposes evil-doing upon the man who begins his career in evil, that a man's whole existence has to bear the weight of his first transgressions, that for him who has exhausted its living sources within himself, happiness is henceforth radically impossible. The whole series of Lovelace's triumphs is a lingering expiation, and when at last he falls beneath the sword of Colonel Morden, his punishment has already long ago begun.

Thus, in spite of the author's concessions to convention, the character of Lovelace remains an admirable creation, inasmuch as Richardson managed to embody a profound characteristic of human nature in the living picture of a man of his time.

His portraits of the Harlowe family constitute a richly furnished gallery of base characters, though their meanness and repulsiveness are of various kinds. Here is Clarissa's brother, an English country squire, coarse, spiteful and avaricious, caring for nothing in the world but to add to the money he has got together, and hating his sisters with the hatred of the son and heir whose patrimony they are consuming: his opinion, as he himself affirms, is that "a man who has sons brings up chickens for his own table, whereas daughters are chickens brought up for the tables of other men."[2] He is subject, moreover, to a most violent temper, a constant savage ill-humour; one would take him for a character of Fielding's. Here, again, is the sister, Arabella, sour and treacherous in disposition, and incapable of forgiving Clarissa for having the advantage of her in beauty and good-nature. And here her father, as relentless as he is tyrannical; her uncle James, concealing a kindly disposition

---

[1] Vol. ii., p. 39.   [2] Vol. i., p. 536.

beneath a rough exterior, and her uncle Anthony, whose harshness borders on ferocity. How many variations upon a single sentiment! With regard to this novel we may honestly share the admiration of Diderot for the marvellous diversity of Richardson's characters.

But his women are more lifelike still. He had associated with them more, and had got to know them more thoroughly. His own nature was a feminine one. From childhood he had always had his audience of girls, to whom he was accustomed to relate stories, and had acted as confidant to a circle of ladies, whose love-letters he had been accustomed to write. In later life he is represented as a weak, but kindly and soft-hearted creature, all imagination and sentiment, with a touch of romance to boot. The sight of a woman sharpened his wits : to Lady Bradshaigh he described himself as " by chance lively ; very lively it will be if he have hope of seeing a lady whom he loves and honours ; his eye always on the ladies."[1]   Like Jean-Jacques he was nervous, impressionable and feeble in health. In him too, as in Rousseau, there was something feminine. He never had the courage to mount a horse. Wine, meat and fish were forbidden him. His nerves at last became so excitable that his hand shook too much to allow of his lifting a glass of wine to his lips, and that he held none but written communication with his foreman, so as to avoid speaking aloud.

A man of this sort—capable of shedding tears over Clementina and Clarissa, as though they were members of his own family— must have been as tender-hearted and as sensitive to pain as Cowper or Rousseau. Hence the genius he displayed in writing the biographies of two or three women.

The first of these, the modest little waiting-maid Pamela, is almost too familiar to be regarded as the heroine of a novel. The daughter of peasants, she takes her three meals with hearty appetite, and brings to the service of her employer a practical mind and good sense—we might almost say, a good return. Once married, she says to her master, " I will assist your housekeeper, as I used to do, in the making jellies, comfits, sweetmeats, mar-

---

[1] Quoted by W. Scott, vol. ii., p. 22.

malades, cordials . . . and to make myself all the fine linen of the family, for yourself and me." She wants to convince him that their marriage, great as the honour would be for her, would at the same time be no bad thing for himself.

She is fully sensible, moreover, of differences in rank. When she leaves her place, the servants shed tears and wish to give her little presents in token of their friendship. She refuses, being unwilling to receive anything from " the lower servants "— which is characteristic of her type.

She is fond of admiration and longs to put on her fine silk dress. But then would not her doing so imply a vain disposition ? And she argues the question out before us.—Again, she is timid. Placed in confinement by her master, she wishes to escape ; unfortunately there is in the meadow a bull which has already injured the cook. So, on a certain occasion when she has opened the garden gate she sees the bull glaring fixedly at her with fiery eyes : " Do you think there are such things as witches and spirits ? If there be, I believe in my heart Mrs Jewkes has got this bull on her side." [1] After a few moments she goes out once more, and this time plucks up all her courage. But again it fails her : "Well, here I am, come back again! frighted, like a fool, out of all my purposes." And then, besides the bull, are not thieves said to be wandering about the country ?—This is all very natural and life-like, and gives us a good picture of the little country girl, with her simplicity, folly and timidity.

Pamela loves with a humble and melancholy fidelity. She endures without murmuring a thousand insults and mortifications. Her master insults her, yet she will not have him ill thought of. The old steward sees her setting off and guesses the reason of her leaving : " You are too *pretty*, my sweet mistress, and it may be too *virtuous*. Ah! have I not hit it ? " Proudly she answers : " No, good Mr Longman, don't think anything amiss of my master," and there is something almost heroic in her simple reply. Her master flouts her. She falls on her knees, and before witnesses declares herself " a very faulty and very ungrateful creature to the *best* of masters." " I have been very perverse

[1] Ballantyne, vol. i., p. 77.

and saucy ; and have deserved nothing at your hands but to be turned out of your family with shame and disgrace." [1] She takes a sort of cruel pleasure in abasing herself at the feet of the man she loves. In spite of all his persecution she is unable to hate him, and when, though placed in confinement and grossly insulted by him, she learns that he has just had a narrow escape from death, her joy breaks forth in spite of herself : "What is the matter, that, with all his ill-usage of me, I cannot hate him ? To be sure, in this, I am not like other people ! " She loves, in fact, as few women have loved. When she thinks her master appreciates her, she seems to hear " the harmony of the spheres all around " her. She is filled with terror at the thought that at the day of judgment she may possibly have to accuse the man she loves above everything else, " the unhappy soul, that I could wish it in my power to save ! " A sober expression of the most intense feeling, purer a thousand times than the love-language of a Marianne or a Manon.

Like a true Englishwoman of the lower class, Pamela's religion is at once artless and conscientious. It is odd that Richardson should have been blamed for the very thing which gives his creation the unmistakable impress of truth. Like George Eliot's heroines, whose prototype she is—like Dinah Morris the preacher, she says, with blind faith in God: "Bread and water I can live upon . . . with content. Water I can get anywhere . . . and if I can't get me bread, I will live like a bird in winter upon hips and haws . . . or anything." [2] Pamela's scruples, it is true, are some of them childish, but even this characteristic is eminently faithful to life. One day, in her trouble, she repeats the 137th Psalm, with a few alterations to make it applicable to her own situation. These changes make her uneasy: is it not sinful to introduce them ? The trait is at least as natural as the innocent pride she takes in her first ride in a carriage. It is just this mixture of candour, innocence, and impulsiveness, in an English country girl, possessed with fear of the devil and haunted by the thought of the Judgment Day, that gives this character its charm.

[1] Ballantyne, vol. i., p. 44. [2] *Pamela*, letter xxix.

At times her religion reaches the level of the sublime. On one occasion she slips out of the house, succeeds in reaching the garden, climbs a wall, falls down and injures herself. What is to become of her?[1]

"God forgive me! but a sad thought came just then into my head. I tremble to think of it! Indeed my apprehensions of the usage I should meet with had like to have made me miserable for ever! O my dear, dear parents, forgive your poor child; but being then quite desperate, I crept along till I could raise myself on my staggering feet; and away limped I! what to do, but to throw myself into the pond, and so put a period to all my griefs in the world!—But oh! to find them infinitely aggravated (had I not, by the divine grace, been withheld) in a miserable *eternity*!"

She sits down therefore on the grass, and the devil tempts her:

"And then, thought I (and oh! that thought was surely of the devil's instigation; for it was very soothing, and powerful with me), these wicked wretches who have now no remorse, no pity on me, will then be moved to lament their misdoings; and when they see the dead corpse of the unhappy Pamela dragged out to these dewy banks, and lying breathless at their feet, they will find that remorse to soften their obdurate heart, which, now, has no place there. And my master, my angry master, will then forget his resentments, and say: O, this is the unhappy Pamela! that I have so causelessly persecuted and destroyed! Now do I see she preferred her honesty to her life, will he say, and is no hypocrite, nor deceiver; but really was the innocent creature she pretended to be. Then, thought I, will he, perhaps, shed a few tears over the corpse of his persecuted servant; and though he may give out, it was love and disappointment; and that, perhaps (in order to hide his own guilt), for the unfortunate Mr Williams, yet will he be inwardly grieved, and order me a decent funeral, and save me, or rather *this part* of me, from the dreadful stake and the highway interment; and the young men and maidens all around my dear father's will pity poor Pamela! But O! I hope I shall not be the subject of their ballads and elegies; but that my memory, for the sake of my dear father and mother, may quickly slide into oblivion."

Clarissa, in virtue of the strength and sincerity of her religious feelings, is sister to Pamela. Like Pamela, too, she is essentially English; that is to say, she has a firmness and stability of judgment which distinguish her at once from the heroines of French fiction. She knows what she wants and why she wants it. She has none of the whims and caprices of the pretty woman. She claims for her sex the right to

[1] In reference to this scene, see Saint-Marc-Girardin, *Cours de littérature dramatique*, vol. i., pp. 109-111. Ballantyne, vol. i., p. 86.

show that it possesses prudence and "steadiness of mind," a quality which is denied it by none but the ill-intentioned. She regards herself as the mistress of her own life, and, with all her respect for her parents, intends to keep the disposal of herself within her own hands. Practical, moreover, and quite at home in money matters, she talks of them with the knowledge of a steward; nor will she ever be the one to forget that fortune is an element of happiness. Melancholy as it may seem to the romantic mind, Clarissa is eminently *reasonable*. Such she appears in the earlier letters of the collection, before her passions have been so violently stirred; and such she remains to the end. In the opinion of her friend, the witty and sprightly Miss Howe, she is "over-serious." Nothing, in fact, deceives her; with unerring discernment she unravels the plots which are being woven around her, detects the underhand tricks of her brothers and sisters, defends herself against them to the best of her ability, like a prudent girl who has no advocate but herself, and amidst all her trials preserves a clear and at times a somewhat harsh judgment.

Thoroughly English also, like Pamela, in her prejudices, she entertains the whole stock of opinions common to every middle-class girl who has been properly brought up, and, in particular, a very keen consciousness of *respectability*. Whether she would love Lovelace, if he were a working man or a small tradesman, I cannot say; we may venture to doubt it. She is too well aware of what she owes to herself, and too much wedded to *decorum*. She strongly commends Lovelace for paying his tenants in order to make them attend church, for otherwise they would not go. And it is good for them to go : it is the natural order of things, and belongs to a well-organised state of society. Her ideas on marriage, too, are almost irritating in their good sense: she would have conformity in rank, in family, in fortune and in everything else. Occasionally she is calm and self-possessed to an extent that is depressing; one wants her to be more at the mercy of her impulses, more free and unconstrained. The truth is that Richardson's admirable art would not allow him to make a weak-minded, romantic creature like Julie d'Étanges the heroine of a drama of fierce passion, but led him rather to choose a girl whose strict virtue approaches austerity. And how much more impressive the lesson becomes in consequence, the drama how much more painfully effective! What does it matter, the reader may say, if the heroine is rendered less womanly, provided her portrait is true to nature.

But Clarissa remains a thorough woman. She is gentle, kind, sympathetic, an excellent counsellor and a faithful friend. In the midst of her troubles she retains an unalterable affection for all her relations, even for her weak-minded mother; insomuch that she cannot forgive Miss Howe for a few harmless reflexions upon her parents. She is determined to be always the best of daughters, and such she remains till death. And with all her soundness of judgment, on the other hand, she is never proof against sudden emotion. She never manages to credit the full extent of human malignity. Observe the strange agreement she signs when she is in the hands of Lovelace : if her parents persist in their opposition to her marriage she will remain single. How serious, how candid a pledge to give! With charming reserve she adds that he must not take this promise as a favour, but merely as a sort of recompense for the trouble he has had on her account.

Clarissa, therefore, is a truly living creation. Even if she did not love, she would still be better than the doll of a court or a drawing-room. Hers is the first complete biography of a woman in modern fiction.

But, in order thoroughly to understand Richardson's characters, we must restore the conditions of thought which give them a background of reality and make them live. Some of these ideas have had their day, some are eternal. To quote a remark of Mr Leslie Stephen's, these men and women " show all the weaknesses inseparable from the age and country of their origin. . . . They are cramped and deformed by the frigid conventionalities of their century and the narrow society in which they move and live. But for all that they stir the emotions of a distant generation."[1]

[1] *Hours in a Library*, vol. i., p. 84.

IV

It cannot but be that these ideas were entertained by Richardson himself. Whatever a novelist's power of observation, however versatile his talent, there is always one type of character which he draws in preference to others, because it is more closely related to his own nature. Lesage was especially successful with the vulgar and practical Gil Blas, Marivaux with Marianne—the type of affectation, and Prévost with the weak-minded and susceptible Des Grieux, just as Balzac incarnated himself in his adventurers, Rastignac and Vautrin, and as George Sand put something of herself into Lelia.

Richardson's ideal was that of a noble and tender soul, liable to temptation by reason of its extreme sensibility, but deeply religious and strongly attached to Christianity. Richardson's characters, said Villemain, became one of the forms of his own existence. The form in which his genius by preference embodied itself was the character of Clarissa Harlowe—affectionate, yet prudent ; passionate, yet self-controlled. This single character epitomizes in itself the moral philosophy of the pious printer who was "the greatest and perhaps the most unconscious of Shakespeare's imitators." [1]

Richardson, it is true, moralizes because he is an Englishman, and because the English, as Tacitus had observed, "cannot laugh at vice": from its earliest days the English novel was a school of morals, and ancestors of Richardson have been discovered even in Lyly and Greene.[2] But there are many degrees in this tendency of the race and of this particular branch of literature, and no one has ever moralized more undisguisedly than the author of *Clarissa*. As a child he was given to inventing stories, all of which "carried with them, I am bold to say, an useful moral."[3] When he takes up his pen it is to "turn young people into a course of reading different from the pomp and parade of romance-writing," and "to promote the cause of

[1] Villemain, *xviiie siècle*, lesson 27.
[2] *Cf.* J. Jusserand, *Le roman anglais au temps de Shakespeare.*
[3] *Life*, quoted by Sir W. Scott.

N

religion and virtue." Plainly he is a moralist first and a novelist afterwards. "Why, sir," wrote Johnson to Erskine, who condemned Richardson for being tedious, "if you were to read Richardson for the story, your impatience would be so much fretted that you would hang yourself. But you must read him for the sentiment, and consider the story only as giving occasion to the sentiment."[1] Now "the sentiment," here, means chiefly the moral sentiment. So true is this that the author had appended to his own copy of *Clarissa Harlowe* an alphabetical index of the maxims and moral disquisitions contained in the work, and had taken such pains over it that even the most trivial thoughts were to be found in the list,[2] such as "habits are not easily changed," or "men are known by their companions." Johnson encouraged him in this work, considering that "Clarissa is not a performance to be read with eagerness, and laid aside for ever; but will be occasionally consulted by the busy, the aged, and the studious."[3]

In the *Postscriptum* to *Clarissa*, moreover, Richardson was careful to explain himself as clearly as possible on this point :

"It will be seen, by this time, that the author had a great end in view. He has lived to see scepticism and infidelity openly avowed, and even endeavoured to be propagated from the *press* ; the great doctrines of the Gospel brought into question ; those of self-denial and mortification blotted out of the catalogue of Christian virtues ; and a taste even to wantonness for outdoor pleasure and luxury, to the general exclusion of domestic as well as public virtue, industriously promoted among all ranks and degrees of people. In this general depravity . . . the author . . . imagined, that if in an age given up to diversion and entertainment, he could *steal in*, as may be said, and investigate the great doctrines of Christianity under the fashionable guise of an amusement, he should be most likely to serve his purpose."[4]

In the mind of its author, his novel is an "amusing" apology for religion.

In this demonstration, if the truth be told, the "amusement" is often conspicuous only by its absence. The author is terribly

[1] Boswell, *Life of Johnson.*
[2] D'Israeli, *Curiosities of Literature*, edn. of 1889, p. 200.
[3] *Life of Johnson*, Boswell (Croker's edn., p. 73). In fact a series of extracts was published, entitled : *A collection of the moral and instructive Sentiments, Maxims, Cautions and Reflexions contained in the Histories of Pamela, Clarissa and Sir Charles Grandison*, 1755, 12mo.
[4] Ballantyne, vol. ii., pp. 778-9.

addicted to platitude.   He is the kind of man who will bring a
score of good reasons to prove that the most immaculate virtue
is insecure against a man who is careless of his own honour, or
again, that a man of good principles, whose love is founded upon
reason, and is directed rather to the mind than to the body, will
make any honest woman happy.

As a moralist, moreover, he is a man of a small and narrow
mind; he believes in the most tyrannical social conventions as
though they were so many dogmas; he establishes really too
close a connexion between virtue and the doctrines of the
English Protestant Church; he is at once a Pharisee and a
utilitarian.   Virtue, for him, is a sort of investment at compound
interest, and the beneficiaries are a little too apt to congratulate
themselves on the excellence of their schemes.   "That his
pieces," wrote Jeffrey, "were all intended to be strictly moral,
is indisputable; but it is not quite so clear that they will
uniformly be found to have this tendency."[1]   Coleridge could
not tolerate Richardson's *cant*, and frankly avowed his preference
for the simpler and healthier moral philosophy of Fielding.[2]
Scott detects in Pamela a "strain of cold-blooded prudence . . .
to which we are almost obliged to deny the name of virtue."
Even in his own country Richardson was occasionally considered
more of a preacher than a moralist.

Nevertheless, however disposed we may be to question certain
of his opinions, the fact remains that the feeling which inspires
these big volumes is profoundly moral.   That they affected their
age to the extent they did was due to the fact that the age found
in them what was previously unknown in fiction—the boldly
avowed pretension to treat the most serious problems through
the medium of the novel.   The pleasure which readers derived
from *Clarissa Harlowe* was that of feeling within themselves a
regeneration of those sources of moral emotion which might have
been supposed exhausted.   The author's teachers had been
Berkeley and Bunyan.[3]   But the preaching of philosophers
and sermon-writers only goes down with converts.   Richard-

---

[1] *Edinburgh Review*, vol. v., pp. 43-44.   [2] *Literary Remains.*
[3] J. Jusserand, *The English Novel*, p. 68.

son convinced the worldlings that to be, or to believe oneself, good, might be a source of the keenest pleasure. These works, following their slow and leisurely course like some listless stream, are pervaded by a kind of beneficent calm. Here were men spoiled by excessive indulgence in keen sensations—pleasure, curiosity, and weariness of the worldly life ; men whose individuality, in the torrent of these small impressions, had become attenuated to the vanishing point ; reduced to mere echoes of their restless environment they were no longer capable of giving forth an independent sound. In these unsatisfied readers Richardson created afresh the taste for the inner life, the illusion that they could be and feel themselves useful, and the firm foundation of everyday thought and activity. The study of *Pamela* and *Clarissa* is a lesson in hygiene.

To reproach him with laying too much stress upon the moral of his work would thus be to deceive ourselves as to the nature of his genius. Deprive the *Nouvelle Héloïse* of its moral, and what remains ? Very little. The case is the same with *Clarissa*. The work owed both its novelty and its influence to its moral inspiration.

Further, it effected a transformation in the art of fiction. In Richardson's hands the novel becomes a marvellous instrument of psychological analysis. " The analytical novel," wrote Vigny, " is the offspring of confession. It was Christianity that suggested the idea, through the practice of self-revelation." [1] We might amend Vigny's remark by saying that it is perhaps the absence of the confessional in Protestantism that has given birth to the novel of moral analysis. Richardson, who was a kind of lay spiritual director—" a Protestant confessor," as an English critic calls him [2]—possibly owed his success to the disappearance of the priest from English society in the eighteenth century. However this may be, we have in fiction a branch of literature which is entirely Christian, and by consequence entirely modern. The novel with a moral, unknown to antiquity, is the most perfect expression of the society of to-day. It reflects its anxiety, its morbid uneasiness, its secret unrest. Christian casuistry, the " natural history of the soul," [3] is unrivalled as a teacher of prac-

---

[1] *Journal d'un poète*, p. 192.   [2] Leslie Stephen, *Hours in a Library*.
[3] Taine, *Littérature anglaise*, vol. iv., p. 103.

tical philosophy. To introduce it in fiction was to open up fresh
fields for the novelist's art.

No one could be better versed is casuistry than Richardson.
His dream in early life was to be a theologian, and for lack of a
pulpit he preached in his novels. " It is he," as Diderot justly
observed, " who carries the torch to the very depths of the
cavern, and teaches us to detest the subtle and dishonest motives
that hide or slink away behind the other honest motives which
are always the first to appear." No one can be more deeply interested in questions of conscience. A thousand minor problems
of the moral life, hitherto considered unworthy of good literature
or touched upon only by professional moralists, such as Addison
and Steele, are by Richardson treated seriously and at length.
How should a virtuous girl behave towards a scolding ill-
tempered mother ? What consolation can she find for the little
weaknesses of her lover—for the sight of his untidy boots or
ill-tied neck-cloth ? How should her lover behave towards his
betrothed ? How is he to make himself lovable without sacri-
ficing his manly dignity ? Miss Howe asks her friend's opinion
as to the amount of importance a woman should attach to a
man's physical beauty. Clarissa replies with a carefully ordered
disquisition, in which she approaches the question, (1) from a
general, and (2) from a particular point of view. She considers
the part which love plays in life, in reference, (1) to our *relative*
duties ; (2) to our social duties ; (3) to our highest duties and
when considered from the divine point of view. She numbers
her arguments, underlines those which are most essential, and
distinguishes fresh points of view in those she has distinguished
already.[1] She asks herself whether she loves Lovelace, and finally
accords him " a sort of conditional love." Keeping a journal is
with her a method of determining, supplementing, or amending her
own resolutions and of " entering into a compact with herself." [2]

[1] *Cf.* vol. i., p. 572 *et seq.*

[2] " When I set down what I *will* do, or what I *have* done, on this or that occasion, the resolution or action is before me, either to be adhered to, withdrawn or
amended, and I have entered into compact with myself, as I may say ; having
given it under my own hand to *improve*, rather than to go backward, as I live
longer." (Vol. ii., p. 82.)

This is the method of the casuist, who divides ideas into the slenderest shreds, nay, even into imperceptible filaments.

Moral dialectic is to be found on every page. Is one bound, Miss Howe queries, to rescue a friend from an awkward situation at the risk of falling into one no less, or more, awkward oneself? A delicate question this; it deserves an entire letter. Should marriages be founded on interest or on love? Clarissa's letters contain matter enough for a volume on this point. Ought one to marry contrary to one's own inclination and in obedience to parental desire? In other words, is it Clarissa's duty to marry Solmes? It must not be supposed that the mere prospect of doing so throws her into despair, like a vulgar stage-heroine. She weighs her reasons. By refusing Solmes she will inflict deep pain on her mother; is this a sin? If so, what excuse has she for her conduct? Here is one, perhaps : however the controversy terminates, her mother's troubles cannot last long, for if she marries Lovelace her mother will immediately console herself, whereas, if she marries a man she detests, Clarissa will be for ever unhappy. A temporary sorrow for her mother is therefore preferable to eternal sorrow for Clarissa. It would be impossible to weigh duties more ingeniously, or in a more sensitive balance.

Occasionally the habit amounts almost to a mania. Shall Pamela stay with her master or not? She draws up a balance-sheet of arguments. Reasons for: she will be sustained by divine grace, and a happy future will be secured for her parents, etc. Reasons against : her inexperience, the danger to her innocence, etc. Richardson drew up this balance-sheet with the same perfection of method as he employed in determining the liabilities and assets of his printing establishment.

Yet even this brings his characters nearer to us. It *humanizes* them, as it were, and endows them with life. The heroes of tragedy struggle against love for the sake of honour, or against infamy for the sake of glory. Such motives are noble ones, it is true, but they are somewhat abstract. They do not come home to us so closely, because, as they appear to our eyes, they are deprived of the train of definite and sometimes paltry circumstances by which they are attended in real life. Richardson does not know what " love " and " honour " are. He observes each particular case, describes it, turns it over and over, weighs it twice or thrice, and finally comes to a conclusion upon it—at the price of having to repeat the whole process when the next case occurs. It is the method adopted by spiritual directors and writers of sermons.[1] It had to be introduced into fiction, and this could only be done by an author with a passion for ethical problems.

V

Lastly, if, in addition to his faithful observation of the external world, to the art with which he manages to bring his characters before the reader, and to the richness and abundance of his moral reflexions, we take into account his intensely sensitive nature and his peculiar gift of passionate attachment to his own creations, we shall have included all, or nearly all, the principal characteristics of Richardson's genius.

His sensibility was extraordinary, and, even at that maudlin period, seems to have been sincere. Consequently, the tears of every reader, during his own day, were at his command. When I read *Clarissa*, Miss Fielding wrote to him, " I am all sensation ; my heart glows." Another of his correspondents abandons the attempt to describe her feelings, and lays down her pen: " Excuse me, good Mr Richardson, I cannot go on ; it is your fault—you have done more than I can bear." [2] Richardson's successors in English fiction felt at liberty gently to banter the " enraptured spinsters " who " incensed " the master " with the coffee-pot," kissed the slippers they worked for him, and

---

[1] M. Brunetière (*Le roman naturaliste*, p. 292) maintains that Richardson drew much of his inspiration from Bourdaloue. It is, at any rate, beyond doubt that the works of the French sermon-writer were very popular in England. Burnet said to Voltaire that Bourdaloue had "effected a reformation among English as well as among French preachers." (*Cf. Lettre au duc de la Vallière.*)

[2] Mrs Barbauld, vol. iv., p. 241 (Letter from Lady Bradshaigh).

believed they saw a "halo of virtue" around his night-cap.[1]
Some of the forms taken by sensibility in the eighteenth century
were extremely ludicrous, but does it follow that Richardson
and Rousseau were insincere?

Richardson was not only sensitive, but also—it must be
admitted—sensual. In *Pamela* there is noticeable a singular
freedom in touching upon certain delicate subjects. Pamela
receives from her master a present of a pair of stockings; she
blushes. "Don't blush, Pamela," he says; "dost think I don't
know pretty maids wear shoes and stockings?" Amenities of
this sort are not rare. The author may seem to dwell at too
great length on the advances to which a girl of fifteen is exposed
from her master. Certain details are repulsive, and other
features astonish us. Pamela seems too familiar with the fact
that dejection commonly follows sensual pleasure: "We read in
Holy Writ, that wicked Ammon, when he had ruined poor
Tamar, hated her more than ever he loved her, and would
have turned her out of door."[2] In *Clarissa* there are long scenes
which take place in a disorderly house, and are anything but
chaste. Does the fault lie with the age? Is it not that
with Richardson, as with Rousseau, sensibility borders upon
sensuality?

Works which appeal so constantly and so powerfully to the
stronger emotions certainly cannot be read with impunity. There
is something sickly and sensual in Richardson's melancholy, a
melancholy, as Diderot said, "at once sweet and lasting." It is
too palpably an enjoyment of a morbid state of physical depression. Written for women, about women, and by an essentially feminine writer, these novels did much to prepare the way
for the "vague lachrymosity" of Hervey, Ossian, and Rousseau.
To Richardson must be accorded the most important place in
the history of "melancholy."[3] It was he who made languor
of soul and hidden tenderness fashionable, and developed the
popular taste for soft and melancholy feelings. All his readers

---

[1] Thackeray, *The Virginians*, vol. i.   [2] Ballantyne, vi., p. 35.
[3] On this topic see Leslie Stephen, *History of English thought in the eighteenth century*, vol. ii.

have mourned with Lovelace over the lost reflection of Clarissa, and all have sympathized with his words—

"I have been traversing her room, meditating, or taking up everything she but touched or used: the glass she dressed at I was ready to break, for not giving me the personal image it was wont to reflect of *her*, whose idea is for ever present with me. I call for her, now in the tenderest, now in the most reproachful terms, as if within hearing; wanting her, I want my own soul, at least everything dear to it. What a void in my heart! what a chillness in my blood, as if its circulation were arrested! From her room to my own; in the dining-room, and in and out of every place where I have seen the beloved of my heart, do I hurry; in none can I tarry; her lovely image in every one, in some lively attitude, rushing in upon me. . . ."[1]

The exquisite sadness of passion, though from Rousseau and Goethe it received a more lyrical expression, was already to be found in Richardson. His emotions, like theirs, were constantly being stirred by the thought of love, because, for him as for them, love is what the soul demands with irresistible force. With all its attendant moods of agitation, anxiety and depression, it is the highest and the deepest manifestation of our innermost self. This, for our pious novelist, is beyond doubt. Carlyle once maintained that in the lives of the majority love occupies but an insignificant place. In the novels of Richardson it occupies not only the most important, but every place. Of all moral and social questions it is the chief. Nor is the love here treated of the mere gallantry which formed the staple of French fiction and French drama in the seventeenth century, but rather that "tragic and terrible" love which is a matter of life and death. Love, in the novels of Marivaux, Lesage and Prévost, whatever importance they attach to it, is, it should be remarked, as yet a mere accident or a means to getting on in the world. Nowhere, even in *Manon Lescaut*, does it attain the dignity of a social duty. With Richardson it takes possession of the whole man, and absorbs the entire interest. "Our feelings," Saint-Évremond once said, "are wanting in a certain intensity; the impulses which half-roused passions excite in our souls can neither leave them in their usual condition nor carry them out of themselves."[2] This intensity in which the passions were deficient was expressed

[1] Ballantyne, vol. i., p. 266.   [2] *Sur les tragédies* (1677).

by Richardson with genius, because love, as he conceived it, was no mere accident or stroke of good fortune, but, in a sense, the most essential of human duties.

Love, passionate love, is the main point of all his novels. Pamela loves her unworthy master, Clarissa loves the monster Lovelace, Henrietta Byron and Clementina are distracted with love for Grandison, and innumerable trials are the reward of passion in every case. Pamela is reviled, imprisoned and over-whelmed with outrageous insults; Clarissa is done to death; Clementina loses her reason. Who will say that passion is not tragic? What a subject for study in this lingering anguish of a heart! And what wonder that Richardson devoted so much labour to the task? " *Clarissa*," wrote Alfred de Vigny, " is a treatise on strategy. Twenty-four volumes to describe the siege and capture of a heart : it is worthy of Vauban."[1] Such a feat is possible only to the man who is thoroughly convinced that if love is the source of man's greatest sorrows, it is also the sole principle of his nobility.

But when this man happens to be an Englishman and a Pro-testant, there is also, of course, a moral to be drawn from these adventures in the field of love. Two objects have to be reconciled, that of arousing the reader's feelings and that of instructing him, of being at once impassioned and thoroughly moral, very pathetic and highly improving. And this being so, one subject only is possible : love thwarted yet struggling, whether against external obstacles or against itself. This, in truth, is the only story Richardson has to tell, and the victims of this fatality are always women. All four—Pamela, Clarissa, Clementina, Henrietta—or, if Miss Jervins and Olivia be in-cluded, all six—strive either against their passion or against their duty. By one happiness is sacrificed to innocence, by another to filial duty, and by a third to religion; while Henrietta, who suffers the least of all, heroically leaves the field to her fortunate rival when she perceives that Clementina is the object of Grandison's affection.

Now no one has ever described these inward struggles as

[1] *Journal d'un poète*, 1833.

Richardson has done. Who had thought of depicting the conflict in a woman's heart between love and religion before he
did ?[1] What heroine of fiction or of tragedy had refused, like
Clementina, to give herself to the man she loves rather than
renounce her religion? Or, rather, what novelist had ventured
to transfer such a subject to the days in which he was writing—
to introduce characters, Protestant or Catholic, belonging to
1750? Pathetic is the struggle in Clementina's soul when
she learns that Grandison refuses to renounce his belief. The
noble girl has but to say one word in order to ensure her happiness : she need not even sacrifice her faith ; but that one word
will impair the dignity of her love. So she refuses to say it,
and it is under these circumstances that she writes Grandison
the following admirable letter :[2]

"O thou whom my heart best loveth, forgive me !—Forgive me, said I, for
what ?—For acting, if I am enabled to act, greatly ? The example is from thee,
who, in my eyes, art the greatest of human creatures. My duty calls upon me
one way : my heart resists my duty, and tempts me not to perform it. Do thou,
O God, support me in the arduous struggle ! Let it not, as once before, over-
throw my reason. . . . My tutor, my brother, my friend ! O most beloved and
best of men ! Seek me not in marriage ! I am unworthy of thee. Thy *soul* was
ever most dear to Clementina ! Whenever I meditated the gracefulness of thy
person, I restrained my eye, I checked my fancy : and how ? Why, by meditating the superior graces of thy mind. And is not that *soul*, thought I, to be
saved ? Dear, obstinate, and perverse ! And shall I bind my soul to a soul
allied to perdition ? That so dearly loves that soul as hardly to wish to be
separated from it in its future lot. O thou most amiable of men ! How can
be sure, that, if I were thine, thou wouldst not draw me after thee, by love, by
sweetness of manners, by condescending goodness? I, who once thought a heretic
the worst of beings, have been already led, by the amiableness of thy piety, by the
universality of thy charity to all thy fellow-creatures, to think more favourably of
all heretics, for thy sake. Of what force would be the admonitions of the most
pious confessor, were thy condescending goodness, and sweet persuasion, to be
exerted to melt a heart wholly thine? . . . O most amiable of men !—O thou
whom my soul loveth, seek not to entangle me by thy love ! Were I to be
thine, my duty to thee would mislead me from that I owe to my God. . . ."

The love which inspires such a letter is a noble feeling. It
is rendered greater by contact with the religious sentiment which

[1] We must not, however, forget the famous *Lettres d'une religieuse portugaise*, nor
Mme. de La Fayette's master-piece *La Princesse de Clèves*.
[2] Ballantyne, vol. iii., p. 508.

is mingled with it, and transforms it. Thence spring new shades, delicate and unsuspected varieties, of passion. Observe, moreover, that each of these heroines loves even to the point of absolutely forgetting herself, and even voluntarily abasing herself before the man she loves. In contrast to the cold Astrée or the haughty Alcidiane, they yield themselves beforehand, are all humility and submission, all tenderness and modesty. " O my dear ! " Henrietta cries with humility, " what a princess in everyone's eye will the declared love of such a man make me ! " Like Milton's Eve they would be the last—whatever the witty Miss Howe may say—to think themselves the equals of their masters. But this only renders the struggle more touching. The wonderful resolution with which they struggle against love is due to the fact that they, too, have souls of their own, for which they are accountable to God. The source of their dignity is their faith ; never had the religious sentiment triumphed more brilliantly in fiction than in these love-distracted hearts, which the tortures of passion drive to madness or to death. No scenes of pathos can equal the spectacle of this inward anguish, nor does any language contain anything superior to the last volume of *Clarissa Harlowe*. Let us try for a moment to imagine a happy ending to the book —such as was clamoured for by Richardson's readers : the consequence would be the absolute destruction of its moral, with all that constitutes its exquisite beauty. The death of Clarissa, as a martyr to duty, is essential. It is necessary that Lovelace should love Clarissa, but it is no less so that he should be the victim of his past errors, the recollection of which interposes between her and him. It is inevitable that he should become incapable of loving her as she deserves to be loved. It is essential that it should be for ever impossible for him to become the husband of her whom he has treated as a mistress. It is essential, in the last place, that she should forgive him, as she forgives her parents, and that her obedience to conscience should entail her death. No other *dénouement* is possible.

It matters little that Clarissa seems prudish, bigoted, or pedantic. Gradually, as the drama approaches its end, what is absurd disappears or loses consequence. Just as when, in

real life, we stand before a death-bed, unhallowed recollections
steal away, and above and beyond all paltry or trivial realities
we behold the image of the departing one, purified and already
less human, so, beside the bed of the dying Clarissa, the meek
little zealot, the affected provincial, the prolix and fastidious correspondent of the earlier chapters is forgotten, and all that remains before us is a girl dying because, amidst the most terrible
trials, she steadfastly retained command of her conscience and
her soul.   Slowly prepared by a host of accumulated incidents,
the emotion aroused by the multiplication of painful impressions
is greater even than would be occasioned by a sudden and
violent shock.   Our feelings are deeply rather than abruptly
stirred.

   " Most happy," says Clarissa upon her death-bed, " has been
to me my punishment *here !* "   In this glorification of suffering
as a means of purification lies the whole moral of the work.
This was something altogether new.   No novel had previously
been made the vehicle of such teaching ; none had so deeply
probed such serious questions ; none had conveyed so lofty a
lesson in a drama so moving.   Even to-day, little as it is read,
the last volume of *Clarissa* retains all its beauty.   " I make my
apologies," wrote Doudan in surprise, " to the old bookseller
Richardson, the closing scene of his drama is all of it very
beautiful and very touching."   Every one who reads these
admirable pages without prejudice will be of Doudan's opinion.

VI

   This was all quite new, and, what was more, it seemed so to
the reader.

   The novel had not yet been transformed into a branch of
literature capable of conveying ideas.   Neither Lesage, with
his short-sighted philosophy and indulgent optimism, nor Prévost,
with his purely romantic conception of life, nor even Marivaux,
who, with all his intellectual charm, was of too amiable a disposition, had achieved more than an imperfect success.   The

only work at all comparable, in point of moral significance, to English novels, was a short master-piece called the *Princesse de Clèves*.

Before the novel could become a branch of serious literature it required, first of all, to be re-constructed in point of form, purged of its crude dramatic interest, and shorn of its elements of romance and gallantry. Richardson attempted this, but did not altogether succeed; his work retains something of the romantic element, though but little in comparison with that of his predecessors. He at all events limited the amount of incident in fiction, and confined it to simple events. He wrote big books about little facts.

In the next place new types of character had to be chosen. Richardson selects them from the middle-class, or from the lesser nobility, as much because these strata of society were more familiar to him as because in them he had happened to find more souls that were souls in the true sense of the word —capable, that is to say, of self-communion and of living a fruitful inner life apart. They had to be exhibited as analysing their own minds, and this is why he chose the epistolary form of novel; a form which, even in his hands, did not attain perfection, but proved, nevertheless, an adequate vehicle for that study of the commonplace tragedies of the soul which it was designed to express.

It was necessary to get rid of any preoccupation of a purely literary character which might have hampered observation and detracted from the moral effect. Excellent in point of matter, the work of the carpenter's son, the pedantic and ill-educated printer, is at the same time inferior as regards form.

It was also needful to portray life in the very meanest detail, with the patience of the naturalist who is passionately interested in everything. This he attempted, and with a success which often rendered him tedious, but enabled him at the same time to present such complete and accurate pictures as make him the greatest realist of his time.

But necessary as it was to be an acute observer, it was even more so to be heart and soul a moralist, that is to say, to com-

bine deep religious convictions with the taste for moral problems : a condition, however, essential, but seldom realised
among literary men in the eighteenth century. Richardson,
like Rousseau in his own day, and like Tolstoï in ours, had
the immense advantage of being a believer.

Lastly, it was also necessary that with all these gifts there
should be combined the gift of emotion, intense sensibility,
extreme soft-heartedness, a really feminine partiality to tears,
and, above all, that talent for making his creations live, which,
as Villemain said, render him "the greatest and perhaps the
most unconscious imitator of Shakespeare."

The work which resulted from all these qualities, crude,
pedantic, and unequal as it was, was nevertheless profoundly
original, very English, though at the same time very human, and
undoubtedly, when we consider the period to which it belongs,
very new. Even at this distance of time its power remains
unimpaired, and sufficiently explains—if it does not absolutely
justify—the expression used by Johnson, when, with his rough
good sense, he said to Boswell that " French novels, compared
with Richardson's, . . . might be pretty baubles, but a wren
was not an eagle." [1]

[1] *Life of Johnson*, ed. Napier, vol. i., p. 516.

Chapter V

It has been truly said that *Clarissa Harlowe* is to *La Nouvelle Héloïse* what Rousseau's novel is to *Werther* :[1] the three works are inseparably connected, because the bond between them is one of heredity. But while *Werther* and *Héloïse* are still read, *Clarissa* is scarcely read at all, and this, beyond doubt, is the reason that, while no one thinks of disputing Goethe's indebtedness to Rousseau, it is to-day less easy to perceive the extent to which Rousseau is indebted to Richardson.

To realise how far this was so, we need to recall the unparalleled good fortune which attended *Pamela*, *Clarissa* and *Grandison* from the very moment of their appearance in France. The story of this controversy concerning English fiction constitutes an entire chapter, and not the least curious one, in the history of French literature. It inflamed public opinion almost to the same extent as the controversy over Shakespeare, and its

---

[1] Marc Monnier, *Rousseau et les étrangers* (in *Jean-Jacques Rousseau jugé par les Genevois d'aujourd'hui*).

208

last episode reflected dazzling glory upon Richardson, by proclaiming him the model, and often even the master, of Rousseau.

I

The success of *Pamela* was in the first place due to the fact that it impressed the reader as being at once moral in tendency and true. " An English girl, without birth or property, sets an example which might put to shame the *comtesses* and *marquises* of our most famous novelists."[1] Desfontaines, the accredited champion of literary novelties from England, strongly insisted on the novelty of *Pamela*, declaring that the book departed from the " beaten track " by restoring the credit of woman, who had been insulted in so many fashionable books (Crébillon *fils* had just published [1736] his *Égarements du cœur et de l'esprit*), and by returning to what was simple and natural. In *Pamela* " there are neither daring descriptions, nor lewd suggestions, nor epigrammatic obscurities." " True, these are not the adventures of the princess, *marquise*, *comtesse*, 'or *baronne*, who commonly figures as the heroine in our novels." But if the author " had credited some lofty personage in the upper ranks of society with so much virtue and power of resistance, where would truth to nature have been ? " The style, it is true, has not the " elegant symmetry of a geometrical figure," but it is full of a " happy carelessness." In short, *Pamela*, in spite of being an English novel, was an excellent pattern to set before French authors.[2]

English the book was, unfortunately for Desfontaines, and at that very moment England had declared herself on the side of Marie-Thérèse, in the war of the Austrian succession. A pamphlet appeared in patriotic denunciation of the dangerous tendencies of a novel so loud in its praises of insular virtue.[3] The *Journal de police* proclaims its " indignation against the

---

[1] *Journal étranger*, February 1755.

[2] *Observations sur les écrits modernes*, vol. xxix., 1742.

[3] *Lettre à l'abbé Desfontaines sur Paméla*, Paris, 1742. (See the *Journal de police*, published with the *Journal de Barbier*, Charpentier's edn., vol. viii., p. 158, and *Observations sur les écrits modernes*, vol. xxix., p. 213.)

author of the *Observations* for having written a defence of
Pamela," and its amazement that a license should have been
granted to the translator of a book, "the preface of which is a
panegyric on the English and an insult to the entire French
nation." Just as, at an earlier date, Corneille had incurred the
suspicion of the authorities for having eulogized Spain in the
Cid, so the anglophiles of the eighteenth century were readily
taken for enemies of the State.

Was it out of resentment that Desfontaines translated *Joseph
Andrews*, which is a satire upon *Pamela*? It is possible. But
his efforts to promote the success of Fielding's novel, and to
commend it "as a popular compendium of moral teaching and
knowledge of the world,"[1] were in vain. He had to acknowledge his failure, and laid the blame for it on the ultra-classical
taste of the French. "It is nothing that the entire population
of a country which is the home of intellectual refinement and
good taste is charmed with the original. They are English, it is
said; do they know what a work of genius is?" The book is
supposed to be deficient in interest. "Where, I venture to ask,
is the interest of such novels as *Don Quixote*, *Gil Blas*, and those
of Scarron?"[2] But since its discovery of Richardson the public
would have none of Fielding, and contrasted a novel "so full of
paltry meanness" with the biography of "the discreet and modest
Pamela, whose famous adventures have been the admiration of
such a multitude of readers."[3] Mme. du Deffand was incon-
solable because she had read the new master-piece.[4] "But for
Pamela, wrote Crébillon to Chesterfield, we should not know here
what to read or to say,"[5] and the heroine's name rapidly became
popular. Even at the close of the century the duc d'Orléans gave
it to a girl who was supposed to be his natural daughter.[6]

Richardson's novel provoked continuations, imitations and
burlesques. There were sequels to *Pamela* on the one hand,

[1] *Lettre d'une dame anglaise*, printed with *Joseph Andrews*.
[2] *Observations*, vol. xxxiii., p. 313.
[3] *Bibliothèque française*, or *Histoire littéraire de la France*, 1744, p. 203.
[4] 5th July 1742.
[5] 26th July 1742; see J. Jusserand, *The English Novel*, p. 414.
[6] Lamartine, *Histoire des Girondins*, vol. iv., p. 182, and v., p. 227.

and "anti-Pamelas" on the other.[1] Powerfully yet clumsily treated in English,[2] the subject attracted the attention of dramatists just at the time when La Chaussée had produced his first comedies of middle-class life; but it did not bring them good fortune. In Boissy's *Paméla en France* the modest waiting-maid is transformed into a coquette, who swoons and faints away with almost mathematical regularity. "Faint," says one of the characters to her, in order to save her from an awkward situation. "I would," she replies, "only the public would take it amiss again."

In truth the public accorded a somewhat cool reception to this clumsy imitation of the latest success in fiction. Its hero is a marquis, who, disguised as Cupid, finally marries the maiden he loves in a grand transformation scene.[3] La Chaussée was no more fortunate, in spite of the manifest affinity between his talent and Richardson's genius. In his piece, one of the poorest plays he wrote, the flavour of originality possessed by the novel has entirely disappeared. Pamela reclines "on a sofa of turf." She has some scruples with regard to angling : " Alas ! can an act of destruction be turned into sport ? I could not inflict pain on a living creature, whatever its species." Charming in the original, this touch becomes ridiculous upon the stage. At a certain point one tame and inoffensive line :

> "You will take my carriage, that you may go more quickly,"

provoked such laughter from the audience that the author had to withdraw his piece.[4] A few days later the *Comédiens Italiens* took advantage of the twofold disaster of Boissy and La Chaussée

---

[1] See *Lettres amusantes et critiques sur les romans en général, anglais et français, tant anciens que modernes* [by Aubert de la Chesnaye Desbois], Paris, 1743, 2 parts 12mo.—*Fanny ou la Nouvelle Paméla*, by d'Arnaud (1767): *Histoire de Paméla en liberté* (1776), &c. Upon the parodies of *Pamela* consult H. Harrisse, *L'abbé Prévost*, p. 338. See, for example : *L'Anti-Paméla ou la fausse innocence découverte dans les aventures de Syrène, histoire véritable traduite de l'anglais*, 1743, 12mo.

[2] Clément, *Les cinq années littéraires*, vol. i., p. 234.

[3] *Paméla en France ou la vertu mieux éprouvée :* a comedy in verse, in three acts, played at the Italiens, 4th March 1743.

[4] Played at the Français, 6th December 1743. (See M. Lanson's book on *Nivelle de la Chaussée*, p. 159 *et seq.*)

to play *La Déroute des Paméla*, by Godard d'Aucour, which proved extremely diverting.[1]

But the success of the novel was by no means at an end. Six years later Voltaire, in his turn, borrowed from it not only the plot for his *Nanine*, but even his heroine's name—Nanine for Nanny.[2] "It is Pamela herself, in the guise of a French miniature," a critic was generous enough to remark[3]; but this is a great deal to say. Nanine is beloved by the generous and open-handed d'Olban; there is no obstacle between them but the difference in their stations; hence, all the pathos that arises out of the situation of the enamoured though virtuous waiting-maid disappears. Nanine turns to Richardson's novel for lessons in philosophy: "I was reading."—"What was the work?"—"An English one which has been given me as a present."—"Upon what subject?"—"It is interesting. The author maintains that all men are brothers—all born equal; but such notions are absurd."

A few of these absurd notions, presented in a somewhat insipid style, were unable to redeem the piece.[4] Rousseau afterwards regretted its failure, and accused the French public of incapacity to appreciate a play which treated "honour, virtue, and the natural sentiments in their original purity as preferable to the impertinent prejudice of rank,"[5] and possessed, moreover, what in his eyes was the great merit of being inspired by Richardson.[6]

But if public opinion refused to accept the adaptations of Boissy, La Chaussée, and Voltaire, it had adopted the original work, and when, eight years later, *Clarissa* was translated by Prévost, the earlier effort had prepared popular taste to admire the master-piece.

•

[1] 23rd December 1743.—See the *Mercure* for 1743, p. 2722.

[2] See M. Holzhauser's study on the comedies of Voltaire (*Zeitschrift fur neu-franzötische Sprache und Literatur*, vol. vii., supplement, p. 69) on the subject of Voltaire's indebtedness to Richardson.

[3] Geoffroy, *Cours de littérature dramatique*, vol. iii., p. 7.

[4] Played 16th June 1749.   [5] *Lettre sur les spectacles*, notes.

[6] A version of *Pamela*, by François de Neufchâteau, was played even during the revolutionary period.

If we may believe Voltaire, the success of this second novel was not to be compared with that attained by the first.[1] But Voltaire, who is never a very reliable witness, is particularly untrustworthy when any English book is in question. Everything goes to prove that *Clarissa* was no less, but even more, successful than *Pamela*. The first part, which appeared by itself, caused, it is true, some disappointment : readers found fault, and not without reason, with its prolixity. "Your reflexions weary us to death," wrote Clément de Genève; "a plague on the subtle and weighty reasoner who gives us a disquisition instead of a story ! "[2] But the work created a sensation, and from *Clarissa* onwards, English novels were translated "the whole day long."

On the publication of the English original, there had appeared at Amsterdam a highly appreciative criticism of it in French. The author drew a parallel between Richardson and Marivaux, commending the latter, though without much warmth, for his efforts to bring the novel back to reality, and praising the former to the skies for having made his work true to life in point of detail, and provided it with a lofty moral. This estimate of his work had fallen into the hands of Richardson, who had made use of it in the appendix to *Clarissa*.[3] Once in possession of the entire master-piece, the French public confirmed this opinion and became loud in praise of the work. Richardson, who, after the appearance of *Pamela*, was regarded simply as an original writer, now became a great man. "I do not think," writes Marmontel,[4] "that the age can show a more faithful, more delicate, more spirited touch. We do not read, we *see*, what he describes," and he praises the consummate art of the

---

[1] *Gazette littéraire*, 30th May 1764: "English novels were scarcely read at all in Europe before the appearance of *Pamela*. This type of work seemed highly interesting ; *Clarissa* met with less success, but deserved more."—Observe, moreover, that he contradicts himself elsewhere (Preface to *L'Écossaise*).

[2] *Les cinq années littéraires*, 15th March 1751.—*Cf. Nouvelles littéraires* for 25th January 1751.

[3] This expression of opinion will be found in the *Gentleman's Magazine* (June 1749, vol. xix.). I am unacquainted with the name of the author.

[4] *Mercure de France*, August 1758.

author who "captivates at the same time as he wearies, or rather does not weary simply because he captivates": his genius is life itself. D'Argenson admires English novels for their vigour of thought and freedom from the commonplace. "The great characteristic of English writers and of the whole of that deeply penetrative and thoughtful nation, is a thorough good sense in everything."[1] Voltaire himself acknowledges that the perusal of *Clarissa* "inflamed his blood," and after regaining his self-possession, confesses that the English stand alone as regards their naturalness: in them there is no pitiful desire to present the author when it is the characters only that should be presented, "nor any anxiety to be witty out of season."[2]

Was it reverence for the master-piece or the failure of the adaptations of *Pamela* that preserved *Clarissa* from the playwrights? However this may be, no piece founded upon it was produced for several years. Contemporaries, it is true, insinuated that Beaumarchais had drawn upon it for the subject of his *Eugénie*,[3] but has not Beaumarchais himself confessed that he borrowed his idea from Le Sage? The first attempts to dramatize Richardson's masterpiece, which retained its popularity down even to the time of the Revolution, were those of Née de la Rochelle in 1786, and Népomucène Lemercier six years later.[4]

When, in 1755, *Grandison* made its appearance, the fame of the English novelist was at its height. Nothing affords better evidence of the growth of his reputation than the outcry occasioned by the emendations Prévost had allowed himself to introduce: "One must have a fair opinion of oneself," we read in the *Correspondance littéraire*,[5] "to act as the sculptor of Mr Richardson's marble. In him we have indeed a glorious artist, and if you, his translators, must venture to touch his

---

[1] *Remarques en lisant.*
[2] Letter to Mme. du Deffand, 12th April 1760;—Preface to *L'Écossaise* (1760).
[3] See *Journal encyclopédique*, 1st November 1756.
[4] The drama of Née de la Rochelle is anonymous; *Clarisse Harlowe*, a prose drama in three acts, Paris, 1786, 8vo.—The *Clarisse Harlowe* of Népomucène Lemercier was acted in 1792.
[5] January 1756.

masterpieces, remove, if you can, any trifling specks and any dust which may here and there conceal these admirable statues; relieve them of the soil which occasionally hides their contours; but beware of even touching the statue with profane hands, lest you betray your ignorance and want of feeling."

In this case, however, the feet of the statue were of clay, though at that time the fact was unsuspected. Gibbon recommends the new book to his aunt as greatly superior to *Clarissa*.[1] Marmontel, while he admits that in France its success is not equal to that of the author's preceding novel, warmly refutes those who find the hero's character "too stiff and unnatural." "If we dared," wrote d'Argenson, "we would say that in Sir Charles Grandison another Christ has appeared upon earth, so perfect is he."[2]   But the character of Grandison is, in Marmontel's opinion, "a marvellous and extraordinary one": it is neither extravagant nor romantic: "He is nothing more than a good man, such as it is possible for everyone to be," and the book, taken as a whole, remains "a masterpiece of the most healthy philosophy."[3]   Admiration had become infatuation. This novel, "ineffective," to quote La Harpe,[4] "in spite of all its merit," did not repel French readers[5]: its moral seemed to them a noble one, and its hero became popular. Grandison was a type, and had as good a claim to the title as Tartuffe or Don Juan. The Clementina episode, from which a person named Bastide constructed a play,[6] was considered an unrivalled piece of work, and in popular estimation the author of Clarissa had never before attained such a pitch of excellence. "Antiquity," Marmontel wrote, "can show nothing more exquisite."[7]

[1] *Memoirs*, vol. ii., p. 240.   Translated in 1797.
[2] *Mémoires*, edited by Jannet, vol. v., p. 112.
[3] See the *Mercure*, August 1758; and *Essai sur les romans* (*Œuvres*, vol. x., p. 341).
[4] *Cours de littérature*, vol. iii., p. 190.
[5] See *Journal encyclopédique*, Feb. 1756; *Mercure de France*, Jan. 1756; *Année littéraire*, 1755, vol. viii., p. 136, and 1758, vol. iv., p. 3.
[6] *Gérsoncour et Clémentine*, "tragédie bourgeoise" in prose, in five acts. Played 4th November 1766.
[7] *Mercure*, August 1758.

On the death of Richardson, 4th July 1761, popular enthusiasm rose to frenzy. The admirers of England were not slow to take advantage of so favourable an opportunity. From September 1757 onwards, the *Journal étranger* kept its readers informed as to the great man's health. In the issue for January 1762, after his death, the following lines appeared : " There has fallen into our hands an English copy of *Clarissa*, containing some notes in manuscript. The author of these, whoever he may be, is undoubtedly a man of keen intelligence, but one who was nothing more than this could never have written them. . . . Through all the absence of method and the pleasing carelessness of a pen unconscious of restraint, it is easy to recognise the sure and skilful hand of a great artist."

The " great artist" was Diderot ; " Diderot, the possessed," as Joseph de Maistre calls him, who loaded Richardson " with praise which he would not have bestowed upon Fénelon," [1] and —as his contemporaries with more justice observed—extolled, of all English writers, the one whose genius bore the closest resemblance to his own.[2]

His contemporaries were right. But during the present century many critics, and those not the least eminent, have thought the same, or nearly so, as Joseph de Maistre. The *Éloge de Richardson* seemed to them a mere piece of rhetoric. It almost makes them blush for Diderot, and they would gladly expunge it from his works. The truth is that they fail to appreciate both him and Richardson. The *Éloge* is certainly not perfect : but, pompous as it is, it remains a most interesting piece of criticism.

In the first place, Diderot is absolutely sincere. In the month of October 1760, he wrote from Grandval to Sophie Volland : " There was a deal of discussion concerning *Clarissa*. Those who despised the work regarded it with supreme contempt ; those who thought highly of it were no less extravagant in their esteem, and considered it one of the most marvellous achievements of the human intellect. . . . I shall not be

---

[1] *Soirées de Saint-Pétersbourg*, vol. i., p. 347.
[2] Marmontel, *Œuvres*, vol. x., p. 339.

satisfied either with you or with myself until I have made
you appreciate the truth of *Pamela, Tom Jones, Clarissa*, and
Grandison.[1] His novel *La Religieuse* was written in the same
year, and he wrote it with the lamentations of Clementina
sounding in his ears, "the ghost of Clarissa" hovering before
him; above all, he borrowed not only the English author's
method of presentation and his style of pathos, but almost, even,
his subject as well, since *La Religieuse*, like *Clarissa Harlowe*, is
the story of a girl who is imprisoned and subjected to the worst
form of outrage.

On the death of Richardson, Diderot, seizing his pen, produced within twenty-four hours, and without pausing for fresh
inspiration, a work that was less a study than a funeral oration,
not so much a criticism as a panegyric. By so doing he gratified
the desires of a great number of readers; what strikes us as
declamation seemed, when his encomium first appeared, simply
eloquence and nothing more. The Comte de Bissy, who translated Young, wrote to Arnaud: "I have read, and re-read, this
sublime and touching panegyric; and have been made sensible
of the power and the charm which genius and virtue derive from
one another when found in combination."[2] Diderot, in fact,
had simply accepted a part assigned to him by public opinion,
and had earned its gratitude thereby. His *Éloge* very quickly
became a classic, and was henceforth reprinted in all editions
of Richardson.

Some have regarded it as an indirect attack upon Prévost.[3]
But if it is so, how can we account for the fact that it was
Prévost who first prefixed the piece to his own translation?
Moreover, if certain allusions are applicable to *Cléveland*—the
work which drew tears from Rousseau—had not Prévost himself been the first to condemn the fluent romantic style of his
early works? Again, had not Prévost, the friend of Rousseau,
and doubtless of Diderot as well, been quite recently the editor
of the *Journal étranger*, by which the *Éloge* was published?

---

[1] 20th October 1760. *Cf.*, in the *Œuvres*, vol. xix., pp. 47, 49, 55.
[2] *Journal étranger*, February 1762, p. 143.
[3] Brunetière, *Études Critiques*, vol. iii., p. 243.

Lastly, what grounds have we for doubting Diderot's sincerity, and why should the fact that he praises Richardson be a reason for supposing that he is attacking Prévost? It would be far more reasonable to suppose that the *Éloge* was intended to remind the numerous admirers of the *Nouvelle Héloïse*, which had been published a few months before, that Rousseau—with whom Diderot, as we are aware, had now quarrelled—had had both a predecessor and a master; and this, indeed, as we shall see, is the way in which Rousseau seems to have interpreted its publication.

Having said so much, it would be a waste of time for us to point out the instances of palpable exaggeration in this fragment, did they not afford a singular testimony to the progress of anglomania. Is it not odd to find French novelists condemned for describing the "secret haunts of profligacy," when we recollect the places in which many of the scenes in *Clarissa* take place? Is it not, to say the least, paradoxical to reject Montaigne, La Rochefoucauld, and Nicole in favour of Richardson as a portrayer of the human heart? Is it not a gross mistake to praise in a novelist of a popular, and sometimes of a vulgar type, that delicate art, appreciable only by a very limited number of readers, which is just the very thing he did not possess in the slightest degree? Diderot was thus in error—possibly not without intention—upon certain points. But he distinguished the characteristics of the work as a whole with much truth and eloquence. No; one who has just laid down the last volume of *Clarissa* will find the *Éloge* something more than a mere piece of rhetoric.

He clearly perceived the novelty of Richardson's precise, deliberate and circumstantial art, of his detailed descriptions, of those pictures of his which produce the effect of life, and give us the illusion "of having added to our experience." Every unprejudiced reader of Richardson can say with Diderot: "I know the house of the Harlowes as well as I know my own; I am no less familiar with Grandison's dwelling than with my father's." When Richardson carries his reader away he does so entirely: this is because he has a complete, varied, and penetrative comprehension of the chaos of incidents and trifling events called life. He endeavoured to portray it in its complexity and its totality. This characteristic has been excellently described by Diderot.

" You accuse Richardson of being tedious! Have you then forgotten the trouble, the attention, the manœuvring that are necessary before the humblest enterprise can be brought to a successful issue—before a law-suit can be concluded, a marriage arranged, or a reconciliation effected? Choose of these details which you will, they will all be interesting to me if they call the passions into play and illustrate character. 'They are commonplace,' say you; 'this is what we see every day?' You are wrong; it is what passes before your eyes every day, without your ever seeing it. Beware; in attacking Richardson you are bringing an action against the great poets. A hundred times you have watched the sun set and the stars appear; you have heard the fields ringing with the shrill song of the birds; but which of you perceived that it was the sounds of the day that charged the silence of the night with emotion? Well! It is for you, with moral as with physical phenomena; outbursts of passion have often fallen upon your ears, but you are very far from knowing all the secrets implied in its accents and manifestations. There is not one of the passions but has its characteristic facial expression; all these different expressions succeed one another upon a countenance, without its ever ceasing to be the same; and the art of the great poet or the great painter consists in making you see something that had escaped your notice before. . . . Learn that it is upon this multitude of little things that illusion depends; it is a very difficult thing to picture them; it is a very difficult thing, also, to reproduce them."

Diderot has caught the very essence of Richardson's " realism." But behind the portraiture of the external world, we must look for that of human souls. Richardson has a rare faculty of analysis. He portrays every character and every station in life; but, above all, he discerns the secret feelings, those which escape your indifferent eye, the " fissures," so to speak, of the soul. " If there is a hidden feeling in the depths of the soul of any one of his characters, listen closely, and you will hear a discordant note which will betray its presence." . . . Or again, " it is he who carries the torch to the darkest part of the cavern." He is an admirable anatomist of the moral life.

All this, it must be observed, was most seasonable as a confirmation of Diderot's own theories on truth to nature in art. Similarly, this apotheosis of Richardson—immediately following the publication of *Le Fils naturel* (1757), and the production of *Le Père de famille* (1761)—came at a time most appropriate for the justification of his ideas concerning morality on the stage and in fiction.

How could Diderot fail to appreciate one who used the novel as a pulpit or a rostrum, and wove in with the thread of the story a continuous lesson for the benefit of the reader? The briefest passage affords opportunity for discussion on "the most important questions of morality and taste." Leave *Pamela* or *Clarissa*, he said, lying about upon a table, and those who read them will soon become as passionately attached to the actors in these dramas as though they were living characters. From differences of opinion with regard to them, "secret hatreds" have been known to spring, veiled contempt, in short the same divisions between those bound together by natural ties as might have occurred if a matter of the utmost gravity had been at stake. Strange that such an effect should be produced by a novel! How rare a genius, too, must that be which has rendered the most frivolous branch of literature capable of producing a book worthy of comparison—these are Diderot's words—"to a book more sacred still," namely, the Gospel! The word once out, Diderot can contain himself no longer. "O Richardson, Richardson, you who have no rival in my eyes, it is you whom I shall always read! Under the stress of pressing circumstances I may sell my books, but you I shall keep: you I shall keep, upon the same shelf as Moses, Homer, Euripides and Sophocles!"

Moses, Homer, Euripides and Sophocles! Great names, these, and grand words. We must not forget that it is Diderot who utters them, nor that the date is about 1760, a time of change and regeneration for French literature, which was awaiting its Homer, and believed it had found him. "O Richardson! If, during your lifetime, you did not enjoy all the reputation which is your due, how great will you appear in the eyes of our descendants, when they behold you at the distance from which we look back upon Homer!" The modern Homer: such is Richardson. Here Diderot is in agreement with Gellert and the Germans, because he, like them, felt the need for a new genius who should be capable of directing a virgin literature into fresh paths.

This was extremely daring; so much so that Voltaire became concerned.

Hitherto he had regarded the popularity of English novels
with toleration, if not with favour.   He had even endeavoured,
in *Nanine* and *L'Écossaise*, to shelter himself behind "these remarkably successful English novels."   Now, however, his secret
antipathy came to light.   Already, and not without malice, he
had pointed out the author's faults, at the very time when he confessed that the perusal of *Clarissa* "fired his blood."   He had
called him "a clever fellow . . . who keeps making promises
from volume to volume," but never fulfils them.   "I said, if all
these people were my relatives and friends, I could not feel
interested in them."[1]   In vain Mme. du Deffand maintained that
Richardson "had great intelligence."   "It is painful," he replied, "for an energetic person like me to read nine whole
volumes and find nothing in them whatever."   In reality he
is standing up for his old idea of the novel as a very light
form of literature, unworthy the attention of a serious mind.
But after the appearance of the *Éloge de Richardson*, and as
anglomania gained ground, his mistrust turned into open
hostility.   An article of his in the *Gazette littéraire*[2] finds an
explanation and an excuse for the English taste for such
"twaddle" in the Englishman's habit of spending nine months
out of the twelve on his country estate; without reading, during
his long winter evenings, what would he find to do ?   But in a
letter to d'Argental he throws off the mask, and confesses his
astonishment and contempt : "I don't like those long and intolerable novels *Pamela* and *Clarissa*.   They have been successful
because they excite the reader's curiosity even amidst a medley
of trifles ; but if the author had been imprudent enough to
inform us at the very beginning that Clarissa and Pamela
were in love with their persecutors, everything would have
been spoiled, and the reader would have thrown the book
aside."[3]   He adds, not without some irony and ill-humour :
"Is it possible that these islanders are better acquainted with
nature than your *Welches* ?"   Still, the *Welches* persist in their
admiration, and a certain Jean-Jacques supplies them with

[1] To Mme. du Deffand, 12th April 1760.   [2] 30th May 1764.
[3] 16th May 1767.

books of the same character: it is too much of a good
thing. To read *Clarissa* one must be crazy and have plenty
of time to lose.[1] Is it not really disgraceful that the English
should allow themselves to be imposed upon with such
"jugglers' tricks as novels," and that a nation which has
afforded a pattern to Europe should forsake the study of
Locke and Newton for works of the most frivolous and extravagant kind?"[2] This was Voltaire's last word upon
English fiction. At bottom, no one could have less romance
about him than he; but neither could anyone view with greater
anxiety the infatuation of France with these foreign novels, which
in his opinion were inferior or barbarous. It was this which
led him ultimately to treat Richardson and Sterne as he treated
Shakespeare.

But public opinion was no longer with him. Readers of
Rousseau and the followers of Diderot were all looking to him
for a reasoned opinion on Richardson. He refused to give one.
As Diderot had nothing to say, Sébastien Mercier, one of his
disciples, took upon himself to ask Voltaire the reason of his
silence. "M. de Voltaire, in his numerous writings, which I
have read and re-read, has avoided, so far as I know, all mention
of Richardson, whether favourable or otherwise, though he has
treated of every other writer, however obscure."—In justice it
should be mentioned that in 1773—the year in which Mercier
was writing—Voltaire's opinion, quoted above, had not been
printed. — "It is impossible," Mercier continues, "that the
author of *Nanine* should fail to appreciate *Pamela*; he has
certainly read *Clarissa* and *Grandison*, poems to which antiquity
can produce no worthy rival. He must know that these masterpieces of feeling, truth, and moral teaching have found readers
of both sexes, in every country and of every age. I suppose
that, since M. de Voltaire's manner of writing is diametrically

[1] *Lettres chinoises*, xli. (1776): "My attention is engaged with a problem in
geometry; and straightway there arrives a novel called *Clarissa*, in six volumes,
which the anglomaniacs praise to the skies as the only novel fit for a sensible
man to read. I am fool enough to read it, and thereby I lose both my time and
the thread of my investigations."

[2] *Journal de politique et de littérature* (1777), article on *Tristram Shandy*.

opposed to Richardson's, the silence he has preserved in regard to this author of genius is founded on principle."[1] Mercier had discerned the truth. Voltaire's silence was that of contempt.

But the books he so despised were making the French nation " stupid," as Horace Walpole said. The women became crazy about them. Mme. du Deffand discussed them with Walpole and could not forgive him his contempt. *Clarissa* was certainly not like other novels ; it was " but a poor antidote to depression." But " the play of every day interests, tastes, and feelings, when their subtle gradations are so finely indicated as in Richardson, is enough to absorb my attention and to give me infinite pleasure."[2] How superior it all is to La Calprenède and to French fiction ! " After your novels I find it impossible to read any of ours." Such was the opinion of Mlle. de Lespinasse : she was very fond of Prévost and Lesage, M. de Guibert tells us, but she placed " the immortal " Richardson above everyone else. In vain her friend d'Alembert declared that " it is well to imitate nature, but not to do so to a wearisome extent." She wrote to her lover, in a fit of despondency : " I believe, if I read *Clarissa* to-night, I should find neither love nor passion in it. Good heavens ! can one fall lower than this ? "[3]

But it was not the women only, as Voltaire maintained,[4] who were responsible for the success of these novels. All the associates of Diderot and Rousseau and the whole of the re-forming party adopted them almost without reserve. They held that " there was more philosophy in most English novels than in many a moral treatise."[5] The *Encyclopædia* made them the subject of a pompous eulogy.[6] Marmontel, the faithful disciple of Diderot, placed the English novelist above all writers,

---

[1] *Essai sur l'art dramatique*, p. 326.

[2] See the *Lettres de Mme. du Deffand à Horace Walpole*, especially that of 8th August 1773.

[3] 17th October 1775 ; see also the letter of 7th July 1775.

[4] *Gazette littéraire*, vol. i., p. 334.   [5] *Journal encyclopédique*, 1st March 1763.

[6] In an article entitled *Roman* : " Novels written in this excellent manner are perhaps the only remaining form of instruction that can be given to a nation so corrupt that no other can be of service to it."

ancient or modern. Even Buffon, with all his calmness and his ready contempt for literary novelties, admired him "for his intense truthfulness, and because of his close observation of every object he portrayed."[1]

For more than half a century France remained subject to the spell. Richardson brought the English type of novel into fashion. "Our novelists," said the *Journal étranger*,[2] "are almost compelled to disguise the products of their fancy in this foreign garb if they wish to be read." Who has not seen upon the quays, or hidden away in old provincial libraries, some of these faint and sterile imitations of the master? Some pretend to be sequels, such as *La Nouvelle Clémentine*, by Léonard, or the *Petit Grandison* of Berquin. Others, more candid, actually claim the sanction of his name; for example: "*Les Mœurs du jour, ou Histoire de Sir William Harrington, écrite du vivant de M. Richardson* (sic), *éditeur de Paméla, Clarisse et Grandisson, revue et retouchée par lui, sur le manuscrit de l'auteur.*"[3] Volumes similar to these, or still more obscure, were produced by the dozen: *Les Lettres de Milady Linsay*, the *Mémoires de Clarence Welldonne*, *Milord d'Ambi, histoire anglaise*; a catalogue of them would be long and unprofitable. It is of more importance to note that all the authors in vogue make use of the British hall-mark: Baculard d'Arnaud, the popular author of the *Épreuves du sentiment*, never loses an opportunity of praising Richardson, and brought out in succession *Anne Bell, Sidnei et Silli, Clary ou le retour à la vertu récompensé, Adelson et Salvini*, "an English anecdote," and any number of other books, now no longer read, which ran through sixty editions, and were translated into several languages! English novels, said Rousseau, are either "sublime or detestable." The imitations of them, for the most part, are not sublime. But the foreign livery made everything go down. English novels are not all good ones, it is true, said the *Correspondance littéraire*,[4] but at any rate they are always better than "our insipid French productions of the same sort."

Not a single novelist of note escaped the taint of anglomania.

---

[1] Sainte-Beuve, *Causeries*, vol. iv., p. 364.   [2] February 1757.
[3] See the *Correspondance littéraire*, February 1773.   [4] February 1767.

Crébillon fils announced his *Heureux orphelins* as a translation.[1]
Mme. Riccoboni, who was so famous in her day, and so much
admired by Doudan,[2] wrote the *Mémoires de Miledi B · ·* , and
the *Lettres de Juliette Catesby*, which evoked the congratulations of
Marmontel. " It is by following English models," he said, " that
a woman has attained such great and well-deserved success among
us."[3] Prévost contributed the *Mémoires pour servir à l'histoire
de la vertu*[4]—an inferior work translated from Mrs Sheridan's
Memoirs of Miss Sidney Biddulph. Marmontel derived the inspiration, and even the subjects, for several of his *Contes moraux*[5] from
Richardson. Voltaire himself had *Clarissa* in mind when he
wrote a certain chapter of *L'Ingénu*, describing the sufferings of
the fair Saint-Yves on her death-bed, as a companion picture to
those of the heroine of the English novel.[6]

From 1760 to the end of the century scarcely a novel was
published that escaped this all-absorbing influence. It was
Richardson who furnished Diderot with the inspiration for *Les
Deux Amis de Bourbonne* and *L'Histoire de Mlle. de la Chaux*; it
was from him that he derived his abounding wealth of detail,
the accuracy which makes his presentation almost palpable, and
his slightly crude colouring; and it was Richardson also whom
he had in mind while writing *La Religieuse*. As his editor points
out, the *Éloge de Richardson* explains the immense advance which
this novel marks in comparison with his earlier efforts; in the
interval he had read *Clarissa Harlowe*, and felt that he had been
initiated.[7] Whether Richardson would have acknowledged him
as a disciple is doubtful. It is certain that he would have frankly

[1] *Les heureux orphelins*, a tale imitated from the English (1754).
[2] *Lettres*, vol. i., p. 271.   [3] *Œuvres*, vol x., p. 346.
[4] All the newspapers of the period attribute this novel to Prévost (*Mercure*,
July 1762 ; *Journal encyclopédique*, 15th July 1762; *Mémoires secrets*, 30th April
1762). It has also been included in his *Œuvres choisies*.
[5] See especially *L'école de l'amitié*.
[6] The resemblance has been pointed out by Villemain. See *L'Ingénu*, chap. xx.
(1767): " She made no show of vainglorious fortitude ; she did not understand
the paltry honour of giving a few neighbours occasion to say, ' Hers was a
courageous end . . .' How many there are who praise the pompous death-beds
of those who meet annihilation with apathy ! " &c.
[7] See Assézat, *Œuvres de Diderot*, vol. v., p. 211.

P

disowned Laclos and Restif, though they professed themselves his followers. Contemporaries had pointed out how far the author of *Les liaisons dangereuses* was indebted for the character of Valmont to that of Lovelace; Valmont is simply Lovelace in the guise of a Frenchman.[1] And as for Restif, a coarse but powerful artist, who dealt with the vulgar side of life, he wrote his *Paysan perverti* "under the inspiration of *Pamela*," and boasted of having done so; when he described in detail "the progress of corruption as it invades an upright and innocent heart,"[2] he claimed to be following Richardson. Lavater, one of his numerous foreign admirers, surnamed him "the French Richardson," and his worshippers ranked him higher than the English novelist whose disciple he professed to be, because, with equal genius, he had set before himself a still more ambitious project.[3] Every one of the novelists who belong to the closing years of the century—including the Marquis de Sade[4]—call upon the name of Richardson.

He had therefore quite a progeny of imitators, distinguished and otherwise. Some loved him for his faithful delineation of the vulgar side of existence, others, more numerous, because he surpassed all other novelists in his command of pathos. Many produced bad imitations of him, because they imitated him too closely. Others, who call themselves his disciples, owe him in reality little or nothing. But all speak of him with respect. In fiction his is the greatest name of the century. A French critic of that period states that "*Clarissa*, the greatest among English novels, *has also become the first among our own*."[5]

The eloquent printer's tomb became a resort for pilgrims. Mme. de Genlis, when in England, called upon Richardson's son-in-law, asked to see the great man's portrait, sat in his own

---

[1] La Harpe, *Correspondance littéraire*, vol. iii., p. 339.—Observe moreover the success attained by *Les liaisons dangereuses* in England (Dutens, *Mémoires d'un voyageur qui se repose*, vol. iii., p. 221.

[2] See *Avis de Pierre R · · ·*, prefixed to the *Paysan perverti*.

[3] *Cf.* P. Lacroix, *Bibliographie de Restif de la Bretonne*, pp. 69, 127; and *Mes Inscriptions*, edn. P. Cottin, 1889, p. lxx.

[4] See his *Idée sur les romans*, edn. Uzanne, 12mo, p. 25.

[5] *Journal des savants*, September 1785.

particular seat, and paid a visit to his grave. Another visitor, Mme. de Tessé, threw herself upon the tomb-stone and gave way to such despair that her guide became alarmed.[1]

But a few years had passed when a great poet, lost in reverie on a bright summer's day in the country, summoned before his mind the images of Richardson's heroines: "Clarissa! with Heaven itself radiant in your saintly beauty; free, in all your pain, alike from hatred and from bitterness, suffering without a groan, and perishing without a murmur; beloved Clementina! pure, and heavenly soul, who, amidst the harsh treatment of an unjust household, never lost your innocence with the loss of your reason:—your eyes, bright souls, hold me with their charm; your sweet likeness hastens to fill my fairest dreams!"[2]

What could afford more signal evidence of Richardson's popularity than this tribute of reverence for his genius from André Chénier, the least English of all French poets?

II

Rousseau began to write *La Nouvelle Héloïse* at L'Ermitage in the winter of 1756, when the sensation caused by the still recent publication of *Clarissa Harlowe* was at its height.

Like everyone else, Rousseau read the new masterpiece, and read it in the translation of Prévost, who had possibly shown it to him in manuscript. It is unlikely that he had recourse to the original, for he never knew much English.[3] He was none the less impressed with the originality of this novel, as with that of the master's other works. In a certain place he demands that the composition of novels shall only be entrusted " to well-bred but

1 Mme. de Genlis, *Mémoires*, vol. iii., p. 360.
2 A. Chénier, *Elégie xiv.*
3 On receiving the English translation of *La Nouvelle Héloïse*, he asked Mme. de Boufflers, who was acquainted with the language, to look through it, and tell him what she thought of it, adding: "I do not understand the language well enough" (To Mme. de Luxembourg, 28th August 1761). Three years later, Panckoucke asked him to undertake the abridgment of Richardson, and he declined on the ground of his ignorance of English (25th May 1764).

sensitive persons, whose writings will reflect their own hearts," [1] and on reading Richardson's masterpiece he at once declared that never yet had " a novel equal to, or even approaching, *Clarissa*, been produced in any language whatever." [2]   What Geoffroy's authority may be for discerning in this statement a disparaging allusion to *Tom Jones*, which had recently been translated by La Place, I cannot say. [3]   Nowhere does Rousseau make any mention of Fielding.   On the other hand, at the very moment when he was expressing this opinion in the *Lettre sur les spectacles*, he was himself putting the last touches to *La Nouvelle Héloïse*, in which he had evidently drawn inspiration from *Clarissa*.   Everything therefore tends to convince us that he was expressing quite sincerely, and without the least reservation, an admiration which lasted throughout his life.

When, at a later period, he visited England, he wrote to the Marquis de Mirabeau as follows [4] : " You admire Richardson, *monsieur le marquis* ; how much greater would be your admiration, if, like me, you were in a position to compare the pictures of this great artist with nature ; to see how natural his situations are, however seemingly romantic, and how true his portraits, for all their apparent exaggeration ! "   And he regretted that he came across so many Captain Tomlinsons, and so few Belfords.

On this point Rousseau never swerved from his opinion. Bernardin de Saint Pierre, who knew him during the latter part of his life, tells us that " he never spoke of Richardson without enthusiasm.   *Clarissa*, according to him, contained a complete portrait gallery of the human race ; of *Grandison* he thought less highly." [5]

While writing his novel he undoubtedly kept *Clarissa* before him, and possibly *Pamela* [6] as well.   In his second preface he protests against the foolish affectation of designing the moral

---

[1] *Nouvelle Héloïse*, ii., 21.   [2] *Lettre sur les spectacles*.
[3] See *Cours de littérature dramatique*, vol. iii., p. 262.   [4] 8th April 1767.
[5] *Fragments sur J.-J. Rousseau*, in Aimé Martin's edition of the works of Bernardin de St. Pierre.
[6] *Cf.* a letter written by La Roche, Streckheisen-Moultou: *J.-J. Rousseau, ses amis et ses ennemis*, vol. i., p. 493.   Rousseau also quotes *Pamela* in the *Lettre sur les spectacles*.

of a novel for the benefit of young girls, without reflecting that young girls can have no part in the disorderly life the author condemns; and in a note he adds: "This has reference only to modern English novels," evidently thinking of Richardson. Similarly, when sending the fifth part of *Julie* to Duclos, he adds that he adheres to his belief that reading of this sort is dangerous for girls: "I go so far as to think that Richardson makes a gross mistake when he attempts to instruct them by means of fiction; it is the same thing as setting a house on fire to make the pumps work."[1] On another occasion he interrupts the thread of his narrative in order to refute an opinion of the English novelist: "My heart," says Julie to Saint-Preux, "was yours from the first moment I saw you." Rousseau inserts a note: "Mr Richardson pours a good deal of ridicule upon these attachments at first sight, founded on indefinable affinities. It is all very well to make fun of them; but since there are in reality only too many cases of the kind, would it not be better, instead of wasting time in denying them, to teach us how to conquer them?"[2] Plainly, therefore, *Clarissa*, the success of which was filling the world with its clamour, was in Rousseau's mind when he wrote *Julie*.

It would even seem that this success caused him annoyance. In response to a request from Malesherbes that certain portions of *Héloïse* should be suppressed, he wrote the following significant lines: "A pious woman of the lower class who humbly submits to the authority of her spiritual director, a woman who forsakes a dissolute life for one of devotion, is not a sufficiently rare or instructive subject to fill a large volume; but a woman who is at once lovable, devout, enlightened and reasonable is a newer and, to my mind, a more useful subject. This novelty and usefulness, however, are the very things that the suggested excisions would remove; if Julie has not the sublime virtues of Clarissa, her virtue is of a more prudent and judicious kind, and is independent of public opinion: *deprived of this counterbalancing*

---

[1] 19th November 1760. The expression occurs again in the second preface.
[2] *Nouvelle Héloïse*, iii., 18.

*characteristic, she would have no choice but to hide her face before the
other ; what right would she have to show herself ? "* [1]

After the publication of Diderot's sonorous *Éloge*, Rousseau's
feeling became stronger. Rightly or wrongly—but not without
some appearance of justification—he thought there were signs
that the work was directed against him. He was unquestionably conscious that the parallel between *Clarissa* and *Julie* was
in everyone's mind, and was somewhat concerned in consequence. He himself touched upon this delicate subject in the
Confessions, and, in 1769, wrote a reply to Diderot's *Éloge*. He
points out with regard to his own novel that the simplicity of
its subject and the small number of characters introduced, in
which respects it is a unique work, have not been sufficiently
praised. "Diderot has complimented Richardson very highly
on the prodigious variety of his scenes and the multitude
of his characters. Richardson has, indeed, the merit of
having given each of them a distinct individuality; but as
far as their number is concerned he is on a par with the
most insipid novelists, who make up for the poverty of their
ideas by the quantity of their characters and adventures."
Surely it is a more difficult thing to sustain attention with
but slender resources : "and if, other things being equal, the
simplicity of its subject adds to the beauty of a work, Richardson's novels, which, *whatever M. Diderot may have said about them*,[2]
are superior in so many other ways, cannot, in this respect, afford
any parallel to mine."[3] It is evident that Rousseau is disturbed
by the recollection of the *Éloge*—the publication of which, following close upon the success of *Julie*, had revived Richardson's
glory at the expense of his own—and that he is annoyed with
Diderot in consequence.

Three years after Richardson's death—at the very moment when
the master's glory was at its height—Panckoucke had committed
the indiscretion of asking Rousseau to undertake the task of

[1] Date unknown. *Œuvres et correspondance inédites*, Streckheisen-Moultou, p. 390.

[2] These significant words were suppressed by the first publishers of the *Confessions*, but appear, without erasure or addition, in the manuscript, which is in the
library of the Chamber of Deputies

[3] *Confessions*, ii., 11.

abridging his works. Rousseau replied from Motiers that he had a good many scruples about abridging such books, though "they unquestionably needed it. Richardson's club-conversations, in particular, were unbearable, since he had seen nothing of high life, and was consequently entirely ignorant of its manners." But, no! Rousseau's health, his indolence, the great number of translations it would be necessary to compare, and his own work, all discourage him.[1] Must we not add to the motives which he here admits, a certain repugnance in the author of *Héloïse* to spend labour in magnifying still further the author of *Clarissa*? I am inclined to think so.

However this may be, the parallel which annoyed him was being remarked by all those about him.

We find it difficult in the present day to picture the state of mind of the contemporaries of Richardson and Rousseau who could weigh the two men against one another. But we are acquainted with the whole of Rousseau's work, whereas his contemporaries were not. In 1761 Jean-Jacques had as yet written neither the *Confessions* nor the *Rêveries*. Though his reputation was of ten years' standing he had not hitherto unbosomed himself for the benefit of his readers with all the unhealthy exuberance that characterised his later effusions. He was known only as a philosopher and a politician. Above all, as a novelist he was making a first appearance. Though awaited with impatience, *La Nouvelle Héloïse* was not crowned as a masterpiece until after publication. Is it likely, sensible people asked themselves, that, if the author of the *Discours sur l'inégalité* ventures into the domain of fiction he will excel the author of *Clarissa* at the first attempt? All this explains how it was that, to the amazement of certain historians, critics should have been found who could compare the two works and the two men.

It seems clear that in England the comparison was unfavourable to Rousseau. The work was immediately translated and was frequently republished.[2] Richardson, it is said, derived no pleasure

[1] 25th May 1764.

[2] *Eloisa, or a series of original letters collected and published by J.-J Rousseau, translated from the French.* London, Becket, 1761, 4 vols. 12mo. "Milord Maréchal" speaks of several English editions. (Letter of 2nd October 1762, Streckheisen-Moultou, vol. ii., p. 68.)

from its perusal. A fact of greater significance is that the refined intelligence of Gray, catholic as it was and usually so inquisitive with regard to French works, was repelled by the want of verisimilitude in a book "more absurd and more improbable than *Amadis de Gaule*." In vain he goes on hoping that a wonderful *dénouement* will "bring something like nature and interest out of absurdity and insipidity." If the book is really by Rousseau it "is the strongest instance I ever saw that a very extraordinary man may entirely mistake his own talents."[1]

A lengthy comparison of Rousseau with his rival was published by an English journal, *The Critical Review*, and was immediately reproduced by the *Journal étranger*, in which it appeared—and the fact is significant—a month before the publication of Diderot's *Éloge*, and as though to pave the way for it. "Our ingenious author," says the writer of this article, "has formed his Eloisa on the plan of the celebrated Clarissa, the favourite work of our late countryman, the amiable Mr Richardson." "Eloisa is a less perfect Clarissa, Clara a Miss Howe, as fervent in her friendship, as witty and charming, but less humorous. . . . It is indeed the highest encomium on Mr Richardson, that he has been deemed worthy the imitation of a writer of Mr Rousseau's eminence." But in respect of moral teaching the palm must be awarded to the English author, who is also the more weighty and the more faithful to nature, if he is the less brilliant of the two. "Rousseau's performance is infinitely more sentimental, animated, refined and elegant ; Richardson's more natural, interesting, variegated and dramatic. The one everywhere appears the easy, the other the masterly writer; Rousseau raises your admiration; Richardson solicits your tears." The one is a master of rhetoric of the most brilliant talent; the other is a painter of genius.[2]

Such was the verdict of all the enemies of Rousseau.

In Fréron's opinion, Rousseau was most likely indebted to

---

[1] Letter of 22nd January 1761. (*Works*, edited by Gosse, vol. iii., p. 79.) See Mrs Barbauld, vol. i., p. cvii.: "Rousseau, whose Héloïse alone, perhaps, can divide the palm with *Clarissa*."

[2] *Critical Review*, September 1761, vol. xii., p. 203. *Cf. Journal étranger*, December 1761.

Clarissa for the plot and the principal characters of his book.[1] Grimm—the friend of Diderot—thinks that "it is the fate of great works to give rise to numbers of feeble imitations : *Miss Biddulph* and *La Nouvelle Héloïse* will not be the last." A few pages only of the new novel deserve comparison with *Grandison*. The three novels of the master stand forth as "prodigious works."[2] La Harpe, also, points out the analogies between the two, and gives the credit to Richardson, without, however, failing to appreciate the genius of Rousseau.[3]

In short, the parallel between the two works was a commonplace of eighteenth century criticism. The general public, less partial, was divided in opinion with respect to them. The one, as containing the history of Rousseau's own love-affairs, was more keenly interesting, and possessed the attraction which scandal always affords; the other, for very many people, remained the more truly great work of the two. Readers were by no means rare, who retained, like the duchess de Lauzun, a preference for the English novel, and derived "a thousand times more pleasure"[4] from its perusal. "The one made me weep no less than the other," said Ballanche, refusing to choose between them. Many a reader preferred "the naturalness, the pathos, the truth, and the moral excellence"[5] which render *Clarissa* the masterpiece of modern fiction, to the "artificial" though "dazzling and fascinating" eloquence of Rousseau.

III

To-day we read Jean-Jacques' novel with less prejudiced eyes. But if we restore the conditions which prevailed at the time of its publication, and if, in addition, we read the two works

[1] *Année littéraire*, 1761, vol. ii., p. 306 *et seq.*
[2] *Correspondance littéraire*, February 1761 and June 1762.
[3] *Cf. Cours de littérature*, vol. iii., p. 192.
[4] D'Haussonville, *Le salon de Mme. Necker*, vol. i., p. 239.
[5] Marmontel, *Essai sur les romans* (1787). A curious comparison between Richardson and Rousseau will be found in Ballanche (*Du sentiment*, Paris, 1801, 8vo, p. 221).

with attention, we can account for the comparison drawn by those who were contemporary with their authors.

Héloïse appeared at the precise moment of the eighteenth century when anglomania was at its height. "If a telescope like those of Herschell," said Garat, "and an ear-trumpet of similar range had existed at that period, they would have been directed towards England still more frequently than towards the moon and the other celestial bodies."[1] At no time during the century was this enthusiasm more keen than towards the close of the Seven Years' War. To a few reactionary spirits who were concerned thereat, it was boldly answered: "Gentlemen, there are a thousand whose voices are raised in declamation against anglomania: what they understand by the word I do not know; if they mean the craze for turning a few useful customs into burlesque . . ., they may be right; but if by any chance these ranters should presume to treat it as a crime on our part that we desire to study, to observe and to philosophize like the English, they would certainly make a very great mistake."[2] We have seen how, in his novel, Rousseau had humoured this current of opinion by giving an English colour to the sentiments and manners of his characters. This was one preliminary reason for comparing him with Richardson; but there were others besides.

In the first place the plot of his book recalls that of *Clarissa*. It is, as in Clarissa, the story of an unfortunate girl, who is victimized by her father's endeavour to force her inclinations. In a certain sense, Rousseau's novel even forms a sequel to Richardson's: Clarissa's father schemes to win from his daughter a consent which violence has failed to extract from her, but her flight prevents him from carrying out his design. What is suggested by Richardson is put into execution by Rousseau, and accordingly the baron d'Étanges induces Julie to marry M. de Wolmar. It is true that Clarissa heroically defends her virtue, while Julie yields at the outset. But the analogy is in a manner restored by Julie's marriage; as Wolmar's wife she

---

[1] *Mémoires sur Suard*, vol. i., p. 72.
[2] Letter to the authors of the *Gazette littéraire* (14th November 1764).

resists Saint-Preux, whom she still loves, just as Clarissa resists Lovelace, whom she has always loved and to whom she has once belonged, though against her own will. Love thwarted by duty, and conquered, is the theme of both works.

Again, there is a symmetry in the arrangement of the characters. Julie resembles Clarissa, as Claire resembles Miss Howe: the two former are alike gentle and serious, their two confidantes malicious and sprightly. Just as Miss Howe marries the stupid but excellent Hickman, so Claire becomes the wife of the good-natured and honourable M. d'Orbe, the man of whom she disrespectfully remarks that he lacks the " virile intelligence of strong souls."[1] Like Miss Howe, Claire, whose affection for her husband is of a very tranquil order, loves her friend with an almost inordinate affection, which causes her even to lose her reason when Julie dies. So too, Julie, like Clarissa, has a harsh and unfeeling father, and a good-natured but insignificant mother. As Clarissa finds a protector in Colonel Morden, so Julie and Saint-Preux have a bosom-friend in Lord Bomston. Bomston, like Morden, is the soul of honour, and like him, again, is proud and generous. Wolmar, though as virtuous as Lovelace is profligate, is, like him, an unbeliever, and reasons in a similar manner, if with the best of intentions. Lastly, Julie purposes flight from her father's roof, just as Clarissa does; she corresponds in the same way with her lover through the agency of a friend; her letters are intercepted ; and, like Clarissa, she dies in the end, after philosophizing at much length for the edification of those around her.

Was it then inexcusable, for contemporaries, who remarked all these analogies, to conclude therefrom that Jean-Jacques had copied the plot and the general arrangement of the English novel ? But he owes to Richardson another and heavier debt.

In *Héloïse* there are two works: in the first place a novel of the *bourgeois* type—the newest, most eloquent, most improving of eighteenth century novels, the earliest model for *Delphine*, *Corinne* and *Werther*, and the work which realises, as no

[1] I., 65.

other does, the literary aspirations of the age. In the second place *Héloïse* contains a prose poem, a first "confession" by Rousseau, disguised and incomplete as yet, but, already even, how full of pathos! Here, in germ, is all the lyricism destined afterwards to shine forth in the *Confessions* and the *Rêveries*, the intercourse with nature, the melancholy, the poetic communion with the heart—or, as Fréron said, immediately after the publication of the book, "an exquisite appreciation of nature, physical, and moral, a touch often pleasing and voluptuous, a gentle melancholy which can be known only in retirement."[1] This it was which constituted the unlooked for gift of genius, and herein Rousseau had no teacher but himself. His lyricism springs from himself alone. But the *roman bourgeois* contained in *Julie*, the art of portraying the characters and presenting them in action, "the eloquent language of the heart, the accents of emotion"—Fréron is still the speaker—all this he derived from Richardson.

In the first place he is indebted to him for the epistolary form of novel.

Was Richardson really the inventor of this form? The question was asked even in the eighteenth century: some asserting, others denying, that he had taken the idea either from the semi-romantic letters to be found here and there in the *Spectator*, from Mme. de Sévigné, Mme. Dacier, and Mme. de Lambert, whom, of his own accord, he quoted as models,[2] or, lastly, from the *Lettres portugaises*, or from those of Héloïse and Abelard.[3] The *Lettres portugaises*, especially, had frequently been reprinted, and often in the same collection with those of Héloïse,[4] while amorous epistles were to be found in French novels—in *Polexandre* and in *Cyrus*; and Crébillon fils, who had attained a great reputation in England, had published his *Lettres de la marquise*

---

[1] *Année littéraire*, 1761, vol. ii.   [2] See Mrs. Barbauld, vol. vi., p. 121.

[3] On this subject see Fréron, *Année littéraire*, vol. ii., p. 306; *Journal encyclopédique*, February 1756, p. 32, and February 1775, p. 459. See also J. Jusserand, *Les grandes écoles du roman anglais*.

[4] For example: *Recueil de lettres galantes et amoureuses d'Héloïse et Abélard, d'une religieuse portugaise au chevalier . . . ., avec celles de Cléante et de Bélise*, Amsterdam, 1711, 12mo.

de . . . au comte de R. . . . in 1738.[1] All this, however, in no way detracts from the glory of Richardson. Novels in the form of letters had plainly been published before his time ; but it is no less evident that no one had turned this method to the same account as he did. In *Pamela,* not only is the diary method employed concurrently with the other, but his art is still very uncertain, and shows but few traces of the imitation of good models. In *Clarissa,* on the contrary, the author has, by his own confession, acquired confidence in himself[2]; the correspondents are more numerous, the style has become flexible, and the characters have the leisure to present themselves to us in all the complexity of their nature. The epistolary novel has really become what it should be, a form of the analytical novel. If it is not this it is nothing, and the originality of Richardson consists in the very fact that he made it such. The essence of the novel in epistolary form lies in the invention " not so much of facts as of feelings," and of " observations upon what takes place in the heart " rather than events, however cleverly contrived.[3] A letter is a journal, and in a large measure a *journal intime.* As a journal it throws light upon hidden feelings; and as a letter it is suggestive of romance, intrigue, and the seductive advances of both intellect and heart. It is a confidence, but a confidence tempered by that dose of vanity which each one of us unintentionally mingles with words spoken to another. The epistolary type of novel is thus a delicate one to deal with, one which readily becomes tedious and is very easily rendered unendurable. A bundle of homilies on suicide, duelling, or marriage does not deserve the name of novel, for this demands a thread of events which shall leave its impression now on one, now on another, of a certain number of minds, wherein, with sufficient clearness, but without too much repetition, we are enabled to follow its consequences. The characters must have the capacity and the leisure for writing to one another, and if they are to be interesting, must have the

---

[1] The Hague, 2 parts, 12mo. Crébillon fils, according to Voltaire, is also the author of the *Lettres de Ninon,* published by Damours (Amsterdam, 1752, 2 vols. 12mo).

[2] See the *Postscript to Clarissa.*   [3] Mme. de Staël, *De l'Allemagne,* ii. 28.

inward yearning for confession and analysis. Lastly, it is necessary that the public should have a taste for confidences of this kind—a circumstance which occurs at certain epochs only, and under the influence of certain moral ideas. Now Richardson, in spite of a certain coarseness in the use of his means, is the actual creator of the confession-novel, and this is why Rousseau— the very incarnation of confession—borrows the form invented by him.

In fact, he is the only writer to borrow it from him. For in spite of the publication of Mme. de Graffigny's *Lettres péruviennes* —inspired, it was said, by Pamela [1]—of Mme. Riccoboni's *Lettres de Juliette Catesby*, and Mme. de Beaumont's *Lettres du marquis de Roselle*, the first genuine example of the epistolary novel to appear in France was *La Nouvelle Héloïse*, because it alone corresponds to the definition of the class.

Rousseau's characters, like those in *Clarissa Harlowe*, make their confessions " in the bosom of friendship." Like them they have, as Mme. du Deffand expressed it, the gift of " verbose eloquence." Like them, too, when swayed by strong emotion, they amaze the reader by rushing to the inkstand. Wolmar quits the bedside of his dying wife, and enters his study in order to set down what she has just said to him ; Julie writes to her friend from her deathbed ; Saint-Preux, confined in the apartment where she has promised to meet him for the first time, exclaims: " How glad I am that I have found ink and paper! I give expression to my feelings in order to moderate their violence ; by describing my raptures I check their extravagance." What is there that they do not write ? What suggestions, what odd confidences, they set down! Rousseau, like Richardson, makes an improper use of the method, and gives us sermons in the form of letters : we have a letter concerning gardens, a letter on duelling, letters upon suicide, education, music, and adultery : he gives us not so much a correspondence as a system of moral precepts for everyday life and for solemn occasions. The digressions are even more numerous than in *Clarissa*, and frequently are no more happily expressed. In spite, also, of Rousseau's immense

[1] Fréron, *Année littéraire*, vol. ii., p. 306.

superiority, his style, like Richardson's, is here sometimes, as the preface observes, "pompous and dull," and worthy "of the provincial, the foreigner, the recluse, or the young person," as the case may be, who employs it. Rousseau did not know how truly he spoke: many passages in these letters are just what would be written by an affected *Vaudoise*. "Thou throne of the world," writes Saint-Preux to Julie, "how far above me do I now behold thee!" Or again: "My heart is overwhelmed with the tears which flow from your eyes." Their souls "touch in all points, and everywhere feel an entire coherence." The hut in which Julie receives her lover is "the temple of Cnida," and her "inquietude increases in a compound ratio of the intervals of time and space."[1] Richardson may be suburban, but Rousseau, with all his greatness, is unquestionably provincial.

As for the interest, "it is for everyone, it is nothing at all." Is it worth while to keep a register "of what anyone can see every day in his own or his neighbour's house"? Similarly, Richardson claims to present nothing but what is "true and founded upon nature itself." The two novelists take equal pleasure in tedious and minute descriptions of middle-class manners. But Richardson was the simpler: Rousseau is more aggressive, and accompanies his portraiture of common people with a homily for the benefit of the great. Nevertheless, the change he introduces is important. French works of fiction were essentially "society" and "drawing-room" novels, wherein certain truths were never stated, certain subjects never mentioned, except to raise a laugh. In the works of Prévost and Crébillon fils there was no cooking or washing of clothes, and the housekeeping was carried on behind the scenes. In *Pamela*, for the first time outside picaresque fiction, the public had been treated to descriptions of objects which previously it had always been considered improper to mention: kitchens, saucepans, and scullions. Rousseau, in his turn, tries to get nearer the truth by condescending to enter the larder, and writes a manual for use of the good housewife. Therein we

[1] I., 5; III., 16; I., 11; I., 36; I., 13.

learn how good servants are trained; how oil, bread, worsted
and lace are economically made; how cloth of good quality is to
be distinguished; how a garden should be laid out; and how
out of simple *vin de Lavaux* we can manufacture sherry, rancio or
malaga, as we please [1] : quite a modern *Oikononomikos*.   An article
of " German pastry " is honoured with a full description.   You
must be able " to take a delight in the pleasures of children ":
have two dining-rooms, one for every day use, the other for
entertaining; do not take coffee, except on great occasions;
make yourself acquainted with familiar little recipes for refresh-
ing the mind, and, like the author, abjure all contempt for people
of the common sort, who delight in these simple pleasures.

On the other hand Rousseau intentionally spares us such too
forcible scenes as Richardson's realism would not allow him to
forego; his book contains nothing so distressing as the death of
the woman Sinclair, the imprisonment of Clarissa, or her funeral.
The death of Julie is managed in a becoming and almost cheerful
manner; she is dressed in holiday attire and surrounded by
flowers.   He spares us the coffin, the train of mourners, the
tolling of the bell and the grave.

His one anxiety is to appear truthful; an effect which, in
his opinion, was only to be produced by dealing almost exclusively with the life of the common people.   Like Richardson he
portrays scarcely any characters but those of the lower or upper
middle class.   Neither M. d'Étanges, who is proud of his
name, nor M. d'Orbe, are very lofty personages.   Saint-Preux is
a man of no fortune.   " Let our noble authors choose more
humble models . . ."   Rousseau introduces us to a few plain
citizens of a little Swiss town, who have neither carriages nor
brilliant clothes, and are neither *comtes* nor *chevaliers*.   In Fanchon
Regard and Claude Anet we meet people who are ignorant of
the customs of society.   You find their history dull?   Then
trouble yourself no further; I do not write for you.   The
hearts I lay bare before you are simple ones, neither perfect nor
depraved.   Their virtues are average virtues, their vices average
vices.

[1] V., 2.

Only a *bourgeois* soul could create the *bourgeois* novel. And this is why the first writer who ventured to tell the story of a persecuted little servant-girl is, in this respect also, the master of Jean-Jacques and has the best right to be regarded as his predecessor. Others had openly professed their desire to make the novel a picture of human life. The younger Crébillon had himself spoken of a literature " wherein man might at last behold man as he is, and be dazzled less but instructed more." [1] Similar declarations occur in the prefaces of novelists and dramatists. A theory of literature is easily constructed. But a reformation in fiction demanded a thoroughly plebeian type of art, an eloquent ruggedness of form, and sincere emotion in presence of these fresh and simple materials.

IV

But if Rousseau resembled Richardson in the bourgeois character of his mind, he resembled him also in that he was a Protestant and preached his religion.

It is plain that there were marked differences between his *credo* and that of the pious Englishman, and Richardson would perhaps have treated the author of the *Profession de foi du vicaire savoyard* as he treated the deists of his own country. But this hatred of the philosophizing spirit—though they did not entertain it either to the same extent or in the same manner—was common to them both. Each held that all one could learn in philosophic circles was "how to undermine all the foundations of virtue." The whole ethical system of the philosophers was " the merest verbiage," and its professed teachers were " fit apologists for crime, who never seduced any but those whose hearts were already corrupt." [2] Like Richardson, Rousseau preaches against the idol of the age ; and like him is given to quoting somewhat ostentatiously, though with less reverence, from the Old Testament. [3] As

[1] Preface to *Égarements du cœur et de l'esprit* (1736).
[2] *Nouvelle Héloïse*, ii., 17 and 18.
[3] V., 7: " O Rachel, sweet maiden, beloved with so much constancy . . ."

his novel approaches its conclusion, its moral and religious purpose declares itself. The work assumes not only a more Christian, but even a more sectarian character. It is true that in his letters, Jean-Jacques asserts his wish to avoid hurting any-one's feelings, and even "to draw opposite parties together by a bond of mutual esteem": "Julie, with her piety, affords," he says, "a lesson to the philosophers, and Wolmar, with his atheism, a lesson to the intolerant."[1] But when Malesherbes speaks of excisions he loudly insists on the religious character of his work. He does not imagine that a "Genevan novel" need be appreciated by the Sorbonne. He observes that the suppres-sions have been so carefully made "that his Calvinists have nothing left in the shape of doctrine" but what might be pro-fessed by the most superstitious Catholic: "one might just as well expect every Protestant who is coming to Paris to abjure his religion before he crosses the frontier." Why is not Prévost's *Cléveland* subjected to the same treatment? "It seems rather strange that a Catholic priest may make Protestants express their opinion more freely in his novels than a Protestant may in his."[2] This is plain speaking. If the letter to Voltaire in answer to the *Poème sur Lisbonne*, or the *Profession de foi du vicaire savoyard* should leave us in any doubt as to the sentiments of Rousseau, his novel would suffice to enlighten us. The moral of the book, in fact, lies in Julie's conversion—and even in that of Wolmar. For the conversion of the atheist, as Rousseau himself remarks, is "so plainly indicated that any further elaboration would turn it into a dull sermon." The atheist Lovelace dies of a sword-thrust, and Julie entrusts her husband's soul to Saint-Preux: "Be a Christian, that you may persuade him to become one. Success is not so far off as you think . . . God is just, my trust will not prove mistaken."[3] This is edifying. But is this *coup de la grâce* any less romantic than Colonel Morden's *coup d'épée*?

Julie, on whom all the sympathies of the author are expended, is, like Clarissa, a thorough Protestant, and even a pietist. She makes a study of Muralt's *Instinct divin*, much as Mme. de

Warens, who also had "a somewhat Protestant mind," was influenced by Magny. It is true that she has long neglected religion : incapable of reconciling the worldly spirit with the spirit of the Gospel, she has "reserved her piety for the church, and cultivated philosophy at home"[1]; but on her marriage she returns to the doctrine of "our Church." She prays, and it is from prayer and prayer alone that she derives the strength which keeps her from further transgression : when philosophy fails her, religion comes to her support. She seeks to convert her lover, and quotes St Paul to him. As the wife of an atheist, she sheds bitter tears over her husband's irreligion. On her deathbed she openly avows the faith of her fathers : "I die, as I have lived, in the Protestant communion, which derives its sole precept from Holy Scripture and from reason"[2]; and to confirm her declaration she piously invokes a curse on Catholicism. When the pastor reminds her that a dying Catholic is surrounded by clergy who frighten him "in order to obtain the more control over his purse," she devoutly answers : "Let me thank Heaven that I was not born in the bosom of a venal religion which kills people in order to inherit their property." Is the writer who puts these words into Julie's mouth a philosopher simply, and nothing else ? And what more could Richardson have said ?

In virtue of this, as also of many other characteristics, Julie is the sister of Clarissa. The woman whom Jean-Jacques loved when he was writing his novel assumed a foreign and Protestant character. The fact is significant. He gave her, it is true, a few of the characteristics of Mme. de Warens; her vulgarity, sensuality, and coarse effrontery. But he gave her also the terrible clear-sightedness of Clarissa or Pamela. The reader will remember a certain strange reflexion of Pamela's concerning the dejection which follows upon transgression. In the same way Julie, even in her maidenhood, is aware that "the moment of fruition is a crisis in love."[3] Like her English sister, she is thoroughly familiar with things of which young girls in French novels and plays either are—or pretend to be—ignorant. She knows that she is her own mistress, and why. She is neither an

[1] III., 18.   [2] VI., 11.   [3] I., 9.

Agnes nor a Henrietta. She has been called a highly improbable
character; all that can really be said is that she is not French.
Once her character is restored to its natural atmosphere and
stripped of any unpleasant attributes with which the polluted
imagination of Jean-Jacques has invested it, the picture appears
both real and life-like. " Like Héloïse in your love," says Claire
to Julie, "you now resemble her also in your piety." The
devout Julie is the true one. The other is a phantom, born,
in Rousseau's mind, of the two figures of Mme. de Warens and
Mme. d'Houdetot.

Julie is pious. Her faith is a rule of life, enjoining respect for
lofty problems, and distrust of whatever is merely human.
" The lessons of philosophy need purifying by Christian
morality." But philosophy is brought in merely for form's sake,
as a concession to the age; for " Christian morality " is sufficient
in itself. Under the influence of her belief Julie becomes cold
and argumentative. She considers that virtue, integrity, and
resemblance in certain points of character can take the place
of love between husband and wife, provided only there be
religion as well.[1] Observe how she breaks with Saint-Preux:
she gives him permission to write to her, using Claire as a
medium of communication, but on condition that the latter will
suppress anything that requires it, " if," says she, " you should
prove capable of abusing your privilege." Her perspicacity
is truly appalling: " My dear friend, I have always found you
most agreeable. . . . But I have never seen you in any other
character than that of a lover: how do I know what you
would become if you ceased to love me?" She tells him
frankly that if she were twenty years old and free she would not
have him; she has too clear a perception of the conditions
necessary to happiness. The truth is that women like Julie,
if they can love at all, cannot love as the heroines of French
novels do. They have a much keener sense of their moral
personality. Like their descendants, the heroines of the Norwegian drama, they require love to be consecrated by equality
of rights. Apparently they have an abundance of pride and some

[1] III., 20.

austerity. Clarissa asks whether a man who has nothing but faults can expect to win her esteem, and what, she would like to know, are the virtues of Lovelace ? Yet the gift of such a soul has the greater value. It was his conception of religion and morality that led Rousseau, just as a different conception had led Richardson, to create female characters which were entirely new to French literature.

Are we to say that Rousseau derived his taste for moral problems from Richardson ? Not exactly. But if *Clarissa Harlowe* seemed to him the finest novel in the world, it was doubtless because he discovered in it something of his own aspirations. The author of *Clarissa* was eloquent on behalf of the family; and, similarly, Jean-Jacques pleaded the cause of marriage. We may hold that his pleading is ineffective, and that the first part of his book anticipates and destroys the effect of the second ; we may feel, moreover, that a happiness founded not so much on affection as on " a certain correspondence of character and disposition" does not sound very promising. Yet after all the cause was defended with zeal, and this in itself was something fresh. Marriage, in French literature, was either a means to getting on in the world, or a subject for coarse pleasantry. In the opinion of Molière's Madelon, to start with a marriage was " to begin a novel at the wrong end"; marriage brought upon Dandin the mishaps which every reader will re-collect, while Gil Blas retreated, as it were, into wedlock in the most perfunctory manner, and in order to get it over. Marivaux's Jacob, who fell into the hands of a woman as old as she was devout, never was the same man afterwards. In every instance married life was the source of distressing or ridiculous mishaps. No one had written, or thought of writing, the novel of marriage.

It was this that Richardson, with sorry results it is true, endeavoured to do in *Pamela*, while in *Clarissa* he exhibited the dangers of love without the sanction of marriage. Rousseau, in the second part of his story, attempted a more direct and more complete demonstration. From its very novelty the undertaking gave offence. A novel without passion ! The notion seemed a paradox. But Rousseau had a weakness for this second part :

this "case of morals and conjugal fidelity" seemed to him more original.

The fact is, he was not afraid to preach—we can scarcely help saying—with effrontery. This was not the way with French classical authors. They were not so profoundly convinced that *"the beautiful is nothing but the active form of the good."* They avoided all direct instruction, and Richardson would have horrified them. Above all they did not import into fiction problems which were the peculiar province of the pulpit or the schools. The *Princesse de Clèves* does not contain lengthy dissertations on the duties of a father, nor on suicide, duelling, the relief of beggars, chastity, adultery or free will. Such questions were treated, if at all, only by the way, and with the lightest possible touch. At most Marivaux had seasoned the novel with a dose of worldly morality, tempered with plenty of wit. He never ascended either the pulpit or the tribune. With him it was the novel that carried the moral, not the moral that included and justified the narrative. With Richardson and Jean-Jacques it was the sermon, bare and undisguised, that invaded literature; an effect, I admit, of a philosophizing age, but also, and mainly, the effect of a profoundly religious education, even when, as in Rousseau's case, that education has been incomplete. Education, domestic economy, the functions of a parent, agriculture, religious duties, immorality, suicide—what a list of homilies and sermons for a single novel! It seems as though fiction had inherited the eloquence of an exhausted pulpit. Modesty sets no limits to his preaching. "Every covering of the heart," says Mme. de Staël,[1] "has been rent asunder. No ancient writer would have made his own soul the subject of fictitious experiences in this manner." The same might be said of the classical writers of France, the disciples in this respect of the ancients. But here we find an insatiable curiosity with regard to the moral life, not of humanity, but of each individual. Fiction no longer speaks through the third person, but exclusively through the first. Nothing less than the complete hygiene, the complete pathology, of the soul will suffice for Rousseau.

[1] *De l'Allemagne*, II., 28.

If "cases" are wanting, they are invented. Richardson had already manifested a strange interest in cases of conscience. In the *Nouvelle Héloïse* casuistry flourishes on every page. Wolmar explains to Mme. d'Orbe how it is that Julie and Saint-Preux are "still lovers," though they "are nothing more than friends." How can they be so? The case is a strange one: "He is in love not with Julie de Wolmar but with Julie d'Étanges; he hates me not because I possess the person of the woman he loves, but as the ravisher of her whom he has loved. . . . He loves her in the past, that is the truth of the enigma; take away his memory, and he will love no longer." So Wolmar is perfectly tranquil. "The more they see of one another alone, the more easily they will understand their mistake, because they will compare what they feel with *what they would once have felt in a similar situation.*" Such is Rousseau's way of solving the problem of conscience which, from sheer love of dialectic, he is so kind as to discuss. Hence the numerous paradoxes that have so repeatedly been pointed out in his book.

Hence, too, however, fiction acquires all at once a singular dignity. For Rousseau's very sophistries indicate an unusual interest in moral questions. At certain periods, if the attention of mankind is to be brought back to questions of vital importance, certain truths must be set forth with all the pomp of paradox: moral doctrine, bare and unadorned, seems quite vapid; this our apostles of to-day—Ibsen, Tolstoï, Dumas fils—have clearly perceived. Similarly, Rousseau, in order to inoculate the French novel with the noble and aspiring unrest of English fiction, to give it the character of "a moral treatise, whence obscure virtues and destinies may derive incentives to enthusiasm"[1]—has strewn his work with paradox of the most provocative kind; first of all because he was Rousseau, but also because it was in his case almost a necessity to be over impressive if a strong impression was to be produced at all.

However this may be, no more complete revolution had ever before transformed the novel in France. For centuries the

[1] Mme. de Staël, *De la littérature*, i., 15.

Latin literatures had maintained their position by means of the drama, the epic, and poetry of the classical type. The novel, as an inferior branch of literature, was reserved to beguile a leisure hour. No other branch, however, was so essentially capable of a profound renovation. Sufficiently comprehensive in scope to include and absorb everything essential to the other forms, admirably fitted to develop that obstinate faculty of precise observation which is the distinctive feature of the modern genius, and susceptible also of adaptation to different varieties of talent, and even to the caprices of humour, the novel, in order to win for itself the place left void by tragedy and the epic, simply needed to attack the gravest problems with confidence. And this is what it did in the hands of the English first of all, and afterwards in those of Rousseau. Others before them had written novels characterized by intelligence, subtlety and even pathos; others had charmed or amused their age, or stirred it to emotion. None had introduced, in a work apparently of so frivolous a nature, the same elevation of thought, the same intensity of faith, and, if the expression be allowed, the same fervour of apostleship. None had boldly substituted the portrait of the individual, with his peculiarities and eccentricities, but with all the power of his personal conviction and of his native originality as well, for conventional types and traditional forms of narrative.

In virtue of these characteristics the English novelists deserved to be what Voltaire desired that Locke and his fellow-philoso-phers in England might become, " the instructors of the human race." Through the agency of the former, as has been justly remarked, the purest and healthiest ideas of the latter have been diffused throughout the universe, " as well as all that is noblest and most exalted in the doctrines of English preachers." [1] Thanks to them the novel attained a dignity it had never known; it became the most powerful of all instruments for the propagation of ideas. Thanks to them, in the last place— since they had prepared the way and cleared the ground — Jean-Jacques Rousseau, their brother in genius, was enabled to

[1] J. Jusserand, *Le roman anglais*, p. 69.

write the most eloquent and the most impassioned work in all French fiction.

In this sense, therefore, the *Nouvelle Héloïse* is the offspring of *Clarissa Harlowe*.

V

But because Richardson's work was capable of being further improved upon, and, above all, because he was Rousseau, Jean-Jacques introduced in his novel what they had been incapable of introducing in theirs.

In the first place, their conscientious representation of life required a setting. The novel as exemplified by Richardson was a play without scenery. This Rousseau had perceived. He had one general fault to find with this author, Bernardin de Saint-Pierre tells us, " that of never having connected the idea of his heroes with any locality of which his pictures would have been recognized with pleasure by the reader." "It is impossible," he said, " to picture Achilles without at the same time beholding the plains of Troy. We follow Aeneas on the shores of Latium : Vergil is not only the painter of love and war, he is also the artist of his own country. This characteristic of genius was wanting in Richardson." [1]

It was wanting indeed, to an incredible degree. In this respect he belongs to the age of Queen Anne : Addison, after crossing the Alps, described how his head was still giddy with mountains and precipices ; no one, he said, would credit the delight he felt at once more beholding a plain.[2]   Grandison, as he crosses Mont Cenis, declares that the prospect around him is wretched in the extreme—and this is the only reflection he has to make. Richardson's ideal landscape is "a large and convenient country house, situated in a spacious park," which contains a few structures "built in the rustic taste." Clarissa's garden is merely a place in which she may walk and dream. It is not described in a manner which brings it before us,

---

[1] *Fragments sur J.-J. Rousseau.*   [2] Letters : December 1701.

any more than the famous " willow walk," humorously quoted by Stendhal as a specimen of the seventeenth century's love for nature, is described by the author of the *Princesse de Clèves*.

Rousseau, we need scarcely remind the reader, placed the story of the sorrows of the soul in a setting it is impossible to forget. With his other characters he associated a new actor —nature, who often takes the leading part. " Ah, Eloisa! too much sensibility, too much tenderness, proves the bitterest curse instead of the most fruitful blessing ; vexation and disappointment are its certain consequences. The temperature of the air, the change of the seasons, the brilliancy of the sun, or thickness of the fogs, are so many moving springs to the unhappy possessor, and he becomes the wanton sport of their arbitration ; his thoughts, his satisfaction, his happiness depend on the blowing of the winds."[1] Now it is difficult to imagine the noble and pious Grandison committing the control of his well-regulated person to the winds. We cannot picture him making nature—the friend for all times and seasons—the participator in his restrained enjoyments and formal sorrows. He is too careful of his personal dignity to ask of the " vast sea "—" the immense sea "— " the calm which flies his agitated heart."[2] He would feel himself wanting in the self-possession which marks the gentleman, if in Clementina's presence he gave utterance to a passionate outcry like this: " I find the country more delightful, the verdure fresher and livelier, the air more temperate and serene than ever I did before ; even the feathered songsters of the sky seem to tune their tender throats with more harmony and pleasure ; the murmuring rills invite to love-inspiring dalliance, while the blossoms of the vine regale me from afar with the choicest perfumes. . . . I am tempted to imagine that even the earth adorns herself to make a nuptial bed for your happy lover, worthy of the passion which he feels, and the goddess he adores."[3] This, nevertheless, is the practice of Shakespeare, and also of Milton. But Richardson, in this respect, departs from the national tradition ; his narrow piety closes his eyes.

[1] *Nouvelle Héloïse*, i., 26.   [2] III., 26.   [3] I., 38.

It has been said that Christianity, by concentrating man's thoughts upon himself, dries up within him the sources of the feeling for nature, and that in opening the eyes of the soul it has closed the eyes of the body. The theory is contestable; for it takes no account of the songs of St Francis, of Bossuet's *Méditations*, of the poetry of Lamartine, and many other works which are at once Christian in character and picturesque. But there is a kind of devoutness, such as Jansenism or Pietism, which savours too much of the cloister—too much of the cell. There are heavens which do not declare the glory of God. There are souls which wither and fade away through excessive devotion to the inner life.

Further, it must be confessed, it is but an indifferent sign of moral health to commit one's soul "to the mercy of the winds." Nature, with its purity of atmosphere, with its vast horizons, with so much in it that is primitive or awe-inspiring, may act as peace-maker; but it is none the less true, as Rousseau more than once with sufficient emphasis remarks, that "all great passions are born of solitude," and that Rousseau himself is full of gratitude that it is so. Lastly, to consider that mere sensibility to natural beauties is a virtue, or even, as the disciples of Jean-Jacques would have it, the whole of virtue, becomes a paradox as soon as we cease to admit that wisdom consists in losing or annihilating oneself in nature. A famous follower of Rousseau, the poet Shelley, pushed the master's theory to its extreme consequence, when he wrote that "whosoever is free from the contamination of luxury and licence may go forth to the fields and to the woods, inhaling joyous renovation from the breath of spring, or catching from the odours and signs of autumn some diviner mood of sweetest sadness, which improves the softened heart." [1] This delicious exaltation becomes a recompense, an encouragement, a talent conferred on virtue by "the divine." It differs little, if at all, from virtue itself. But what sort of a virtue is that which totters at the faintest breath? And how much more sure of himself was Grandison than the weak and wavering Saint-Preux!

[1] *Essay on Christianity.*

The truth is that Rousseau's genius was profoundly lyrical, whereas Richardson's was not, or was so only during those rare moments when the pathos of his subject lent him wings and carried him beyond the reach of the sordid things of life.

This lyrical quality of Rousseau's genius is due to his conception of love. For him it is more violent, more enthralling, more sensual. Clarissa cannot help loving Lovelace, but she strives against her passion. Julie acknowledges herself vanquished at the outset, with the excuse that she has "only the choice of her faults." Genuine love, in fact, "is a devouring fire, which inspires the other sentiments with its zeal, and animates them with fresh vigour."[1] Richardson had depicted its matchless power and nobility, but he had also set forth its dangers. Rousseau, thoroughly convinced that "cold reason never did a great deed," reached the same conclusions, but at the same time took a delight in portraying the exquisite agitation experienced by a fiery soul under the sway of passion, a passion "which penetrates and burns even to the marrow." In short, it is repugnant to the poet in Jean-Jacques to bring himself into harmony with the moralist. But what the moralist has lost thereby, the poet, the great poet, has gained.

Moreover, Rousseau describes not only the sensual, but also the melancholy aspect of love. In this there was nothing absolutely fresh : Prévost, in *Cléveland* and *Manon Lescaut*, and Richardson himself, in certain parts of *Clarissa*, had attempted to portray the fierce yet sweet unrest which follows sensual pleasure. But their delight in indulgence was unaccompanied by the same exaltation. Their heroes had never sought love for the sake of the bitter taste it leaves behind it. To them the yearning for "enchanting sadness," for the "languor of the melted and impassioned soul,"[2] were unknown. They had never experienced to the same extent that sense of the irreparable which accompanies transgression and leaves the heart "empty and swollen

[1] I., 12.

[2] "O enchanting sadness ! O languor of the melted and impassioned soul ! By how much you surpass the stormy pleasures, the wanton gaiety, the passionate delight, and every other transport, which the unbridled desires of lovers can derive from passion unrestrained."—I., 38.

like a balloon filled with air."[1] They had not fostered within themselves "the sweet yet bitter recollection of a lost happiness." Rousseau is infinitely their superior, and all comparison would be futile. No novelist had shed tears so sincere over "the sweet charm, now vanished like a dream, which attends on virtue." No poet had said to his mistress, with a richness of language previously unknown: "Our souls, exhausted with love and anguish, melt and flow like water."[2]

Nor, lastly, had any one clothed sentiments so sincere in so poetical a form. "It may be very funny," wrote Voltaire, "to see a soul flow; but as for water, it is usually just when it is exhausted that it ceases to flow."[3] Voltaire says no more than he is entitled to say; but neither do we when we assert that Voltaire understands neither Rousseau, nor what constitutes the essence of lyricism, nor what separates the author of *Julie* from the author of *Clarissa*. Richardson wrote a novel, and Rousseau writes a poem. The one is a very great novelist, but a very bad writer; the other is an incomparable artist in words. The one has no style at all; the other renewed the French language from its very foundation.

Feeling for nature, melancholy, the lyrical faculty :—in each of these respects, which at bottom may be reduced to one, Rousseau excels Richardson by the full stature of genius.

Nevertheless, something of Richardson is transmitted to every one who reads Rousseau. It should be remarked that for nearly a century, most of the disciples of Jean-Jacques have been disciples of Richardson as well. All the romantic writers who preceded or followed the Revolution piously associated his name with that of his glorious imitator.

From Rousseau Bernardin de Saint Pierre learned to love and imitate the author of *Clarissa*.[4] André Chénier praises him in the warmest terms. Mme. de Staël acknowledges that the abduction of Clarissa was "the great event of her early life."[5] "Let neither man nor woman, of grovelling mind or corrupted

[1] II., 17.   [2] I., 26.   [3] *Lettres sur la nouvelle Héloïse.*
[4] See *Fragments sur J.-J. Rousseau.*
[5] Lady Blennerhasset, *Mme. de Staël et son temps*, vol. i., p. 185.

heart, dare to touch the books of Richardson, . . . they are
sacred!"[1]   Chateaubriand earnestly invokes a revival of his
reputation.[2]   Charles Nodier admires his nobility and freedom
from affectation.[3]   Sainte Beuve, in his earliest lines, recalls
with emotion "the pure passion" of Clarissa and Clementina.[4]
Lamartine, as well as Michelet, makes Richardson one of the
studies of his early life.[5]   George Sand is enthusiastic in her admiration of the writer whom Villemain describes as "the greatest
and perhaps the least conscious of Shakespeare's imitators,"[6] and
of whom Alfred de Musset says that he has written "the greatest
novel in the world."

[1] *Du sentiment*, 1801, p. 221.   [2] *Essai sur la littérature anglaise*, pt. v.

[3] *Des types en littérature*.   [4] *Poésies complètes*, p. 352.

[5] F. Reysslé, *La jeunesse de Lamartine*, p. 89; Michelet, *Mon journal*, p. 81.

[6] *XVIIIe siècle*, lesson 27.

Book III

ROUSSEAU AND THE INFLUENCE OF ENGLAND DURING THE LATTER HALF OF THE EIGHTEENTH CENTURY

Chapter I

ROUSSEAU AND THE DIFFUSION OF THE LITERATURES OF NORTHERN EUROPE

I. Development of English influence in the latter half of the century—Intercourse with England—Influence of English manners.
II. Growth of the cosmopolitan idea—Diffusion of the English language and literature : newspapers and translations.
III. Wherein Rousseau assisted the movement—The revolution accomplished by him in criticism—Manner in which he effected the union of Germanic with Latin Europe.

THE influence of England had paved the way for the literary revolution accomplished by Rousseau, and, conversely, during the latter half of the century, the influence of Rousseau furthered the spread of English and of the Northern literatures generally among the French. The cosmopolitan spirit in France was born of the union of the Latin with the Germanic genius in the person of Jean-Jacques Rousseau.

By the year 1760, the date of the appearance of *La Nouvelle Héloïse*, " an experiment extending over a period of thirty years "—to use the expression, already quoted, of an eighteenth century writer [1]—" had been made upon one of the neighbours of France, namely England : it had long been impossible to doubt that the crossing of races is beneficial to every species of plants and animals ; and it was a necessary conclusion that in the human species, which the faculties of thought, speech, and conscience render so especially capable of being brought to perfection, the

[1] Garat, *Mémoires sur Suard*, vol. i., p. 153.

255

crossing of minds, since they, too, have their races, would produce a species little short of divine." In the preceding pages we have endeavoured to show what we are to understand by this crossing of races and of minds. We have attempted to prove that Jean-Jacques Rousseau inoculated the French mind, as Mme. de Staël says, with "a little foreign vigour." We have striven to draw the reader's attention to a fact which has been too little noticed, "the union of the French with the English mind, which, if its immense consequences are borne in mind, is the most important fact in the history of the eighteenth century." [1] It has been our object to exhibit the effect of the example set by a great French writer—the most popular of his epoch—in frankly imitating an English model: even were Rousseau's debt less important than it really is, it would be none the less true that his contemporaries thought they perceived it, and that they hailed with delight—without, at the same time, very clearly discerning its consequences—the influence exercised by England upon his genius. The ancient prestige of the Latin spirit in France had received a blow from which it never recovered.

It remains to show how the revolution in French taste accomplished by Rousseau has in its turn facilitated the comprehension of the noble literature of a neighbouring country; how, from 1760 onwards, he came to be pre-eminently the spokesman of those who, wearied by the long domination of the classical spirit, dreamed more or less vaguely of a renovation of art through the agency of the English genius; and how, thanks to him, France was invaded by foreign works which up to that time had been misunderstood and regarded with suspicion, or admired, if at all, only by a few elect spirits.

I

In the latter half of the eighteenth century, from the close of the Seven Years' War down to the Revolution, the social and intellectual influence of England was on the increase in France. The movement inaugurated by Voltaire, Prévost, and Montesquieu

[1] Buckle, *History of Civilization in England*, vol. ii.

attained during these decisive years its full strength.   Since these are just the years when the genius of Jean-Jacques was revolutionizing French literature and unsettling what up to that time had been recognized in France as the principles of criticism, it is necessary briefly to call to mind the extent to which circumstances lent their assistance, unsuspected by Rousseau, to a work of which he himself doubtless failed to gauge the true import.

Between 1760 and 1789, the intercourse between the two countries became closer and closer.   The favour with which everything English was received in France attracted thither a large number of distinguished foreigners, including adventurers like Hales, poets like Gray,[1] novelists like Smollett,[2] economists like Arthur Young, actors like Garrick, critics like Johnson, and philosophers such as Hume or Dugald Stewart.   In the same drawing-room—d'Holbach's, for example—such visitors as David Hume, Wilkes, Shelburne, Garrick, Priestley, and Franklin the American would come and go one after the other.   Some of these guests created a sensation; among them "the English Roscius," as Diderot calls Garrick, who inspired Mme. Riccoboni with a "warm, indeed a very warm, friendship,"[3] and dreamed of converting Voltaire to the worship of Shakespeare[4]; Wilkes, described by Jean-Jacques as "that mischief-maker," who posed as a great victim, astonished all Paris by his fiery eloquence, and went about everywhere with his daughter, "like Oedipus with Antigone"[5]; Hume, whom people rushed to behold as they formerly crowded "to see a rhinoceros at a fair"—David Hume—"heavy and silent," described by Rousseau, who at first befriended him but afterwards became his enemy, as "the truest philosopher I know,

---

[1] Gray's visit was paid some years earlier.   See the journal of his tour in France and Italy in *Gray and his friends*, by Duncan C. Tovey (Cambridge, 1890).

[2] See *Peregrine Pickle*, ch. xxxv.-l.

[3] See the dedication to the *Lettres de Mme. de Sancerre*.

[4] *Cf*. Ballantyne, *op. cit.*, p. 271.

[5] Garat, *Mémoires sur Suard*, vol. ii., p. 91 *et seq.*   (*Cf.* Légier, *Amusements poétiques*, Paris, 1769, p. 182 :

> Ce républicain intrépide
> Qui brave les plus grands revers,
> Des mains d'une beauté timide,
> Vient à Paris prendre des fers).

and the only historian who ever wrote in an impartial manner "[1];
and many others as well. The name of Englishman, said
Gibbon, who came to Paris in 1761, was *clarum et venerabile nomen
gentibus*,[2] and a key to the door of every *salon*.

Conversely, the French learned to cross the Channel, and the
"pilgrimage to England" became almost obligatory. Buckle
observes with pride that during the two generations which
separated the close of the reign of Louis XIV. from the commencement of the Revolution, there was scarcely a single
Frenchman of note who did not cross the straits. With
regard to the period anterior to 1750, the assertion would
be hazardous. Messieurs de Conflans and de Lauzun, Mmes. de
Boufflers and du Boccage were quoted as having been to England.
A writer of the day remarks with interest that Mme. de Boufflers
is the first lady of quality to attempt the journey.[3]   But during
the latter half of the century a trip to England formed a part
of the education of every intelligent man. The practice was
adopted by the majority of such scholars and men of learning
as Buffon, La Condamine, Delisle, Élie de Beaumont, Jussieu,
Lalande, Nollet, and Valmont de Bomare; by the greater
number of politicians and economists, from Montesquieu to
Helvetius, from Gournay to Morellet, from Mirabeau to
Lafayette or Roland; and, to a constantly increasing extent,
by ordinary men of letters—Grimm, Suard, Duclos, and many
others. In the philosophical circle of which Rousseau was so
long a member, what was preached was also practised. Helvetius's friend, the abbé Le Blanc, spent several years in England,
and on his return brought back three great volumes of letters,
heavy in style, but not lacking in discernment, which complete
the work of Voltaire and Muralt.[4]   Raynal, the author of

[1] Letter to Mme. de Boufflers, August 1762. See also *Confessions*, ii. 12.

[2] *Miscellaneous Works*, p. 73. On English travellers in France during the
eighteenth century, see Rathery : *Les Relations sociales et intellectuelles* . . ., 4th part,
and A. Babeau, *Les Voyageurs en France*.

[3] Dutens, *Journal d'un voyageur*, vol. i., p. 217.

[4] Le Blanc's *Lettres* were translated into English in 1747 (London, 2 vols. 8vo)
and discussed by English critics. See *Mémoires de Trévoux*, May and June 1746 ;
Nouv. litt., January 1751 ; Clément, *Les cinq années littéraires*, iii. 26 ; Tabaraud,
Histoire du philosophisme anglaise, vol. ii., pp. 443-444.

the *Histoire philosophique des deux Indes*, so highly esteemed by Franklin and Gibbon, visited London and became a member of the Royal Society.   Helvetius, who crossed the straits in 1763, came back "quite crazy about the English," and talked of "packing up his wife and children" to go and settle in London.[1] But the only thing which d'Holbach, who was less of an anglomaniac, found to his liking in that land of liberty was that " the Christian religion was almost extinct there "; nevertheless, on his return he became a voluminous translator of English books, especially of such as had as little flavour of Christianity about them as possible.[2]   Grimm was charmed " with the simplicity, naturalness and good sense" he met with in England, and would have been glad to remain in that happy country.[3]   Necker, his wife, Duclos, Morellet and Suard are scarcely less enthusiastic. It should be observed, as a highly interesting fact, that the prevailing fashion even led several youths to complete their education in England: young Walckenaer, who was sent by his uncle to Oxford, and afterwards to Glasgow, was four years absent from France; while Fontanes spent eighteen months in England shortly before the Revolution, and there acquired a love for the poetry of Gray and Ossian.[4]

What was taking place was, in short, a revolution in French habits, big with significant consequences.

Of these consequences the first is the growth of the influence of English customs.   " Anglomania," says Grimm, a thoroughly trustworthy witness, " and the appalling progress it makes, threaten alike the gallantry, the social disposition, and the taste in dress of the French nation."   In a more general sense, it endangered a whole tradition of genial grace and sociability, which formed as it were the stay of French classical literature. In France, as elsewhere, it tended to replace the social spirit by individualism; in other words, by its very negation.

[1] Diderot, *Œuvres*, vol. xix., p. 187.   [2] *Ibid.*, vol. xx., pp. 246 and 308.
[3] E. Scherer, *Melchior Grimm*, p. 254.
[4] Observe also the great number of accounts of travels in England ; Grosley's oft-reprinted *Londres* ; and books by Lacombe, Chantreau, de Cambry, etc.   We may call especial attention to that curious document, *Un voyage philosophique en Angleterre*, by Lacoste (Paris, 1787, 2 vols. 8vo).

A certain pleasant comedy of the day satirizes English ways in a very agreeable manner. Éraste is an anglomaniac—that is to say, he turns his garden into a heap of ruins, has Hogard and Hindel (*sic*) always on his lips, drinks nothing but tea, rides none but English horses, and reads no authors but Shakespeare, Otway, and Pope: "The teachers of mankind have been born in London, and it is from them that we must take lessons. I am going to see this land of thinkers." His craze is flattered by Damis, who makes fun of him: "In France people laugh at everything; but you must know, sir, that in England, though men sometimes hang themselves, they never laugh." Note, especially, that "in London every one assumes just what character he pleases; there you surprise no one by being yourself."[1]

Accordingly, anglomaniacs make a point of being like no one else. Women are dressed "in hat, chemise," and short skirts, as in *Émile*, that they may take their constitutional in comfort; men, in frock coat and vest, "walk with their chins in the air and assume a republican bearing."[2] A learned justice of the period wants to know how Frenchmen are benefited by such close intercourse with England: "It only introduces queer tastes, less courtesy in tone and manners, and an increase of obnoxious absurdities. . . . Would you recognize this ecclesiastic, this magistrate, this new favourite of Fortune, with his high shoes, a whip or light cane in his hand, his hair turned up beneath a broad-brimmed hat which flaps about his eyes, his frock-coat fitting so tightly that it scarcely covers his back, and his neck muffled in a thick cravat? Will you have time to get out of the way of this young madcap, seated like a quack in a carriage as flimsy as it is dangerous, driving like the wind at the risk of his own life and of those of the passers by, hatted, dressed and booted like his jockey, in a manner which befits the back seat of his carriage quite as well as the front, and makes it impossible for any one to say which is the master and which

---

[1] Saurin, *l'Anglomane ou l'Orpheline léguée*.

[2] See Grimm, *Correspondance littéraire*, May 1786; Mercier, *Tableau de Paris*, vol. vii., p. 38; Quicherat, *Histoire du costume en France*, p. 601.

the servant ? " [1] The English type of coxcomb, " bundled up in a hideous great cloak," splashed with mud up to his shoulders, and with a comb under his hat, sets up for a philosopher, quotes Addison and Pope, and seems to say: " Now am I a *thinker*." This thinking creature, "dressed in green," whose coat shows not a single crease, whose hair is innocent of powder, and whose head is always covered—is the anglomaniac. " Well ! " said one of them to the abbé Le Blanc, " what do you think of me ? Don't I look thoroughly English ? " [2]

Touches like these, absurd as they are, afford evidence of a social transformation which struck the attention of all who were contemporary with it. The fashion was a democratic one, and was adopted by the common people. It reflected a ruder and more primitive form of society, or rather a society which was ambitious of being so. Louis XV. strove against the infatuation, but Louis XVI., who, at Necker's instigation, had made a study of England, encouraged it. [3] From 1774 onwards, everything was in the English style—costumes, horse-races, and clubs. [4] The evening meal is taken in the English fashion, about four or five o'clock ; and as for intellectual refinement, who would any longer expect it of the French ? A *club à l'anglaise* is a place of perdition, where, as Fox is surprised to find, you eat the vilest dishes, drink *ponche* made with bad rum, and read the news-papers: " I am very glad," Fox concludes after an evening of this kind, " to see that as regards imitation we cannot be more ridiculous than our dear neighbours." [5] This fresh social

[1] Rigoley de Juvigny, *De la décadence des lettres et des mœurs*, Paris, 1787, 12mo, p. 476.
[2] *Préservatif contre l'anglomanie*, Minorca and Paris, 1757. Le Blanc, *Lettres*, vol. i., p. 63.
[3] Tabaraud, vol. ii., p. 451.
[4] Ladies wore head-dresses said to be the outcome " of the union between France and England " (Mercier, *Tableau de Paris*). In many shops English signs were displayed and English goods sold. Grimm (*Correspondance littéraire*, May 1786) says that horses, carriages, furniture, jewellery, and woven materials were sent over from England. *Vauxhalls* were built at Paris in imitation of London, and there were a Coliseum, a Ranelagh, and an Astley's circus, the latter of which drew all Paris to see it. For horse racing there was quite a mania (see Le Blanc, *Lettres*, vol. iii., p. 151), etc.
[5] Quoted by Rathery.

influence modifies the French disposition. "Elegance consisted in having none. Society had been spoilt by dinners attended by men only, by those who supposed themselves to be men of intelligence, or by military men who were destitute of it. Platitudes about liberty and abuses made them fancy themselves Englishmen ; how many times have I not said to them—the speaker is the Prince de Ligne :—' Let them alone, these enormously long newspapers which you cannot read. What have you to do with Pitt and Fox, who ridicule anglomaniacs every day ? You don't even know the name of the lord-lieutenant of your own province '[1] . . ." Social life is disappearing, and with it a part of the heritage the French have received from their ancestors. A drawing-room is now an ante-chamber, where everyone remains standing, including even the women : " You praise the hostess's wit, but what good does it do you ? A lay figure placed in a chair would do the honours of an evening like this quite as well. There she is bound to remain until three o'clock in the morning, and she will go to bed without having had a glimpse of half the people she has received. . . . And that is what is called an *assemblée à l'anglaise*."[2]

II

In a society of this type, the highest virtue is to be a cosmopolitan in an intellectual sense. The word "cosmopolitanism" is of earlier origin, but it was at this period that it came into

---

[1] Prince de Ligne, *Mémoires*, vol. iv., p. 154. We read in the same author that " Horses and traps for the morning drive are ruining the young fellows in Paris. The French will take more harm from the English habits they adopt than from all the English fleet. . . . All these *clubs* will be the end of them. Farewell to good manners, to gallantry, to the desire to please. Now we talk of Parliament and of the House of Commons. We read the *Courrier de l'Europe*, and talk horses. We bet ; play at *creps* ; we drink wretched pale wine instead of the champagne which used to make our ancestors merry and inspire them with song. Barbarians ! You should give the tone; never receive it " (*Œuvres*, ed. 1796, vol. xii., p. 173).

[2] Mme. de Genlis, *Mémoires*, vol. v., p. 101, and vol. vii., p. 10.

general use.[1] " The true sage is a cosmopolitan," says a writer
of comedy.[2] "Happy the man," exclaims Sébastien Mercier,
" whose literary taste is cosmopolitan ! "[3] A traveller declares
that " the highest title in Paris, after that of woman, is that of
foreigner."[4] And Franklin also remarks that a foreigner is
treated with the same respect in France as a lady is in England.[5]

Thanks largely to this infatuation for everything exotic,
Frenchmen began to have a more accurate acquaintance with
at least one foreign language, and the knowledge of that
language increased in a very remarkable manner.

English had long repelled the student by the harshness of
what La Harpe—who never knew the language—called its
" inconceivable" pronunciation. None " but a northern ear,"
thought Le Blanc, "could endure sounds so harsh that they
seem to conflict with the principles of human articulation."[6]
"I cannot imagine," wrote Fréron naïvely to Desfontaines,
" how so subtle and so keenly intellectual a nation can employ
such a language for the composition of works of genius. Can
I conceive of *Gulliver, Pamela,* or *Joseph Andrews* as having
been written in so harsh a language as this ? " And he uttered
the hope that soon the English would make up their minds to
write their books in French, which was " smooth, expressive,
flowing and harmonious."[7] Louis XV., moreover, was opposed
to the teaching of English, and when Paris-Duverney, the super-
intendent of the military school, suggested the institution of
classes in that language, for the benefit of naval recruits, he
replied peevishly : " The English have destroyed the intelligence

[1] In the sixteenth century the word appears chiefly in the form *cosmopolitain*.
In 1605, a Swiss writer published at Berne *la Comédie du cosmopolite* (Virgile Rossel,
Histoire de la littérature française en Suisse, vol. i., p. 464). The form *cosmopolite* is
mentioned in the Trévoux Dictionary in 1721, and was recognized by the Academy
in 1762. In 1750, a writer of the name of Monbron published *Le Cosmopolite ou le
Citoyen du monde*, and in 1762 Chévrier produced *Le Cosmopolite ou les Contradictions*.

[2] Palissot, *les Philosophes*, iii. 4.

[3] Sébastien Mercier, preface to *Jeanne d'Arc*.

[4] John Moore, *Lettres d'un voyageur anglais*, Paris, 1788, vol. i.

[5] *Correspondance*, translated by Ed. Laboulaye.

[6] *Lettres*, vol. i., p. 75 *et seq.*

[7] *Observations sur les écrits modernes*, vol. xxxiii. (1743), p. 286.

of my kingdom; let us not expose the rising generation to the danger of similar perversion." [1]

Voltaire had been the first to resist this prejudice. On his return from England, he had converted Thiériot, Mme. de Châtelet, and the abbé de Sade.[2] To a young man who asked his advice with regard to journalism as a profession, he boldly replied, in 1737: "A good journalist ought at least to have a knowledge of English and Italian, for these languages contain many works of genius, and genius is scarcely ever translated. I consider these the two European languages most necessary to a Frenchman."[3]

A few years later his efforts at dissemination had borne fruit. About the middle of the century it was the fashion for women, even in the provinces, to learn English. "Not an Armande or a Bélise" could be found who did not devote herself to the study of it.[4] The means thereto were multiplied: Boyer's grammar and dictionary gave rise to numerous imitations.[5] In 1755 the *Journal étranger* gave a long account of Johnson's dictionary, with a translation of the preface.[6] But, so early as 1739, Prévost declares that the study of English has become an essential part of "fine literature."[7] An English traveller was struck by the change that had taken place: "Thirty years ago a Frenchman with a knowledge of two or three foreign languages would have been looked upon as a marvel; to-day there are many people who read the speeches delivered in Parliament in the original."[8]

In the reign of Louis XVI., a *Société philosophique* was founded in Paris with the object of promoting the study of foreign languages, and of assisting foreigners in the acquisition of

---

[1] Tabaraud, vol. ii., p. 447.

[2] Letter to the abbé de Sade, 13th November 1733.

[3] *Conseils à un journaliste: Œuvres*, vol. xxii., p. 261.

[4] Le Blanc, *Lettres*, vol. ii., p. 465. See also La Harpe, *Cours de littérature*, vol. iii., p. 224.

[5] *E.g.* the grammars of J. Wallis, Mauger et Festeau, Peyton, Siret, Rogissard, Lavery, Gautier, Berry, O'Reilly, Flint, Dumay, &c.; and the dictionaries of Boyer, Brady, Chambaud et Robinet, &c.

[6] June 1755 and December 1756.   [7] *Pour et Contre*, vol. xviii.

[8] *Premier et second voyage de Milord . . . à Paris*, vol. iii., p. 153.

French.[1] Grimm states that the language of Shakespeare[2] is the only one which forms an essential part of the scheme of a fashionable education.   Mercier observes that the reading of English papers has become as common in Paris as fifty years ago it was rare.[3] Every week *Les Papiers anglais*, a journal devoted to the study of English, published in both languages the most interesting articles from English journals, and Fréron remarks on the success of the idea, which enabled students at one and the same time to learn the language and to make themselves familiar with the events of the day.[4] Buckle has drawn up a long list of all the well-known Frenchmen who, during the eighteenth century, took the trouble to learn English ; it includes all, or nearly all, the noted writers of the period,[5] and enables us to estimate the depth and extent of English influence better than many general considerations would do.   This knowledge, it is true, was not uniformly accurate or thorough, but it was most widely spread, and indeed almost general—a fact which speaks volumes.   A considerable number of English words, which were introduced into the French language at that time, bear witness to the fashion ; new customs bring new words : men go to the *club*, drink *ponche* and play *whisk* ; now-a-days, says Voltaire, "your major-domo serves up *rostbifs* of mutton . . . our poor French tongue must simply make the best of a bad case."[6]   In truth the anglomaniacs put it to some pretty severe tests : *dame* becomes *ladi*[7] ; *loi* becomes *bil*[8] ; while *monsieur* is replaced by *sir*, even when every rule forbids its use.   " Sir, voulez-vous du thé ?" may pass muster, but " à Sir donnez un verre d'eau "[9] is neither

---

[1] Babeau, *Paris in* 1789, p. 339.   [2] *Correspondance littéraire*, May 1786.

[3] *Tableau de Paris*, vol. xi., p. 128.

[4] There was also a goodly number of *Musées à l'anglaise* in several towns : the *Musée de Paris*, the *Société olympique*, etc.

[5] Buckle, vol. iii., p. 81.

[6] Letter to Linguet, published in the *Journal encyclopédique*, September 1769

[7] Prévost, *Mémoires d'un homme de qualité*, vol. ii., p. 254 : " C'est une charmante ladi."

[8] Francois de Neufchâteau, *Paméla*, iv. 12 :

> Dans vos bills dès longtemps mon supplice est écrit.

The word is found even in the Trévoux Dictionary (1704).

[9] *Ibid.*, ii. 12.

English nor French. *Un plaisant sérieux* becomes *un homme d'humour*,[1] and it is good form to have the *spleen* rather than the *vapeurs*.[2]

In the latter half of the century the " demon translator " raged furiously. Every publisher had his translating staff.[3] Desfontaines, Mme. du Boccage, Dupré de Saint-Maur, Du Resnel, Saint-Hyacinthe, and Van Effen had led the way. His version of *Paradise Lost* had even obtained for Dupré de Saint-Maur a chair in the Academy. Their successors were legion, from Leclerc de Septchênes to Frenais, the translator of Sterne; from the abbé Yart, the author of a voluminous *Idée de la poésie anglaise*, to the " inevitable M. Eidous," who, if Grimm is to be believed, translated a volume every month. Women took part in the work, and produced their " traductionette," in order to gain the reputation of being authors[4]; Mme. de Boufflers translated English songs, the wife of the president de Meynières turned her attention to the historians, and the duchess d'Aiguillon attacked Ossian. Prominent writers such as Prévost, Diderot, d'Holbach, and Suard devoted themselves to translation. Others, more modest or less capable, attribute all their success to their knowledge of English; among them the first adapter of Shakespeare, La Place, who flattered himself that he knew two languages because he had been educated in the college of the English Jesuits as Saint-Omer, whereas in reality he did not know one. His knowledge of English, however, was " the cause of any little success he had had." La Place produced a translation of Otway's *Venice Preserved*, a *Théâtre anglais* in eight volumes, a version of *Tom Jones*, and translations of everything that came in his way; thanks to all these versions and to Mme. de Pompadour, he became editor of the *Mercure*.[5] Another, the

---

[1] Suard, *Mélanges de littérature*, vol. iv., p. 366. Muralt is responsible for the first definition of *humour*. See also Le Blanc, *Lettres*, vol. i., p. 79. Attempts were also made to distinguish *humour*, or, as Garat spells it, *hyumour* (*Mémoires sur Suard* vol. ii., p. 92) from *whim* (see *Journal encyclopédique*, 1st June 1786).

[2] On the spleen or *vapeurs anglaises*, see Prévost's *Cléveland*; Le Blanc, vol. i., p. 169; Bezenval, *Mémoires*, vol. iv., etc.

[3] *Journal encyclopédique*, February 1761.   [4] Mercier, *Tableau*, vol. xi., p. 130.

[5] La Harpe: remarks on La Place, in the *Cours de littérature*.

celebrated Letourneur, described by Voltaire as "secrétaire de la librairie, mais non secrétaire du bon goût," extended this branch of commerce still further, founded together with Fontaine-Malherbe, the Comte de Catuélan, the chevalier de Rutlidge, and others, a regular translating firm, rendered Shakespeare, Richardson, Young, and Ossian into French, and, in addition to this mass of work, was able at his death to leave behind him certain fragments of translation in manuscript which were piously published by his friends, together with his biography.[1]

A fact of greater importance is that, in order to satisfy this increasing taste for foreign productions, journals were started—not, as heretofore, at the Hague, or in London—which allotted the greater part of their space to English affairs, or were even exclusively devoted to them.

Most of the literary journals of the period declare that the cosmopolitan spirit gives rise to "a social intercourse thoroughly worthy of the enlightened nations of which the European federation consists."[2] Those even who had once been hostile to the movement ultimately fell in with the fashion: Fréron, who had at first shown no disposition to welcome foreign literature, now became very curious about it: assigned much of the space in his *Année littéraire* to German and English books, became intimate with Letourneur, and corresponded with Garrick. Pierre Rousseau's *Journal encyclopédique* is a mine of information for the student of the relations between France and Europe during the eighteenth century, and as much might be said of the *Esprit des journaux*—an immense series containing a most curious selection of the best articles from every periodical in the world, and the delight of Sainte-Beuve. Those who have never turned over the pages of the two hundred and eighty-eight volumes of the *Journal encyclopédique*, or the four hundred and ninety-five volumes of the *Esprit des journaux*,[3] have no

[1] *Le Jardin anglais*, or Varieties both original and translated: a posthumous work with a notice of the author, Paris, 1788, 2 vols. 12mo.

[2] *Correspondance littéraire*, August 1772.

[3] *L'Esprit des journaux français et étrangers* appeared from July 1772 to April 1818. The *Journal encyclopédique* appeared from 1756 to 1773.

idea of the curiosity which foreign productions aroused in France.

But, in addition to these magazines of a general character, special reviews were established : following the example of the *Bibliothèque germanique* and the *Bibliothèque italique*, there was a *Traducteur*, which gave a summary of the English periodicals, a *Bibliothèque des romans anglais*, a *Censeur universel anglais*, or " General, critical, and impartial review of all English productions " [1]—a list of efforts which would have greatly astonished Ariste, one of the characters of Father Bouhours, who considered " that people of refined intelligence are somewhat rarer in cold countries."

The most famous of these cosmopolitan magazines, and the one most worthy of remembrance, was the *Journal étranger*, which was issued from 1754 to 1762, and edited successively by Grimm, Prévost, Fréron, Arnaud, and Suard.

Established in April 1754, the *Journal* was by turns mainly scientific in character under Prévost, political under Fréron, and literary under Arnaud and Suard. Its title, and the sections into which it was divided, were frequently altered.[2] After Fréron left it, in October 1756, the scope of the magazine was enlarged ; regular correspondents were secured in the East, and in Rome, Leghorn, Florence, Gottingen, Leipzig, Dresden, Stockholm and London, and foreign contributions became both more accurate and more abundant. But the spirit of the magazine remained unchanged; from the outset its object had been to combine "the genius of each nation with those of all the others," to bring " writers of every nationality" into relation with one another, " to decide

---

[1] See Hatin, *Histoire de la presse*, vol. iii., p. 114.

[2] The descriptions of the *Journal étranger* given in bibliographies have, as a rule, been inaccurate. Its successive titles were *Journal étranger, ouvrage périodique ; à Paris, au bureau du Journal étranger*, . . . then *Journal étranger, ou notice exacte et detaillée des ouvrages de toutes les nations étrangères, en fait d'arts, de sciences, de littérature, etc.*, by M. Fréron . . . (Paris, Michel Lambert). In 1760 it bore on the title-page the name of the abbé Arnaud, and appeared under the patronage of the Dauphin. The entire collection extends from April 1754 to August 1762 (42 vols. 12mo); though no issue was made for December 1754, nor during the whole of 1759. Prévost's editorship lasted from January to August 1755 ; Fréron's from August 1755 until October 1756.

those idle differences of opinion upon questions of taste which set the peoples of Europe at variance with one another," and to teach France "no longer to lay exclusive claim to the gift of thought, the mere pretension to which would almost afford evidence of its absence, no longer to venture upon the unseemly jests which are enough to make one people detested by all the rest, nor any longer to evince that offensive contempt for estimable nations which is nothing but a relic of the brutal prejudice due to former ignorance."[1]   In short, the *Journal étranger* proposed to resume, and at the same time to develop, the idea which had guided the refugee critics in the work of editing their magazines.   Side by side with a letter on the condition of literature in Poland, it inserts an account of the German fable-writers.   Here it speaks of Portuguese writers, and there of the poets of Arabia. Winckelmann, Kleist, Klopstock, and Lessing are mentioned in the same breath with Goldoni and Metastasio.   But England, above all, furnished the material for whole numbers of the magazine.   "We are aware," wrote the authors, "how necessary to our journal English literature has become.   The lively and almost exclusive interest which is everywhere taken in the productions of the British intellect makes it imperative that we should conform in this respect to the general wish."[2]   From the earliest volumes the journal derived its materials largely from Hume, Johnson, Foote, Glover, Milton, and even from Chaucer, Spenser, and Ben Jonson, either in the shape of translated excerpts from their works, or of biographical articles.   Under Suard's influence the journal was still further devoted to the study of English writers.

Suard, a man of subtle and acute intelligence—of whom it has been said that he was, "as it were, the full length portrait of a Frenchman"[3]—had made England peculiarly his own province. He had a thorough knowledge of the language, translated Robertson, and possibly Mrs Montague's *Essay on Shakespeare*, visited London thrice, once in the company of Necker, and saw

---

[1] April 1754.   Compare Arnaud's *Discours préliminaire sur le caractère des principales langues de l'Europe*, which occurs in the year 1760.

[2] September 1757.   [3] Garat, *Mémoires sur Suard*, vol. i., p. 133.

Garrick play *King Lear*. He became remarkable, his biographer tells us, for his "absolute and unshaken confidence in the knowledge of Great Britain he had thus acquired." The moment England was in question he "seemed, as it were, to take the chairman's seat,"[1] and his drawing-room was the rendezvous for all the anglomaniacs in Paris.

In 1764 the *Journal étranger* was succeeded by the *Gazette littéraire*,[2] under the same management and conducted in a similar spirit. The *Gazette* forms a natural continuation of the *Journal*. Like its predecessor it was "intended especially to afford information concerning foreign literature, the knowledge of which has more to do with the progress of reason and good taste than may be supposed."[3] It would rely for its information upon the diplomatic staff, and would enjoy the support of the minister for foreign affairs.[4]

Voltaire became a contributor, and wrote for it accounts of several English books, more especially of Sidney's *Discourses upon Government*, and Lady Mary Montagu's letters. But these distinguished contributions appeared irregularly; the directors, too, were negligent, being too much occupied with the *Gazette de France*, which they edited as well. When, in August 1765, the *Gazette littéraire* ceased to appear, they had at least proved to every European nation that, as the abbé Arnaud expressed it, "no one was at liberty to assume a tyranny over others."

"In the absurd dispute concerning the ancients and the moderns, the partisans of antiquity justly required that before forming an estimate of Homer we should transport ourselves to the period of which the manners and characters are described by the poet. *We owe a like justice to everything which comes to us from abroad. We must place ourselves at their point of view if we are to judge of the way in which foreigners live.*"[5] Thus it came about

[1] Garat, *Mémoires sur Suard*, vol. i., p. 78.
[2] *Gazette littéraire de l'Europe*, printed in Paris at the printing office of the *Gazette de France*, Louvre Gallery (March 1764, August 1765), 6 vols. 8vo.
[3] Vol. i., p. 7.
[4] This official protection caused the *Journal des savants* much concern; it considered that its rights were infringed upon, and, through Choiseul, raised an ineffective protest.
[5] *Journal étranger*, January 1760.

that periodical literature, always a faithful mirror of public opinion, provided nourishment for the confused aspirations of all who hoped to see France and the Teutonic nations drawn more closely together.

III

The common bond between all the vague aspirations which the study of English works aroused in France was provided by Rousseau. He gave them vigour, life, and substance. Thanks to him—and to his writings—Frenchmen read and appreciated Sterne, Ossian, Young, Hervey, and Shakespeare himself, all of whom had uttered in another language sentiments similar to those expressed by Rousseau, and all of whom were, like him, sensitive, melancholy, and lyrical. The admirers of these writers—most of whom preceded him—are the very people who admired Jean-Jacques. Between the two currents which, in France on the one hand, in England and in Germany on the other, were guiding literature towards a renewal of the sources of inspiration, a junction was about to take place. France, a Latin-speaking country, was for the first time to be conscious that her feeling, her imagination and her thought were those of the German-speaking nations, and those who seek for the ancestors and forerunners of Rousseau must look for them not in a classic antiquity, but beyond the borders of France.

Henceforth criticism could not fail to distinguish, with Mme. de Staël, a northern genius—represented by the English, by Rousseau, and by the Germans who drew their inspiration from him—and a southern genius, developed by the Latin nations without foreign admixture. The distinction, it is true, cannot be strictly maintained, and is perhaps not even a natural one. But here we are writing the history of an idea which has borne fruit in the world, rather than examining the accuracy of a theory.

The cosmopolitan idea in literature has its origin in Jean-

Jacques Rousseau—because Rousseau altered the very foundations of criticism.

Before his time no one, in France at any rate, had doubted that there were certain rules which must regulate the composition of a book, whether it be an epic or a satire, a drama or a sermon. Though the nature of these rules was disputed, their existence was never called in question, and there was a pretty general agreement with regard to certain essential principles bequeathed by ancient criticism. It was believed, in short, that there was an art of correct thought and even of correct feeling and imagination. Jean-Jacques felt and imagined in defiance of every rule. He boldly declared that he was not made like any man he had seen, nor, he "ventured to believe, like any man in existence." There was nothing in merely saying so; but he gave a practical exemplification of the fact, and claimed for the individual the right to like and to admire without consulting any other guide than himself.

This was a momentous revolution, but it was a revolution in France alone. It is in vain, Rousseau declared, to pretend to remould every mind "according to a single pattern." To change a mind you must change a character, which is itself dependent on "a temperament." For temperament—or sensibility—is the substratum of the man. "It is thus not a question of altering the character and subduing the disposition, but, on the contrary, of pushing it to its utmost limits." Yet as much had been said by his English predecessors, and Young, the author of *Night Thoughts*—in his *Conjectures on Original Composition*, which, published in the form of a letter to Richardson, enjoyed some reputation in the eighteenth century—had, long before, expressed himself as follows: "By a spirit of imitation we counteract Nature, and thwart her design. She brings us into the world all *originals*: no two faces, no two minds, are just alike; but all bear Nature's evident mark of separation on them. Born originals, how comes it to pass that we die copies? . . . Nature stands absolved, and the inferiority of our composition must be charged on ourselves." The remedy he suggested was that proposed by Jean-Jacques: let us commune with ourselves, and seek to develop that which is our very own property—our temperament. "Know thyself. Of ourselves, it may be said, as Martial says of a bad neighbour,

> . . . *Nil tam prope, proculque nobis.*"

Rousseau never said more than this; perhaps, even, he did not deduce the inevitable consequence of his principle quite so rigorously as Young, who contrasted all the endeavour of antiquity with the boundless horizon of the future. "Who hath fathomed the mind of man? Its bounds are as unknown as those of the creation." "Men as great, perhaps greater than the great ones of antiquity (presumptuous as it may sound) may, possibly, arise."[1]

The part played by Rousseau in the evolution of criticism was that of substituting the notion of a relative æsthetic, variable both from one period, and from one country, to another, for that of an absolute æsthetic—which has found perfect expression in a few works of genius. Æsthetic discernment, he expressly declares, is nothing more than the faculty of judging what pleases or displeases the greatest number."[2] See how man varies according as he dwells in the North or in the South, and according as he is born in the first century or in the fifteenth. See him in the earliest stages of his development, try to picture his rude yet simple life, the slow awakening of his intelligence to a more complete form of existence, his struggle with a soil "surrendered to its natural fertility, and covered with immense forests never yet mutilated by the axe."[3] What affinity has this uncultivated creature with the modern society man, whom books would foist upon us as the type of humanity?—And so we find St Preux making the tour of the world, and endeavouring to acquire the illusion of remoteness in time by transporting himself to remote distances in space; traversing "the stormy seas of the antarctic zone," the Ocean, where man is the enemy of man, and "those vast, sorrow-stricken lands which seem to have no other destiny than to people the earth with droves of slaves."[4] What

---

[1] *Conjectures on Original Composition*, London, 1759, p. 42.
[2] *Émile*, i. iv.   [3] *Discours sur l'inégalité*, part i.   [4] *Nouvelle Héloïse*, iv. 3.

analogy is there between the Hottentot, the Indian of the Congo, or the cannibal of the Antilles,[1] and the heroes of our tragedies and novels. Again, to return to our own doors, can we help thinking of the countless souls never mentioned in our books and scarcely better known to our writers than the souls of African negroes or the inhabitants of China? Thus no one could be more conscious than Rousseau of the almost infinite diversity of human nature—a consciousness entirely unknown to classical criticism; and he deduces therefrom the consequence that, if the types are almost infinite in number, almost the whole of humanity still remains to be portrayed. "One would suppose," says Rousseau's faithful expositor, Mme. de Staël, "that logic is the foundation of the arts," and that the "unstable nature" spoken of by Montaigne is banished from our books. This unstable nature we must restore to the position suited to it, and must convince ourselves that taste does not consist in confining it within the narrow limits of French and Western logic.

This, however, had been vaguely perceived by many writers —Young, for instance—before Rousseau. The superiority of Jean-Jacques lies in the fact that he proved it by his own example, and found the most signal justification of his ideas within himself. It is this that made him the guide and master of Europe. France, but Germany, England, Italy, and Spain no less—all those, of whatever nationality, who had already found their own consciousness voiced by English writers— felt themselves still more completely reflected in Rousseau. No writer has made so many countries his own at the same time; none has appealed to so many hearts or so many minds; none has thrown down more barriers or removed more boundaries. In him, European, as distinct from national, literature takes its rise.

By German writers he was hailed as a deliverer. Schiller nourished his mind upon *Julie*, and composed *The Robbers* and *Fiesco* under the inspiration of its author. The youthful Goethe was fascinated by him, and every day, at Strasbourg, made extracts from his works. Herder addressed him in passionate

---

[1] See the curious notes to the *Discours sur l'inégalité.*

terms: "It is myself that I would seek, that at last I may find and never again lose myself; come, Rousseau, be you my guide!"[1] Lessing entertained for Jean-Jacques a "secret respect." Kant hung his portrait in his study. Lenz demanded that a statue should be erected in his honour, opposite to that of Shakespeare. Many writers of the period regarded him as an apostle, or, as Herder said to his betrothed, as "a saint and a prophet. I am almost tempted to address him in prayer." At his decease, Schiller extolled him as a martyr: "In these enlightened times the sage must die. Socrates was martyred by the sophists of old; and Rousseau, who endeavoured to render Christians more manly, must suffer and fall beneath their hands."[2]

In England, the home of his literary predecessors, his success was scarcely less. There, to tell the truth, his art did not perhaps seem quite so new as in Germany; since many of the sentiments he expressed were already familiar to English literature. Richardson, Fielding and Sterne had created the sentimental novel of middle class life before Rousseau. Even in his lyrical quality there was nothing absolutely fresh. "Thirty years earlier than Rousseau, Thomson had given expression to the same sentiments, and almost in the same style."[3] An entire school of poetry had sung the praises of melancholy before he did, from Young's *Night Thoughts*, which appeared in 1742, down to the first fragments of Ossian, which were published in 1760. But these same sentiments were expressed by Rousseau in a more truly poetical manner. This is why he became one of the masters of the English romantic school; of Cowper, by whom he was addressed in beautiful lines; of Shelley, who is never tired of appealing to Rousseau as his teacher; and of Byron, who read him in youth and remained faithful to him in maturer years.[4] Many an English poet of the eighteenth, and even of the nine-

---

[1] C. Joret, *Herder*, p. 323.

[2] See Marc Monnier: *Jean-Jacques Rousseau et les étrangers*, in *Rousseau jugé par les Genevois d'aujourd'hui*. With regard to Rousseau's popularity in Germany consult also Erich Schmidt: *Richardson, Rousseau und Goethe*.

[3] Taine, *Littérature anglaise*, vol. iv., p. 224.

[4] See O. Schmidt, *Rousseau und Byron*, Greifswald, 1889, 8vo.

teenth, century could have said with George Eliot : " Rousseau's genius has sent that electric thrill through my intellectual and moral frame which has awakened me to new perceptions [and] . . . quickened my faculties."[1] It would be impossible to write any portion of the history of European, as distinct from national, literature during the last one hundred and fifty years without pronouncing his name, for the reason that in him the genius of Latin Europe became one with that of Teutonic Europe.

But if his philosophical work is mainly an expression of the Latin genius, it was mainly the Teutonic genius, or, as Mme. de Staël said, the literatures of the North, that benefited by the revolution he accomplished. Rousseau's triumph marks the advent of these literatures ; his influence was henceforth inseparable from theirs. And this union dates from the eighteenth century, and from pre-revolutionary times.

I do not propose to write here the history of the intercourse of France with England and Germany between 1760 and 1789. I shall simply attempt to show how the success of Jean-Jacques Rousseau brought success to certain foreign writers whose careers preceded, or were contemporary with, his own, whose genius was very closely related to his, and whose influence became blended with that which he exerted.

[1] *George Eliot's Life*, vol. i., p. 168.

Chapter II

ENGLISH INFLUENCE AND THE SENTIMENTAL NOVEL

I. Sterne and the sentimental novel—Sterne, like Rousseau, brought the
sentimental confession into fashion—His visit to Paris—His amours—The
culte-du-moi.
II. The eighteenth century failed to understand his humour, but appreciated the
way in which, like Rousseau, he affected to talk of himself, and to be deeply
touched by his own condition—Nature and extent of the influence exerted
by his work in France.

I

SOME months after the appearance of *La Nouvelle Héloïse*, and simultaneously with the publication of Diderot's famous *Éloge de Richardson*, there appeared in Paris one of the most remarkable characters
of the age. Laurence Sterne was a man of weak health, effusive
disposition, profound sensibility and singular genius. A contemporary says that " by the frank simplicity, the readiness and
the touching character of his own sensibility, he inspired sensitive
hearts with fresh emotions."[1] Suard once asked him to explain
his own personality. Sterne replied that he could distinguish
three causes which had made him like nobody else : the daily
reading of the Bible, the study of Locke's sacred philosophy,
" without which the world will never attain to a true universal
religion or a true science of ethics, and man will never obtain
real command over nature "; lastly, and above all, the possession
of " one of those organizations, in which the sacred constitutive
principle of the soul is predominant, that immortal flame by
which life is at once nourished and devoured."[2] Endowed with
the originality of an Englishman, Sterne, like Rousseau, was also
sensitive, passionate, and, at times, lyrical.

[1] Garat, *Mémoires sur Suard*, vol. ii., p. 135.　　　[2] *Ibid.*, p. 149.

When he arrived in Paris, *Tristram Shandy*—the first volume of which had recently appeared—was already famous there; so that Sterne wrote to Garrick : "My head is turned with what I see, and the unexpected honour I have met with here. *Tristram* was almost as much known here as in London."[1]

The Seven Years' War being then at its height, it was necessary to find a guarantor for one's good behaviour; accordingly d'Holbach became his patron and admitted him to his *salon*. There he met with all the anglomaniacs of Paris, and astonished them, now by his exuberant gaiety, now by his philosophical gravity. But what gave most pleasure was his ostentatious contempt for the "eternal sameness" of the French mind and disposition. Being asked whether he had not found in France some character which he could introduce in his novel: No, he replied, Frenchmen are like coins which, "by jingling and rubbing one against another, . . . are become so much alike you scarcely can tell one from another."[2] This sally in the manner of Jean-Jacques was immensely successful. "What sort of a fellow is this?" cried Choiseul in astonishment.—On another occasion he halted before Henri IV.'s statue on the Pont-Neuf; a crowd gathered around him; turning round, he called out : "What are you all looking at me for? Follow my example, all of you!"—and they all knelt with him before the statue. "The Englishman," says the narrator, "forgot that it was the statue of a king of France. A slave would never have paid such homage to Henri IV."[3]

Just as Rousseau, who had his Thérèse, fell in love with Mme. d'Houdetot, so "the good and agreeable Tristram," as a contemporary calls him, though possessed of a devoted helpmeet, loved Eliza Draper, the wife of another man, and neither the one nor the other, nor both together, could keep him from falling in love with every woman he met. "By loving them all," says Garat, gravely, "in such a transient manner, the minister of the Gospel maintained his religious belief in all its purity."

To Eliza, "wife of Daniel Draper, Esq., chief of the English

---

[1] Traill, *Sterne*, p. 67.
[2] Garat, vol. ii., p. 147.   *Sentimental Journey*, ch. li.   [3] Garat, p. 148.

factory at Surat," he addressed the most passionate letters, " with the easy carelessness of a heart which opens itself any how, every how . . ." [1] She, writing to him, said : " Think of me waking, and let me, like an illusion, glide through your fancy while you sleep." In reply he tells her about himself, his low spirits, the age of his body, and the youth of his soul, and proposes to marry her if both should be bereaved of their partners. Eliza, at twenty-five, was consumptive, and made preparations for a journey to India, whence there was little hope that she would ever return. " Best of all God's works," writes Sterne, "farewell ! Love me, I beseech thee; and remember me for ever ! " The romantic story deeply affected its readers. When Eliza died at the age of thirty-three, Raynal wrote a panegyric on her in the *Histoire philosophique des deux Indes.* " Land of Anjinga," he cried, addressing her country, " in thyself thou art nothing ! But thou hast given birth to Eliza. A day will come when the emporiums which Europeans have founded upon Asiatic shores will no longer exist. The grass will cover them, or the Indian, avenged at last, will build upon their ruins. . . . But if my writings are destined to endure, the name of Anjinga will dwell within the memories of men. Those who read me, those whom the winds shall carry to these shores, will say : ' There was the birthplace of Eliza Draper,' and if among them a Briton should be found, ' the offspring,' he will hasten to add, ' of English parents.' "

Thus Sterne, like Jean-Jacques, permitted the public to feed its curiosity upon his private life. Like him, he gloried in his own failings. Like Mme. de Warens and Mme. d'Houdetot, Eliza Draper—the beloved of Laurence Sterne, who, after all, forgot her—became the theme of novelist and poet. " Deign, noble Eliza," writes the excellent Ballanche,[2] " to accept my homage : pattern of true friendship, Heaven brought thee forth in a calm and peaceful hour : God presented thee to weak mortals as a convincing proof of his unspeakable goodness, of which thou wert a faithful image upon earth. . . . Accept my homage, woman without a peer. . . . Let all whose souls are alive to

---

[1] *Letters from Yorick to Eliza.*   [2] *Du Sentiment*, p. 219.

feeling gather around this monument, erected in friendly rivalry by Sterne and Raynal."[1]

Sterne was received in Paris with open arms. He became a frequent visitor at the houses of d'Holbach, Suard, Choiseul, the Comte de Bissy—an ardent anglomaniac, who supplied the material for an amusing chapter in the *Sentimental Journey*—and Crébillon fils, with whom he formed the project of carrying on an extraordinary controversy, in which each was to accuse the other of immorality, in order to catch the ear of the gallery[2]— a scheme, however, which was never carried out. Diderot he also met, who was delighted by his eccentricities, and commissioned him to procure him English books. A lady submitted to him *Le fils naturel*—whether with or without the author's consent we do not certainly know—and under the impression that it was " English in character," suggested that he should induce Garrick to play the piece. Sterne, however, considered that the speeches in it were too long, and " savoured too much of preaching " ; what was more, it had " too much sentiment " to suit him.[3]

The last and not the least amusing act of this comedy[4] was a sermon preached by Sterne at the English embassy before the most prominent free-thinkers in Paris, Diderot, d'Holbach, David Hume, and others. He chose as his text that passage from the Book of *Kings*, in which Isaiah reproaches Hezekiah for his vanity in showing his treasures to the Babylonish ambassadors : " All the things that are in mine house have they seen : there is nothing among my treasures that I have not shewed them." The text lent itself to allusions, the significance of which did not escape the audience, and in the evening, at the dinner which followed, Hume rallied Sterne upon his sermon. " David was disposed to make a little merry with the parson, and in return the parson was equally disposed to make a little merry with the infidel. We laughed at one another, and the company

---

[1] *Lettres d'Yorick à Elisa*, followed by Raynal's *Éloge*.
[2] Traill, p. 71.   [3] Traill, p. 70.
[4] The *Magazin encyclopédique* (1799, vol. vi., p. 121) mentions the title of a vaudeville which was founded on Sterne's visit to Paris—viz., *Sterne à Paris ou le Voyageur sentimental*, by Révoil and Forbin.

laughed at us both."[1]   A strange party, forsooth, and a strange man !

Though at the present day we do not take Sterne very seriously, his contemporaries not only appreciated him as a humorist, but delighted especially in the depth and originality of his genius, in his "gloomy and mournful appearance," and in what his translator called "an aroma of sentiment, and a suppleness of thought, impossible to define."[2]   By his country-men he was praised for his joyous spirit, while in France he was looked upon as a kind of prophet of the new religion just brought into fashion by Rousseau, the religion of the *self*.

II

Sterne's works very quickly became known in France, where they met with a success not inferior to, though very different from, that which they attained in London.

It was in May 1760 that the *Journal encyclopédique* first made mention of "that famous book, *Tristram Shandy*." In England this singular work of fiction gave rise to keen controversy. Those whose well-balanced minds were full of respect for tradition spoke of it only with pity. Goldsmith and Johnson did not disguise their contempt; Richardson pronounced it execrable ; it made Walpole "smile two or three times at the beginning, but in recompense" made him yawn for two hours; "the humour," he says, "is for ever attempted and missed."[3]   But the public in general, by Walpole's own showing, went wild over the new novel : a portrait of the author, who but yester-day had been leading an obscure existence in the retirement of his parish, was painted by Reynolds, and a frontispiece for his works was designed by Hogarth. Gray asserts that it was impossible to dine with the author without making the engage-ment a fortnight beforehand.[4]   But the success of the book was due to curiosity more than to anything else, and readers were

---

[1] Traill, p. 86.   [2] Frenais's translation of the *Sentimental Journey*, p. 223.
[3] April 1760.   [4] Letters, 22nd June 1760.

amused by Tristram's eccentric humour rather than convinced of the depth of his genius.

Abroad, however, it was by no means the same. Sterne's reputation increased when it crossed the water. The Germans hailed him as a philosopher. Lessing was taken with him, and when Sterne died, wrote to Nicolai that he would gladly have sacrificed several years of his own life if by so doing he could have prolonged the existence of the sentimental traveller. Goethe writes : "Whoever reads him, immediately feels that there is something free and beautiful in his own soul."[1] The philosophy of Sterne is the most brilliant invention of eighteenth century anglomania.

In France the *Gazette littéraire* published extracts from *Shandy*, and three translators contended for the honour of producing a complete French version of the work.[2] The *Sentimental Journey* was translated in the year following its publication ; the *Sermons*, which the author was enabled to publish by the subscriptions of d'Holbach, Diderot, Crébillon fils, and Voltaire, were also issued in French, as well as the famous *Letters to Eliza*, which were regarded as a precious autobiographical document.[3]

His chief work, that wonderful, amazing, wearisome book, *Tristram Shandy*, with its extraordinary medley of every language and every art—French, Greek, Latin, medicine, theology, and the art of fortification; with its parentheses of two volumes, its dedica-

---

[1] See Hettner, vol. i., p. 508, and, for the numerous German imitations of Sterne, vol. v., p. 410.

[2] Frenais's translation of *Tristram Shandy* (Paris, 1776, 2 vols. 12mo) contains only the first part of the novel. Two translations of the remainder were published concurrently in 1785, by de Bonnay and G. de la Baume. (See *Journal encyclopédique*, 15th March 1786.) Finally, the two translations of Frenais and de Bonnay were reprinted together (1785, 4 vols. 12mo).

[3] *Voyage sentimental*, by Mr Sterne, under the name of Yorick, translated from the English by M. Frenais, Amsterdam and Paris, 1769, 2 vols. 12mo (often reprinted). *Sermons choisis de Sterne*, translated by M. L. D. B. [de la Baume], London and Paris, 1786, 12mo. *Lettres de Sterne à ses amis* (translated by the same), London and Paris, 1788, 8vo ; another translation (by Durand de Saint-Georges), the Hague, 1789, 12mo. *Lettres d'Yorick à Elisa* (translated by Frenais), Paris, 1776, 12mo. A volume entitled *Beautés de Sterne*, Paris, 2 parts, 8vo, was also published, and several editions of the *Œuvres complètes* (1787, 1797, 1803, etc.).

tions in the midst of chapters, its insertion of a chapter xviii. after
chapter xxviii., and its serpent-like twisting and turning of words;
" this great curiosity shop," as Taine calls it, excited amazement
rather than genuine admiration.   How indeed should it have
been appreciated ?   " Mr Sterne's pleasantries," says his translator, " have not always struck me as particularly happy.   I have
left them where I found them, and have put others in their place."
Let us see what this heavy hand makes of the humorist's delicate
fabric.   Speaking of a village midwife, Sterne says that her
fame was world-wide : and by the " world," he says, we are to
understand a circle " about four English miles in diameter."
The irony is subtle, or at all events delicate.   Frenais remarks :[1]
" But let us not deceive ourselves : he does not allude to the
whole of the world.   She was not known, for instance, to the
Hottentots, nor to the Dutch at the Cape of Good Hope, who, it
is said, bring forth their children in the same manner as Mme.
Gigogne; the world, for her, was but a small circle," &c.
Sterne's eccentricities become absurdities.   The public looks for
subtle and lively satire; and getting nothing but " a riddle to
which there is no answer,"[2] it seeks in vain for " some deep
meaning in drollery which contains none."

Yet, even in the mutilated versions of his translators, Sterne
delighted Voltaire.   According to him " the second English
Rabelais " had drawn " several pictures superior to those of
Rembrandt and to the sketches of Callot."[3]   Elsewhere, however, he makes certain reservations; in an article on *Tristram
Shandy* in the *Journal de politique et de littérature*,[4] he pronounces it
" from beginning to end a piece of buffoonery after the style of
Scarron."   The book is empty—empty as the bottle which a
certain charlatan had promised to enter.   " There was philosophy
in Sterne's head," nevertheless, queer fellow as he was.   In

---

[1] Vol. i., p. 22.

[2] *Gazette littéraire*, 20th March 1765.   The first two volumes " excited the
curiosity of their readers, who took them for a subtle and lively satire in which
the sage hid his face behind the jester's mask.   The sage has published four other
volumes which tbe public has read with eagerness, but, to its amazement, has
entirely failed to understand."

[3] *Dictionnaire philosophique* : article on *Conscience*.   [4] 25th April 1777.

him, as in Shakespeare, there were flashes of a superior reason.

In truth, the eighteenth century failed to understand Sterne's inimitable *humour*. What impressed it was the spasmodic, disconnected progress of his thought, the tangles in the thread of his ideas, the abrupt flights taken by his imagination, all so opposed to French classical habits of systematic and coherent exposition. Diderot endeavoured to adopt some of his methods : " How did they meet ? By chance, like every one else. Whence did they come ? From the next place. Whither were they going ? Which of us can tell whither he is going ? What did they say ? The master said nothing, and Jacques said his captain had told him that everything that happens to us here below is written above." This passage, at the opening of *Jacques le fataliste*, is worthy of Sterne : it is even taken from Sterne, literally.[1] Diderot borrowed freely from *Tristram Shandy* : the young woman who receives Jacques when he is wounded is the one who has already given shelter to Toby ;[2] and a certain broad anecdote is derived from the same source.[3] These instances of borrowing are palpable, and they are not happy. Diderot delighted in this roving, disconnected mode of progress—and he, too, wrote his *Jacques le fataliste* at odd times, in the postchaise which carried him to Holland and to Russia.[4] The superficial character of the work he succeeded in reproducing, but the fine edge of Sterne's humour escaped him. The Englishman's true heirs in this respect came after the Revolution, in the persons of Xavier de Maistre and Charles Nodier.[5]

The eighteenth century appreciated Sterne primarily as the disciple of Richardson, the minute and punctilious painter of everyday life, " a life wherein there can be no sublimity either in

---

[1] See de Wailly's translation, ch. cclxiii.

[2] Diderot, *Œuvres*, vol. vi., p. 14.   [3] *Ibid.*, p. 284.

[4] *Ibid.*, p. 8.   M. Ducros, in his *Diderot*, has given a most acute study of that author's imitations of Sterne.

[5] See especially *Un voyage autour de ma chambre*, chaps. xix. and xxviii., and Nodier's *Histoire du roi de Bohême et de ses sept châteaux*. An imitation of Sterne may also be found in V. Hugo's *Bug-Jargal*, in which Captain d'Auverney and Sergeant Thadée are reminiscences of Captain Toby and Corporal Trim.

events or things or thoughts, a life which has always lacked observers, as though it were unworthy anyone's interest because it is that which each one of us leads."[1]

Following Richardson's example, Sterne observes insignificant facts and faint fluctuations of thought: he writes the novel of gesture. "I paused," says Henrietta Byron, "I hesitated. . . . Then I stopt, and held down my head."—"Speak out, my dear," said Lady L. "Thus called upon; thus encouraged—and I lifted my head as boldly as I could (but it was not, I believe, very boldly). . . ."[2] Such is Richardson's method of presenting his characters, whether in action or in repose. He sees them completely, and at each successive moment. Sterne does the same, and thereby earns the compliments of his French readers, who at the same time mildly banter him for carrying the process too far. Of one of the characters in *Faublas* we are told that "by a mechanical movement, his left arm was raised in the air, where it became fixed " . . .; and the writer adds: "Why, fair lady, am I not Tristram Shandy? I might then tell you to what height it was raised, in what direction and in what position."[3] This hits the mark; Sterne's work is so distinctly the novel of gesture that his characters even resemble automata or wax-work figures.

In the second place he displays the most exquisite art in painting tiny gems of pictures in the smallest of frames. Sometimes he drops into triviality; but on the other hand, when he is at his best, he brings to light forgotten yet delightful recesses in the lives of the humble, both animals and men. His province, as a phrase of singular felicity has described it, is that of mental entomology.[4] He seizes the most delicate impressions in their flight and deftly pins them down. "Sterne's merit," wrote Mme. Suard, his passionate admirer, "lies, it seems to me, in his having attached an interest to details which in themselves have none whatever; in his having caught a thousand faint impressions, a thousand evanescent feelings, which pass through

[1] Garat, *Mémoires sur Suard*, vol. ii., p. 143.   [2] Ballantyne, vi., p. 35.
[3] Edition of 1807, vol. iii., p. 8.
[4] See Émile Montégut's fine study of Sterne.

the heart or the imagination of a sensitive man. He enters the
human heart, as it were, by portraying his own sensations, . . .
he adds to the stores of our enjoyment."[1]

But he would add nothing to them were he not gifted with
sensibility. The slightest agitation, the faintest tremor of the
soul, is enough to excite his emotion. A hair upon a hand, a
spot upon a cloth, the crease in a coat, will provide the matter for
a paragraph, and even for a chapter. Moods, whims, fits of
unaccountable dejection, passion in its rudimentary stages, the
germs of great crises, these constitute the province of Sterne.
This is the secret of the unrivalled popularity attained in the
eighteenth century by that charming little volume, so witty, so
unconstrained, with all its tearfulness and affectation, the *Sentimental Journey in France and Italy*.

"Sentimental?" wrote John Wesley in his journal,[2] "what is
that? It is not *English* : he might as well say, *Continental*." With
the appearance of *Clarissa Harlowe*, however, in 1749, the word,
as well as the thing it denotes, had come into fashion. "The
word sentimental," wrote Lady Bradshaigh, "is much in vogue
amongst the polite."[3] Be this as it may, Sterne's little book won
the hearts of all readers who had taken alarm at the eccentricities
of Shandy and of *Shandeism*. It even pleased Horace Walpole.[4]
It was shorter, more lucid. It spoke to the French, and spoke
to them of France. True, it did not treat them altogether
kindly. La Fleur, one of the characters, has "a small cast of
the coxcomb," is simple, of good address, and ignorant as a
Frenchman, though the best fellow in the world. But then
every one knows that Englishmen, like medals which have been
kept apart, and have passed "but few people's hands, preserve
the first sharpnesses which the fine hand of Nature has given
them."[5] Then, how could one resist an author who, after being
hurried from one salon or from one party to another all over
Paris, loudly proclaims that such rewards are but "the gain of a
slave," and, sickened by the "most vile prostitution" of himself

---

[1] M. Suard's *Mélanges*, vol. iii., pp. 111-122.   [2] 11th February 1772.
[3] L. Stephen, *Hours in a Library*, vol. i., p. 58.
[4] Letter dated 12th March 1768.   [5] *Sentimental Journey*, chap. li.

"to half a dozen people" of high position, calls for his post-chaise and makes his escape from the good friends that flattery has given him. That is all one need do to acquire the reputation of a philosopher.

The *Sentimental Journey*, "one of the most inimitable productions existing in any language,"[1] charmed all France by the sensibility Sterne had breathed into it, and provoked a whole school of imitators.

Sterne was the kind of man to set a fly at liberty with a sermon and a tear : "'Go,' said he, lifting up the sash . . . 'go, poor devil, get thee gone, why should I hurt thee ? This world surely is wide enough to hold both thee and me.'"[2]

His admirers were touched by the noble-mindedness of a butcher who renounced his occupation rather than kill a sheep he had grown fond of.[3] Mlle. de Lespinasse, in a couple of chapters, after the manner of Sterne, told the story of Mme. Geoffrin's milkwoman, who, on the loss of her cow, received one or even two others from her kind-hearted patroness : she described how Sterne himself, on hearing of this kind act, clasped Mme. Geoffrin in his arms, and embraced her with ecstasy : " My soul," he said, " had a moment of rapture. . . . It will make me the more worthy of my Eliza : she will mingle her tears with mine when I tell her the story of Mme. Geoffrin's milkwoman ! "[4]

For Sterne's contemporaries that sensibility which made the hearts of his readers swell within them was merely the outward sign of a profound yet genial philosophy. " If you do not *feel* this author, you will often find him over-solicitous about trifles, frivolous, extravagant, and childish ; but fathom the secret of his genius and you will perceive one of the great teachers

---

[1] *Correspondance littéraire*, December 1786.   [2] *Tristram Shandy*, chap. xii.

[3] *Le voyageur sentimental ou une promenade à Verdun*, by Vernes, Lausanne, 1786, 12mo. There were also a *Nouveau voyage sentimental* [by Gorgy], a *Voyage dans plusieurs provinces occidentales de la France* [by Brune], a *Voyage sentimental dans les Pyrénées*, &c. The *Nouveau voyage de Sterne en France*, translated by D. L. . . . (Lausanne, 1785, 12mo), is taken from Tristram Shandy.

[4] The anecdote told by Mlle. de Lespinasse has been reprinted in the *Œuvres posthumes de d'Alembert*, 1799, vol. ii., pp. 22-43. On this subject, see Garat, *Mémoires sur Suard*, vol ii., p. 150.

of mankind." He shows you, on every hand, "fresh sources of
interest, sensation, and enjoyment." *Shandeism* is the philosophy
of the man who is "clever and emotional, and loves his fellow-
men."[1] Sterne declares that when he travels he does so "with
his whole soul," and this, at that precise period of French history
which extends from 1760 to 1789, was the best of recommenda-
tions.—Yet he is lively, and even broad.—As Voltaire said, he
resembles "those little satyrs in ancient times which were
meant to hold precious essences." Now, the precious essence in
Sterne is simply his capacity for emotion where no one had been
affected before, and of shedding a flood of tears when a few modest
drops had previously sufficed. He provides, it was said, "a feast
for tender hearts."[2] In reality he is changeable and impressionable as a woman, his intelligence is at the mercy of the slightest
whisper, he surrenders his heart to the first breath of desire, and
throws wide the portals of his soul before the idle and the
inquisitive. He does not blush to shed tears when tears are
becoming, nor even when they are not : therein lies the whole
secret of Sterne. He wrote confessions before Rousseau,
and with no more false shame than he. He is more "personal,"
and if the neologism be allowed, more frankly an "impressionist"
than any other writer of his age.

Upon us, who read him to-day, he no longer produces, to the
same extent, the effect of novelty. But we can understand that
his method must have seemed new in his time. Sterne writes
without a plan, without arrangement, one might almost say
without an object : he lets his soul wander where it lists. His
whole work is, in reality, nothing more than a long account
of journeyings—always sentimental—through the world. Does
he discover in the courtyard of an inn an old "*desobligeant*,"—
forthwith Sterne grows sentimental over the fate of the forgotten
vehicle, falling to pieces where it stands.—An old Franciscan
monk presents him with a horn snuff-box. He preserves it that
it may "help his mind on to something better"; and one day, on

---

[1] *Journal encyclopédique*, 1st August 1786.
[2] Garat. Michelet, too, found the *Sentimental Journey* a book "after my own
heart" (*Mon Journal*, p. 122).

his way through Calais, he visits father Laurent's grave, and seating himself beside it takes out the horn snuff-box and bursts into a flood of tears. Elsewhere, in *Tristram Shandy*, we have the story of Marie de Moulines, by Garat considered superior to Clementina's madness or the funeral of Clarissa, and again, in the *Journey*, the incident of the starling. Sterne, alone in Paris, is without a passport, and in danger of the Bastille; a starling, hanging in a cage, begins to sing; forthwith the miseries of confinement present themselves to his mind: he *sees* a captive in his dungeon, pale and wasted by fever, a rude calendar of notched sticks by his side; he sees him take a rusty nail and scratch the little stick in his hand; his chains rattle with the movement; he gives a deep sigh. . . . Here, as on so many other occasions, Sterne's heart overflows, not without satisfaction to himself. "Dear Sensibility!" he exclaims elsewhere, "source inexhausted of all that's precious in our joys, or costly in our sorrows!"[1]

Sterne's readers, like himself, felt some self-gratitude for their own emotion. Like him they easily persuaded themselves that the gift of tears is a proof of the excellence and loftiness of our nature, and exclaimed when their tears were over: "I am positive I have a soul!"[2] With him, said one of them, "we become more susceptible of every possible emotion of the heart, and of enjoying the multitude of good things strewn by nature in every path of life, yet lost to all, because their hearts are dried up by poverty or wealth, by meanness or by pride."[3]

Accordingly Sterne commits himself to the turbulent current of his impressions. His manner of confession is not only ingenuous, but cynical. And he too, moreover, flatters the sociable tendencies of his age. One evening he reaches, at nightfall, a farm in Anjou. Everyone is seated at table: the bill of fare consists of a wheaten loaf, a bottle of wine, and lentil soup —a "feast of love and friendship." Invited by his hosts the traveller takes a seat; with the old man's knife he cuts himself a large slice of bread, and reads in every eye an expression of gratitude for the liberty he takes—a subject ready to hand for

---

[1] *Sentimental Journey*, The Bourbonnois.
[2] *Ibid.*, Maria : Moulines.   [3] Garat, *ibid.*

T

a Greuze. Supper over, there follows a dance on the sward to the sound of the *vielle*; youths and maidens dance together in decorous freedom; in the midst of the second dance the traveller notices that all eyes are raised heavenward, and "I fancied," he says, "I could distinguish an elevation of spirit different from that which is the cause or the effect of simple jollity." He questions the father of the family, who explains that it is in this manner they express their gratitude to God, believing "that a cheerful and contented mind is the best sort of thanks to Heaven that an illiterate peasant can pay." This combination of the religious spirit with the spirit of enjoyment, of moral improvement with the pleasures of a ball, this uplifting of conscience amid the intoxication of a dance, seemed delightful to the readers of Jean-Jacques. Sterne was hailed as a philosopher, and it was even complacently asserted that he stood "above all philosophers and above all preachers in his power of solving the most mysterious problems." Suard went further,—he compared Laurence Sterne to the Bible.

Such was the revolution effected by the influence of Rousseau in the manner of judging the productions of literary art. Let us suppose that the work of Sterne, disconnected, paradoxical, and almost maudlin in its pathos, had made its appearance in France thirty or forty years earlier, and had come under the observation of Montesquieu or Fontenelle. I imagine it would have caused a certain amount of astonishment, and would have incurred some contempt. It was not the practice, in 1730, to present a succession of desultory impressions to the public as a work of art. A traveller's note book, which was neither novel, pamphlet, moral treatise, nor satire, but each and all of these at the same time, and was also meant to be a noble monument of literature, could never have been offered to the world.

Still less would an author have been forgiven for speaking of himself with such unblushing sentimentality. The man of feeling, "the sport and plaything of temperature and season, whose happiness is at the mercy of the winds," has got on in the world since that day. His soul, sometimes joyful, sometimes disconsolate, has been allowed to roam hither and thither at the mercy of northern gales or western breezes; to them he has shouted his sorrows and his victories; he has found a strange delight in fusing himself with the elements, in incorporating himself with the universe, in feeling that, puny creature as he is, his life forms a part of the mighty symphony or tempest of the heavens.

Of this melancholy and poetic race Rousseau was the first representative. Was Sterne the second? To-day we can hardly connect the two names without hesitation, for we no longer have the same belief in Sterne as readers who were contemporary with him. Yet such readers—and the fact is significant—were conscious of a gift in him similar to that of Rousseau. "Man, under Sterne's treatment," to quote Garat once more, "is not so much held captive, as *tossed hither and thither*." His characters, "in some vague borderland between sleeping and waking, tread the brink of every form of error and of crime, like the somnambulist upon the verge of roof or precipice." In a word, Sterne, like Rousseau, reveals "the somnambulist" in man—the creature of instinct, given over to the fluctuations of sensation and of feeling.

And he reveals himself also, quite artlessly it would seem, in his true colours—passionate, sensitive, and not particularly *reasonable*. "He makes us smile," said Ballanche—one of his warmest admirers—"but it is the smile of the soul; he makes us weep, but the tears we shed are gentle as drops of dew." It gave the impression of perfect sincerity, and this was the secret of his success. His readers were grateful to him for speaking of himself, and of himself alone. The time had come when, impelled by the genius of Rousseau, literature was becoming ever more and more narrowed down to "the confession of a soul," and when all that was needed to obtain the public ear was to tell the story of oneself,—provided only one happened to be Yorick, "jester to his Majesty the King of England."

Chapter III

NOT only however did Rousseau excite in readers of his day the taste for sentimental confession ; he opened their eyes at the same time to physical nature, and inspired them with the taste for melancholy. Sensibility, the feeling for nature, and the sadness of the poet are simply three forms of the same disposition of soul, and constitute the whole of Rousseau's lyricism.

How far, in this further respect, was he in harmony with foreign writers, both among his predecessors and his contemporaries ?

I

" The picturesque "—wrote Stendhal—" like our good coaches and our steam-boats, comes to us from England," [1] and he adds, " a fine landscape is no less essential to an Englishman's religion than to his aristocratic station." Frenchmen of the eighteenth century had already remarked this characteristic, and, in the frenzy of their anglomania, had endeavoured to appropriate it themselves. Fashion, following the example set by the English, had driven them to live in the country,—" certainly one of the best customs," wrote Arthur Young, " they have

[1] *Mémoires d'un touriste*, vol. i., p. 87.

taken from England."[1] And it was in imitation of the English that they planted those strange parks in which crooked paths, flights of winding steps and mazes took the place of the broad avenues of Versailles; in which antique statues were replaced by grottoes, tombs and hermitages; in which you beheld a castle in flagrant discord with a Hindoo temple, or a Russian cottage with a Swiss chalet, and in which Petrarch's urn stood side by side with the tomb of Captain Cook. They merely mimicked nature, under the impression that they were imitating her. The English garden was a school of virtue: " When you are thinking," wrote a famous amateur,[2] " how to make a ravine shady, or trying to control the course of a stream, you have too much to do to become a dangerous citizen, a scheming general or a plotting courtier. One whose head is full of his stand of flowers, or his clump of judas-trees," cannot be a bad man. Preoccupied in so virtuous a manner, one cannot commit a guilty act. " One would scarcely arrive in time to take advantage of the frailty of a friend's wife, and afterwards would hastily make one's escape to the country, there to expiate the sweetest of crimes."

Such was the character of descriptive literature from 1760 to the Revolution. Rousseau's beautiful pages apart, it is inferior and insipid, nor did the influence of Rousseau bear fruit until five-and-twenty years after the publication of *La Nouvelle Héloïse*.[3] The love of nature is not a feeling to be acquired in a day. It demands a whole education of eye and heart. And it may be that certain races, prepared by certain climates or certain conditions of social life, can more easily sustain that abrupt disturbance of the moral equilibrium which must precede the love of physical nature. It was neither central nor northern France—the France which produced most of the French classical writers, the gentle France of Touraine or Anjou, the nursery of the Pléiade—that gave birth to Rousseau, Chateaubriand, and Bernardin de Saint-Pierre : one of them came from the Alps, the others from the sea.

---

[1] *Travels*, vol. i., p. 72.
[2] The prince de Ligne, quoted by de Lescure : *Rivarol*, p. 310.
[3] Bernardin de Saint-Pierre : *Études de la nature*, 1784; *Paul et Virginie*, 1788.

But the English had loved and described the material universe long before Rousseau. The feeling for nature is common to all their great poets : Shakespeare is full of it, a fact which had been noticed even by Letourneur ;[1] Milton abounds in admirable descriptive passages which would have greatly astonished his French contemporaries ; and in the least productive years of the century, Thomson, Gray, Collins, and Chatterton, not to come down to Burns and the lake poets, are great painters of nature. What French writer in 1739 would have said, with Gray, during the ascent to the Grande-Chartreuse : "Not a precipice, not a torrent, not a cliff, but is pregnant with religion and poetry. There are certain scenes that would awe an atheist into belief."

It was in 1730 that Thomson—the only one of these poets to obtain any celebrity in France—had published his admirable poem *The Seasons*,[2] so shamefully misrepresented by Saint-Lambert and by Roucher. It is true that in this work man as a social being still occupies too large a place. Thomson cannot describe winter without giving a sentimental picture of the horrors of cold, nor spring without introducing a hymn to Love. Too frequently also there are suggestions of the *Georgics*, and apostrophes to those "who live in luxury and ease," or to the "generous Englishmen" who "venerate the plough." Nevertheless, Thomson has the painter's eye. His winter and his spring are no mere adaptations from Vergil. He has a true and deep understanding of the English landscape. With delicate subtlety he renders the impressions produced by spring or autumn, the charm of the indefinite periods when season gives way to season, the approach of rain, the forebodings of storm, the scudding of heavy clouds across skies grey and overcast. Even in the awkward French version something of the charm of these pictures lingers yet.

> Rising slow,
> Blank, in the leaden-colour'd east, the Moon
> Wears a wan circle round her blunted horns.
> Seen through the turbid fluctuating air,
> The stars obtuse emit a shiver'd ray ;

---

[1] See the introduction to his version of Shakespeare.
[2] See Léon Morel's able book : *James Thomson, sa vie et ses œuvres* (Paris, 1895).

> Or frequent seen to shoot athwart the gloom,
> And long behind them trail the whitening blaze.
> Snatch'd in short eddies, plays the wither'd leaf;
> And on the flood the dancing feather floats.[1]

It is in these grey-toned pictures that Thomson excels. But in others he revels in precision of detail : there is one of a farm, for instance, redolent of the dunghill, damp grass, and new milk ; another of a flower-garden with its " velvet-leaved " auriculas, variegated pinks, and " hyacinths, of purest virgin white, low bent, and blushing inward " ;[2] the whole perceived with the artist's glance and described in the language of a poet. Occasionally, too, Thomson can command richness of colouring and splendour of imagery.[3]

> The downward Sun
> Looks out, effulgent, from amid the flush
> Of broken clouds gay-shifting to his beam.
> The rapid radiance instantaneous strikes
> The illumined mountain, through the forest streams,
> Shakes on the floods, and in a yellow mist,
> Far smoking o'er the interminable plain,
> In twinkling myriads lights the dewy gems.
> Moist, bright and green, the landscape laughs around.

What French author wrote in this style, in 1730 ?

The author of the *Seasons* had visited France as a young man, without, however, attracting any notice. But since then Voltaire had made the public acquainted with his name, if not with his talent.[4] The *Seasons*, if Villemain is to be credited, came as a revelation in 1759 :[5] a certain Mme. Bontemps had taken upon herself to introduce the work to the French public in a translation which she described as " scrupulously simple," adding, at the same time, an earnest apology for the "extravagant and almost hideous" images employed by its author. Villemain affirms that the climate of the North, the Scotch mountains,

---

[1] *Winter*, l. 122.   [2] *Spring*.   [3] *Spring*, l. 187.

[4] Voltaire represents his own play *Socrate* (1759) as a posthumous work of Thomson's. In 1763 Saurin produced *Blanche et Guiscar*, a tragedy imitated from Thomson, who had himself, it was said, taken his subject from *Gil Blas* (see the *Journal encyclopédique*, March 1764). See an English letter of Voltaire's on Thomson, published by Ballantyne, *Voltaire's Visit to England*, (pp. 99-101).

[5] Lesson xxvi.

and the exultation inspired by storm and tempest, fascinated men's minds and prepared them for the admiration of Ossian a few years later. To me it seems that just at first the work surprised French readers still more than it captivated them. The *Mercure* finds fault with its *disgusting* images : the description of fields *putrid* with decaying locusts is unendurable.

Grimm, while recognizing its wealth of imagery, found the poem monotonous.[1] Fréron complains that the reader seems to be breathing an atmosphere of coal-dust.[2] Even in translation the work remained too faithful to fact and gave the impression of triviality.

Its success was due to its philosophy and its love of humanity. Thomson was considered a worthy pupil of Addison, Pope, and Steele, and his poem was ranked with *Paradise Lost* and the *Essay on Man*.[3] The truth is that in Thomson there was not only the faithful painter of nature as she appears in England, but also the philosopher in whom the emotions aroused by the thought of eternal life or conjugal happiness found vent in beautiful verse. It was the latter more especially who was imitated by Léonard, Bernis, Gentil-Bernard, Gilbert, Dorat, and Delille[4] ; the "gentle bard" whose melancholy genius was celebrated in an admirable poem by Collins was beyond their comprehension.[5] Saint-Lambert ventured to praise him because he had "embellished" nature, and had seen the peasant "in his picturesque aspect"; he congratulated him on having done for the labourers what Racine and M. de Voltaire had done for their heroes—on having "elevated our species." The true descriptive poet, he said, will mention only the nobler birds: he will not speak of the jay or magpie. Nevertheless Thomson had given a minute description of the hen and "her chirping family," the crested duck, the turkey-cock, the thrush, the linnets that warble "o'er the flowering furze," and the jay

---

[1] *Correspondance littéraire*, June 1760.   [2] *Année littéraire*, 1760, vol. i., p. 142.
[3] *Journal encyclopédique*, March 1760.
[4] Imitations of the *Seasons* were innumerable. With regard to translations the most important, next to that by Mme. Bontemps, which was several times reprinted, are those by Deleuze, Poulin, de Beaumont (1801, 1802, 1806), &c.
[5] *Ode on the death of Mr. Thomson.*

himself with his "harsh, discordant pipe."[1] But this did not prevent Saint-Lambert from saying : "That which Homer, Tasso and our dramatic poets have done for the moral world should be done for the material world also: it should be magnified, beautified, and made interesting."[2] The country is for him merely the temple of Love; thither he escorts "Doris, his sweet and gentle friend"; he brings nature within the reach of "those enlightened judges of manners and of pleasures" who dwell in towns. He is vapid, false and arid.

Voltaire's admiration for these would-be disciples of Thomson was not indeed shared by the whole of the eighteenth century.[3] "It is the very essence of sterility," said Mme. du Deffand of Saint-Lambert's work, "and without his reeds, and birds, and elms with their branches, he would have very little to say."[4] "Saint-Lambert," wrote Buffon, with more severity, "is nothing but a cold frog, Delille a cockchafer, and Roucher a bird of night. Not one of them has succeeded, I will not say in depicting nature, but even in placing clearly before us a single characteristic of its most striking beauties."[5] Thomson had his worshippers, who read him for his own sake. When Mme. Roland was taken to prison, in 1793, she took with her Tacitus, Plutarch, Shaftesbury, and Thomson, to console her in captivity, and of the last of them she said : "He is dear to me for more reasons than one."[6] But neither Mme. Roland nor any of her contemporaries did full justice to his descriptive gifts. What they sought in Thomson, as in Gessner, whose incredible popularity dates from the same period,[7] was descriptions in which man, and man of the eighteenth century, still occupied an important place. André Chénier, who borrowed freely from

[1] *Spring*. [2] Preface to the *Seasons* (1769).
[3] *Cf.* the letter to Dupont, 7th June 1769 : "If the decision rested with me, I should have no difficulty in giving the preference to M. de Saint-Lambert. He seems to me not only more charming, but more serviceable. *The Englishman describes the seasons, and the Frenchman tells us what should be done in each.*"
[4] "Les roseaux, les oiseaux, les ormeaux, et leurs rameaux."
[5] To Mme. Necker, 16th July 1782. [6] Letter to Buzot, 22nd June 1793.
[7] *Der Tod Abels* was translated by Huber in 1759; the *Idyllen* in 1762. On Gessner in France see Th. Süpfle's book, *Geschichte des deutschen Cultureinflusses auf Frankreich*, Gotha, 1886-1890, vol. i.

"the Good Swiss, Gessner" and from Thomson, adopted from
both the art of blending professions of philanthropy with quiet
pictures of nature in her milder manifestations. The following
lines are a fairly close rendering of a passage in Thomson's
Autumn.

> Ah ! prends un cœur humain, laboureur trop avide,
> Lorsque d'un pas tremblant l'indigence timide
> De tes larges moissons vient, le regard confus,
> Recueillir après toi les restes superflus.
> Souviens-toi que Cybèle est la mère commune.
> Laisse la probité que trahit la fortune,
> Comme l'oiseau du ciel, se nourrir à tes pieds
> De quelques grains épars sur la terre oubliés.[1]

This somewhat mawkish kind of work no longer affects the
reader as it did. But we must not fail to realise that these little
pictures, with their modest colouring and their disguised yet not
ungraceful sentiment, enchanted our forefathers. From 1760
until the Revolution, and even afterwards,[2] Thor,son and
Gessner were regarded as great poets, and the English and

---

[1] *Bucoliques*, LX., ed. Becq de Fouquiéres. *Cf.* Thomson's *Autumn.*

> Be not too narrow, husbandmen ! but fling
> From the full sheaf, with charitable stealth,
> The lib'ral handful. Think, O grateful think !
> How good the God of Harvest is to you,
> Who pours abundance o'er your flowing fields ;
> While these unhappy partners of your kind
> Wide hover round you, like the fowls of heaven,
> And ask their humble dole.

See also Becq de Fouquiéres (*Lettres critiques sur André Chénier*, p. 182 *et seq.*) upon
Chénier's indebtedness to Gessner, from whom the following exquisite lines are
taken :—

> Ma muse fuit les champs abreuvés de carnage,
> Et ses pieds innocents ne se poseront pas
> Où la cendre des morts gémirait sous ses pas.
> Elle pâlit d'entendre et le cri des batailles
> Et les assauts tonnants qui frappent les murailles ;
> Et le sang qui jaillit sous les pointes d'airain
> Souillerait la blancheur de sa robe de lin.

[2] Legouvé, *La Mort d'Abel* (1792). Translations of Thomson were published
even during the time of the Revolution (*Épisodes des saisons de Thomson*, Paris,
an vii., 8vo., &c.).

Germans were believed to have created "descriptive poetry."[1] Diderot admired Gessner and imitated him;[2] Mlle. de Lespinasse detected "the charm of Gessner, combined with the vigour of Jean-Jacques," in the man she loved. Chênedollé, who read the *Idylles* as a youth, said that he had rarely fallen under "a spell like Gessner's."[3] Grimm calls him "a divine poet." In the judgment of the *Almanach des Muses* "he has the pure and lofty soul of a Fénelon; in his artless descriptions of simple scenes he surpasses Theocritus; as we read him we seem to behold nature herself, and when we see him we believe in virtue.[4] Such, also, was the verdict passed by Jean-Jacques himself. He, too, was doubtless an admirer of the *Seasons*, and discovered therein his own manner of feeling and thinking. At any rate it is certain that his *Lévite d'Éphraïm* was written in Gessner's artless, rustic fashion, and that he wrote to Huber, who had sent him the *Idylles*: "I feel that your friend Gessner is a man after my own heart. . . . To you, in particular, I am extremely grateful for your courage in throwing aside the senseless and affected jargon which falsifies imagery and renders sentiments unconvincing. Those who attempt to embellish and adorn nature have neither souls nor taste, and have never come to know her beauties."[5]

Neither for Rousseau nor for his contemporaries was there any "senseless and affected jargon" in Gessner or in Thomson. They considered that these poets portrayed nature "with the nicety of a lover enumerating the charms of his mistress."[6] They relished these artificial pastorals, these highly-sweetened idylls, and the languid grace of these descriptions. It should be noted that the famous *Lettres à M. de Malesherbes*—which contain Rousseau's finest descriptive passages—were not published before 1779, that the *Confessions* appeared in 1782, and that the *Rêveries d'un promeneur solitaire* are also posthumous. Between 1760 and 1780 Thomson and Gessner shared with Rousseau the glory

---

[1] Saint-Lambert, Preface to *Les Saisons*, p. 9.
[2] In *Les Pères malheureux*. (See *Œuvres*, vol. xiii., p. 19.)
[3] Sainte-Beuve, *Châteaubriand et son groupe*, vol. ii., p. 149.
[4] *Almanach des Muses*, 1786.   [5] Letter to Huber, 24th December 1761.
[6] Dorat, *Recueil de contes et de poèmes*, the Hague, 1770, p. 118.

of having drawn the attention of the French public to nature. Of these two, one—the Zurich printer—cannot for a moment be compared with Jean-Jacques; the other—the author of the *Seasons*—was a true poet, and gave expression, long before Rousseau, to many sentiments which the latter introduced into the great current of French literature. The pious Thomson sang of golden broom and purple heather before he did, just as he anticipated him also in raising his thoughts to the incomprehensible Being in whom all things are contained.

> The rolling year
> Is full of Thee. Forth in the pleasant Spring
> Thy beauty walks, thy tenderness and love.
> Wide flush the fields; the softening air is balm;
> Echo the mountains round; the forest smiles;
> And every sense, and every heart is joy.[1]

Thomson anticipated Rousseau, but was not his teacher. It would scarcely be paradoxical to say that Rousseau discharged the debt he had incurred towards English literature when he made it possible for Frenchmen to appreciate Thomson, Young, and Ossian.

II

Just as Rousseau inspired his contemporaries with a feeling for physical nature, so also he was the great poet of melancholy. He it was who became the interpreter of those burning hearts that, in the words of Chateaubriand, " have felt themselves strangers in the midst of mankind "; he, who " with a full heart dwelt in an empty world," he, who knew what it was to be miserable in the midst of happiness, and had lost every illusion before he had exhausted anything. By the right which genius gives, he is father to René, Oberman, and Adolphe.

But in the history of European literature he had his own predecessors in the English, and here dates speak more eloquently than any argument can do. Not to mention Shakespeare or the

[1] *Hymn* which concludes the *Seasons*.

author of *Il Penseroso*, from whom every poet of melancholy in modern times has drawn his inspiration,[1] Thomson's *Seasons* appeared in 1730, Young's *Night Thoughts* from 1742 to 1744, Collins's *Odes* in 1747, and Gray's *Elegy in a country churchyard* in 1751, while the earliest fragments of Ossian are earlier by a year than the *Nouvelle Héloïse*, and by several years than the *Rêveries*. Long before Rousseau had written anything the poetry of melancholy in England was very rich, and was prolific of powerful and characteristic works if not of masterpieces.

English melancholy had long been proverbial in France, and French authors were not slow to turn it into ridicule. In Favart's *L'Anglais à Bordeaux* there is a certain Milord Brumton, who is proud, gentle, brave, sensitive and melancholy,—a distant cousin of Hamlet. Brumton envies the wanton French gaiety which he can never acquire ; at sight of a timepiece he exclaims : " While for me this swinging disc numbers the steps of approaching death, the Frenchman, at the mercy of every breath of desire, regards the dial but as the record of a round of pleasures ! " As for him, Locke, Newton and Haendel's severe music are his study. In vain an attractive *marquise* who secretly loves him says prettily : "Cease to seek for reasonings in which your melancholy may find its daily food. You think ; we enjoy. Trust me and cast your philosophy aside : it gives men the spleen and hardens their hearts. Our gaiety, which you call foolishness, colours our minds with smiling hues. . . ." Brumton remains melancholy, and, in reality, the *marquise* does not object to it. As the century advances melancholy becomes an ever more certain mark of the English genius. Another comic poet and man of good sense becomes indignant at it, and favours these islanders with some plain speaking : " Your melancholy vapours make your very tastes more gloomy, and the same dark gloss covers both your books and your arts. Seeking everywhere the funereal aspect of things you would like to find cemeteries even in your gardens."[2] But the " cemetery " which gave such offence to François de

---

[1] See William Lyon Phelps: *The beginnings of the English romantic movement*, Boston, 1893, especially chap. v. : *The literature of melancholy*.

[2] *Paméla*, by F. de Neufchâteau, ii. 12.

Neufchâteau was just what fascinated sensitive souls. Mme. de Genlis declares that in England lovers are accustomed in the evening to meet by moonlight among the tombs, and considers that no love but that which is "honourable, deep and pure" can express itself in such a spot.[1] Ducis praised the "sombre, melancholy" genius of the English before the whole Academy, and Sébastien Mercier makes immense efforts, he says, to give men some idea of "these sad and melancholy souls"[2]: Know, O Frenchmen, whose "false gaiety" is so highly extolled, that "frivolous minds can neither reason nor enjoy!"

Prévost, in his *Cléveland*, had already imitated the English in some pages of a strange and penetrating melancholy, which give, as it were, a foretaste of Chateaubriand. Already, too, Gresset, in his *Sidnei*, which appeared in 1745, had rendered the depression of Hamlet into verse of some beauty:

"To the pleasures I once adored I am now indifferent; I know them no longer, and in those self-same joys I now find nothing but vanity and sorrow. Life, with its scenes of changeless monotony, cannot awaken my soul from its torpor. . . . The world I have exhausted, it affects me not. . . . Destitute of feeling, dead to every pleasure, my soul is no longer capable of delight.".

Accordingly the poet Gray, who had read much of Gresset, called him a great master, and his tragedy a fine work.[3] But it is necessary to point out that Gresset—himself the offspring of an English family which had settled in France a century earlier—simply imitates, and imitates closely, the soliloquy of Hamlet,[4] so that the Frenchman who, in this respect, anticipated Rousseau, had recourse, like Prévost, to foreign sources.

---

[1] *Mémoires*, vol. iii., p. 357.

[2] See *Discours de réception à l'Académie francaise*, by Ducis, and Mercier's *Essai sur l'art dramatique*, p. 207.

[3] See *Gray's Works*, ed. Gosse, vol. i., p. 123, and vol. ii., p. 182, 183, &c.

[4] See in particular the long speech which occurs in act ii., scene 1, and also the one in act ii., scene 2: "In the noisy pageant, amidst which I have dwelt so long, there is nothing which I have not seen and seen again, nothing that I have not tasted and known; I have had my day upon this frivolous stage: if each one of us quitted it when his part was ended, everything would be as it should be, and the public would no longer see so many everlasting people of whom it is weary."

It is beyond doubt that Young, Ossian, and Gray, whose works were all introduced into France between 1760 and 1770, shortly after the appearance of *Héloïse*, owed their success in that country mainly to Rousseau. He had tapped the spring, and the French public fell with avidity upon these English poets whose genius was so nearly related to his.

Gray was not so well known as the others. The only one of his poems to be read in France was the *Elegy written in a country churchyard*, which was translated by the *Gazette littéraire* in 1765, and was freely copied by French poets, from Lemierre to Marie-Joseph Chénier, and from Fontanes or Delille to Chateaubriand. The *Elegy* is quite the most popular of Gray's works, but it by no means represents the profound and unique originality of the author of *The Bard* and the *Descent of Odin*, than whom few poets have been more sincere. Nevertheless this work, so modern in the sentiments it expresses yet at the same time so subtly classical in taste, attained something like celebrity in France. Gray's studious and highly cultivated talent provided, as it were, a connecting link between new aspirations and the classical methods to which Frenchmen were accustomed ; he was spoken of as a ," sublime philosopher, and a child of harmony." [1] A few who were curious as to foreign literature sought information about him : Bonstetten went to see him at Cambridge ; Fontanes, on a visit to London in 1786, made the acquaintance of Mason, Gray's biographer, and learnt from him a few details concerning one who was among his favourite poets. Voltaire, even, had attempted to enter into correspondence with him, but Gray had declined : his devout and gentle soul could scarcely conceal its aversion to the author of so many irreligious works, and to a friend who was starting for France he said : " I have one thing to beg of you. . . . Do not go to see Voltaire ; no one knows the mischief that man will do." [2]

Melancholy, Gray once said, was his most faithful companion : it rose with him, retired to rest with him, was with him when he went abroad and when he returned. The *Elegy written in a*

---

[1] *Journal encyclopédique*, 1st November 1788.
[2] *Gray's Works*, ed. Milford, vol. v., p. 32.

country churchyard is his most perfect expression of this deep inward feeling :

> The curfew tolls the knell of parting day,
> The lowing herd winds slowly o'er the lea,
> The ploughman homeward plods his weary way,
> And leaves the world to darkness and to me.
>
> Now fades the glimmering landscape on the sight,
> And all the air a solemn stillness holds,
> Save where the beetle wheels his droning flight,
> And drowsy tinklings lull the distant folds ;
>
> Save that from yonder ivy-mantled tower
> The moping owl does to the moon complain
> Of such as, wandering near her secret bower,
> Molest her ancient solitary reign.

By virtue of the sincerity of his religious feelings, of the delicious vagueness of his impressions, and of his serene and lofty inspiration, Gray is beyond dispute the predecessor of Chateaubriand and Lamartine, and of Rousseau before them. "With him," says his translator, the author of *René*, "begins that school of the melancholy poets, which in our day has been transformed into a school of poets of despair."[1] A valuable testimony, considering the authority with which it comes.

Collins, Chatterton, and Cowper were known to Frenchmen in the eighteenth century only through rare allusions to them in the newspapers.[2] The author of *Night Thoughts*, on the other hand, was famous not only in France, but throughout Europe, much more so, even, than in his own country.

Edward Young, the "sepulchral Young," as he was called, was really a survivor from the seventeenth century, having been born before Pope, in 1684. From whatever standpoint we consider him there is something singular about the man. He was nearly sixty years old when he revealed himself, not as a great poet, but as an eloquent interpreter of the melancholy of his age. He had in succession been a candidate for parliamentary honours, taken holy orders, aspired to a bishopric, enriched himself by

---

[1] *Essai sur la littérature anglaise.*
[2] On Chatterton, see *Journal encyclopédique*, 1st March 1790.

marriage with a lady of fortune, and had been throughout insatiable. He excited the pity of Europe in his behalf, but appears to have lied in the history of his misfortunes. He stated that he had lost his wife, his step-daughter, and the betrothed husband of the latter, within a few months. A serious matter, and one which should cover the French nation with confusion, is that this girl, who seems to have died at Montpellier, whither she had been taken by her father for the sake of her health, was refused burial by the unfeeling inhabitants of the country, on the ground that she was a Protestant :

> For oh ! the cursed ungodliness of zeal !
> While sinful flesh relented, spirit nursed
> In blind infallibility's embrace,
> The sainted spirit petrified the breast ;
> Denied the charity of dust, to spread
> O'er dust ! a charity their days enjoy.
> What could I do ? what succour ? what resource ?
> With pious sacrilege, a grave I stole ;
> With impious piety, that grave I wrong'd ;
> Short in my duty ; coward in my grief !
> More like her murderer, than friend, I crept,
> With soft-suspended step, and muffled deep
> In midnight darkness, whisper'd my last sigh.
> I whisper'd what should echo through their realms ;
> Nor writ her name, whose tomb should pierce the skies.[1]

The gruesome story of the father burying his daughter in secret went the round of Europe ; and a lugubrious engraving representing Young interring Narcissa by the light of a lantern was introduced as a frontispiece to the second volume of Letourneur's translation of the *Night Thoughts*. Such intolerance on the part of the French seemed monstrous. Young, the victim of fate, appeared also to be the victim of fanaticism, and for many a long year English visitors made pilgrimages to the melancholy grotto where this drama had been enacted. Unfortunately for the poet's sincerity, the story is of his own invention. The death of Young's step-daughter did actually occur in France, but at Lyon, as a learned inhabitant of that town has shown, and not at Montpellier : she was buried at the

[1] Night iii.

U

latter place, not in a nameless grave, but in the enclosure formerly reserved for Protestants, and not by stealth, but with all befitting ceremony. At most it appears that the cost of interment was excessive, and it was this trifling grievance that was dramatically treated by Young.[1]

Thus a strong suspicion of insincerity lingers about the nine books and the ten thousand lines of *The Complaint* or *Night Thoughts*, which legend asserts to have been written by the light of a candle burning in a skull. To our ears there is a false ring about his misfortunes as depicted in his poetry, however real they may have been. But the actual Young, the satirist and intriguer, was unknown in France. Whereas in his own country he enjoyed but a moderate celebrity and had fallen somewhat into disrepute, Young was looked upon by Frenchmen as an eloquent victim with strong claims to compassion, and his book as " the noblest elegy ever written upon the miseries of human existence.[2] At heart insatiably ambitious, the man enjoyed in France the reputation at once of a priest and a philosopher, fond of retirement and obscurity, who lived in quiet wedlock with a virtuous woman, and whom nothing but the sense that he had a duty to perform had driven forth into the world. The story went that he had served as almoner during the war in Flanders, and that even at that period his " dark and brilliant imagination " constantly subjected him to fits of absent mindedness: having on one occasion wandered away from the English camp with a copy of Æschylus in his hand he came upon the French troops, who, taking him for a spy, brought him before their general; but he, on learning the prisoner's name had him safely escorted back to his friends, thus doing sincere homage to his genius.[3] Stricken in the hour of his happiness Young " went down alive into the tomb of his friends, buried himself with them and drew a curtain between the world and himself." His genius, like a sepulchral lamp, burnt for ten years in honour of the dead; then

[1] See Breghot du Lut, *Nouveaux mélanges bibliographiques et littéraires*, Lyon, 1829, 8vo, p. 363; where there will also be found a note by Dr Ozanam on the same historical point.

[2] *Les Nuits*, a translation by Letourneur, vol. i., p. 7.

[3] *Journal encyclopédique*, 15th September 1772.

he himself died, forgotten. No bell tolled for him ; the very poor whom he had befriended neglected to follow his body to the grave, " and the frame to which a virtuous soul and a glorious genius had lent such lustre did not even receive the commonest funeral honours." His soul was " by nature majestic "; his character serious and noble. Men compared him to Pascal. But this need cause the sensitive no apprehension : though solemn, Young was no misanthrope ; " death and the grave were not always on his lips " ; he was fond of pleasure, and even started a bowling-alley in his parish. His was a gentle melancholy, though profound.

Such was the eighteenth century legend with regard to Young.[1] His book, like its author, has a legend of its own.

In 1760 there appeared anonymously a little collection entitled *Pensées anglaises sur divers sujets de religion et de morale.*[2] It was a selection of thoughts taken from *The Complaint*, which had been published sixteen years before, and was intended by the compiler to be a sort of manual of holy dying. Some of these reflexions are commonplace to the last degree ; others appear profound, because they are obscure ; while some owe their singularity to the form in which they are expressed, such as : " Night is a curtain drawn by Providence between man and his vanity "; or, " The firmament, like the vestment of the high priest under the law, is strewn with precious stones, which utter oracles."[3] Some, too, are of an apocalyptic type :

> Silence how dead ! and darkness how profound ! . . .
> Creation sleeps. 'Tis as the general pulse
> Of life stood still, and nature made a pause ;
> An awful pause ! prophetic of her end.[4]

This seemed original, though fantastic and disconnected. Some praised the freshness and singularity of the ideas ;[5] others were in ecstasies over the gloomy yet powerful character of the English imagination.[6] The appetite of the passionate admirers

---

[1] See Letourneur's *Nuits*, Introduction.   [2] Amsterdam, 1760, 12mo.

[3] These fragments are not literal quotations from Young, but appear to be imitations of certain passages from that author.

[4] Night i.   [5] *Journal encyclopédique*, October 1760.

[6] Fréron, *Année littéraire*, 1762, vol. vii., p. 47.

of England was whetted ; they asked for a more complete translation. In 1762, the *Journal étranger*, always on the watch for
foreign works, gave a version of the first Night.

The translator was the Comte de Bissy, lieutenant-general of
Languedoc and member of the French Academy, the same whom
we have already met with as the patron of Sterne. Though
according to Collé his knowledge of French was very poor and
his spelling still worse, Bissy was a determined anglomaniac and
had translated—some said by means of a substitute—Bolingbroke's
letters on patriotism. His translation of Young was accompanied
by a curious address which shows clearly what it was that the
eighteenth century admired in the author of *Night Thoughts* :

Works of this character—filled with grand and gloomy, yet exquisitely pleasing ideas ; works which leave an impression of melancholy behind them, and
plunge the reader in the depths of meditation—are unknown to French literature.
With our authors, the soul is, so to speak, all on the outside ; more devoted to
pleasure, less solitary, than English authors, they dwell too much with other
men, and since, as a rule, they only meet them in the fashionable world, where
none but cheerful thoughts are recognised as pleasing, they suit their works to
what their observation leads them to suppose the taste of the greatest number of
readers. But why do we not follow these readers to the privacy of their study ?
Then we should see that the works which please and captivate the most are the
sad ones.

Returning to Young, Bissy added : " I will venture to say
that in point of depth this poet is what Homer and Pindar are in
point of grandeur. I should find it difficult to explain the effect
produced upon me by my first perusal of this work. I might
experience much the same impression in the heart of the desert
on a dark and stormy night, when the surrounding blackness is
pierced at intervals by flashes of lightning." [1]

Bissy had touched a sensitive cord : his *Nuit* proved a great
success. For twenty years translators vied with one another
in producing, either in prose or in metre, a version of one or
more of the Nights.[2] And when the *Night Thoughts* were

---

[1] *Journal étranger*, February 1762.

[2] The first Night was translated by Sabatier de Castres, and by Colardeau
(1770) ; the second, which was translated in the *Gazette littéraire* (vol. ii., p. 101),
was rendered into metre by Colardeau (1770) ; the same writer also produced
versions of the fourth, twelfth, and seventeenth (1771), and a further translation,
by Doigni du Ponceau, was published in the same year ; the fifteenth was translated again, by L. de Limoges (1787). There were also *Vérités philosophiques*

exhausted they betook themselves to the satires, the tragedies, and the minor works, until the whole of Young had been dealt with.[1] Of these versions, the most famous, and the only approximately complete one, was that by Letourneur,[2] which created a sensation. It was prefaced by a curious dissertation intended to introduce "a great poet, who is certain to share the immortality of Swift, Shaftesbury, Pope, Addison, and Richardson." We have seen what Letourneur said of Young as a man; as a writer he praises him no less. "Born to be original," incapable of slavish adherence to a model, he was distinct from all others. Letourneur is lavish of big words: the French have laid themselves open to the charge "of cowardice in the field of genius": they restrict their talent "by keeping it in bondage to fixed rules of art." Will no one rouse the soul with the "shock" it needs? Will no one give it an impulse in the direction of new beauties? Writers must do what Young has done; they must be themselves. Each should "express his ideas and sensations as they are received"—a doctrine which is pure Diderot, and also pure Sterne. Now of this poetic method Young affords the best example, by giving expression to "that vague and confused feeling called *ennui*, the true remedy for which lies in rousing the emotions of the soul."

With all his admiration for Young's work Letourneur did not feel bound to give a faithful rendering of it: he suppresses, or relegates to his notes, everything which seems to him to savour of the preacher: "these passages," he says pleasantly, "belong exclusively to theology." Young is no longer a Christian, though still a philosopher.

tirées des Nuits d'Young (by Mouslier de Moissy), Paris, 1770, 8vo; Le triomphe du chrétien, one of the Nights, translated by Dom Devienne, Paris, 1781, 8vo, &c. Various scattered fragments of Young will be found in the magazines of the day. (See, especially, Journal encyclopédique, 15th October 1784, 15th July 1786). The Abbé Baudrand published: Esprit, Maximes et Pensées d'Young, Paris, 1786, 12mo.

[1] Œuvres diverses by Young, translated from the English by Letourneur, Paris, 1770, 2 vols. 8vo. Satires d'Young . . . a free translation by Bertin, London and Paris, 1787, 8vo.

[2] Les Nuits d'Young, translated from the English by Letourneur, Paris, 1769, 2 vols. 8vo, (copyright, 2nd May 1769). Frequently reprinted, four editions being issued between 1769 and 1775.

He is still, also, quite sufficiently " sepulchral." The majestic harmony of blank verse, which renders certain pages of Young, justly quoted in anthologies, so admirable as self-complete passages, has of necessity disappeared, as well as the truly oratorical pomp of phrase, and the breadth of effect Young obtained from his ample use of poetical platitude. His rhetoric appears in all its poverty. His persistent denunciations ring false. In truth, Young in translation is too barren of ideas. We know moreover that wit is simply the art of " combating truth with sophisms," and having read Jean-Jacques are aware that nothing is more uncommon than that " precious wisdom which examines thoroughly and goes to the root of its subject." The theme of the author of *Night Thoughts* is the old opposition between the social and the natural man. Every other element in the book—its expression of fellowship with nature, its appeal to the human conscience, its sincere conviction of man's miserable condition, has since been expressed by many others whose voices are more persuasive than his.

Yet it may be that, if we carry our minds back to 1742 and 1744—the years in which Young's collection of poems appeared —and especially if we reflect on the condition of French lyrical poetry just at that time, we shall feel, even to-day, the partly vanished charm of such lines as these :

> O majestic Night !
> Nature's great ancestor ! Day's elder-born !
> And fated to survive the transient sun !
> By mortals and immortals seen with awe !
> A starry crown thy raven brow adorns,
> An azure zone thy waist ; clouds, in heaven's loom,
> Wrought through varieties of shape and shade,
> In ample folds of drapery divine,
> Thy flowing mantle form, and, heaven throughout,
> Voluminously pour thy pompous train.
> Thy gloomy grandeurs (Nature's most august,
> Inspiring aspect !) claim a grateful verse . . . .
> Heaven's King ! whose face unveil'd consummates bliss ;
> Redundant bliss ! which fills that mighty void,
> The whole creation leaves in human hearts !
> Thou, who didst touch the lip of Jesse's son,
> Rapt in sweet contemplation of these fires,
> And set his harp in concert with the spheres ! . . . .

Loose me from earth's enclosure, from the sun's
Contracted circle set my heart at large,
Eliminate my spirit, give it range
Through provinces of thought yet unexplored ;
Teach me, by this stupendous scaffolding,
Creation's golden steps, to climb to Thee.[1]

Can we not recognise, in these lines, something of the true poet that at times was revealed in Edward Young ? Are our wearied perceptions entirely proof against the spell which so fascinated our fathers ?

The influence of this spell was almost universal. Twice translated into German, the book created quite a revolution in Klopstock's circle. In spite of Lessing's protestations, Kremer, in the *Northern Spectator*, declared that the author was a greater poet than Milton and full " of the spirit of God and of the prophets." Klopstock, the leading spirit, wrote a poem on Young's death.[2] Young brought death and moonlight into fashion in literature : by moonlight Werther roams about the forest in order to soothe his soul, and by moonlight he bids farewell to Charlotte. For many a long year Young reigned supreme as the poet of night.[3]

In France he encountered sceptics, Voltaire among the foremost. Voltaire had made his acquaintance when staying with Bubb Doddington at Eastbury, in the days before Young took holy orders. He had found him witty, sarcastic, and worldly. Young had even made him the object of a somewhat caustic epigram.[4] At a later period the poet dedicated to the philosopher certain lines as a reminder that

Life's little drama done, the curtain falls !—
Dost thou not hear it ? I can hear,
Though nothing strikes the listening ear ;
Time groans his last ! Eternal loudly calls ![5]

---

[1] Ninth Night.   [2] Imitated in the *Journal encyclopédique*, 1st December 1785.
[3] See Erich Schmidt, *Richardson, Rousseau, und Goethe*, p. 190.
[4] They were arguing together about the characters Death and Sin in *Paradise Lost*. Young addressed Voltaire in the lines :

You are so witty, profligate, and thin,
At once we think thee Milton, Death, and Sin.

[5] Letourneur translated the piece and published it together with the *Nuits*, vol. ii., pp. 318-321.

I do not know if Voltaire was offended by this sermon, but to Letourneur, who had sent him his translation of *Night Thoughts*, he replied: "Sir, you have conferred a high honour on my old acquaintance Young; the taste of the translator appears to be better than the author's. You have done all that could be done in the way of bringing order into this collection of confused and bombastic platitudes." And after contrasting the poem on *Religion* with the *Night Thoughts*, he concluded by saying, "I think that every foreigner will prefer your prose to the poetry of one who is half poet and half priest, like this Englishman."[1]

A certain Abbé Rémy went further. Writing in the character of a "black musqueteer," he published *Les Jours, pour servir de correctif et de supplément aux Nuits*;[2] in which he pleaded the cause of laughter, and protested that "the man who introduced so simple, so innocuous, and so universally accessible a form of enjoyment as the use of tobacco would deserve an altar (*autel*) in every heart, had he not already sufficiently brilliant ones in the homestead (*hôtel*) of every farm."

If a book is parodied it is being read. In fact, the *Night Thoughts*, in spite of Voltaire, were all the rage. "It is an unanswerable proof," said Mme. Riccoboni, "of the change that is taking place in the French mind."[3] Everyone who desired to see a reformation in French poetry caught the infection. One writer describes the poem as the masterpiece "of a melancholy imagination and a sensitive soul,"[4] another—Baculard d'Arnaud—regards it as a perfect example "of the sombre type" of literature: "my soul," writes this lover of tears, "has buried itself among the tombs. . . . I have penetrated and explored a new nature to its very heart! Ah! what wealth have I not discovered therein!"[5] Mercier, who of course gave his opinion, thinks that the book translated by Letourneur will give the French language "an entirely fresh appearance."[6] Another, one of the same clan, compares Young to Æschylus in respect of

---

[1] 7th June 1769.
[2] London and Paris, 1770, 12mo. (See *Journal encyclopédique*, 15th June 1770.)
[3] Garrick, *Correspondence*, vol. ii., p. 566.
[4] *Journal encyclopédique*, 15th August and 1st September 1769.
[5] Preface to the *Comte de Comminges*.　　　[6] *Essai sur l'art dramatique*, p. 299.

" his colossal imagination, and the frenzy of his oriental style."[1]
Grimm is more calm, and considers that the work is magnificently
sombre ; but is it nothing to get oneself read by a people " whose
disposition it is to see everything in rosy hues ? "

Encouraged by his success Letourneur translated Hervey's
Meditations among the Tombs, another work of the same stamp, and
the *Journal encyclopédique* bears witness to " the strange revolution
which French literature has been undergoing for some years
past."[2]

But Young had more famous admirers still.

Grimm had ventured to express some doubt. He was of
opinion that Young's poetry, with its " fitful and uncertain
gleams," could not succeed in France. " It is all too full of
tolling bells, tombs, mournful chants and cries, and phantoms ;
the simple and artless expression of true sorrow would be a
hundred times more effective."[3] Grimm was right enough.
But Diderot was on the watch, and rated him soundly. " Do
you ever retract what you have said, Mr Shopkeeper at the sign
of the *Evergreen Holly?* If so, here is an excellent opportunity
for you." It may be well to inform you that Letourneur's translation is " most harmonious, and characterized by the greatest
richness of expression," that the first edition has been exhausted
in four months, " and that nothing but exceptional merit could
induce a frivolous and light-hearted nation to read jeremiads "
such as this. . . . " Ah! Mr Grimm! Mr Grimm! Your conscience has assumed a very heavy burden ! "[4] How could Grimm
help bowing to the decree of " Cato Diderot ? "

And so he submitted, and the entire French public with him.
The *Night Thoughts* continued to cause a " a general ferment."
They were accused of spreading suicidal mania.[5] It is beyond

---

[1] *Essai sur la tragédie,* by a philosopher, 1773, 8vo.

[2] 15th November 1770. It was in 1770 that Letourneur's translation appeared
(Paris, 8vo). Concerning Hervey see also *Méditations sur les tombeaux,* translated
[by Mme. d'Arcouville], Paris, 1771, 12mo ; *Les Tombeaux* [by Bridel], Lausanne,
1779, 8vo ; *Abrégé des œuvres d'Hervey,* Bâll, 1796, 16mo ; and the imitations in
verse by Baour-Lormian. See also, on Hervey, Leslie Stephen's *History of English
Thought,* vol. ii., p. 438.

[3] May 1770.   [4] *Correspondance littéraire,* June 1770

[5] See the *Gazette universelle de littérature,* 1777, p. 236.

doubt that Young's work, unequal as it was, yet heady, eloquent yet false, declamatory and at the same time poetic, exerted a great influence over many minds. Robespierre kept it under his pillow during the days of the Revolution. Camille Desmoulins read it through once more, together with Hervey's *Meditations*, on the eve of his death; "you wish to die twice over, then," said Westermann, jocosely.[1] Above all, Chateaubriand, Byron, and all the leading romantic writers, both English and French, were readers of Young, and this is why it may be said, with Villemain, that his power is not yet exhausted. Like Rousseau, and earlier than he, Young had perceived the charm of "enchanting sadness"; like him had known "the mighty void which the universe leaves in the heart of man"; and like him, in the words of Chateaubriand, had created the "descriptive elegiac" style, of which "the after effect is a sort of lamentation, as it were, within the soul."[2] If melancholy is one of the sources of modern poetry, few have a better claim than Young to the honour of having anticipated the poets of the present day.

III

It was at the very time when France became subject to the spell wielded by Young that she acquired an enthusiasm also for Ossian, and this again, if we examine it closely, is but another natural result of the revolution effected by Rousseau.

Young's melancholy seemed a natural characteristic of the poet and the sage. But his lamentations were only for the present, for man's corruption, his sufferings and his approaching death. He never allows his imagination to wander among vanished centuries or ancient civilizations. He is insensible to the depth and the poetry which sorrow acquires from regret for the past. Nevertheless, it was practically inevitable that the poetry of melancholy should become the poetry of the past. The past, because it has vanished, has a melancholy of its own,

---

1 Lamartine, *Histoire des Girondins*, vol. viii., p. 51.
2 *Essai sur la littérature anglaise.*

and of this, Rousseau, who had known "the sweet yet bitter recollection which stimulates our anguish with the vain sentiment of departed happiness," was well aware. But, just as the individual, in the decline of life, turns back with delight to his earliest years, so too, the race, when it has known the intoxicating consciousness of its own energy, when it has enjoyed to the full its own virility and proved it vigorous and keen, feels itself smitten with fond yearning for centuries that are past, a longing which seizes it like a mighty desire to become once more a child. It dreams of finding again the freshness of its first impressions; again it crosses the seas of remembrance, and, by the diffused light of imagination, recognises in a mysterious distance the vague and wavering lineaments of humanity as once it was and now can be no longer. The very fierceness of primitive man seems then like a sign of vigorous adolescence : distance attenuates and, if one may say so, shades away his savage and monstrous aspects; his haughty stature, his native fidelity, daring and nobility are all that strike the eye. So may the marble faun shine through the mist like the statue of Apollo.

The eighteenth century, like many another age, surrendered itself to this spell. With Rousseau, with Ossian, with Chateaubriand in his youth, it fell in love with the past. The twilight ages of the human race supplied a marvellously appropriate setting for the need of reverie which was beginning to torment the men of that day. What books for the pillow like Homer and the Bible, wherein man is tempted to bury himself in his hours of weariness, not because of their eloquence or sacredness alone, but also because of their antiquity? But Homer, who moreover was little known, was regarded with suspicion by the innovators as the fountain-head of classical literature; while the Bible, of which it has been justly remarked that "it has never been a French book,"[1] was looked upon with twofold more suspicion than Homer.

Thus the new literature, the ideal of which was taking vague shape in certain minds, was in need of ancestors which should

[1] J.—J. Weiss, *A propos de théâtre*, p. 168.

be peculiarly its own. It became necessary to discover, in the past history of humanity, a race whence the descent of a whole line of poets could legitimately be traced, and worthy of being placed in opposition to an antiquity properly so called, that is to say, to Greece and Rome. Lastly, it was needful, as Garat expressed it, "to supply the somewhat effete poetry of the south with images, scenes, and manners wherein poetic talent might renew its youth as in a freshly created world."[1]

This modern Homer, so eagerly sought, was discovered by a very clever man. Macpherson's Caledonia, and Ossian, its poet, were accepted with enthusiasm by the whole of Europe.[2]

For years already there had been shaping itself among the English a movement which drew the attention of many distinguished minds towards a past, not perhaps more remote than classical antiquity, but at any rate more mysterious and more pregnant with the unknown. Some, like Walpole, Warton, and Hurd, sought to bring mediæval poetry and architecture once more into fashion.[3] Others devoted themselves to the collection of old songs—English, Irish, or Welsh. Percy's famous book, which appeared in 1765, is simply the most celebrated collection among a long series which began in the early years of the century.[4] Others again, with more ambition, restored in its entirety the dead civilization of the Celts and of the Northern races in general, contrasting it triumphantly with the worn-out civilizations of Greece and Rome. In some fine stanzas, written in 1749, Collins sang the praises of ancient Scotland, and of her highlands,

> where, beneath the showery west,
> The mighty kings of three fair realms are laid ;
> Once foes, perhaps, together now they rest,
> No slaves revere them and no wars invade ;

---

[1] *Mémoires sur Suard*, vol. ii., p. 153.

[2] See *The Life and Letters of James Macpherson*, London, 1894, 8vo, by Bailey Saunders.

[3] Thomas Warton, *Observations on the Faery Queen* (1754). Richard Hurd, *Letters on Chivalry and Romance* (1762).

[4] A very accurate account of this movement will be found in Mr Phelps's book : *The beginnings of the English romantic movement*, ch. vii. (*Revival of the past*). Percy's collection was known in France. (See Suard, *Mélanges de littérature*.)

Yet frequent now, at midnight solemn hour,
'The rifted mounds their yawning cells unfold,
And forth the monarchs stalk with sovereign power,
In pageant robes, and wreathed with sheeny gold,
And on their twilight tombs aërial councils hold.[1]

This, however, was merely the presentiment of a poet. It was a historical work—one of importance in the evolution of the literature of the age—that provided restless imaginations with the material they required. This was Mallet's *Introduction à l'histoire de Danemark*, published in 1755, and followed after a short interval by *Monuments de la mythologie et de la poésie des Celtes et particulièrement des anciens Scandinaves*.[2]

Paul-Henri Mallet was a Genevan. At the age of twenty-two he had become professor of literature at Copenhagen,[3] where he had been seized with a strong passion for the then unknown literatures of the North, and had taken upon himself the task of revealing them to Europe. With the help of Danish or Swedish versions he read and translated the *Edda*, and it was a German version of his translation which inspired Klopstock and his school with their taste for *bardic* poetry.[4] Mallet was thus the occasion of a European movement which had only been awaiting a vivifying impulse. His book was translated by Percy, and attained great celebrity in England. Gray read it with avidity,[5] and Percy produced some *runic* poems in the style of the Scandinavian sages. Through Mallet a whole generation of poets and critics was made acquainted with northern Europe, and from him Mme. de Staël herself derived a large number of her ideas.[6] A new antiquity had come to life. An entire civilization made its appearance ; one very different from those of Greece and Rome, untouched as yet by the imitator, and offering a fine field to the eager imagination. Such ungracious spirits as found fault with Mallet's undertaking, or blamed him for resuscitating "childish

[1] *An Ode on the popular superstitions of the Highlands of Scotland.*   [2] 1756.
[3] See Sismondi, *De la vie et des écrits de P.-H. Mallet*, 1807, and Sayous, *Le xviiie siècle à l'étranger*, vol. ii., p. 46 *et seq.*
[4] Joret, *Herder*, p. 20.
[5] See *Gray's Works*, ed. Gosse, vol. ii., p. 352.
[6] See *De la littérature* : Preface to the 2nd edition.

fables,"[1] were very few in number. It is not too much to say of his book that it was the starting-point of the entire Ossianic literature.

In 1760 Macpherson brought out his *Fragments of ancient poetry, collected in the Highlands, and translated from the Gaelic or Erse Languages.* In 1762—or perhaps at the close of 1761—he produced *Fingal,* and in 1763 *Temora.* Such was the birth of Ossian.

From these dates it will be seen that Ossian came into existence at the very moment when Rousseau was giving a new direction to French literature—in the same year, or nearly so, as the *Nouvelle Héloïse.* Besides, Macpherson owes as little to Rousseau as Rousseau owes to Macpherson : there is a remarkable coincidence between them, but neither was influenced by the other. Macpherson, moreover, was by no means a reformer in literature : his individual taste was extremely diffident, and he good-humouredly derides the old English poets—for instance, Spenser, with his giants and his fairies. He has a very poor opinion of those who imitate them, and of their "romantic compositions," so "disgustful to true taste."[2] It is as an antiquary that he publishes Ossian, not as a poet : he does it to gratify contemporary taste for literary curiosities. He would have been amazed to learn that critics of the succeeding generation regarded him as one of the best authenticated ancestors of romanticism.

Nevertheless Ossian very soon effected a revolution. He was almost immediately recognised as the leading spirit of the new literature—"the modern Homer" of Mme. de Staël. In England every genuine adherent of the classical school regarded him with distrust and uneasiness. "It tires me to death," wrote Walpole, "to read how many ways a warrior is like the moon, or the sun, or a rock, or a lion, or the ocean."[3] Johnson, an Englishman and a member of the classical school, detects in Macpherson, the Scotchman, an impostor and a dangerous innovator. He indulges in amenities of this sort : "I received your foolish and impudent

---

[1] Preface to the edition of 1773. [2] Note to *Cathloda.*
[3] 8th December 1761.

letter . . . I hope I shall never be deterred from detecting what I think a cheat, by the menaces of a ruffian."[1]   Macpherson, however, but yesterday a schoolmaster and salaried tutor, could already count as his warm admirers all who believed in his Caledonia. Even those who were doubtful as to the authenticity of the fragments discovered in them a singular beauty which excited their admiration. The subtle intelligence of Gray found them "full of noble wild imagination,"[2] and "infinite beauty." What does it signify whether they are by Ossian? "I am resolved to believe them genuine, spite of the Devil and the Kirk." Beyond doubt "this man is the very Daemon of poetry," and if there be really no fraud in the case, imagination must have "dwelt many hundred years ago in all her pomp on the cold and barren mountains of Scotland."

Macpherson was soon enabled to make the proud assertion that Ossian had achieved a European success.

Ossian was translated into Italian by Cesarotti; there were two versions of him in Spanish, several in German, one in Swedish, one in Danish, and two in Dutch, of which one was by Bilderdyk. In Germany, especially, he created a furor. The true originator of Northern poetry was found at last; "Thou, too, Ossian," cried Klopstock, "wert swallowed up in oblivion; but thou hast been restored to thy position; behold thee now before us, the equal and the challenger of Homer the Greek." "What need," wrote Voss to Brückner, "of natural beauty? Ossian of Scotland is a greater poet than Homer of Ionia." Lerse, in a sonorous discourse at Strasburg, acknowledged three guides of the "sacred art of poetry": Shakespeare, Homer, and Ossian—two Northern poets to a single classic. Herder wrote a comparison between the Homeric and the Ossianic epics, spoke of Ossian as "the man I have sought," and contemplated a journey to Scotland in order to collect the songs of the bards. Bürger imitated him, and Christian Heyne constituted himself his champion at the Uni-

---

[1] Boswell, *Life of Johnson*, ed. Croker, 1847, p. 430.
[2] Letters of 29th June 1760, July 1760, 17th February 1763.

versity of Göttingen. Lastly, Goethe, need we remind the reader, drew inspiration from him in *Werther* and elsewhere. When his spirits are high Werther's taste is for Homer, but in sorrow he feeds upon Ossian, and when "it is autumn within and about him," he cries: "Ossian has completely banished Homer from my heart!" It is a fragment of Ossian—the lamentation of Armin over the death of his daughter—that throws the distracted Charlotte into the disorder which almost proves her undoing :

> Why dost thou awake me, O gale?
> I'm covered with dew-drops, it says,
> But the time of my fading is near,
> The blast which my foliage decays.
>
> To-morrow the traveller shall come,
> Who once saw me comely and bold ;
> His eyes shall the meadow search round,
> But me they shall never behold ! [1]

In his *Memoirs* Goethe has given an admirable explanation of the Caledonian bard's popularity. It was Macpherson who developed among young people in Germany the taste for "the gloomy reflections which lead him who yields to them astray in the infinite." It was he who, with Young and Gray, excited and "stimulated these fatal workings within them." "That all this melancholy might have a theatre adapted to it Ossian had carried us away to distant Thule, where, as we traversed the vast and gloomy heath, amid the moss-grown stones of tombs, we beheld the surrounding herbage swayed by a mighty blast, and above our heads a sky leaden with cloud. Then the moon changed this Caledonian night into day ; dead heroes, and women, beautiful yet pale, hovered around us ; we dreamed at last that we saw, in her own awful form, the very spirit of Loda." [2]

Nothing affords a better proof of the growing interest taken by the French in foreign matters than the rapidity with which Ossian became known among them. It is worthy of remark

---

[1] From Gotzberg's translation of *Werther*, letter xci. On Ossian in Germany, see Erich Schmidt, *loc. cit.*, p. 225 *et seq.*

[2] *Memoirs*, part iii.

that, contrary to received opinion, he was famous in France almost before he had become so in the countries of the North.[1]

Macpherson's first volume was issued early in 1760, and in September of that year the *Journal étranger* published two fragments of "ancient poetry, translated into English from the Erse, the language of the Scotch highlanders," these fragments being *Connal and Crimora* and *Ryno and Alpin*. The translator commented upon " the singular way in which the action advances, the rapid movement from one idea to another without any transition, the accumulation of images, the frequent repetitions, and, in addition, all the defects of what we call the oriental style." From these examples he concluded that the imagination of the northern nations was no less poetic than that of the Asiatics. " A race which speaks a barren language, and has made no progress in the arts, is obliged to make frequent use of figures and metaphors. . . . Grandeur and profusion of imagery, daring methods of expression, and a certain irregularity in the sequence of ideas, must of necessity characterize its poetry."

This writer, the first Frenchman to translate and to criticize Ossian, was Turgot.[2]

The experiment proving successful, the same journal inserted two other fragments, with a brief notice on Macpherson's selection. This time it was remarked that Erse poetry was more akin to Homer than to Pope or Dryden, whence it was concluded that poetry " knows neither nation nor language." It may even be that " heroic poetry, as it was conceived by the ancients, belongs rather to races which are still in a state of barbarism than to more educated and more civilized nations." Uncivilized men whose soul, so to speak, is entirely " on the outside," whose passions are held in check neither by education nor by law, whose intelligence speaks no language but that of the imagination, because it is incapable of accommodating itself to abstractions—such men as these are poets by nature.

---

[1] On the success of Ossian in France see Mr Bailey Saunders's book above-mentioned (chap. i.), and two articles by Arvède Barine (*Journal des Débats*, 13th and 27th November 1894).

[2] See *Œuvres*, vol. ix., p. 141 *et seq.*

"By the art of introspection the soul is in a manner detached from external objects; the practice of reflection and of thought blunts the sensibility and the imagination, and restrains the activity of the passions; the intelligence becomes more austere and less tolerant of *that vague and indefinite latitude in respect of ideas which poetry demands.*"[1]　This, more clearly expressed, was the theory of Diderot and Rousseau. Man is poetical only in the primitive stage, and consequently the primitive man alone is a poet.

We know for a certainty that these fragments achieved a brilliant and European success. "It is as beautiful as Homer," wrote Grimm.[2]　Accordingly the *Journal* published successive translations by Suard of *Fingal, Lathmon, Oithona, Dar-Thula,* and *Conlath and Cuthona,* all of them "poems from the Erse."[3] A new translator, the duchess d'Aiguillon, produced a version of *Carthon.*[4]　This gave rise to a great controversy upon the authenticity of all these poems, the conclusion of the dispute, which filled the columns of the *Journal des savants,*[5] being "that the honour of having created these sublime and touching poems was quite as great as that of having been so fortunate as to discover them."

For ten years the Ossianic dispute occupied the attention of critics, but neither in France nor in England did anyone manage to convict the fortunate Macpherson of imposture. How should French journalists have succeeded[6] where the cleverest members of the most learned societies in Scotland had failed? For fifty years and more, bardic, Erse, Runic or Gaelic poetry, as it was variously called, maintained its popularity in France.

In 1764 the *Gazette littéraire* contrasted this new type of

---

[1] *Journal étranger,* January 1761.　　　[2] *Correspondance littéraire,* April 1762.

[3] December 1761, January, February, April, and July 1762.

[4] *Carthon,* a poem translated from the English by Mme. ——, London, 1762, 12mo. On this subject the *Mémoires secrets* (20th February 1763) may be consulted. Quérard asserts that the duchess—who was the mother of the opponent of La Chalotais—had a collaborator named Marin.

[5] February and November 1762; May, June, September, December 1764. *Gazette littéraire* (1st September 1765); Cesarotti's reflections upon Ossian.

[6] See Mr Archibald Clerk's edition of Ossian's poems (London, 1870, 2 vols. 8vo).

poetry with that of the Greeks, just as Herder himself or Goethe might have done, and while recognising in it "that quality of enthusiasm which the Greeks called *poetic frenzy*," it pointed out the differences due to climate, race and religion. "The poems of the North abound in awful and impressive images, but rarely contain such as are pleasing or cheerful. . . . All their imagery is representative of mournful skies, the wildest scenes of nature, and savage manners." In them, nevertheless, is to be found that essential gift which constitutes the poet, the power of "realising the phantoms of one's own imagination": may it not be that "what we call the days of barbarism were in very many respects favourable to poetic genius?" Now Ossian, though less ancient, appears a hundred times more uncivilised than Homer: his inspiration is simpler, more artless, more faithful to nature. It is like a gushing spring. Better still, "it is genuine, heartfelt poetry, for throughout we can detect a heart stirred by noble feelings and tender passions."[1]

Opinion was thus occupied by the question of the Erse poems, and was leaning towards the cult of the new divinity, when Letourneur, an indefatigable purveyor of foreign literature, brought out his translation of the "Gaelic poems of Ossian, the son of Fingal," with the addition of a few "bardic" poems by John Smith,[2] and achieved therewith a prodigious success. Letourneur's translation, however, was far from deserving the praises which La Harpe generously bestowed upon it; the harmony of the prose-poetry, so admired by Gray, and, to Macpherson's honour, not indeed invented but brought into fashion by him, is difficult to recognize in the somewhat inferior prose of Letourneur; as a parallel case we may imagine *Atala* translated into the style of Johnson. Letourneur's *Ossian* remains, nevertheless, a book of much importance in the history of French literature.

---

[1] *Gazette littéraire*, 1764, vol. i., p. 238; 1st July and 1st August 1765.

[2] *Ossian, fils de Fingal, poésies galliques*, translated by Letourneur from the English of Macpherson, Paris, 1777, 2 vols. 8vo. Frequently reprinted, the principal editions being those of 1799 and 1810, the former containing additional matter, the latter a preface by Ginguené. A translation of *Temora*, by a writer named Saint-Simon, had appeared at Amsterdam in 1774.

"I no longer believe," Chateaubriand once wrote, "in the authenticity of Ossian's works. . . . Yet still I listen to the sound of his harp, as one might listen to a voice, monotonous indeed, yet sweet and plaintive."[1] This voice we hear, even to-day, and find, when we take the trouble to look for it, just what Chateaubriand found in the false Ossian, "a lofty and noble spring of poetry," as an excellent judge expressed it, "through which, whatever others may have said, there breathes a blast as mighty as the storm-wind."[2] On the other hand, we no longer believe either in Fingal or in Oscar. The "Caledonian" civilization, which had for eighteenth century readers the charm of something new and striking, seems to us an artificial compound of heterogeneous elements. Macpherson's clans and bards and druids no longer wield their ancient spell: we have admitted—a little too readily perhaps—that Macpherson was nothing more than a dexterous impostor. But those who seek to explain the vogue of the Ossianic poems must not forget that contemporaries held a very different opinion. They believed, with the faith that imagination gives, in the Caledonians, sturdy men with white skins, fair hair, and blue eyes. They believed in the druids, who fulfilled the functions of priests and legislators, and in the bards, who were not only poets but also ambassadors. They believed in that singular race which had neither industries nor agriculture, knew no metals but gold and iron, launched their rash barks upon the ocean, and chose the loftiest sites for their dwellings that they might be near to Heaven. They believed in that vague and poetic religion, according to which the clouds were inhabited by souls who commanded the winds and storms, spoke to the living at solemn seasons, and challenged them to combat. They believed that the gods, in the darkness of night, waged mysterious warfare with men—and they loved the sombre poetry of their idea.

The wan, cold moon rose in the east. Sleep descended on the youths! Their blue helmets glitter to the beam; the fading fire decays. But sleep did

---

[1] Preface to the translation of *Poèmes traduits du gallique.*

[2] Angellier, *Burns*, vol. i., p. 59. Mr. Clerk admits the authenticity of the poems of Ossian.

not rest on the king: he rose in the midst of his arms, and slowly ascended the hill, to behold the flame of Sarno's tower.

The flame was dim and distant: the moon hid her red face in the east. A blast came from the mountain, on its wings was the spirit of Loda. He came to his place in his terrors, and shook his dusky spear. His eyes appear like flames in his dark face; his voice is like distant thunder.

Fingal defies the spirit.

Dost thou force me from my place, replied the hollow voice! The people bend before me. I turn the battle from the field of the brave. I look on the nations and they vanish: my nostrils pour the blast of death. I come abroad on the winds: the tempests are before my face. But my dwelling is calm, above the clouds. . . .

The hero does not quail before him.

He lifted high his shadowy spear! He bent forward his dreadful height. Fingal, advancing, drew his sword, the blade of dark-brown Luno. The gleaming'path of the steel winds through the gloomy ghost. The form fell shapeless into air, like a column of smoke, which the staff of the boy disturbs, as it rises from the half-extinguished furnace. The spirit of Loda shrieked, as, rolled into himself, he rose on the wind.[1]

Scenes like this, though they bear too close a resemblance to those of Homer or the Bible, are not without their grandeur. But they do not affect us as they affected the contemporaries of Macpherson. We find them less original. Of the two poets, one epic, the other lyric, that go to the making of old Ossian, we prefer the latter, who really is original. But eighteenth century criticism was largely occupied with the former, the poet whom it was possible to compare with Homer.

Some years before the publication of Letourneur's translation, Voltaire had already introduced in one of his plays an amusing conversation between a Florentine, an Oxford professor, and a Scotchman, who had met at Lord Chesterfield's house.[2] The Scotchman stands up for Ossian. "How beautiful," he exclaims, "were the days of old; Fingal's poem has passed from mouth to mouth down to us of to-day for nearly two thousand years, without ever having been altered: such is the power of genuine beauties over the minds of men!" And he

[1] *Carric-thura. The Poems of Ossian*, London, 1812, p. 171.
[2] *Dictionnaire philosophique : Anciens et modernes*, 1770.

recites a translation or rather a paraphrase of the opening lines of Fingal.[1] "Ah!" says the Oxford professor; "there you have the true Homeric style; but what pleases me still more is that I can detect in it the sublime eloquence of the Hebrews." And the man proceeds to quote a few passages from the Psalms, carefully selected by Voltaire, as the reader will perceive, so as to give an idea of the "oriental style." The Scotchman grows pale with rage. But the Florentine, with a smile, engages to hold forth in this so-called "oriental style" for any length of time; with a little dexterity any one can "reel off bombastic lines of irregular metre," "pile one combat on another," and "describe idle flights of fancy." In fact he improvises on the spot a nonsensical fragment on the first subject suggested to him. The satire was cheap, but not altogether unjust. Ossian is monotonous; he does cultivate "the oriental style"; and will anyone venture to maintain that he never "described empty dreams?"

But Voltaire fails to perceive, or pretends not to see, that the true cause of his success lay elsewhere. To not a few superficial minds the Caledonian epic undoubtedly seemed to be the successful rival of the Homeric: "Farewell the tales of ancient days, the gods of Greece and Troy! Hail to the heroes of the clouds, in their aerial palaces!"[2] But Ossian's epic qualities by no means exhausted his merit. What made English and French readers so fond of him was the lyric, still more than the epic, poet in him—more indeed than anything else: the poet who gave form, or at all events a new setting, to the love of nature, to melancholy, to "passion's vague unrest," the sweet pain which they had experienced in the pages of Rousseau. It was the poet who, by the mouth of the blind bard, addressed the following pathetic apostrophe to the sun:

O thou that rollest above, round as the shield of my fathers! Whence are thy beams, O sun! thy everlasting light? Thou comest forth in thy awful beauty; the stars hide themselves in the sky; the moon, cold and pale, sinks

---

[1] Cuchullin was seated by the wall of Tura, "by the tree of the rustling sound." Voltaire gives a parody of these lines.

[2] Creuzé de Lesser.

in the western wave; but thou thyself movest alone. . . . But to Ossian thou lookest in vain, for he beholds thy beams no more; whether thy yellow hair flows on the eastern clouds, or thou tremblest at the gates of the west. But thou art perhaps like me, for a season; thy years will have an end. Thou shalt sleep in thy clouds, careless of the voice of the morning. Exult then, O sun, in the strength of thy youth! age is dark and unlovely; it is like the glimmering light of the moon when it shines through broken clouds, and the mist is on the hills. . . .[1]

It is in fragments such as this, full of deeply impressive yet hidden poetry, that the real Ossian is to be found, the poet of whom Chateaubriand could write that he had "added to the melody of the Muses a note until his time unheard."[2]   It was this poet whom the readers of Letourneur appreciated and understood.   "Why can I not dwell among the snow-clad mountains which hem the happy sons of Scotland round; while my dreams, as I watch the seas which bathe Norwegian coasts, are lulled by the sound of the wind beneath a lowering sky, and the dweller among those rugged rocks recites, it may be within my hearing, the mournful hymns which Ossian erstwhile sang upon the self-same shores." Such was the impression produced by the French Macpherson upon one of his earliest readers, Fontanes, then quite a young man, who, addressing the translator of Ossian with ill-restrained emotion, adds: "O Le Tourneur! whose bold prose ventured almost to imitate the inimitable melody of daring verse, more than once have you revealed treasures unknown to the poets of our day."[3]

These lines are of no great merit; but the feeling they expressed was sincere, and Fontanes composed his *Chant du Barde* after the manner of Ossian, in order, as he wrote to Joubert from London, to try his hand at reproducing "that sweet, slow music which seems to come from the distant shore of the sea, and to linger echoing among the tombs."

Thus, even in the eighteenth century, Frenchmen discerned the originality of one who was to be among the teachers of Chateaubriand and Lamartine. They divined his subtle poetry,

[1] *Carthon. Poems*, p. 190.   [2] Preface to *Poèmes traduits du gallique.*
[3] *Œuvres*, 1839, vol. i., p. 398.

if they did not succeed in making it fully their own. They delighted to read him, like Mme. de Genlis, seated on a green bank "shaded by a pair of poplars," "a wild yet melancholy scene before them," and an Æolian harp within hearing.[1] Like Fontanes they attempted to reproduce the music of his strange flights of melody. With La Harpe they praised that "sort of melancholy imaginativeness," which calls up before the reader "a remote and dismal region where the mountain-mists, the monotonous sound of the sea, and the soughing of the wind among the crags, inspire the mind with a contemplative sadness which becomes habitual."[2] Before the Revolution, thanks to Ossian, "the poetry of the North" counted its adherents in France: "sorrowful as their ever cloud-wreathed skies, turgid as the sea that whitens their shores, dense and dismal as the curtain of mist wrapped thickly round them in their gloomy isle,"[3] the northern poets seemed destined to renew the exhausted literature of France. They were not imitated as yet, or if they were, they were imitated badly.[4] But a time was at hand when a Chateaubriand was to make all that was best in their genius his own, and when, an exile in Macpherson's own land, he was to prepare himself for the composition of *René* by translating the poems of Ossian.[5]

Ossian's fame lasted from 1789 down to the imperial epoch. Arnault borrowed the subject of a tragedy from him ;[6] Labaume and David de Saint-George produced a continuation of Letour-

---

[1] *Mémoires*, vol. iii., p. 353. [2] *Cours de littérature*, vol. iii., pp. 214-217.

[3] André Chénier, *Elégie XXI*.

[4] See *Athos et Dermide*, the matter for which is derived from a note by Macpherson. (*Journal encyclopédique*, 1st June 1786); *Essai d'une traduction d'Ossian en vers français*, by Lombard (Berlin, 1789, 8vo), etc.

[5] "When, in 1793, the Revolution drove me to England, I was a devoted adherent of the Scottish bard: lance in rest I would have maintained his existence in the face of the whole world, and against that of old Homer himself. I read with avidity a host of poems unknown in France. . . . In the fervour of my zeal and admiration, ill, too, and extremely busy as I was, I translated certain Ossianic pieces by John Smith." (Preface to *Translations from the Gaelic*.) These pieces are *Dargo*, and *Duthona and Gaul*, and are included in Chateaubriand's works; they are imitations rather than translations.

[6] *Oscar, fils d'Ossian*, 1796.

neur.[1] The story goes that under the Directory those who
lived in the Bois de Boulogne were one day alarmed to see a
great blaze amongst the trees, and that when they came close to
it they perceived some men, attired in Scandinavian fashion,
endeavouring to set fire to a pine and singing to the accompaniment of a guitar with an air of inspiration : they were admirers
of Ossian who intended to sleep in the open air and to set the
trees alight in order to keep themselves warm, like the heroes of
Caledonia.[2] Under the Consulate Ossian enjoyed a far greater
vogue, even, than before ; the first consul had made him " his
own poet," thereby enlisting the sympathies of Mme. de Staël ;
he read him on board the vessel which brought him back from
Egypt, as at a later period he read him on his voyage to St
Helena.[3] " How beautiful it is," he said to Arnault. It has
been said that he imposed the Ossianic stamp upon the art of his
time. It would be more just to say that having been brought
up in the literary traditions of the eighteenth century, he shared
the veneration of his contemporaries for the Caledonian bard.
It was under the Consulate, and at his suggestion, that Baour
Lormian composed his *Poésies galliques*, that Girodet painted his
picture of Fingal and Ossian welcoming the shades of the French
warriors, and that Lesueur wrote his opera *Les Bardes*, which
Napoleon proclaimed a " brilliant, heroic and truly Ossianic "
piece.[4]

When, after the Revolution, Mme. de Staël and Chateaubriand
attempted to lay down the rules of a new theory of poetry, both

---

[1] *Poèmes d'Ossian et de quelques autres bardes*, intended as a sequel to Letourneur's
Ossian, and translated from the English by Hill (pseudon.), Paris, 1795, 3 vols.
18mo.

[2] G. Renard, *De l'influence de l'antiquité classique sur la littérature française pendant les
dernières années du xviiiᵉ siècle et les premières années du xixᵉ.* Lausanne, 1875, 8vo.

[3] See the *Journal de la traversée d'Angleterre à Sainte-Hélène*, by an English officer,
published in the *Journal des Débats*.

[4] The *Poésies galliques* belong to 1801. Girodet's picture was exhibited at the
Salon of 1802. Lesueur's opera was played in 1804. See also *Catheluina*, or the
Rival Friends, a poem written in imitation of Ossian (by General Despinay),
Paris, 1801, 8vo ; *Traductions et imitations de quelques poésies d'Ossian*, an old Celtic
poet, by Charles Arbaud Jouques, Paris, 1801, 8vo ; *Traduction libre, en vers, des
chants de Selma*, from Ossian, etc., by J. Taillasson, Paris, 1801, 8vo, etc.

accepted Ossian as a precious legacy from the century which had just come to a close. Through them he became appreciated by the youthful band of writers that was destined shortly afterwards to form the romantic "Pleiad": "Ah, plaintive harp, once, as the faithful comrade of Ossian, wont to sing of love and heroes! No longer shalt thou hang in mournful silence on these walls."[1]

These lines are by Alphonse de Lamartine, and were written in 1808. All his life Lamartine remained faithful to the object of his youthful admiration, and even in the *Confidences* he placed Ossian on a level with Dante and above Homer.

> The harp of Morven is the emblem of my soul.

Many indeed were the imaginations whose dreams were haunted by Ossian, between 1800 and 1830! Edgar Quinet, as a youth, in the depths of his native province, was amazed at an infatuation he did not share, and remarked with curiosity the unrivalled popularity of Fingal, Malvina, and Carril.[2] Distributions of prizes, Villemain says, resounded with the names of the Caledonian heroes, Oscar and Temora, and it is possible that Bernadotte owed the throne of Sweden to the Ossianic forename borne by his son.[3] Nodier, like everyone else, became fascinated with Macpherson's prose, and George Sand consoled herself for the sorrows of her married life by reading *Fingal*.[4] "Four moss-covered stones"—Chateaubriand had written in his *Génie du Christianisme*—"stand amid the Caledonian heather to mark the tomb of the warriors of Fingal; Oscar and Malvina have departed, but nothing has changed in their lonely land. Still the Scottish Highlander loves to recite the songs of his ancestors: still he is brave, generous, and obliging; but the hand of the bard himself, if the image be allowed, no longer strikes the harp; what we hear is the tremulous vibration of the strings produced by the touch of a spirit,

---

[1] Letter to Mme. de Virieu, 1808. [2] *Histoire de mes idées*, p. 132.

[3] See Brunetière, *L'évolution de la poésie lyrique*, vol. i., p. 82.

[4] Nodier, *Essais d'un jeune barde* (1804). G. Sand, *Histoire de ma vie*, vol. iv., chap. i.

when, at night, in a deserted hall, it forebodes the death of a hero."[1] Many and many are the readers who, from the close of the eighteenth century down to the appearance of the romantic generation, have heard this murmur from the strings of Ossian's harp.

IV

Yet such readers heard it and, above all, appreciated it, mainly because Rousseau had written.   Just as there was an occasional coincidence between Thomson's or Gessner's manner of feeling and portraying nature, and Rousseau's, so it was mainly because Jean-Jacques had led the way that Young, Ossian, and even *Werther*—which made its somewhat unsuccessful appearance in France about the same time[2]—found it so easy to obtain a hold over the minds of Frenchmen.   They may indeed be, in the history of European literature, his precnrsors; that, in fact, is what they are.   But in the history of French literature, they are merely his successors.   He owes nothing to them, nor they to him.

What, however, admits of no doubt, is that their melancholy is but a form of his melancholy, their lyricism a variety, or a development of his lyricism.   "But behold, alas, the inconceivable swiftness of that fate which is never at rest.   It is constantly pursuing, time flies hastily, the opportunity is irretrievable, and your beauty, even your beauty, is circumscribed by very narrow limits of existence: it must some time or other decay and wither away like a flower that fades before it was gathered. . . . O fond, mistaken fair! you are laying

---

[1] *Génie du Christianisme*, pt. iv., ii. 5.

[2] On this subject, see Th. Süpfle (*Goethes literarischer Einfluss auf Frankreich*, in the *Goethe-Jahrbuch*, 1887, p. 208), and F. Gross, *Werther in Frankreich*, Leipzig, 1888.   Besides translations by Seckendorff and Aubry, there was a play by La Rivière, *Werther ou le Délire de l'Amour* (la Haye, 1778).   On the subject of Goethe's novel, the *Correspondance littéraire* (March 1778) says: "All that we have found in it is ordinary events set forth without art, unpolished manners, a *bourgeois* tone, and a heroine apparently utterly uneducated and absolutely provincial."

plans for a futurity at which you may never arrive, and
neglecting the present moments which can never be retrieved.
You are so anxious, and intent on that uncertain hereafter, that
you forget that in the meantime our hearts melt away like snow
before the sun."[1] If the writer of these lines followed Ossian
and Young in order of time, he preceded them in order of
genius, and for this reason may be regarded as the creator of
modern lyric poetry.

Nevertheless—and the fact is one which Frenchmen are too
apt to forget—the sentiments he expresses were also expressed
in foreign works, and through them were introduced into France
as soon as, or even earlier than, through the pages of Rousseau.
To the new art which he created, English literature furnished
ancestors, Germany disciples. What more inevitable than that
those who were weary of classical tradition and impatient to
escape from the leading strings by which they felt they had been
confined for ages, should turn with an ever more and more lively
curiosity to England, in their eyes the intellectual birthplace of
Rousseau, and to Germany which welcomed him—and English
writers as well—with such youthful enthusiasm? "Every
method of imitating the ancients," it was said, "has been exhausted. Let us therefore fathom these deep mines (of English
literature); let us separate the gold from the dross which conceals it; let us polish it and turn it to a useful purpose."[2] But
thus to imitate foreign models was to reject the heritage, hitherto
enjoyed exclusively by the French nation, bequeathed by Greece
and Rome. It was to break with all the traditions of French
classical literature. Rousseau himself, who owes so many ideas
to the ancients, is not indebted to them for a single one of his
artistic methods; rather is his art the very negation of theirs.
Thus, with the growth of foreign influence, whether English or
German, in France, the influence of Rousseau proportionately
increased, while that of antiquity, and even of the national
classics, was further and further undermined. "O Germany,"
wrote a French critic in 1768, "the days of our greatness have

---

[1] *Nouvelle Héloïse*, i. 26.
[2] Yart, *Idée de la poésie anglaise*, vol. i., preface.

departed, and thine are only in their dawn. Within thy breast dwells every quality that can raise one race above the others, and our conceited frivolity is compelled to do homage to thy mighty offspring ! "[1]

In the Germany of the eighteenth century we have the incarnation of what Mme. de Staël was to call the Ossianic literatures, of the "genius of the North," of everything that was novel, poetic and disturbing in Rousseau, in so far as he seems to personify the influence of the Germanic nations. "I can see," says Chateaubriand, "that in my early youth *Ossian*, *Werther*, the *Rêveries d'un promeneur solitaire*, and the *Études de la nature* must have become wedded with my own ideas."[2] He makes no distinction between them ; on the contrary he treats the genius of Rousseau, the genius of Ossian, and the genius of Goethe as one. So too Mme. de Staël, when writing off-hand, speaks of "Rousseau and the English," or of "Rousseau and the Teutonic ideal" ; the idea in her mind is always the same, whether she speaks of the Teutonic spirit as opposed to the Latin, or of the genius of the North as opposed to that of the South.

There is no doubt whatever that this substitution of the cosmopolitan and exotic spirit for the old-fashioned humanism which satisfied our fathers was a revolution of very great importance. To tell the truth, it only came to fulfilment during the present century, with Mme. de Staël and the romantic school. But we have seen that it was in preparation before '89. The five-and-twenty years which preceded the Revolution paved the way for the invasion of Europe by the literatures of the North. Can we wonder that Herder, blinded by prejudice, thought himself justified in writing : "French literature has had its day"?[3]

The only thing that had had its day, and that after three centuries of glory, was one particular form of the French spirit, one of the fairest it ever assumed, but in which, whatever may be said to the contrary, it neither exhausted itself nor revealed the whole of its limitations.

[1] Dorat, *Idée de la poésie allemande*, 1768, p. 133.
[2] *Essai sur la littérature anglaise.*   [3] *Lebensbilder.*

Chapter IV

"THERE exist, it seems to me, two entirely distinct literatures,
that which springs from the South and that which springs from
the North, one which finds its primal source in Homer, another
which had its origin in Ossian.   The Greeks, the Latins, the
Italians, the Spaniards, and the French of the age of Louis XIV.,
belong to that branch of literature which I shall call the literature
of the South.   The work of the English and the Germans, and
a few writings by Danes and Swedes, must be ranked as belonging to the literature of the North."[1]   In these lines Mme.
de Staël expressed with remarkable clearness the very principle
of cosmopolitanism in literature as she herself conceived it.   A
few years later she gave her idea still greater precision in the
following words : " On every occasion during our own times
when the French habit of strict conformity to rule has been
supplemented by a little fresh life and spirit from abroad, the

---

[1] *De la littérature*, i. 11.

French have been enthusiastic in their applause: Jean-Jacques Rousseau, Bernardin de Saint-Pierre, Chateaubriand, etc., are all, in one or other of their works, *though they may not be aware of it themselves*, members of the Germanic school." [1]

Thus the course of French literature has been successively directed, according to the period we consider, either towards antiquity or towards Germanic Europe, towards humanism or towards cosmopolitanism, and the most important agent in the transformation has been Rousseau. The eighteenth century had an obscure perception of Mme. de Staël's theory, but did not formulate it in a clear and definite manner. Previously to the publication, in 1800, of *De la Littérature*, cosmopolitanism had been rather an undefined aspiration than a theory properly so called. It took some time for Rousseau's influence, personified in Mme. de Staël, to develop its extreme results. It was long before the opposition between cosmopolitanism and humanism became as distinct as was to be desired.

I

The reason is, in the first place, that if the twenty years which preceded the Revolution witnessed an incipient renovation and broadening of taste, they witnessed also the dawn of a genuine classical reaction. With the spread of anglomania, the admirers of the great French writers felt the need for a sturdier defence of a cause which was ever more and more threatened. "When we had once tasted of the springs of English literature," says a critic, "a revolution quickly took place in our own: the Frenchman, who readily becomes an ardent partisan, no longer welcomed or valued anything that had not something of an English flavour about it. . . . Our genius deteriorated from its unnatural fusion with a genius foreign to its character." [2] It was against this perversion of the national genius that the classical party, headed by Voltaire,

---

[1] *De l'Allemagne*, ii. 1.   [2] Dorat, *Idée de la poésie allemande* (1768), p. 43.

rose in revolt. The cause was good; what a pity it was that it should have been so badly defended!

Herein, in truth, lay the danger of the cosmopolitan spirit. Briefly, the question at issue was, whether or not the French mind would remain faithful to the ideal of universality and humanity which for two or three hundred years had been the strength of French literature, and had been inherited by it from the literatures of antiquity. The ideal of the classical writers of France had been to portray man by means of all the most general and least accidental qualities of his nature—not indeed *in abstracto*, for that would have been to deprive him of all reality —but in so far, at anyrate, as he resembles that "ideal of humanity" which everyone bears within himself. "I acknowledge," said Voltaire in reference to Shakespeare, "that we ought not to condemn an artist who has understood the taste of his countrymen; but we may pity him for having pleased no other nation." From this principle Voltaire never departed, and therefore always obstinately refused to admit that the object of literary criticism is to make us admire what is most national in the genius of each people. In his youth he felt a curiosity with regard to the geniuses of the different nations, but simply because they struck him as singular. He could understand that one could write a comparative history of customs and laws; but he never fully recognised, though he sometimes advocated, the comparative and disinterested criticism of literatures; and therein he remained truly French and truly classical. "We have long taken upon ourselves to utter generalities for the edification of the universe. We are manufacturers of good rough furniture for general purposes and of the fashionable article as well." This neat phrase of Doudan's[1] is one which Voltaire might have acknowledged. He claimed the manufacture of "furniture for general purposes" as an honour to the French intellect.

He considered, also, with the pure classicists of his time, that everything had been said, and that form alone was renewed. "There is no more poetry to write," said Fontanes, speaking of Racine. All the books are written, thought the classical school.

[1] *Lettres*, vol. ii., p. 346.

"The imitation of the beauty of nature," wrote d'Alembert, "seems confined to certain limits which are reached in a generation or two at most ; *nothing is left for the succeeding generation to do but to imitate.*"[1] If this is the case, and if poetry is the art of enhancing an old theme with a fresh variation, those who come last are at a great disadvantage, and for us who have to follow the masters it is a high honour to succeed through beauty of form alone. Innovators, on the contrary, admit that in literature there are, as Sébastien Mercier said, "austral lands," where everything still remains to be discovered. They hold that the last has not yet been said concerning man. They believe that literary progress is limited only by the confines of the human intellect itself, and that these have not yet been determined. They extol Dante for his "stupidly extravagant flights of imagination,"[2] Milton for descriptions which "sicken every one whose taste is at all delicate,"[3] or Ossian, again, because he expresses bombastic platitudes in pompous verse. Voltaire, faithful to the tradition of the *grand siècle*, was honestly unable to comprehend. "What is it to me," he wrote to an Englishman, who had vaunted Shakespeare to him, "that a tragic author has genius, if none of his pieces can be played in all the countries of the world ? Cimabuë had genius as an artist, yet his pictures are of no value ; Lully had great talent for music, but his airs are never sung beyond the borders of France."[4] . . . And this is his final verdict, not only upon Shakespeare, but also upon Young, Ossian, Milton, Dante, Swift and Rabelais. The mark of genius is universality, and do we not find the Transylvanian, the Hungarian and the Courlander, uniting, as Voltaire observes, with the Spaniard, the Frenchman and the German, in admiration of Vergil and Horace ? These, the great masters, belong to every age. Dante belongs merely to the thirteenth century,

---

[1] *Discours préliminaire.*

[2] Voltaire to Bettinelli, March 1761 : "I think very highly of your courage in daring to say that Dante was a madman and his work monstrous. . . . Dante may find his way into the libraries of the curious, but he will never be read."

[3] See *Candide,* ch. xxv.

[4] Letter published by G. Bengesco, *Lettres et billets inédits de Voltaire* (1887), p. 12.

and Milton to the seventeenth; the one is but an Englishman, the other only an Italian.

Nor was Voltaire the only writer to lay himself open to the charge of narrowness. He is simply the mouthpiece of a tradition to which many intelligent people remained faithful. The "literature of the North" irritated them, because it was neither human nor artistic, qualities which are practically identical. For the art of writing is not what Sterne and Young would have it to be—the art of giving expression to "one's sensations and impressions," or of recording, as inspiration may dictate, the variations of a "temperament"; it consists in speaking to the understanding in a language that every educated man can understand: "what is accurately conceived is clearly expressed."

Now, the conceptions of Young and Sterne are inaccurate, and their expression of them is obscure; indeed, these writers can scarcely be said to think; they are content to feel, and to abandon themselves to the flow of trivial impressions. Rousseau, speaking of himself, said: "He is largely dependent on his senses."[1] So, in reality, are all these innovators, and they glory in being thus dependent. But if the art of writing consists in arranging correct ideas in a harmonious whole, how then can they be writers? Shakespeare, who knows nothing of orderly arrangement, is no writer, and Letourneur gives us nothing but an "abominable jargon." Hence the transcendent superiority of the great French poets. "In Shakespeare, genius and sublimity gleam forth like flashes of lightning during a long night, but Racine is always Racine." Whence comes this thought? From Voltaire? No; from Diderot.[2] Genius begins where art begins, and cannot get on without it. Such was the opinion of all who had been brought up on tradition, and in whose eyes the reverence for foreign models was responsible for "that anti-national taste, the ravages of which were only too obvious";[3] and some even of those who spoke of reforming everything could not succeed in shaking off the prejudices they had imbibed

---

[1] *Rousseau juge de Jean-Jacques*, second dialogue.   [2] Article entitled *Génie*.

[3] *Discours sur les progrès des lettres en France*, by Rigoley de Juvigny (Paris, 1773, 8vo, p. 190).

in the course of their education. Sufficiently clear-sighted to perceive that classical art is not the whole of art, they found it difficult to believe that in breaking away from it they were not lapsing into barbarism. This explains how Condorcet could write to Voltaire, in reference to Necker, that he had no hopes of a man who " took Shakespeare's tragedies for masterpieces," [1] and how it was that Marie-Joseph Chénier, one of the best critics of his time, asserted that the degree to which Shakespeare " carried passion and indecency was enough to put humanity to the blush." [2] We are amazed to find opinions like these enter-tained by anyone besides Voltaire. We can understand them, however, if we reflect that revolutions in taste are, with most men, changes in their manner of feeling rather than in their manner of judging. For many men in the eighteenth century the intellectual revolution had already taken place, while the revolution in feeling was yet to come.

Some, like Voltaire, remained absolutely faithful to the objects of their youthful admiration, refusing to associate with them other and fresh objects which could not be brought under their conception of beauty. Classical beauty, the object of their devotion, was compounded of art and of humanity. Now it is quite true that the cosmopolitans took credit to themselves for extending the boundaries of the intellect, and for widening the province of art. In reality, however, they restricted them by substituting for the antique ideal, which up to that time had been generally accepted by all nations, the imitation of what is most exclusively national, that is to say least communicable, in each one. " Though I am no great admirer of the human mind," wrote Vauvenargues in reference to Shakespeare, " I nevertheless cannot dishonour it so far as to place a genius so defective and *so defiant of common sense* in the first rank." [3] If each people and each race have their special modes of sensibility to which other nations are strangers, it can no more be possible to transfer incommunicable beauties from one country to another

---

[1] Sainte-Beuve, *Causeries*, vol. iii., p. 342.
[2] Fragments appended to his *Tableau de la littérature*.
[3] *Œuvres*, ed. Gilbert, p. 486.

without defying common sense than to make palm-trees grow in Norway or to rear reindeer under the equator. This was forcibly expressed by Rivarol in his famous treatise[1] on the universality of the French language, where, after granting that English works "will be the eternal glory of the human mind," he added that those works had nevertheless "not become the common possession of all the world." They have never left the hands of certain people ; "precaution and tentative effort are needful if one is not to be repelled by the husk of the fruit and its foreign flavour." In short, the Englishman makes a book "out of one or two sensations"; he is dull, taciturn, gloomy and solitary; he writes for himself alone, and it follows therefrom that English literature "suffers from the isolation of the people and of the writer." The Frenchman, on the other hand, "looks for the humorous side of things"; he is all elegance, wit, and subtlety, and has conquered the universe by means of a sociable disposition. Are the French wantonly to sacrifice a position of influence so laboriously attained in order to take lessons of a nation whose originality has gone so far as to obscure its own conception of humanity ?

The classical revolution witnessed by the close of the century was thus founded on two ideas and supported by two principles : respect for art and the tradition of humanism. And at bottom these two ideas are reducible to one,—the imperious necessity that the writer should win the ear of all men and not that of his countrymen only—should be read in all ages, and not by his contemporaries alone. So that for the first time in the history of French criticism the defenders of the national genius found, or supposed, themselves engaged in the defence of the genius common to humanity. For the question as to the pre-eminence of the ancients or the moderns had been discussed even in the seventeenth century. But the dispute had never gone beyond the frontiers in any country. For Italy of the Renaissance, the only rival to Greek or Latin antiquity was Italy, for France of the following century it was France; and the most resolute upholders of the idea of progress persistently

[1] 1784.

refused to take up any other position. Neither Perrault nor La Motte contrasted the sterility of the French intellect with the literary fertility of England or even of Italy. The controversy was between Vergil and Racan, Horace and Boileau, Euripides and Racine. It was a courteous debate in which the adversaries were agreed as to first principles, and only disputed as to the degree of success with which this or that writer had applied them. But even the most zealous of the " ancients " no more revolted against an alleged aberration of the national genius than the most resolute of the " moderns " appealed to exotic influence. Now, on the contrary, it was a question, in the mind of Voltaire, of rescuing not only the national tradition, but also the still more sacred tradition of humanity, from the sacrilegious hands of barbarians. " Imagine, gentlemen," he said to the Academy, " Louis XIV. in his gallery at Versailles, surrounded by his brilliant court : a Gilles in battered garments forces his way through the crowd of heroes, great men and beauties of whom it consists, and suggests that they shall forsake Corneille, Racine, and Molière for a mountebank who makes a few happy sallies and pulls wry faces. How do you suppose such a proposal would be received ? " [1]

The wry-faced mountebank was Shakespeare, but it might as well have been Richardson, Young, Sterne, Ossian, and everyone who owned no authority but " his own temperament," and pretended to substitute individual caprice for that worship of beauty which had been established in France by communion with antiquity, and had made the Latin genius the very type of human genius in general. For Voltaire, therefore, cosmopolitanism is individualism, which is as much as to say it is barbarism. " He is what nature has made him," wrote Jean-Jacques of himself.[2] Now nature, unassisted by the art which restrains and the reason which guides it, can do nothing. Abandoned to itself it is mere disorder and caprice; it can only make occasional " happy sallies "; it produces nothing but monstrosities, such as *Hamlet* or *Tristram Shandy*.

[1] First letter to the Academy on Shakespeare.
[2] *Rousseau juge de Jean-Jacques* (second dialogue).

But when he assumes the post of defender of the national genius Voltaire does not see as clearly as we do that cosmopolitanism may after all be nothing but a new form of humanism. For him it is no bond between nations, but rather merely an element of discord and of mischief. He seems to have no suspicion that when Rousseau, whom he detests, appeals to what is most individual in man, he may be simply giving expression to sentiments common to the whole of a new generation that is more disposed to find its own feelings reflected in him and in foreign writers than in the classical poets of France. Voltaire does not argue, he has recourse to abuse: "The abomination of desolation is in the temple of the Lord"; the French are the prey of "savages" and "monsters," and, when Letourneur translates Shakespeare, are going to be "devoured by Hottentots."[1] Observe that by making Shakespeare the object of his attack he obtains an advantage: of all the writers introduced to the French public during the eighteenth century Shakespeare was the least understood because he was the most English and the most original. Accordingly he makes Shakespeare the point of his attack upon all the anglomaniacs. He is anxious for a combat in the lists, a tournament. "Either Shakespeare or Racine must be left dead upon the ground!" We must cry, "Long live Saint-Denis Voltaire and death to George Shakespeare!"[2] A strange method, truly, of stating the problem!

Unfortunately for Voltaire he proves but a poor advocate of a cause which deserved to be well defended. He fights "like an old hussar against an army of freebooters," blindly, and with any weapon that comes to hand. Was it not he who, before the assembled Academy, appealed, on behalf of Racine, "to our princesses, to the daughters of so many heroes who know how heroes should speak";[3] and, imploring the duc de Richelieu's protection against Shakespeare, summoned up the spirit of the great cardinal "who did not like the English?"[4] Methods like these savour of burlesque. Public opinion daily

[1] Letter of 24th July 1776. [2] D'Alembert to Voltaire, 20th April 1776.
[3] First letter. [4] 11th September 1776.

became more clearly conscious of the weakness of such criticism ; it felt the inanity, the pompousness, and the utter want of exact information and accurate knowledge such criticism betrayed; it had an impression that in attacking Shakespeare Voltaire was attacking a rival of his own fame as a tragedian ;[1] and even those who were the most disturbed at the prevalence of anglomania regretted that it should be met with such weapons as those he employed.

The classical reaction, whether it fell foul of Shakespeare or of Ossian or of Rousseau, was thus more violent than really effective. Voltaire speaks of English authors without having studied them closely. La Harpe, his most eminent disciple, who supposed himself destined to administer a rebuff to the " stage-playing barbarian," criticizes *Othello* without knowing a word of English,[2] but, as Grimm says, " wit makes up for everything." It was La Harpe, again, who declared that certain "madmen" wanted " to bring Bedlam and Tyburn upon the French stage, and to erect the huts of savages round the colonnade of the Louvre."[3] " Whatever Shakespeare has copied out of Plutarch," wrote Marie-Joseph Chénier, " is well enough, but I cannot admire what he has added himself."[4] How indeed was it possible to argue with prejudice so inveterate, or with ignorance so gross, as this ? The influence of Voltaire, who was now old and embittered, was in this case disastrous. Like every other champion of the same cause he needed a little more information upon the subject of which he treated. *Vir est*, said Johnson, *acerrimi ingenii et paucarum litterarum.* As foreign literatures became more widely known, and as Rousseau inspired the French mind with a more perfect sense of the diversity of epochs

---

[1] At the meeting of the Academy of 25th August 1776, when d'Alembert had finished reading the famous letter against Shakespeare, he went up to Mrs. Montague and asked her whether she was annoyed by its contents. " Not in the least," she replied, " I am not one of M. de Voltaire's friends." " The union between England and France is an accomplished fact," wrote Grimm (*Correspondance littéraire*, July 1776). . . . " Such is our memory of old hatreds."

[2] Mme. de Genlis, *Mémoires*, vol. iii., p. 193.

[3] *De Shakespeare (Œuvres nouvelles*, 1788, vol. i).

[4] Letter to André Chénier, 17th February 1788.

and of races, the inadequacy of classical criticism became more irritating and almost more scandalous.

Nevertheless, during the years which preceded the Revolution, the ground was admirably prepared for a renaissance of the classical literature of France. Antiquity was restored to unexpected favour. The discovery of Herculaneum and Pompeii gave fresh life to the science of archæology. Historical as well as æsthetic criticism of carved monuments was founded by Winckelmann, in his *Histoire de l'art chez les anciens*.[1] Brunck published his *Analecta* in 1776, and Villoison his notes on Homer in 1788. Journeys in the East and in Greece were made by such travellers as Wood, Choiseul-Gouffier and Guys.[2] The abbé Barthélemy produced a condensed yet spirited statement of the results of classical scholarship in his delightful *Voyage d'Anacharsis*, published in 1788. In 1780 David initiated the school of painting to which we owe the *Serment des Horaces* and the *Enlèvement des Sabines*. A few enthusiasts talked of "denationalizing themselves and of becoming Greeks and Romans in soul."[3]

But the whole movement, which was of real importance, remained without influence upon the criticism of works of literature. Its effect was neither to extend the controversy nor to define the point at issue. Its consequences were mainly political, nor did it result in any renovation of the French genius, as this was understood by Voltaire. "Our public education," said Bernardin de Saint-Pierre, going back to his school-days, "alters the national character . . . .: men are made Christians by means of the catechism, pagans by the poetry of Vergil, Greeks and Romans by the study of Demosthenes and Cicero, but Frenchmen never."[4] In truth the very study of antiquity, as Winckelmann or Barthélemy understood it, was as yet nothing

---

[1] Twice translated into French before 1789; first of all at Amsterdam in 1766, and afterwards at Leipzig in 1781.

[2] Guys, *Voyage littéraire de la Grèce* (1776). Choiseul-Gouffier, *Voyage pittoresque en Grèce* (1782).

[3] The phrase is quoted by Chamfort. On the movement as a whole see the interesting study by M. G. Renard, quoted above.

[4] *Œuvres posthumes*, p. 447.

more than a means of getting away from one's own country and one's own environment. Left to its own strength and to the impetus it had acquired, the classical influence produced Delille's *Géorgiques*, or the *Éloge de Marc Aurèle* of Thomas; no very brilliant result. Refreshed by archæology and by the breath of individual inspiration, it was the source of Chénier's most beautiful lines.

Chénier alone, during the last twenty years of the century, is a true disciple of the ancients: " A devout worshipper of the great ones of old, I would bury myself in the sacred relics they have left." He alone triumphantly contrasts the faultless beauty with the disturbing charm of Ossian or of Shakespeare: " Seek the tempting banquets provided by this bright train of Greeks; but avoid the sodden intoxication of the treacherous and stormy waters of Parnassus with which the harsh singers of the misty North assuage their thirst."[1] He alone, having read and, during his residence in London,[2] translated portions of Milton, Thomson, and Shakespeare,[3] and having spoken of Richardson in the manner we have mentioned, boldly proclaims the superiority of ancient art: " Too proud to be slaves, English poets have even cast off the fetters of common sense."

But antiquity, as Chénier conceived it, was no longer the antiquity which France of the seventeenth century had loved and understood, and one feels some concern as to what Voltaire would have said of it. On the other hand Chénier was entirely without influence during the eighteenth century, since no one

---

[1] Ed. Becq de Fouquières, *Poésies diverses*, xi.

[2] Chénier seems to have been depressed by his residence in London as though it were an exile. He found England, as Alfieri told him, " more bitter than absinthe " (Becq de Fonquières, *Doc. nouv.*, p. 21). Writing from London in 1787, he said: " Bereft of parents, friends and countrymen, forgotten on the face of the earth and far from all my relatives, cast up by the waves upon this inhospitable island, I find the sweet name of France frequently on my lips. Alone, by the ashes of my fire, I lament my fate, I count the moments, I long for death." On the other hand his brother writes to him (7th February 1788): " You are enjoying yourself in London ; I thought you would. . . ."

[3] In addition to the imitations of Thomson quoted above, Chénier translated a fragment from Shakespeare. His admiration for the piece provoked his brother's condemnation.

read his poetry. It neither stimulated criticism nor furnished it with a text.

More effectually than was possible through the agency of any books, the controversy was cut short by the Revolution.

II

The primary effect of the Revolution was to restore the worship of antiquity to a degree not far short of superstition.

The innovators had at first looked to it for the regeneration of art. In a curious letter to the authors of the *Journal encyclopédique*,[1] Daunou anticipated Mme. de Staël in giving expression to the idea that "the monotony of a despotic form of government" confines poetic genius to a narrow circle of ideas, adding that "the Revolution now about to regenerate the French empire may infuse genius with new vigour, render talent more fruitful, ennoble the subjects of art, extend its methods, multiply its forms and revive not poetry only but also eloquence and history." This hope was disappointed, at all events at the outset; far from renewing poetic art, the Revolution led it back to classical or pseudo-classical sources, to an art the very antithesis of that of Rousseau, whose political theories it rated so highly while it failed to recognize his literary genius.

The Revolution marked at first a step backwards in the progress of cosmopolitanism, because it occasioned a rupture, lasting from 1789 to 1814, with the rest of Europe, and with the Germanic section of it in particular. Within the course of a few months France found herself as isolated—to employ the metaphor used by a historian—as an island in mid-ocean. How was it possible, during these troublous years, to maintain literary relations with England or with Germany? Great Britain was spoken of as a "guilty island, haughty Carthage."[2] In 1792, when the Institute had received a scientific memorandum from a

---

[1] 15th March 1790. On the classical reaction in France see M. L. Bertrand's book : *La fin du classicisme et le retour à l'antique* (Paris, 1897, 16mo).

[2] In an opera entitled *La Reprise de Toulon*.

German, Roland, who was minister of the home department at the time, added the following brief, but expressive, marginal note : " We cannot look to Germany for any light on such subjects as this." [1] Under the Empire matters were still worse. We know what Mme. de Staël's praises of Germany brought upon her, and Napoleon made no secret of his contempt for " German nonsense, the admirers of which are constantly disparaging French literature, French newspapers and the French drama, for the sake of magnifying the absurd and dangerous productions of Germany and the North at the expense of our own." [2]

Sundered, therefore, by political circumstances, the threads which had been stretched from the continent to the North and *vice versâ* remained broken for twenty years and more. Several prominent revolutionists remained, it is true, faithful to the objects of their youthful admiration : Robespierre read Gessner and Young; Camille Desmoulins Hervey and the author of *Night Thoughts*; Mme. Roland Thomson, and Collot d'Herbois Shakespeare, whose *Merry Wives of Windsor* he had formerly imitated.[3] There were translations and adaptations of various German writers : Lessing, Goethe, Wieland, Klopstock [4] and the writer whom the *Moniteur* called " Monsieur Scheller," " a strong advocate of the republic against the monarchy, a true Girondist," of whose plays several met with considerable success upon the French stage.[5] We may go so far as to say that a

[1] J. Simon, *Une académie sous le Directoire*, p. 213.

[2] Esménard's report, in Welschinger : *La Censure sous le premier Empire*, p. 249.

[3] *L'amant loup-garou ou M. Rodomont* (1777).

[4] Lessing's *Dramaturgie* was translated in 1795, *Laocoon* in 1802 ; *Nathan der Weise* provided M.-J. Chénier with the inspiration for a drama. Werther was imitated several times (*Stellino cu le nouveau Werther*, 1791, etc.). *Stella*, translated by *Du Buisson*, was played at Louvois in 1791 ; Wilhelm Meister was translated by Sévelinges in 1802, under the title of *Alfred*.

[5] 12th February 1792. *The Robbers* was adapted by La Martelière [Schwindenhammer, the Alsatian] in 1793 and by Creuzé in 1795 ; in 1799 A. de Lezay translated *Don Carlos*, and in the same year La Martelière published his *Théâtre de Schiller* (Paris, year viii.); in 1802 Mercier brought out his *Jeanne d'Arc*, an imitation of Schiller. See Dr Richter's work, *Schiller und seine Räuber in der französischen Revolution*, Grünberg, 1865, 8vo, and Th. Süpfle's book already quoted.

certain limited public took a lively interest in German literature, and William de Humboldt wrote from Paris in 1800 that "people here have German names on their lips more than ever."[1]

But it must be added that the public in general remained indifferent to these foreign productions, and that those even who claimed to be connoisseurs spoke of writers from beyond the Rhine upon hearsay only. "Frenchmen think they are very well informed concerning our literature," writes the same witness; "they suppose themselves thoroughly familiar with it and very fond of it. . . . But you only need to hear them talk a little to know what to think of their knowledge of it and their fondness for it. . . . The French are still too different from us to be capable of understanding us in respect to those points upon which we too are beginning to be a little original." The influence of the intellect of Germany upon that of France acquired substance with the publication of *De l'Allemagne* in 1812. With regard to English literature, the novelists, Richardson, Sterne, Miss Burney and even Anne Radcliffe still found an audience, and even playwrights who adapted their works for the stage,[2] nor were the reputations of Young and Ossian on the wane.[3] Shakespeare himself supplied the French stage with the subject of a drama almost every year.[4] Are we to conclude therefrom that these writers were more highly appreciated and better understood? A glance at François de Neufchâteau's *Paméla*, or at the *Jean sans Terre* of Ducis, will suffice to convince us that the contrary was the case.

In short, the literature of the Revolution, like its criticism, was pseudo-classical, that is to say inferior. The men of the period, who had antiquity always upon their lips, knew in truth but little

---

[1] Lady Blennerhasset, *Mme. de Staël*, vol. ii., p. 560.

[2] *Paméla*, by F. de Neufchâteau (1793). *Clarisse Harlowe*, by Népomucène Lemercier (1792).

[3] Young's *Nuits*, translated into French verse by Letourneur, Paris, 1792, 4 vols. 12mo.

[4] *Jean sans terre*, by Ducis (1791); *Othello*, by the same (1792); *Epicharis et Néron*, by Legouvé (after *Richard III*.) (1793); *Timon d'Athènes*, by Sébastien Mercier (1794); *Imogènes*, by Dejaure (after *Cymbeline*) (1796), etc.

about it. How could they find the leisure and the means to acquire a knowledge of the ancient languages? Was it not Lakanal who complained before the Convention that lads spent all their time "in jabbering Greek and Latin"? Was it not the revolutionary government that gave science and modern languages the preference over the classics in its syllabus of instruction,[1] and proposed to substitute schools of arts and handicrafts for the Sorbonne and the *collèges*? The educational work of the Convention was, it is true, of much importance, but who would venture to maintain that it did anything to promote the knowledge of ancient literature? Whatever admiration the democrats of the period may have felt for Socrates, Scaevola, Brutus or Cato of Utica, there are reasons for doubting whether they had read much of Plutarch or Tacitus. "My friends," said Camille Desmoulins, "since you read Cicero, I will answer for you; you will be free"; but how many of the Revolutionists were readers of Cicero?

Nevertheless, considered from a merely superficial point of view, the literature of the revolutionary epoch does draw its inspiration from the antique. Just as the art of David, Letronne and Lemercier derives its subjects from antiquity, so the poetry of Delille and Lebrun-Pindare is cast in traditional moulds. "It did not require much effort," says Charles Nodier, "to pass from our schoolroom studies to the pleadings in the forum and the Servile Wars. We were already convinced admirers of the institutions of Lycurgus and of those who played the tyrannicide at the Panathenaic festival."[2] The *Contrat Social* not only begot constitutions; it inspired tragedies and odes.

But greatly as the influence of Rousseau's political theories increased, it might almost be said that to the same extent the influence of his genius as novelist and poet waned. Of his subtle and tender comprehension of the heart, of his deep and sincere feeling for nature, of his "enchanting sadness," of all the qualities, in fine, which make him a poet of the highest order, little enough is to be found in the second-rate works the indiscriminate

[1] See Condorcet's report to the Legislative Assembly.
[2] Jeanroy-Félix, *La littérature française sous la Révolution*, p. 349.

aggregate of which constitutes the literature of the revolutionary period—practically nothing, indeed, save an insipid and faithless copy, not unlike the grimace of a mimic. Mme. de Staël, at the close of the century, complained that the public had forgotten "the writer who more than any one else had infused language with warmth, vigour and life," and ought to be "the friend, the beguiler, the leader of all!"[1] He was no longer read, and, though some affected to quote him, was no longer understood. Ten or twelve unfruitful years were to pass, and Chateaubriand would simply need to resume the poetic traditions of Rousseau, and to find anew, in the author of the *Contrat Social*, the poet whom the public had forgotten to seek in him.

And just as the purely literary influence of Rousseau decreased almost, in fact, to the vanishing point, so a comprehension of the foreign works which Rousseau had rendered popular became more and more rare. The superstitious veneration for a little understood antiquity shut off every approach to that English literature which, but a few years earlier, had raised so many hopes. Mythology rose again from its own ashes, and ancient Olympus dethroned the gods of the North. "Long life to Homer and to his Elysium, to his Olympus and his heroes, and to his muse, on whom the god of Claros smiles! Apollo keep us all, my friends, from Fingals and from Oscars, and from the lofty sorrows of a bard who sings amid an atmosphere of fog!"[2] The majority of the public agreed with Lebrun-Pindare, and allowed themselves to fall once more beneath the bondage of a tradition which the genius of Jean-Jacques had nevertheless impaired. Very few were those who said with the still youthful Béranger: "Neither the Latins nor even the Greeks should be taken as models. They are torches, which one must learn how to

---

[1] *De la littérature*, 2nd preface.

[2] The poem continues, "His rivers have lost their urns; his lakes are the prison of the dead, and their silent naiads stand like spectres on their gloomy shores. In his heaven, as in his verses, Hebe and her ambrosia are alike unknown; his vague and dismal poetry is daughter to the rocks and to the seas." (Lebrun: *Ode sur Homère et Ossian*, in book vii. of the *Odes*.)

use."[1] Under the Revolution antiquity was rather mimicked than imitated sympathetically, and this is why such imitation remained unfruitful.

When order was restored, and criticism attempted to explain the course which literature had followed, it was quite natural that men like Geoffroy, Dussault, and Fiévée should join the broken links in the chain of tradition. In 1800 or thereabouts there was, as Sainte-Beuve says, a sort of " solemn restoration " of classical criticism ; in the *Débats*, under Dussault and Geoffroy ; in the *Mercure*, under Fontanes, Bonald, Guéneau de Mussy ; and at the Lycée, in La Harpe's lectures on literature. It was just at this time that proposals were made to re-establish the old French Academy, that Delille, the " French Vergil," was recalled from London, and that the classical spirit awoke once more to a measure of its old vigour and brilliancy. The time had come for putting some check upon such as would again attempt to lay hands upon the sacred ark : " It is almost certain," wrote Fontanes, " that those who are incapable of passionate admiration for masterpieces which have been the wonder of every age ; who would abate the enthusiasm they inspire, and would compare with them to their disadvantage *some of the barbarous productions which are generally condemned by men of taste,* have not received from nature that sensibility of the organs, and that accuracy of judgment, without which it is impossible to speak well concerning the fine arts."[2] It seemed that in the face of Europe in arms France felt, as it were, the need of meditation, and of returning yet once more to the great masters who had obtained for her a time-honoured supremacy in the intellectual sphere.

Thus, to look no further than the borders of France, the Revolution marks a temporary cessation of the development of cosmopolitanism in France. But neither Bonaparte nor any of his coadjutors had the least suspicion that to those who, instead of studying its consequences at home, followed its results beyond the French frontier, the Revolution was shortly to appear in an entirely different light.

The effect of the emigration in driving from France some

[1] *Ma biographie.* [2] *Œuvres*, vol. ii. p. 183.

thousands of the most enlightened members of the community was in reality very similar to that produced by the revocation of the Edict of Nantes. In spite of political hostilities, it had promoted the formation of new bonds between France and Europe. For many minds it had been a painful but often fruitful introduction to a knowledge of the interests of other nations.

In the solitude of exile, during the long years of expatriation, the *émigrés*, such as Chateaubriand, Narbonne, Gérando and even Fontanes, could not but learn and retain something of the manners, the art and the literature of neighbouring countries. A history of the literature of the *émigrés* has been written by a foreign critic.[1] There is room also for a history of the influence which the emigration exerted upon French literature, for, diffused and fragmentary as this influence was, it was also extremely fruitful. Many indeed were those of whom it might be said, as it was said of Mme. de Staël by Lamartine, that "they made English and German thought their refuge,"[2] and yielded to the attractions "of the only nations whose life was at that time sustained by moral ideas, by poetry and by philosophy."

They sought shelter chiefly in Germany, England and the Low Countries. They certainly had no literary prepossessions when they arrived, and they abused their exile as Fontanes abused Hamburg, when he requested to be transported to Corfu, rather than remain in Germany. But necessity compelled them to learn the language of the country, and to observe the manners of its inhabitants, so that a very natural curiosity, begotten of enforced leisure, soon brought them into contact with foreigners who were able to open new horizons before them. Narbonne, de Gérando and Camille Jordan settled at Tübingen, and issued translations or studies, the first of them of Schiller's *Wallenstein*, the second of the German philosophers, and the third of Klopstock. Mounier became the manager of a boarding-school at Weimar and formed an intimacy

---

[1] M. G. Brandes, *Die Emigranten-Literatur*. See Joseph Texte, *Les origines de l'influence allemande dans la littérature française du xixe siècle* (*Revue d'histoire littéraire de la France*, January 1898).

[2] *Des Destinées de la poésie.*

with Wieland, while at Hamburg Rivarol, Sénac de Meilhan, Chênedollé, Esménard and Delille witnessed the performance of German and English plays in the theatres of the town where Lessing had written his *Dramaturgie*. Intimate relations were formed between the *émigrés* and several of the great German writers : de Serre, the marquis de la Tresne and Chênedollé conceived a warm admiration for Klopstock, sought his acquaintance, and learnt through him to appreciate the poetry of the North. Of northern literature, at that time little known in France, and still counting its most famous representatives among the living, they formed a lofty opinion. "It is when I read men like Goethe, Schiller, Klopstock and Byron," wrote Chênedollé, "that I feel how small and insignificant I am. I declare with all the sincerity of which I am capable, and with the deepest conviction, that I have not a tenth part of the thinking power, talent and poetic genius of Goethe."[1] Many others too there were, who confessed that light as was the esteem in which she was held, Germany was the storehouse of unknown and precious treasures.

In England were to be found not only Montlosier, Lally-Tollendal and Cazalès, but also Rivarol, de Jaucourt, Delille, Fontanes and Chateaubriand.[2] Some of them, it is true, like Saint-Évremond at an earlier date, persisted in maintaining their French habits of life, and in holding aloof from the English. "I don't like a country," said the incorrigible Rivarol, "where there are more apothecaries than bakers, and where sour apples are the only ripe fruit to be got."[3] But others resigned themselves to their exile and even profited by it. Chateaubriand, who spent eight years away from France, delighted to remind himself of all that he owed to his prolonged intercourse with foreigners[4] : in his long conversations with Fontanes, on the banks of the Thames at Chelsea, they used to talk of Milton—whom he translated—of Shakespeare and of Ossian. He prides himself upon having, in the course of his exile, learnt "as much of

[1] In Sainte-Beuve, *Chateaubriand et son groupe :* the article on Chênedollé. On the *émigrés* in Germany see Lady Blennerhasset, *Mme. de Staël et son temps*, and *Rivarol et la société française*, by de Lescure.
[2] See de Lescure, *ibid.*, book iii., and *Mémoires d'Outre-Tombe*, ed. Biré, vol. ii.
[3] De Lescure, p. 414.   [4] *Essai sur la littérature anglaise :* preface.

z

English as any man can learn of a foreign language," and it was during these fruitful years that he translated the Ossianic poems, which he acknowledges had inspired him with a strange liking, and were more than once in his mind when he wrote *René* and the *Martyrs*. Then, too, it was that he collected the materials for his *Essai sur la littérature anglaise*. Then it was, above all, that he acquired that varied and sympathetic comprehension of the genius of each of the different peoples of Europe, which ranks him, with Mme. de Staël, as the greatest critic of the early years of this century.

Examples might be multiplied to show that the result of the Revolution, as of all great historical movements, such as the crusades or the revocation of the Edict of Nantes, was the mixture of races and the crossing of intellectual strains. But for the Revolution there could never have been a career like that of Chamisso, who, the offspring of natives of Champagne, became, in consequence of the emigration, page to the Queen of Prussia, then, after his return to France, a master in a French *lycée*, next, during a second residence in Prussia, the occupant of a post at the botanical gardens in Berlin, and finally, after his death, one of those classics of German literature whom the French schoolboy has to construe at college. Nor, but for the Revolution, which led to his banishment, would Charles de Villers, a French officer, have settled at Göttingen and Lubeck, become acquainted with Goethe, Jacobi, Klopstock and Schelling, or have made German his second mother-tongue and Germany his intellectual fatherland.[1] Sufficient notice has perhaps scarcely been taken of the fact that the Revolution marks the appearance of such cosmopolitans in literature as Benjamin Constant, Bonstetten, Sismondi and Mme. de Staël, all of them imbued no less with the Germanic than with the Latin spirit, and all, through the agency of Rousseau, heirs to the literary criticism of those who were refugees in the early part of the eighteenth century.

[1] See the curious essay by Charles de Villers : *Idées sur la destination des hommes de lettres sortis de France et qui séjournent en Allemagne.* (In *le Spectateur du Nord*, 1798, vol. vii.)

If any doubt were felt as to whether this was really one of
the results of the revolutionary period, one would but need to
turn the leaves of one of the Reviews which were established
under the Directory with the co-operation either of the refugees
or of foreigners, such as the *Bibliothèque britannique*, the *Journal de
littérature étrangère*, the *Décade philosophique*, the *Magasin encyclopédique*, or better still the · *Spectateur du Nord* or the *Archives
littéraires de l'Europe*. Of the two last-mentioned journals the
former, which was started at Hamburg by an émigré de
Baudus, and counted as its contributors Chênedollé, the abbé
Louis, Delille, Rivarol, and Charles de Villers, was designed to
propagate German literature and philosophy [1] in France, and was
for that reason suppressed in 1798 ; the other, with a staff consisting of Schweighäuser, de Villers, Morellet, Vanderbourg,
and Quatremère de Quincy, published in its first issue an article
by de Gérando on "literary and philosophical intercourse between the nations of Europe," [2] in which the author endeavoured
to prove that, rightly interpreted, patriotism authorizes and even
justifies literary intercourse between one people and another, and
that those who manage to borrow in season thereby prove themselves rich.

It is therefore permissible to say of the French spirit that
it migrated during the revolutionary period ; that unconsciously,
and, above all, unintentionally, it became broader and less im-
pervious to external influences through contact with the rest of
Europe, and that through this intercourse between races and
individuals it acquired a thirst for new forms of knowledge.

III

There is a book, not so much the first of the nineteenth as the
last of the eighteenth century, which not only summarizes these

[1] The *Spectateur du Nord*, a journal of politics, literature, and morals, Hamburg,
January 1797-December 1802, 2 vols. 8vo. (See Süpfle, vol. ii., p. 93, and
Hatin, *Histoire de la presse*, vol. vii., p. 576.)

[2] *Archives littéraires de l'Europe*, a literary, historical and philosophical miscellany, by an association of literary men. Tübingen and Paris, 1794-1808, 51
numbers, 8vo.

acquisitions, but at the same time marks a revival, in criticism, of the influence of Rousseau and of the northern literatures. Published in 1800, the book entitled *De la Littérature considérée dans ses rapports avec les institutions sociales* closes one epoch in the history of criticism and opens another. It is the first properly thought out, though as yet imperfect, expression of cosmopolitanism in all the dignity of a theory. It is an unquestionable indication that the movement which has been the object of this study had come to a head.

No one was more plainly indicated than Mme. de Staël for the delicate task of determining the two great classes of mind which, according to her, were henceforth to divide European literature between them. The most faithful of all Rousseau's disciples, she may without hesitation be said to have completed and crowned the work of which he laid the foundation. In truth Mme. de Staël's criticism is nothing more than a statement of Rousseau's theories with regard to poetry and beauty, selected from his works by the most brilliant of commentators.

She, like him, was of Genevan origin, a Protestant, born on the confines of two races and where two distinct types of genius met. With her, as with him, this was a source of pride, and at times also of sadness. "Heavens!" she wrote one day to a foreign friend, Frederika Brün, "if only there were but a few sparks from your hearth in this country of mine, this land of my mother tongue, what would I not make of myself! I know I have faculties which are capable of more than I have accomplished; but *to be born French with a foreign character*, with French tastes and habits, and the thoughts and feelings of the North, is a contrast which ruins one's life." [1] Everyone who came near her was struck with this contrast: "To me," wrote Humboldt to Goethe, "as to you, it has always seemed that the French atmosphere into which she was thrown during her education was too narrow for her. . . . It is a strange phenomenon, the fact that we sometimes find in a nation intelligences animated by a foreign spirit." [2] To this fruitful antithesis Rousseau owed at once his greatness and his misfortune. Like him Mme. de Staël

---

[1] 15th July 1806 (Lady Blennerhasset, vol. iii., p. 223).
[2] 18th October 1800 (*ibid.*, vol. iii., p. 11).

may be described, in a happily expressed formula, as " a European mind in a French soul." [1]

The extent to which she was indebted to Rousseau, and the manner in which she had dedicated to him one of her earliest and most interesting works, are sufficiently well known. It was not with her, as with many of her compatriots, admiration only, or a mere passing infatuation, that attached her to Jean-Jacques. It was that in him she found again her own innermost aspirations, whether religious, political or literary ; or rather that in him she came to a consciousness of herself. In his school she had been trained ; she had grown up in the habit of respect for his name ; and to his influence she remained faithful throughout her life, even in error.

Very early too she had felt herself drawn towards the countries of the North. In Mme. Necker's *salon* she had been brought into close and frequent contact with the most determined anglomaniacs of the age, such as Grimm, Raynal, Diderot and Suard. Her father, like a true Genevan, had directed her early attention to the English constitution as a pattern for all nations. Her mother had been careful to make her learn English, and she took to Milton, Thomson, Ossian and Young as naturally as though they had been old favourites, as well as to Richardson, her reading of whom had marked an epoch in her early life, and whose manner she had endeavoured to imitate in one of her first attempts. [2]

Like everyone else during the eighteenth century, she felt, even in 1800, but little curiosity with regard to Germany, and the fact is worthy of remark. She had not yet met Charles de Villers, who introduced her to German literature, nor Wilhelm Schlegel, her principal teacher next to Rousseau. It is difficult to-day to imagine Mme. de Staël unacquainted with and indifferent to German concerns. She was so, nevertheless, when she wrote her book *De la Littérature*. The whole of the chapter it devotes to Germany is irresolute and vague. She praises, though not very accurately, Wieland, Schiller, Gessner, and " the one book above all others which the Germans possess," namely Werther. In reality she merely retailed the opinions of Chênedollé, who was

---

[1] E. Faguet, *Politiques et moralistes*.   [2] *Pauline*, a novel.

on his way back from Hamburg, and happening to be thrown into her society just at the time when she was writing her book—during the winter of 1798—endeavoured to inspire her with a little of his own enthusiasm. But she did not know German, and replied to Goethe, who had sent her his *Williamsmeister* (sic), that she was no judge of the value of his gift : " As it was in German," she writes to Meister, "I could do no more than admire the binding."[1] In 1797, the same Meister wrote from Zürich asking her to come and see Wieland. She answered with vivacity : " Go to Zürich for the sake of a German author ? You will never find me doing that. . . . I think I know everything that is said in German, and even everything that will be said in that tongue for the next fifty years." It was not until afterwards that she learnt the language and studied the people at close quarters. In 1800, Humboldt reproached her because the phrase of father Bouhours : "Can intellectual refinement exist in a German ?" was too often on her lips, and because in speaking of his country she displayed a want both of " philosophy and erudition."[2]

With England, on the contrary, she was familiar. Her acquaintance with it dated almost from her birth, for she had grown up in a circle which was enamoured of all things English. She had spent several months there in 1793, and had become intimate with Miss Burney, one of the most prominent writers of the period.[3] She had read all that an intelligent man of the eighteenth century would be likely to know of English writers, and on more than one point she shared that century's prejudices. In a disquisition, somewhat wanting in knowledge and discernment, upon " the bards of the fourth century," she simply follows Mallet ; she considers that Spenser is " the most tedious stuff in the world " ; she believes, on the authority of Voltaire, who never

---

[1] Lady Blennerhasset, vol. ii., pp. 564-565.
[2] 30th May 1800, in a letter to Goethe on the subject of *De la Littérature*.
[3] Mme. de Staël's second residence in England took place in 1813 and 1814. On that occasion she became acquainted with Byron, Rogers, Sheridan, Coleridge, Godwin, Kemble, and others. It was during this visit that she conceived the idea of doing for England what she had done for Germany, but only the political portion of the contemplated book was written, and this was inserted in the *Considérations sur la Révolution française*.

departed from his erroneous opinion, that "blank verse presents very few difficulties"; above all, like everyone else in the eighteenth century, she innocently supposes Ossian, who was a Celt, to be a Saxon and the father of Germanic poetry.

Failings like these, however, may be set down to the age in which she lived. The philosophers, on the other hand, Bacon, Hobbes, Locke, Hume, and even Ferguson, whose utilitarianism "has given, if I may use the expression, so much substance to the literature of the English," received adequate treatment at her hands. She read the political writers, including Bolingbroke and Junius, the moralists, like Addison, and, among dramatists, Shakespeare, Congreve and Sheridan. Like all her contemporaries she did not greatly care for the humorists, and remembered nothing of them except the philosophy of Swift, whom she admired, it seems, partly upon hearsay. But Shakespeare, Ossian, Milton and the novelists, the very writers that were most closely akin to Rousseau, were the objects of her especial admiration. They were the typical specimens she had in mind when she contrasted the English with the French spirit, the North with the South, a literature founded upon the social instincts with one based upon reverence for the individual as a moral being.

But while she drew attention to this contrast, it must be admitted that as yet she failed to shake off certain of the prejudices of eighteenth century criticism.

In the first place she belongs to her century by her inability to comprehend antiquity, the spirit of which escaped her. Her acquaintance with it was in truth no better than that of Voltaire or d'Alembert. She admired its great characters upon trust, but her reading of ancient writers was very limited.

For her the unpardonable fault of the ancients is that their literature is essentially masculine. It is masculine because it knows nothing of the power of love : "Racine, Voltaire, Pope, Rousseau, Goethe, etc., have portrayed love with a kind of delicacy, reverence, melancholy and devotion" which the ancients never knew. Their literature is neither tender, pensive, sorrowful nor despairing ; it is uninfluenced by intercourse with women. It is masculine because it is calm and undisturbed ; because in the work of the Greeks there is neither the horror of death, the anguish of despair, nor the despondency caused by the irreparable. But the only great poetry is the poetry of sadness. Theirs is masculine because it refuses to recognize the existence of pain : the Greeks bear up under misfortune and stand erect beneath whatever blows may fall to their lot. With them it is a part of their primitive conception of decency not to admit their suffering. They look with distrust upon the representation of "secret passions"; they are not lyrical in the least.

It is they who have restricted literature to the study of man as a social being, and have observed society "just as one describes the growth of plants." Thereby they have cut themselves off from the principal province of art, which is the representation, inspired by lofty moral sentiment, of our most intimate affections. The Greek race was "non-moral": "they neither blamed nor approved : they simply transmitted moral truths in the same way as physical facts." They are said to be profound; but who could compare Thucydides with David Hume? What they wanted, if they were to inspire emotion, was the mighty power of sensibility : "The human race had not yet reached the age of melancholy." Hence it follows that the Greeks, being neither sensitive nor sad, "left few regrets behind them."

We see, therefore, the narrowness of Mme de Staël's ideal. She judges Euripides, Thucydides and Homer by the ideals of Richardson and Rousseau. Small wonder that she failed to understand them.

In common with her age and with her master, Rousseau, she preferred the Romans. They were better known, and "the sublime Montesquieu" had made it fashionable to admire them. She loved their republican dignity. She praises them because they had " more of true sensibility than the Greeks had, because they attributed more importance to woman, because they gave expression, however discreetly, to a certain "vague tenderness not unmixed with philosophy," which had found utterance in the works of Tibullus, Propertius and Vergil. She considers them more truly poetical and also more philosophical.

Taken as a whole, however, the literature of antiquity has one incurable defect; it portrays man, not as an individual, but as a social being. It is political, satirical, epic, but never lyrical. Now, Mme. de Staël's models are "*Tancrède, La Nouvelle Héloïse, Werther,* and the English poets." To put it in more general terms, she is for the North as against the South: she prefers Thomson, she says, to Petrarch, and is more affected by Gray than by Anacreon. The reason why "almost all the French poets of the age," from Rousseau, its typical example, downwards, have imitated the English, is that they are lyrical and passionate.

But let us understand what we mean. Poetry is not simply the art of speaking of oneself with emotion. The emotion must also be moral: "it is only the most subtle moral teaching that can produce the lasting beauties of literature," and, by consequence, "literary criticism is very often a treatise upon ethics." This is Rousseau pure and simple; but here is something more characteristic of him still. Poetry, eloquence, reverie "should act upon the organs"; virtue must be an involuntary impulse, an intellectual "movement passing over into the blood," the virtue-passion dear to Rousseau. Lastly—and this is the third and most important condition—the literature of a nation should be sober; for "human nature is serious." The Northerner, in contrast to the Greek, the Roman and the Frenchman, likes only "those writings which appeal to the reason or move the feelings," by preference the latter. At all costs we must avoid what Dante called "the inferno of insensibility."

If, therefore, we consider modern literature "in its relations to virtue, glory, liberty and happiness," we shall "detect two different ways of judging, which to-day form, as it were, two distinct schools"—those who stand by the Southern literatures, and those who stand by the literature of the North. This is the central and, at the same time, the most definite idea in the book. Mme. de Staël had no intention of writing a treatise on the poet's art; on that point she is content to accept current opinion, and refers us back to Voltaire, Marmontel and La Harpe, whom she has read and does not as yet repudiate. But to inspire literature with the idea of progress, nay, even, by setting up fresh models as rivals to those of antiquity, to give definite shape to the confused aspirations which had been agitating men's minds for a century, was indeed a fruitful achievement. It was a resumption of the long-standing quarrel between the ancients and the moderns upon broader grounds than heretofore, and with Rousseau's example, and others from various modern literatures, in the shape of evidence. The *Journal des Débats*, criticizing Mme. de Staël's work, maintained "that men have always been the same, that nothing in their nature is capable of change, and that rules for present guidance are only to be found in the lessons of the past."[1] A very precise statement of the opposite thesis to that maintained in *De la Littérature*.

The weak point in Mme. de Stael's book is her attempt to explain the historical origins of the movement she is defending. She reminds the reader how the invasion of the barbarians, which was one of the most fertile events in the history of the world, resulted in the crossing of races and the fusion of intellects; how Christianity came to be "the connecting link between the peoples of the North and those of the South"; how from the whole era of the middle ages the modern Christian world emerged as from a sort of crucible; how the North remained more faithful to woman, to melancholy, to "a truly sympathetic moral philosophy," and the South to the artistic sentiment, to the love of sensuous pleasure, and to the worship of form.[2]

In this part of her work, full of ideas as it is, there is a good deal of confusion. In what manner, by the operation of what laws, and under the influence of what circumstances, did this separation of Europe into two intellectual groups become accentuated? How are we to account for the supposed fact, above all how are we to prove, that antiquity had lost its

---

[1] See 11 and 14 messidor, year viii.

[2] It may be remarked, in this connexion, that Mme. de Staël is extremely ill-informed as regards the literature of the South. She knows nothing of Spain and very little of Italy. She believes that "there is nothing remarkable in Italy beyond what comes from France." The fine lectures of her friend Sismondi upon *Littératures du Midi de l'Europe* were not delivered until 1804; and she did not herself cross the Alps before 1806. See M. Dejob's book: *Mme. de Staël et l'Italie* (1890).

power over the Teutonic nations ? If there is so much difference
between France and certain other nations, how is it that she has
exercised so deep and lasting an influence upon them? This
Mme. de Staël does not explain, or at any rate does not explain
correctly. In virtue of her general opinions upon history she
remains a child of the eighteenth century, and of the epoch of the
Encyclopédie. She borrows freely, even in the form of expression,
from d'Alembert.[1] Like him, she holds that the history of the
human mind during the interval between Pliny and Bacon,
between Epictetus and Montaigne, "between Plutarch and
Machiavelli" presents no features of interest ; thereby frankly
contradicting herself. Like him, she fearlessly asserts that
"from the time of Vergil down to the institution of the Catholic
mysteries, the human mind, in the sphere of art, has been simply
receding towards the most preposterous barbarism."[2] Lastly,
she actually affirms, by a still more strange contradiction,
that since imitation is the essence of the fine arts, "all that
the moderns do, or ever can do, is to repeat the work of the
ancients "[3]—a proposition which entirely destroys her thesis.

We see, therefore, how deeply *De la Littérature* was rooted in the
century which had just reached its close. Evidently the author
was writing at the point where two epochs met. She dreams of
a new art, but like Rousseau himself cannot make up her mind
to break with the art of the classical era. Having proclaimed
that taste is merely observation of nature—which is characteristic
of Jean-Jacques—she comes round to the statement that good
taste is absolute—which is the opinion of d'Alembert. She holds,
with Voltaire, that Shakespeare is too English, and that this
greatly detracts from his glory[4] ; and again, with Ducis, that
one must be on one's guard against the incoherencies of the
English and German writers of tragedy. In short, she seeks a
compromise, and declares that "talent consists in importing into

---

[1] See especially book I., chaps. viii. and ix.; compare d'Alembert, *Discours
préliminaire*, ed. Picavet, p. 81, *et seq.*

[2] Gibbon somewhere points out, as one of the most striking evidences of the
decrease of the influence of antiquity during the eighteenth century, the easy way
in which d'Alembert treats Justus Lipsius and Casaubon as mere pedants.

[3] I., viii.   [4] I., xii.

our literature all that is beautiful, sublime and touching in the melancholy aspect of nature portrayed by the writers of the North, without, at the same time, ceasing to respect the true laws of taste."

But these contradictions and hesitations notwithstanding, the book in other passages gives clear expression to what the eighteenth century had but dimly perceived. Had Mme. de Staël entertained any doubts upon the point, the tone of official criticism would have been enough to convince her that she had attained her object, seeing that she was reproached with taking no account of "the experience of the ages," and with "wandering off into idle theories."[1]

"The experience of the ages," she was told, proves that the French mind keeps to its natural path only when it follows the footsteps of the Latins and the Greeks. Her answer was: It is true that all modern literature is founded upon the ancients: the English and Germans themselves owe them much. But it is none the less clear that, taken as a whole, northern, that is to say Germanic and Protestant, literature — and to this literature Rousseau belongs—has new and original beauties of its own, which have nothing in common with those of classical works, whether Greek, Latin, or French.

In the first place, the philosophical spirit, by which, if pressed a little, she is found to mean the capacity for the life of meditation, coupled with a sense of the solemnity of existence. In this sense the Frenchman is rarely a philosopher; he sees "the humorous side of things," and sees it readily. Ossian, on the contrary, is a philosopher.—He scarcely ever reasons ?—What of that ? He "disturbs the imagination" in a manner which predisposes it to the most serious meditations.—But in this sense Homer is a philosopher too ?—Yes, but he is not melancholy, or is so merely by way of exception. It is only the "northern imagination" that can find a pleasure on the sea-shore, in the sound of the winds, upon the desolate heath; it alone can pierce the clouds which skirt the horizon and seem to typify "the dim passage from life to eternity." All that

[1] *Journal des Débats, ibid.*

Rousseau, Young and Ossian had known of the poet's sadness she feels keenly and expresses with power. Three years later, and *Atala* and then *René* were to justify her vague previsions. Mme. de Staël, the interpreter of those aspirations of her age which had been kindled and quickened by the Revolution, in this respect anticipated Chateaubriand.

If Ossian and Shakespeare are melancholy, they owe it also to their climate, which encourages meditation rather than activity; to their passionate temperament—for like Rousseau Mme. de Staël thinks the passions are fiercer in the North than in the South—and to their sensibility to the beauties of nature, which implies a restless soul. To their other characteristics must be added a certain spiritual elevation, an aloofness from life, due to the rugged nature of their country; the passion for heroism, enthusiasm tempered by deliberation, unreserved exaltation in the presence of the sublime; lastly, the strong emotional capacities of the northern writer, reverence for woman, and that indefinable romantic thrill in virtue of which Goethe, and even Thomson or Pope, must always appeal directly to the heart of man as Petrarch can never do. But herein what does Mme. de Staël add to the aspirations of the eighteenth century ? All she does is to state them in definite form.

On one point only did she go beyond them, as Rousseau had done. She declared that the superiority of the " Ossianic " literatures had its source in Protestantism.

Rousseau, as we have seen, had gloried in being a Protestant, and in the most eloquent manner had proved or attempted to prove that no Christianity is consistent with the spirit of Christ but that which recognizes the moral consciousness as the only court of appeal. Religious individualism was the mainstay of his philosophical teaching, and the nutriment of his eloquence. He congratulated himself even at the close of his life on having continued faithful to the " prejudices " of his childhood, and on having " remained a Christian "[1] in the midst of a Catholic environment. Thus by merely generalizing an idea of Rousseau's Mme. de Staël came to represent Protestantism as the chief cause

[1] *Rêveries d'un promeneur solitaire*, iii.

of the greatness of northern writers. The thesis had already been propounded by the refugees, and Charles de Villers, Bonstetten, Sismondi and Benjamin Constant successively devoted their attention to its demonstration.[1] For them, as for their friend Mme. de Staël, the Reformation was " of all the epochs of history the one which most effectually promoted the perfectibility of the human species."

The idea was not in all respects a new one, even in literary criticism. Montesquieu had already observed that the North is Protestant because " in the northern nations there is and always will be a spirit of independence which the peoples of the South do not possess," and he was not afraid to add " that religion gives an infinite advantage " to the former.[2] But he established no connexion between religion and art. He simply commended Protestantism because it had made the nations more prosperous; of its moral influence he said nothing, and even considered that Catholics are " the more invincibly attached to their religion." Generally speaking, no intimate connexion was shown during the eighteenth century to exist between the literature and the beliefs of the English. With regard to the latter, Frenchmen were content to accept Voltaire's pleasantries concerning the Quakers. They did not perceive how the Reformation had infused the English mind with a calm and dignified gravity, with intense and imperious conviction, though at the same time with narrowness and false pride. Similarly, the Protestantism which was so prominent an element in Rousseau's character earned him no gratitude in the *salons* of Paris; in the eyes of his French admirers it was merely one peculiarity the more; indeed there were not a few who thought it a blemish. To an Englishman who once called upon him, Diderot explained that the only fault of the British nation was that they had " mixed up theology with their philosophy," adding " *il faut sabrer la théologie*—we must put

---

[1] Charles de Villers: *Essai sur l'esprit et l'influence de la réformation de Luther* (1803). This book was crowned by the Institute, passed through four editions in one year, and was thrice translated into German, twice into English, and once into Italian.—*Cf.* Bonstetten, *L'homme du Midi et l'homme du Nord;* Sismondi, *Histoire des littératures du midi de l'Europe;* Benjamin Constant, *De la religion.*

[2] *Esprit des Lois,* xxiv. 5, and xxv. 2; *Lettres persanes,* cxviii.

theology to the sword."[1] Protestantism was simply so much more theology to be put to the sword. The refugee critics alone had attempted to show how English literature had originated in the Reformation. But they had convinced no one except themselves. So that when Mme. de Staël adopted the same thesis she introduced into literary criticism a new element of the highest importance. Hitherto it had been customary to compare nations with one another in respect of their laws, their manners, and their theories of philosophy and art. The difference between their religions had not indeed escaped notice, but no one had detected in it the most important source of the other differences, and one which might possibly give rise to them all. If it is not exactly true that the religion is the race, at anyrate no definition of a race is conceivable without a definition of its religion.

As it happens, Mme. de Staël is guilty of exaggeration. She chooses to invest even the poems of Ossian with a tinge of Protestantism and to say that the poetry of the North does not imply nearly so much superstition as Greek mythology,—a very doubtful proposition. Is it likely that "in the maxims and fables of the Edda" there is, as she maintains, something more philosophical than in the myths of the southern religions, and that the religious ideas of the North are almost all "consistent with the loftiest reason?" It is odd, too, to find her, under the influence of her distrust of Catholicism, reducing the miraculous to what she vaguely calls the "philosopher's predilection for the marvellous," and committing herself to the statement that Dante "lacks intelligence."

On the other hand, it is scarcely too much to say that it was that part of her criticism which dealt with religion that revealed to Mme. de Staël, and through her to her fellow-countrymen, the majority of the great writers of the North, Shakespeare for example.

The eighteenth century could not tell what to make of the witches in *Macbeth*, of the dialogue between the gravediggers in *Hamlet*, and of the soliloquies of the Danish prince: this "predi-

[1] Memoirs of Sir Samuel Romilly, quoted by J. Morley, *Diderot*, vol. ii. p. 247.

lection for the marvellous" in a tragic dramatist seemed odd and at times scarcely sane. In reality the age failed to appreciate the resulting effect of grandeur. It regarded the introduction of the marvellous as a mere piece of stage-craft, like that employed by Voltaire when he brings the shade of Ninus upon the stage. Shakespeare's philosophy went unsuspected, as did the reason why he was the great painter of death and pity. This Mme. de Staël explained for the first time, and explained it remarkably well. She understood not Shakespeare's mind only, but also his soul. She knows how it is that he makes us feel "the awful shudder of horror which comes over a man when in the full vigour of life he learns that death is at hand; how it is that he can excite our pity for an insignificant and sometimes contemptible creature;" why, in short, he has put his own pity, his own terror, his own conception of life and death into his plays, instead of the tragic dramatist's conventional platitudes concerning man. He felt that the wretched tragi-comedies of our interests and passions required a background of mystery and grandeur. He is aware that at certain moments it is the fate of human reason— which the classical literature of France represents as so self-confident—to founder when it attempts to fathom this mystery. And he understands that "man owes his greatest achievements to his painful sense of the incompleteness of his destiny."

Nowhere had the French drama given expression to this bitter and painful feeling; where, in the plays of Racine and Corneille, are we to look for their philosophy? What did they think of those great problems which bring such anguish to lofty souls? There is nothing to tell us. There was then in France, there still is, a sort of divorce between religion and secular literature. A modesty, deserving of all respect, restrained the poet, the novelist and the dramatist from putting their own innermost selves into their work. Thereby French literature lost, as, by the admission of M. Jules Lemaître, it loses even to-day, "something of moral depth." With this characteristic of "depth" Rousseau had aspired to invest it. He had been the first to break this silence and to venture upon giving prominence to the religious question in a work of fiction. He had been the first

Frenchman to follow the English in mingling the sacred with the profane and in boldly employing a distinctly secular work as the vehicle of earnest convictions. Thus in following Rousseau over the same ground Mme. de Staël merely consolidated and justified in the sphere of criticism a revolution which had already been accomplished in that of imaginative literature.

But by so doing she did but place one gulf the more between the "French and Catholic" spirit, and the "Teutonic and Protestant" spirit. She introduced an entirely fresh element, afterwards, as every one knows, turned to account by Taine, into the definitions of Southerner and Northerner respectively. She gave a more rigorous statement of the problem of race, upon which cosmopolitanism depends. She made her readers keenly sensible of a fact which the Protestant books of Ibsen and George Eliot have since given us occasion to repeat, that to a large extent "the differences between literatures are bound up with the profound differences between peoples."

Conclusion

I

To give precision to an idea is to render it fruitful.

De la Littérature, the book we have been discussing, gave form
to the aspirations of the eighteenth century; it was the logical
outcome of the work undertaken and continued, from the close
of the seventeenth century onwards, by the refugees, by Prévost, by Voltaire and by Diderot; from the books of Rousseau
and the English it extracted, not perhaps such a theory of
poetry as might have been written by Rousseau, but at any
rate that of which his books contained the germ. Through
Mme. de Staël, and because she identified the influence of
Jean-Jacques with the influence of the northern literatures,
the " genius of the North " became, in a manner, conscious
of itself. It became a power in literary criticism, and
from the standpoint of classical tradition a danger. More
or less explicitly it assumed an attitude of opposition to the
ancient tradition of France. It definitely took its place in the
concert of European powers, never again to surrender it. But
a few years, and Lamartine, on submitting his earliest poems,
entitled *Méditations*, to Didot the publisher, received the characteristic reply : " Give up novelties like these, *which would
denationalise the French genius.*" [1]   Again a few years and the
romantic school, in the name of " the literature of the North ",
made war upon the " French genius"; one of its members, in the
heat of battle, going so far as to exclaim : " The English and the
Germans for ever ! Give me nature in all its fierceness and

[1] See *Raphaël.*

370

brutality ! " [1] And Stendhal was found to say with a sort of fierce joy : " Spite of all the pedants, Germany and England will win the day against France ; Shakespeare, Schiller and Lord Byron will prevail over Racine and Boileau." [2]

To-day there is no longer any doubt that Stendhal was wrong, that neither Lord Byron nor Schiller have caused or will cause Racine to be forgotten, and that romanticism was in no sense a defeat of the French by the German intellect. There is even something puerile in the very idea. If it were true, France would have given up reading French books from 1823 down to the present time, and like Germany during the early years of the eighteenth century would have handed itself over, bound hand and foot, to foreign influences. What period of French literary history has been more fruitful than that which extends from 1820 to 1848? What writers have been more truly and entirely national than Hugo, Vigny and Michelet ? What literature has exerted greater influence, or shone with more lustre in Europe during the past fifty years, than the French ?—On these points facts speak so plainly that they require no commentary. " The true strength of a country "—wrote Mme. de Staël, indiscreetly enough—" lies in the character natural to it, and the imitation of foreign nations, in any respect whatever, implies a lack of patriotism." I am not so sure of this ; I really do not think that Corneille was wanting in patriotism because he borrowed *le Cid* from Spanish sources, or Molière because he took *l'Étourdi* from the Italians, or Racine because he went to the Greek authors—who also, after all, are " foreigners "—for the subjects of his tragedies. Imitation is not abdication, and it would be the easiest of tasks to show that Lamartine is none the less Lamartine because he imitated Byron, and Musset none the less Musset because his comedies are inspired by Shakespeare. At no period in its history—not even, nay, least of all, in the middle ages—has the literature of France been shut up within itself. " The literature that confines itself within its own frontiers," writes M. Gaston Paris, " especially at a period so stirring and so fruitful as our own, thereby

[1] L. Thiessé, *Mercure du xixe siècle*, 1826 (quoted by Dorison, *Alfred de Vigny*).
[2] *Racine et Shakespeare*, p. 246.

condemns itself to a stunted and withered existence." French romanticism avoided this narrow-minded course. By calling to mind what it owes to neighbouring literatures we do not diminish its originality. No one, in fact, disputes that the great writers who followed Rousseau and Mme. de Staël are "French" writers in the full sense of the word. If they were not, it would not be worth while to investigate the origins of the revolution they have accomplished, nor would it take us long to learn all that there is to know about the spirit by which they were animated.

But it is because they are strongly individual, full of life, and, when all is said and done, highly original, that it is, to say the least, imprudent to claim for them a function they did not fulfil, that of inauguration. Just as of old the literatures of antiquity, working like a leaven within the French mind, occasioned the rise of the classical literature of France, so the "literatures of the North," during the last century and the present one, have caused the germination of the great harvest of romanticism. To employ the apt phrase of Arvède Barine, they imparted to the French race a powerful intellectual shock, the vibrations of which have since "lost themselves in that vortex of forces whose resultant is the French genius." And this in two ways; firstly and principally through Rousseau, who not only supplemented that genius by a turn of mind, an imagination, and a sensibility which were already of a northern cast, but also, as Mme. de Staël expressed it, infused it with "foreign vigour"; and, in the second place, through the English works which, during the present century, have been followed by those of the Germans and the Russians, and have exerted a profound influence, not altogether distinct from that of Rousseau himself, upon the whole of the romantic generation. If romanticism was in reality "a rebellion against the spirit of a race which had become latinized to the core"— the phrase is M. Brunetière's,—it was truly Rousseau who raised the standard of revolt. Benjamin Constant, said Sainte-Beuve, is "of the lineage of Rousseau, with a tinge of Germanic blood in his veins." Most of the French romantic school are of the same extraction as Benjamin Constant.

Mme. de Staël said precisely the same, and we must congratulate her thereon.

But even had we to leave this problem of the foreign sources of romanticism unsolved, we should none the less be justified in closely following the fortunes of the " cosmopolitan " idea during our own century. A question that blocks our way is not to be set aside as unimportant or obscure by a mere stroke of the pen. The mere fact that this question has occupied the minds of several generations of men, including certain writers of genius, gives it a right of citizenship in the history of ideas. Attempts were formerly made to convict Macpherson of skilful imposture. But the poems of Ossian, whether authentic or not, remain a monument in the literary history of Europe, and nothing can alter the fact that Chateaubriand ranked Ossian higher than Homer.— Similarly, it is impossible for the most sceptical of critics, the most incredulous with regard to "the French spirit" and "the Germanic genius," to change the fact that this entity—"northern literature"—has exercised a most powerful influence over the men of our own epoch. Doubtless it will be open to him to dispute the strength of the historical scaffolding with which Mme. de Staël supported her theory; he will be free to scoff at her misty and mythical Ossian, and to deny the Caledonia of the poets; he may spare himself the trouble of following the author of *De la Littérature* and her critic, Fontanes, in their inquiry " whether the progress of the arts is from the North to the South, or from the South to the North." If, lastly, he calls in the assistance of ethnography, he may adduce proofs against Taine that his theory of the European races is false, that there is neither a purely " Latin " nor a purely " Germanic " group of peoples, and that the English nation contains many other elements than that which consists of a cross between Norman and Saxon.[1] We may even admit, should he insist upon the point, that none of the European races has a genius peculiar to itself. Will the historian be, on this account, any the less bound to recount the vicissitudes of the " cosmopolitan spirit in literature " during the nineteenth century?

[1] *Cf.* Angellier, *Robert Burns*, Introduction, and the first volume of M. J. Jusserand's fine work, *Histoire littéraire du peuple anglais*.

There can be no doubt as to the reply. The triumph of Rousseau's influence marked also the triumph of cosmopolitanism. Romanticism endeavoured to counteract the classical influence by the example of non-Latin Europe. In *De l'Allemagne* Mme. de Staël resumed the thesis of *De la Littérature*, enlarging its application, and supporting it by fresh arguments. In France, after Ossian and Shakespeare, we had Byron and Walter Scott; after Goethe and Schiller, the whole series of German romanticists, succeeded by the romanticists of the North—and we admired them all, possibly without much discrimination or discretion, but with a sincerity that admits of no reasonable doubt. "*The true romantic poetry*," wrote Stendhal, "*is, I repeat, the poetry of Shakespeare, Schiller, and Lord Byron.* The mortal combat is between Racine's methods of tragedy and Shakespeare's. The opposed armies are the French men of letters, led by M. Dussault, on the one hand, and the *Edinburgh Review* on the other."[1] The cosmopolitan spirit has become so closely interwoven with the fabric of the literary history of this period, that by attempting to separate it therefrom we should run the risk of rending the fabric itself.

It will be observed that it is nothing to the point to dispute, as is so often done, the fact of a certain form of influence being exercised by this or that foreign writer upon this or that French author. What does Lamartine, it may be asked, owe to Goethe? or Musset to Schiller? And was not Victor Hugo ignorant of the simplest elements of the German language? Undoubtedly. But will anyone deny that the appetite for foreign, and especially for northern, works was one of the essential factors of the romantic revolution? And who can help seeing that "the genius of the North" gained all the ground which the "genius of antiquity" had lost? Romanticism is the same thing as cosmopolitanism, not because, as has been innocently remarked, French writers have plagiarized from English or German poets, but because, through the instrumentality of Rousseau, they too had learnt to infuse themselves with some of that "foreign vigour" with which he had grafted the old national stock.

[1] *Racine et Shakespeare* (1823), p. 253.

Nisard, speaking of the Renaissance, says somewhere or other: "The French spirit, holding fast to the spirit of antiquity, is Dante led by Vergil, his gentle teacher, through the mysterious circles of the *Divine Comedy*." In two or three centuries' time, perhaps earlier, Jean-Jacques Rousseau will seem, as it were, to be the Dante of modern times, the writer who has opened before us the portals, not of the ancient world, but of that northern and Germanic section of Europe which has wielded so powerful a spell over the French genius during the present century.

It will be objected that the cosmopolitan spirit in literature did not rest content with being, as Sainte-Beuve expressed it, a "Germanic spirit," and nothing more; and that the curiosity of the romantic, as of the following, generation was extended to Spain, to Italy, to the East, and even to antiquity. And, indeed, the cosmopolitan spirit has endeavoured, during the present century, to justify its definition: it has aimed at embracing "the literature of the world." But I venture to assert that, in France, the influence of the North has always been at the bottom of the movement, just as it was its point of departure in Rousseau. The characteristic which the French mind has appreciated above all others in southern literatures is precisely that which reminded it of the literatures of the North, and it may be, as Doudan very shrewdly remarks, that what we love in the East and in the South is the attributes with which Northern imaginations have invested them. "We want blue spectacles in order to look at this sun. After all, we shall always understand Shakespeare better than Calderon." More exactly, we shall appreciate in Calderon what we love in Shakespeare, and in Alfieri, and Leopardi—as in Ibsen and Tolstoï—what they owe to Rousseau. And this because we are before all things of the literary posterity of Jean-Jacques, and because in him nineteenth century literature takes its rise.

II

Thus, at the close of the present century, the cosmopolitan spirit in regard to literature has become a feature of every thoughtful mind.

Is this a cause for lamentation? In particular, have we, as Frenchmen, any reason to tremble for the integrity of our country, regarded as an intellectual entity? Are we to look upon " exoticism " as nothing more than a solvent of the national genius?

Sismondi had already asserted that for a vigorous nation "there was no such thing as foreign literature." J. J. Weiss almost wished that there was no such thing for France when, referring in eloquent language to her classical authors, he said: " In them we have still a happy reserve, a storehouse—long the property of the nation, and always at our command—of positive wisdom, of practical good sense, of cogent moral philosophy, of applied political science, of heroic ideas and heroic sentiments. *It is there that France is to be found.*" [1] Many writers of superior intelligence have likewise feared " lest, in becoming European, our national genius should at length become less French." Many, like J. J. Weiss, have asked: " Where is France? "

That their fears are not altogether imaginary it would be childish to deny. Certainly France claims as her own alike Malherbe and Hugo, Voltaire and Chateaubriand, Molière and Renan. But Hugo, Chateaubriand, and Renan, however French, are nevertheless not French in the same way as the others. They represent a different and, so to speak, a more European side of the national genius.

Above all, they broke with " tradition." With regard to Mme. de Staël it was remarked by Fontanes that she " treated the age of Louis XIV. almost as lightly as Greece "—which, as we have seen above, is saying a good deal—and he also expressed the fear that her fondness for Rousseau had made her " care very little for Racine." " Why! " said Stendhal, in a significant passage, " we should be rejecting the most fascinating pleasures *simply and solely in order to imitate Frenchmen!* " More recently an advanced critic boldly declared: " It is upon the national tradition that we are making war."

And therein lies the danger which exoticism in literature may occasion in a distant future. But every European literature is

[1] *A propos de théâtre*, p. 168.

obscurely threatened by the same danger. Perhaps, in Europe of the twenty-fifth century, the idea of the literary fatherland will have grown as weak as that of the political fatherland. From one end of this little European continent to the other, what, a number of books are published, Italian, Dutch, Portuguese, and Russian, which have the same tendencies and wear the same livery ! How is it possible to withstand the incredible facility of exchange, the frequency of intercourse, the multiplicity of translations,—and, what may yet come, the coalescence of tongues ? " In our days," writes M. de Vogüé, " above all preferences founded on party or nationality, a European spirit is being formed." Suppose this movement were to grow much more rapid : what would happen then ? Did Rivarol merely dream when he longed to see mankind " form itself into one republic, from one end of the earth to the other, under the sway of a single language ? " Would it be so absurd if, from the comparison, the juxtaposition, and, let us admit it, the confusion of so many works from every country in Europe, there should result a sort of composite idea consisting of elements artificially compounded so as to form a literature no longer either English, or German, or French, but simply European—until the time should come when it would be universal ? Should such a day ever arrive, across the frontiers—if any remain—there will be stretched a network of invisible bonds which will unite nation to nation and, as of old during the middle ages, will form a collective European soul.

Nor is this dream—or, shall we say, this danger, which threatens alike the literatures of the Old World and the New— a merely visionary one. But at anyrate the peril is not imminent ; there are formidable obstacles in its way. Held together by community of race, of language, and of historical tradition, men will for long years to come remain citizens of a country or of a province in the first place, and be citizens of the universe only in the second. Long enough yet will last the sway of that imperious necessity which binds man to the soil and makes him a citizen of his native burgh. For long years yet each people will hand down, as a sacred legacy, the literary works which in past ages have sprung from the efforts of its national genius. It may indeed be that cosmopolitanism, when it is truly the worship of " the literature of the world," abjures its own principle in exhausting the consequences of it, and that it is then nothing more than a resuscitated form of " humanism," the name of which thus becomes synonymous with its own. But at the present moment the triumph of such an idea is impossible of realization. The struggle between the races is waged more fiercely than ever, and it is incumbent on the literature of France, as on all other literatures—more so, indeed, than on any other—to uphold the time-honoured position of influence it occupies in the world. As one of its own teachers has said[1]: " The literature that would give proof of its youth-fulness and vital energy, that would secure for itself fresh life and influence in the future, will spread the knowledge, and acquire a comprehension, of every great, new or beautiful work that is created beyond its own borders; will turn it to account, not as a pattern merely, but by assimilating it and converting it to a form appropriate to its own nature; will amplify, without destroying, its own individuality, and thus, while remaining always the same, will be perpetually changing, always European yet never renouncing its nationality."

I have endeavoured to show that one man above all others has acted as a connecting link between France and Northern Europe; that, while, by reason of his foreign extraction, he was especially qualified to make the French acquainted with foreign literature, and was moreover greatly helped by the fact of his having been educated in a French-speaking country, circumstances also lent him powerful assistance in the accomplishment of this task; that his intellect, the most complex and the most richly endowed of any in that age, really called into being a sort of European literature, the future of which is henceforth assured; and that, if after all he did not succeed in transferring the literary hegemony of Europe from France to the Northern nations, he at least enabled one nation to understand the original genius of the others, and thereby deserved the gratitude of all.

[1] G. Paris, *Leçons et lectures sur la poésie du moyen âge* (1895), preface.

"It would seem," says M. Renan, "that if it is to produce the best that is in it the Gallic race requires to be from time to time impregnated by the Germanic: the finest manifestations of human nature have sprung from this mutual intercourse, which is, to my mind, the source of modern civilization, the cause of its superiority, and the best guarantee for its persistence in the future."[1]

If this be the case, then no one, assuredly, has deserved better of the Gallic race than Jean-Jacques Rousseau.

[1] *Essais de critique et de morale*, p. 59.

CONCLUSION

...
...
...
...
...

Index

www.ingramcontent.com/pod-product-compliance
Lightning Source LLC
Chambersburg PA
CBHW021336110726
47900CB00005B/1491